The
Diviner

Also by Marilyn Harris

KINGS EX
IN THE MIDST OF EARTH
THE PEPPERSALT LAND
THE RUNAWAY'S DIARY
HATTER FOX
THE CONJURERS
BLEDDING SORROW
THIS OTHER EDEN
THE PRINCE OF EDEN
THE EDEN PASSION
THE WOMEN OF EDEN
THE PORTENT
THE LAST GREAT LOVE
EDEN RISING

THE
DIVINER

Marilyn Harris

G. P. Putnam's Sons
New York

C.4

Library of Congress Cataloging in Publication Data
Harris, Marilyn.
The diviner.

I. Title.
PS3558.A648D5   1982   813'.54   82-13216
ISBN 0-399-12739-9

PRINTED IN THE UNITED STATES OF AMERICA

Third Impression

. . . and yet there are certain rare spirits, diviners, who have the power to rise above the demands of the flesh and with passionate concentration to devote themselves to the contemplation and accomplishment of the supernatural.

Cicero—*De Divinatione*

The fact is indisputable that when our ordinary waking consciousness goes to sleep or rests, in that instant an entirely different power takes command of the myriad forces of memory. This power knows things hidden from me and can do what I cannot.

Charles Leland

Lovers battle against evils of the past
that dominate the present.

August 24, 1942

Naval Air Technical Training Center
Farwell

"Thank you, God, for Rita Manning."

"Huh?"

"Look. There she is."

The two seamen-third-class commissary men gaped across the mahagony bar of the Officers' Club through the arched door in which Rita Manning had just appeared.

August-hot and the end of the day, the club was filled with officers relaxing with their wives, girlfriends and lovers, all sitting at the small, round bamboo-and-glass tables like little enclaves of sensuality and quiet seduction.

With Rita Manning's appearance the chatter stopped. Each inconclusive sexual game came to a halt as well, and all sat now in quiet condemnation, all eyes save those of the two focused on the woman in the doorway who, having once appeared, seemed more than willing to stand posed forever and let them look their fill, as though she knew better than anyone the caliber and quality of her beauty, her body adorned in red jersey which, highlighted from behind by the dying sun, outlined in perfect detail the classic curve of hips, thighs and calves, terminating in two shapely ankles, the whole form the sculpted creation of a godly artist.

7

Now, from where she stood, she shifted slightly from one high-platformed, ankle-strapped heel to the other. At the same time her left hand made a quick caressing motion starting at her throat and sliding in an enviable passage down over her left breast, a sculpted mound with a matching twin that becomingly objected to the mild restraint of red jersey.

"What's she doing?" the second bartender whispered under his breath, his lips not moving, as though he didn't want anyone to know he'd spoken.

"Looking for you-know-who," the first bartender replied, speaking in the same tight-lipped manner.

"My God, but she's gorgeous!" the second bartender prayed. "If she were mine she wouldn't have to come lookin' for me."

The other bartender snickered. "If she was yours," he repeated derisively, "you'd have to look for her. Something like that don't belong to one cock. She's everybody's and nobody's, not even her husband's."

With that pronouncement he peered around the side of the bar toward one of the small round tables on the sun terrace, the red-tiled room which gave a view of the high stand of trees marking the southern boundaries of the base, a no-man's land of about five blocks stretching between Halsey Avenue and the high, barbed-wire fence. On Friday and Saturday nights the thickly wooded area was alive with copulating couples. It was impossible to walk five feet in any direction without stumbling over prone bodies. In attempts to discourage the inevitable and increase the water supply for the base, the Navy Corps of Engineers was in the process of erecting a water tower and drainage ditch in the middle of the no-man's-land. Thus far the earthmovers and Caterpillars had discouraged nothing.

"Lookee," Bartender No. 1 whispered and pointed to a man and woman seated at one of the tables on the sun terrace.

The second bartender snickered. "Well, son-of-a-bitch, it's hubby himself!"

Alec Manning appeared to be focusing all of his attention on the construction of the drainage ditch, apparently oblivious to both the frightened woman who sat opposite him, nervously opening and closing the toy paper parasol in her Singapore sling, and ignoring with equal calm the new, tense silence which had fallen over the Officers' Club with the appearance of his wife Rita Manning in the arched doorway.

"Don't he even know?" muttered the first bartender, his head swiveling between the arched doorway to the far table.

8

"Offhand I'd say he didn't," replied his mate, and for the first time since Rita Manning's appearance, he began slowly to polish the highball glass in his hand. As though that were a signal for life to resume, one officer standing by the jukebox punched a button, and a moment later the meandering, rhapsodic and altogether too appropriate flowering of "Blues in the Night" drifted forth in tinny rendition, sax predominant and wailing.

The first bartender grinned and sang along under his breath for two bars.

"Ain't she never goin' to move?" his mate whispered, a tinge of anger in his tone as though the posed woman was beginning to annoy him.

"When she gets ready to," the first bartender replied. "When she thinks everybody's looked their fill and when the one she's come here to see looks her way."

"That ain't never goin' to happen," the other bartender replied, " 'cause Lieutenant Manning's happy comforting the chaplain's pretty little wife, like he does every night for . . ."

"Whoa, there," the first bartender interrupted, and once again froze in his limited activity of sponging the bar's surface.

The warning in his voice dragged their attention back to the small table by the terrace window where Alec Manning was saying something earnestly to his companion, Brett Simpson, wife of the Episcopal chaplain who'd been assigned to the *Lexington* on a tour of duty in the Pacific.

"The preacher's wife sees her all right," muttered the first bartender, nodding his head toward Mrs. Simpson, the fragile blonde who had never fully recovered from the birth of her son a year ago and who had taken her husband's absence very hard.

It was common knowledge on the base that these four—Alec and Rita Manning and Brett and Gerald Simpson—had been the best of friends during their assignment here, but the war and duty tours had interceded, and something else as well, though no one knew precisely what.

Brett Simpson now stood with a suddenness that suggested breaking nerves. The chair legs scraped, creating a deeper silence. Alec Manning extended one quick hand in her direction and instantly withdrew it, as though it had encountered an invisible heat midway between them.

Rita Manning, still standing in the door, was momentarily forgotten as the fascinated eyewitnesses recorded and digested the pain on Brett Simpson's face as she looked down on Alec Manning.

Then without warning Brett Simpson turned away, a wrenching movement, a small square of white handkerchief pressed to her lips, her delicate figure resembling a child's more than a woman's, enhancing her vulnerability. She ran on noisy spiked heels through the door which led down onto the outside red-bricked terrace and disappeared around the corner of the club.

"Do you suppose he's going to go after her?" mused the second bartender, relaxing a bit into the drama, his attention, along with everyone else's, still focused on Alec Manning, who stood in a crouched position over the table, half in his chair, half out, his body fixed in a bent position.

"Naw, he ain't going no place," the first bartender ventured. "Not with that one watching him."

Both men stood frozen behind the bar, their focused attention fixed on the woman in the door, who now—as though standing still no longer suited her purpose—without lifting her eyes from the far table where her husband sat alone, moved one step forward, the clinging red jersey brushing against and outlining hips, thighs, knees.

As she moved slowly down the two steps to the level of the club itself, someone spoke to her from the near table, a male voice. "Good evening, Rita," it said.

Her sole response was a soft half smile in the general vicinity of the voice, a slight tilting of her head which gave her an instantaneous vulnerability as though she were being misused. In that moment every male in the club would have killed for her.

Save one.

Only Alec Manning sat with his back to his approaching wife, who had effortlessly and casually captured the attention and desire of every man in the club.

As she was now approaching the bar, the two bartenders drew back toward the low shelves and the pyramid arrangement of sparkling glasses as though she were a fatal destiny eagerly anticipated and yet dreaded.

"What's she want?" the first bartender whispered.

"Sssh," the second man scolded, a new tenderness on his face, as though suspecting the woman was within hearing distance and did not want to hurt her feelings.

Still she came, the essence of all things subtle and proclaiming, sensuous and childlike, a riot of contradictions that had made her the favorite topic of gossip and conversation on the base for the last two years since she'd emerged a highly respectable town girl, then spectacularly pregnant, the favorite daughter and only child of Dr. Karl Butes, professor of Greek at the university, who

10

tended to view his daughter's swollen condition with the resigned disappointment of a man who had known all along how things would turn out.

The accused had been the brilliant naval officer Alec Manning, a most unlikely seducer. But he'd accepted her accusation, had married her, and with all the docility of a reformed culprit, had moved off the base and into Dr. Butes's large Victorian house on the corner of Sorrento and Capri, allowing Rita to play the dual role of wife and daughter. Rita's mother had died seven years earlier, and since then Rita had tended to the house and to her father with the soft devotion of daughterly obedience. No one was quite certain how she and Alec Manning had ever gotten together in a position intimate enough to produce a child, but Dr. Butes had permitted Rita to work two nights a week with the Methodist Church on a volunteer basis at the USO. Apparently it had been there that her breathtaking beauty had shattered the good judgment of the brilliant young naval officer, and obviously a rendezvous had taken place, for only last year a squalling, rosy-cheeked baby daughter had slipped from Rita Manning's womb, and all four—mother, father, infant and grandfather—had taken up a splintered and uneasy residence in the large three-story house in town.

Rita Manning took one step closer to the bar. "May I have a bit of Scotch in one of those glasses?" she asked, the complete sentence drifting liquidly out, conveying the simple request yet manifest with mystery.

"Coming up," Bartender No. 2 responded, and with admirable energy proceeded to move awkwardly around the obstacle that was Bartender No. 1, who stood fixed like a human pillar anchored to the bar floor.

While the "bit of Scotch" was being prepared, Rita Manning briefly lowered her head and appeared to be studying her own hand. The scrutiny lasted only a moment. Then, with her head still in a bowed position, she turned slowly to the left in the direction of the glassed-in sun terrace and the man sitting alone at the table, his attention still riveted on the emptiness beyond the glass.

Still it held, that frozen dead tension, though it was clear from the strained delight in all faces that the life in the room had merely gone underground inside the mind, as in infinite variation and interpretation everyone—male and female—re-created the well-known drama which had led to this marvelous moment— The Confrontation.

There were four basic elements. One: Two officers, best of

friends, divided and separated by quarreling, incompatible wives. Brett Simpson's and Rita Manning's antagonism to each other was legend and had reached the point where the two couples could not be invited to the same dinner party on the base. Two: Gerald Simpson shipped out on the *Lexington* and Alec Manning had been seen on more than one occasion coming out of the Simpson house in the officers' compound, comforting the wife left behind with an infant son.

Then came the tragic word that Gerald Simpson had gone down on the *Lexington,* and for two weeks Alec Manning had been a model of deportment, visiting the bereaved Simpson house only once and then in the company of his wife.

But then, two weeks after the death announcement and the memorial service held in the very chapel on base where Father Simpson had officiated at so many similar services, it was rumored that Alec Manning had walked out of the Victorian house near the campus, carrying two packed bags, one quite large and bulky, the other smaller, and while no one followed him or called him back, the moment after his car had pulled away from the curb, all the lights had gone out in the large house and a woman's sobs had been heard all night and well into the next day. Yet perhaps it had signified nothing. Other officers had found it difficult, if not impossible, to live in town and still be accessible to the demands of the war machine. Some ensconced families in the normalcy of town life and then they themselves moved back into bachelor quarters, alternating between the two worlds as best they could, satisfying all the various demands placed upon them by both.

So undoubtedly this was what Alec Manning had done. In fact for the first week following his late-night departure from his wife's house, Alec Manning went no place at all except where official duty called him—to conduct his classes in training naval air personnel, official conferences concerning new inductees, the endless red-tape paperwork demanded of him from the Navy Department and, most difficult, redistributing to the families the possessions of men recently killed in the line of duty. Including Gerald Simpson.

So it was that the first time he went back to the Simpson house he went on official business, carrying with him the plain brown carton, Navy issue, which contained all that could be found of the personal possessions belonging to Captain Gerald Simpson.

It was reported that he entered the Simpson bungalow shortly after seven P.M. on a Thursday evening and was seen emerging shortly before seven A.M. on Friday morning. And of course everyone knew that Navy Captain Gerald Simpson did not leave that many earthly possessions.

Still, the all-night visit might have been reported and forgotten if that had been the only incident. But the truth was that that visit was repeated every night, Alec Manning arriving shortly after seven in the evening, leaving shortly before seven the next morning, and on occasion he'd even been seen sitting on the small front porch, rocking Brett Simpson's infant son.

As for Rita Manning? Until tonight, she'd not been seen at all since the belabored memorial service for Gerald Simpson four weeks ago. At least she'd not been seen on the base. There were those who claimed to have seen her pushing a baby carriage up and down in front of the house near campus, but certainly no one had approached her or spoken to her until tonight.

So this in essence was the excitement that was cartwheeling through the minds of all those private witnesses who continued to gape at Rita Manning as though transfixed, she apparently having looked her fill at her distant husband as though she wished more than anything that he would in some way respond to or acknowledge her presence. Of course he hadn't, and wasn't likely to, considering the depth and degree of his concentration on the green-foliage emptiness beyond the large picture window.

Slowly Rita Manning abandoned her vigil on her distant and unresponding husband. Turning away from him, she allowed her head to bow completely, the humble position of a penitent. Her long, luxuriant auburn hair fell forward as well in thick, becoming locks and obscured her profile.

"Here you go," Bartender No. 2 announced, and presented to the bowed woman a sparkling highball glass with two fingers of "a bit of Scotch" and nothing more.

Then slowly, as though despite the pain of the moment she knew she was being watched, she lifted the glass, studied it carefully, as though looking for a clue in the amber liquid. Once she even moved it toward her lips to take a fortifying sip, but she apparently changed her mind at the last minute and lowered the glass and held it cupped in both hands and gave bartenders a half smile and lowered her head once again, and this time closed her eyes as though suffering a momentary weakness.

At last she lifted her head and turned toward the sun terrace and the man sitting alone, disengaged, distant. Her pace was slow, almost measured, as she started across the tile floor, her platform heels sending out a mournful yet rhythmical tap-tap, the female sound of one who moves easily and gracefully.

Rita Manning stopped short of her husband's table by about five feet, still fingering her "bit of scotch" which she had yet to sip. Then she did. All at once. Placing the rim of the glass to her lips, with a quick upward motion of her head she drained the liquid, her eyes resting briefly on the acoustical tile ceiling before she pinched them shut from the effect of the strong, hot booze.

Of course her motivation was clear to all those gaping eyes. She needed the fortification in order to face the unresponding man still seated with his back to her, although he would have had to have known about her presence from any number of sources—the proclaiming tapping of her heels, the awesome silence which had descended upon the previously chattering club, the sudden departure of Brett Simpson.

She was standing less than two feet from him now, her head slightly bowed, obscuring her features, though from the faint movement of her shoulders it could be assumed she was still fingering the empty highball glass.

"Christ, is he a rock?" the first bartender marveled, though it was less marvel than condemnation.

"Cold fish."

"Dead, you mean."

"Sssh."

The shush had been prompted by Rita Manning, who suddenly stepped toward the chair recently abandoned by Brett Simpson. In the process she placed the empty highball glass on the table and with that simple gesture at last attracted the attention of her husband who, very slowly, very reluctantly, looked up—not at her but at the empty glass as though it were the prime offender in his life and wanted smashing.

If Rita Manning saw or felt the hostility, it was her turn now to ignore and be passive. Accordingly she sat slowly on the very edge of the bamboo chair. For several moments she appeared to sit obediently before her husband, head down, hands folded simply in her lap, nothing moving either within or without.

"Lord, help!" the second bartender whispered, his face awash with pity for the unhappy two and the merciless focus of the rest of the club. "Give 'em a break!" he muttered further, but did nothing to turn away himself, instead moved closer to the end of the bar, enhancing his position in order to see everything that was happening—which for the moment was exactly nothing.

The two continued to sit in their peculiarly rigid positions as though physically bound to the chairs. Then her eyes were raised in one direct glance to her husband, an unfortunate moment for

14

anyone quick enough to catch it, for mirrored in that flawless cameo was the wretched grief of every betrayed woman the world had ever created.

Rita Manning's left hand then broke free of her right and, ascending to the tabletop, headed in a faltering movement of love and need in the direction of her unresponding husband, the hand stopping halfway toward its clear destination as though it had collided with an invisible barrier. Which indeed it had, for Alec Manning's mood was now being conveyed not just to Rita Manning but for the benefit of everyone in the club who could feel anger building in the quiet facade, the turmoil being manifested in small but concise ways—the nervous twitch in the fingers of his right hand, a slight increase in the rate of breathing, the manner in which the once slumped, relaxed position had suddenly assumed a crouched aspect, as though a force within were making ready to spring.

Her lips moved, though the voice behind them was so depleted that no one heard—perhaps not even Alec Manning himself, although he looked up for the first time, a quizzical expression on his face blending with the pain and anger there, and for a moment it appeared a question would evolve out of his bewilderment.

Now the unsuccessful communication had come to a halt, both man and woman staring hopelessly at each other, as though a last ploy had been launched and failed.

But Rita Manning spoke once more—still inaudible, still short—something that required less than three words. The last word had no more than left her lips when the smoldering volcano of a man seated opposite her exploded.

The movement was so fast that for several seconds no one reacted with anything more than the rather stunned, hypnotic state that had marked the entire unhappy evening. It wasn't until the sound of glass shattering exploded throughout the club that the sequence of events clearly registered with all those eyewitnesses, the realization that in answer to Rita Manning's short and whispered entreaty, Alec Manning by way of reply had grasped her recently abandoned highball glass and in a lightning-fast movement had hurled it through the broad plate-glass picture window on the sun porch.

The shattering echoed endlessly. From someplace near the back of the club a woman screamed, one short, sharp sound of fear. Following the scream there were several sounds of chairs scraping. One or two of the passive witnesses were no longer

15

passive. The two bartenders shifted suddenly. The first started forward reflexively with the air of a man who might be held acountable for another man's insane destruction. Strangely, the second bartender withdrew for perhaps the same reason.

The initial impact of the glass on glass multiplied and spread, new cracks and fissures widening, mammoth shards shattering on the tile floor, some striking perilously close to the chair where Rita Manning sat, now in a crouched position, her left arm uplifted at a defensive angle, the fear on her face a mirror-image reflection of everyone else in the club.

Alec Manning seemed literally to derive strength from the destruction. The force with which he'd hurled the highball glass through the window had, in the process, dragged him to his feet, and the forward momentum had left him in a peculiarly aggressive position halfway across the small table.

Since he was already on his feet and since there was no conceivable way for him to add to the statement of contempt he'd just made regarding his wife and her presence before him, most of the witnesses fully expected him to depart immediately through the door to the left. For all intents and purposes, he had the upper hand and by rights should have dominated this last pathetic moment. Instead, he appeared to have faltered, to have realized something he'd not realized before. His expression altered as he looked down on Rita Manning, as though seeing her for the first time and seeing something that provoked a curious remorse in his face.

"Too late now, you stupid bastard!" the first bartender whispered with contempt.

"Atta girl!" the first bartender grinned in a whisper, spotting new movement coming from Rita Manning, her left hand lifting to her right, her fingers encircling her right wrist, a peculiar gesture as though recently she'd worn handcuffs, some sort of bondage, and now freed, it was imperative she rub life back into the numb appendage.

The slight massage lasted only a moment, then ceased. Without lifting her eyes to anyone or anything, she pushed effortlessly up and out of the curved bamboo chair, displaying none of the effects of extreme emotion that one might expect. Instead her movements seemed light, almost buoyant. At last she stood, apparently undiminished in any way, in fact displaying for one and all a pronounced sense of relief, as though something obligatory had forced her here tonight to play out this dreadful scene,

16

and, having completed it, she now was free to leave, indeed was looking forward to it.

This peculiar turnabout of roles, so clear for all to see, held the communal attentions riveted. No way of safely predicting this one. What they had assumed to be Alec Manning's apparent victory now seemed to have shattered about his head like the window glass itself.

Then she was moving toward the south door. Seeing her direction and apparently something else, Alec Manning appeared to lose his balance, grabbed hold of the table at the last moment and righted himself in the direction of his departing wife. For a moment he appeared to expect her to turn about with no command spoken, as though she were capable of reading his mind. When she didn't, he started after her.

When she still didn't turn about and proceeded on in an almost relieved, light manner—her head erect, her platform heels sending back that same magical sound—he lifted his head in a sudden movement and spoke her name, a curious utterance. Yet, despite the fine edge of desperation in his voice, he didn't stop her. Rita Manning could be seen now through the jagged glass, a perfectly perceived form of grace and beauty, both enhanced by the almost insupportable weight of sorrow which she appeared to bear as close to her skin as the red jersey.

Her direction and ultimate destination were not yet clear. At the end of the path the direction divided. Left led back toward the heart of the base, right, toward the extreme edge of the base and the dark, narrow strip dubbed no-man's-land, with deep ravines which were being excavated for the new drainage ditch, sewer line and water tower.

As Rita Manning approached the fork in the path, all eyes in the club looked beyond through the jagged remains of the glass, as though they were under some sort of compulsive obligation to stay with the woman until she was out of their sight.

"Hey!" the first bartender gasped, and pointed toward the frieze of green trees and the woman, who took two steps toward the left and home, then stopped abruptly and turned slowly and stared pointedly toward the right, as though someone had called to her.

"Why in the hell has she gone to the right? That leads into no-man's land." The second bartender's bewilderment was joined with everyone else's in the club who—now relieved of Rita Manning's presence—began to chatter compulsively among themselves. Nothing loud and boisterous, just frenzied whispers, various interpretations of the awful scene, which undoubtedly would be repeated in all quarters of the base in countless variations for weeks to come.

Only at the last minute did everyone seem to realize there still was one player present in the form of Alec Manning, who appeared to physically buckle with his wife's decision. The small collapse lasted only a minute, and then he, too, was moving as rapidly as circumstances would permit in the opposite direction from his wife, back into the club itself.

Ultimately he found his way to the arched door and disappeared through it, clearly on his way to one of two destinations: the safe fortress of the low, rambling, stucco bachelor officers' quarters, his present official residence—or the more hazardous but ultimately more rewarding fortress of Brett Simpson's small bungalow.

Strangely enough, no one seemed interested in Alec Manning's decision of a destination, and, once Rita Manning was out of their sight, even the significance of her choice seemed to fade to relative unimportance.

"Something's fishy," the first bartender grumbled ominously, the only one who seemed loath to abandon his vigil on the now empty path.

"Something's always fishy with that pair," his mate confirmed, indulging in a bit of healthy cynicism. "God, I hope Manning realizes he's responsible for . . ."

"Be back in a minute," the first bartender announced suddenly. Stripping off his white jacket, he hurried toward the end of the bar. He was moving at such a rate of speed that he was halfway across the sun porch before the second bartender realized what he was doing.

"Hey! What the hell? Wait a minute! You can't . . . I can't . . ." At the same time the second bartender caught the condemning eyes of several officers seated at near tables. It was as he'd suspected. They were thirsty, as were their female companions, and as he heard the first shouted order behind him, he looked heavenward toward the god who looks after harried bartenders and scooped up the abandoned white jacket with a resigned expression and started toward the first table and vowed to do the best he could in true Navy tradition.

Despite the fact Amos Foster had grown up in Santa Monica in close proximity to Hollywood and a varied assortment of the most beautiful women in the world, still never in his life had he ever seen anything or anyone quite like Rita Manning.

In point of fact he was a dedicated, world-class Rita Manning watcher, had been in on the drama from the beginning, had indeed been jerking sodas at the USO on the very night that the dilapidated yellow bus from the First Methodist Church had brought their choicest blossoms out to the base to do their part in the war effort.

Even then Rita Manning had stood out from the others, though precisely how it was still difficult to say. At the moment, as Amos hurried down the flagstone path which led to the fork—which in turn would lead him in pursuit of his pleasant and harmless obsession—he really wasn't all that interested in the beginning. Suffice it to say, that he—along with every red-blooded male who laid eyes on her—had responded with a dedicated fascination and on occasion an irrational zeal, which included a passive willing-ness to sacrifice life and even soul for her.

Why the right path? Amos pondered now, still baffled, thinking that if Rita Manning had gone left he'd have felt no compulsion to follow after her. The front gate and home would have been her clear and ultimate destination.

As he approached the fork in the path, he stole a quick backward look toward the Officers' Club. He saw first the jagged, shattered plate-glass window, and it reminded him of abandoned duties. He must hurry. Frank would need all the help he could get after the tense drama which recently transpired in the Officers' Club.

Still hesitating at the fork, he glanced back a third and final time to the place of his abandoned duties. Seeing no visible sign he was immediately needed, he quickly started off down the path, which narrowed as though the geography itself were making a moral warning on the direction of the path, the concealment of thick foliage, so dense in places as to be impenetrable, the one area on the base the Navy had been contented to leave as nature had created it. Of course the Navy was now altering the extreme southwest edge of the base because the volume of human waste produced by seventy-six thousand men every day required an expanded drainage and sewage network.

The machines were quiet now, he observed, as he hurried down the narrow path toward no-man's-land. Why in the name of God had she gone in this direction? To walk? To be alone? To meet someone of her own? That was a thought. Perhaps Alec Manning's liaison with Brett Simpson had been motivated by self-defense.

Alec Manning, Amos brooded, breaking his pace somewhat as the terrain underfoot became less steady and reliable, what a stupid son of a bitch he was! On this specific thought, Amos stumbled and glanced down. The path was untended here, little more than a trampled-down place cleared by the repeated passage of sailors and their girls in search of a dark and secluded place.

Now to the left through the dense, green-black foliage he spotted the first white Navy middy, like a single spotlight, locked in close and hungry embrace with a female whose identity was obscured by the crush of their two bodies. Not Rita Manning, he knew, for he saw not a sign nor a flutter of red jersey.

Amos paused, thinking the unthinkable. Did she have a lover, some very discreet young officer who had literally accomplished what everyone else merely dreamt about?

Sensing the end of daylight, Amos stepped off the end of the discernible path. Nearby, though out of sight, he heard pleasurable groans and thought of "Green Knees," the parody on the song "Greensleeves," which was the favorite ditty in the Monday-morning laundry. Raunchy beyond comment, still it described with graphic accuracy precisely what was going on behind those rocks and bushes.

For a few moments Amos looked curiously up at the high terrain, debating whether or not he should launch a specific bush-by-rock search.

No—

For some reason he knew very well that Rita Manning was not flattened beneath some sweaty boot. He didn't know where she was, but he knew with almost infallible wisdom where she wasn't.

So no need to scramble up to the high embankment, rather proceed straight ahead to—what? The end of the road? The place where the earthmovers had been digging for three days, scooping out a deep ditch in the already hilly terrain which marked the south edge of the base?

But what the hell would she be doing there?

Softly he shook his head as though part of him—perhaps the most rational part—still couldn't understand this obsessive fascination. But it didn't matter. The other part that did understand it was by far the most powerful and now urged him on despite the diminishing light and the ultimate dead end of the drainage ditch, in the irrationality that Rita Manning had taken this path which led absolutely nowhere.

Then a grim thought occurred, one that for a moment literally took his breath away. Irrational? Of course she was irrational. She'd just endured a very public humiliation at the hands of her husband. Come to think of it, she wasn't such a big girl either. No more than early twenties. Not really sophisticated, just the opposite. Protected. Overprotected by her old man. In fact now that he thought about it, it was a certain childlike quality that first appeared to capture everyone's attention and interest in Rita Manning.

Then maybe she did need help. This thought occurring so simply worked a profound effect on him, and suddenly he was no longer standing still gazing numbly into the fading light of day but breaking into a run—at least as much of a run as the terrain would allow—and simultaneously called out—

"Mrs. Manning!"

—and heard his voice echo over the dark woods and heard nothing that spoke of a response. He tripped once over a protruding tree root and righted himself reflexively just in time, tried to accelerate again and tripped again and glanced down to his right on the narrow, one-lane, blacktop road that served as an artery for the south edge of the base. Easier going down there. Now feeling speed was of the essence, he half slid down the steep embankment, aware of loose dirt spilling over the sides of his shoes, aware he'd have to stay up to polish them tonight— whenever he finished with the mess at the Officers' Club, that is. A report would have to be filed on the broken window, some temporary security devised.

God, he'd be up half the night and all because of—

Where the hell was she?

"Mrs. Manning?"

Again his voice echoed strangely about him, and as he hit the bottom of the embankment, he stepped eagerly up onto the blacktop and tried to look ahead to the place about two blocks away where the excavation had been going on. In what was left of day, he was looking very specifically for a fragment, a glimpse, of red jersey. She would be so easy to spot.

Briefly he fantasized that he did indeed spy her directly up ahead. Just there in that small clearing about fifty yards away.

Mrs. Manning, don't cry. The bastard isn't worth it. Here, lean on me.

But of course it wasn't her. It wasn't anything, just a deserted stretch of blacktop road.

21

Still he proceeded on down the empty road, thinking he'd follow it directly to the end of the excavation site, find nothing and return to the club to clean up the mess there, send Frank to the barracks, delicately send the officers to their respective quarters and close up after a long and most unusual night. As for Rita Manning, if he didn't catch sight of her within the next few minutes, she clearly wasn't here to catch sight of.

It was dark, almost, save for the mysterious light which lingers at the beginning of night like a reflection from some unknown source.

Atop an embankment a stand of trees had been cleared and in their place he saw one enormous earthmover with huge jaws in an open position. Quite a distance away it was. He glanced up, thinking he'd hate to be the guys who'd gotten it up there or—worse—the ones who had to get it down. The area appeared newly scarred. All grass and foliage had been scraped clean like a shaved body for a surgical procedure. In fact he observed now that the red dirt even resembled dried blood in the fading light.

He gaped upward, thinking for a moment he'd heard something, the growl of a machine. But the nearest machine was that one perched on the cliff. He stopped again after two steps and squinted his eyes into the distance toward that newly made mound of displaced earth.

He closed his eyes briefly to clear and sharpen their focus, then quickly opened them again to the highest point where—in addition to hearing the growl of the machine—he thought he had seen—

Nothing. Gone. Something.

He had seen something—or imagined it and heard it as well. A reed-thin figure that did not belong to the natural landscape.

"Mrs. Manning?"

If it was her, why was she playing games? Or was it his eyes playing games, visible one minute, gone the next?

Then shifting light? No. The light of day as well as its source were completely gone, and the high embankment, made higher by the mounded earth, was still visible and—

"Mrs. Manning?"

This time he had seen something. The clear figure of a woman. Not just any woman but the gorgeous red-jersey silhouette of Rita Manning. Standing atop the highest point she was, directly in front of the earthmover. How in the hell had she gotten up there?

"Mrs. Manning, watch . . .!"

Then he was running, experiencing a curiously mixed emotion, part relief, part fear, part incredible excitement. So his instincts had been correct. Follow her and gain for himself what few sailors on this base had ever gained, a few moments alone with that face and those eyes, that voice, and the entire miraculous combination made even more appealing and hopefully vulnerable by the fact of her recent humiliation at the hands of Alec Manning.

"Mrs. . . ."

He started to call again but heard only the ominous growl of the machine. What in the hell?

"Hey, up there!"

Half running, half stumbling, Amos Foster moved jerkily down the blacktop, standing dead still now, and, once reversing his direction altogether, then starting off again, never taking his eyes off the spot about a hundred and fifty yards away where the highest embankment looked down on the deepest ditch.

"Wait!" he called out foolishly to nothing, thinking that at each step the mystery would be clarified, the puzzle solved.

But suddenly she slipped from view as though she'd stepped behind something—or never been there.

"My God!" he was shouting hysterically to the night. Curious how breathless he was. He'd not run that far or that fast and yet—

Still for several moments as he gulped painfully for air, he lifted his head now and then, not precisely sure what it was he'd imagined or not imagined. The figure of the woman clad in red jersey, perfectly clear and visible one moment and then gone, then reappearing, then—

Again he heard the growl of a large machine. Yet he looked closely at the one at the top of the embankment and noticed that it had not moved.

Then once again he caught a clear glimpse of Rita Manning standing on the precise edge of the embankment, the tilt of her body leaning precariously into the edge of the cliff itself.

"Oh, my God, no!" he gasped, seeing her clearly now, seeing for the first time a telltale vibration of the large earthmover directly behind her. Still frozen in his position of recognition a distance away, nonetheless he was close enough to see the earth's slight landslide caused by the pressure of her weight on the loose and already disturbed earth.

"Mrs. Manning!" he cried. He was moving at top speed down the blacktop, trying to find a way across the deep ditch and up the embankment.

Then he saw that something was different about her in the hazy half-light which still lingered on the periphery of blackness. He saw Rita Manning absolutely motionless, the vibration coming from the machine but nothing moving.

All at once he looked behind him, thinking he needed help, thinking in that moment that help was close by. But he was alone. My God, where were all the make-out artists who usually inhabited this deserted area of the base, turning every concealment of bushes into natural brothels?

"Mrs. Manning, look out behind!"

Even the peripheral light was fading now, the blackness a tight-knit fabric that seemed literally to press against him.

"Hey," he whispered and shivered. "Hey, what's . . .?"

Abruptly he turned in all directions, a spastic, disjointed movement, as the roar of the machine increased. He sensed something moving toward him, coming closer.

"Hey, who's there?" he called out and heard the fear in his voice.

"I'm warning you!" he called out full voice over the roar of the machine, hearing disembodied movement now, first in front of him and then behind him, little more than a pronounced displacement of air, more a sense of something approaching very slowly, taking its own time.

"Are you there?" he called out foolishly. My God, what was it? Where was it?

"Hey, I'm going to go on back now, Mrs. Manning," he called out with a false bravado, and took one step backward, hearing the movement increase. To his left now. No, to his right.

"You can stay out here and play your little game if you want to," he called out, and stepped back once again, a single step, and heard a new rush of air as though something with wings were following slowly after him. The cool breeze was stirred by the rapid movement of wings, something trying to stay aloft yet not quite ready to approach him directly.

"Mrs. Manning, just say 'Okay,' if you're okay and I'll get on back to the club. A hundred things are waiting . . ."

There it was again, something hovering in the air not too far in front of him—five feet—something airborne, something emitting a curious sound like breathless whimpering as though it were unhappy.

"Screw you!" muttered Amos, and the growl of the machine atop the embankment seemed to be growing louder. Now he summoned all the courage he could muster under the circumstances and turned with admirable conviction and started off into the darkness which resembled a deep pit.

He managed three steps before he felt the first sharp pain, as though someone had thrown a dart at his back, and with this, a rush of wings, as though something had swooped low and sharply pecked at him.

"Goddamn it!" he gasped, and reached awkwardly toward his back, his left arm twisting about in an attempt to reach the spot in the center of his back which still smarted. Despite the stiff angle, his fingers found the area, and went on to find the small coin of spreading moisture in the place where obviously the skin had been broken.

"What in the . . .?"

Though it was pitch black, he rapidly drew his hand back and looked at it as though he were capable of seeing the moisture, identifying it and being shocked by it. In a curious, futile, belated gesture he lifted both arms and flailed wildly at the air in an attempt to frighten away whatever it was attacking him. But whatever it was that still hovered close beside him seemed to approach with a bit more daring now, for he could hear the bizarre noise quite clearly, a heavy, breathless whimpering. Not a human sound. He'd never heard a human make that sound—nor, for that matter, anything else.

Get the hell out of here, his good sense suggested, and wisely he followed the suggestion, though foolishly he took his first three steps in a backward manner as though it were important to keep his eyes on what he could not see. In the process he stumbled and flailed out on either side in frantic search for something to break the fall and found nothing but heard the soft thud of wings beating against the air. He felt something brush up against the side of his face as he fell, and at the precise moment that he struck ground, he felt something hovering directly over him.

In a witless and terrified attempt to see, he opened his eyes wide, searching the black for recognizable features, something which would give him a clue.

But he saw no clue, saw nothing, for the knife-sharp object that had plucked at his back now drove full force into his left eye, causing a howl of anguish. The burning, tearing sensation persisted, and he belatedly tried to cover his eyes, but the pointed object simply commenced assaulting his hands. Screaming for help continuously now, he tried to roll to one side in an attempt to escape the murderous attack, though somehow he knew no one would hear.

As the rush of wings increased, he froze on his side, paralyzed by pain, by the sensation of a red-hot poker being driven deeper and deeper. Something hot, wet and sticky was running in unchecked torrents between his fingers even while the assault continued. His shirt was in shreds now, the sharp talons moving indiscriminately over his shoulders and back, emitting a rancid odor.

For the first time he noticed that the breathless whimpering had stopped as though whatever it was had found relief and satisfaction in the attack itself.

His last conscious thoughts were how in hell would he explain his wounds to the infirmary, and when would it cease, and what would be left of . . . and why didn't the bastard in the machine up there see him, help him, and what had happened to Mrs. Manning, and why hadn't he had the good sense to stay in the club along with Frank?

All at once he felt searing pain in his back, a bizarre, wet, tearing sound. Still holding his useless left eye, he reflexively lifted his head as far as he could manage, a prolonged, sirenlike scream of his own agony filling the still, hot, black night—

Base Infirmary

"It's the goddamndest thing I've ever seen in twenty years of doctoring. I want you to . . ."

Dr. Lee paced nervously in the small area of the examination room. He noticed bloodstains on the left side of his white coat. He should have changed but there had been no time. The officer of the day, Lieutenant Evans, had arrived, looking slightly pissed and sleepy-eyed. No matter. All that would change soon.

"Where did you say he was found?" Evans asked, making an attempt to straighten his tie. Obviously he'd dressed hurriedly.

"On the blacktop near no-man's-land. Some poor boot out for a dawn jog found him. We've got him under sedation back there. He said that from a distance he thought it was a piece of meat, like a freshly butchered carcass of a critter. It wasn't until he was right over it that he saw what it was."

Evans looked up. "Well, what do you make of it?"

"That's why I called you," Dr. Lee said wearily. "I'm not paid to have theories."

At that Lieutenant Evans looked sharply over his shoulder as though trying to determine if Dr. Lee was joking or not.

He wasn't.

"All right," Lieutenant Evans nodded. "How many others saw him?"

Dr. Lee could have predicted that. It was cover-up time. "I had to send a couple of my boys out to get him."

"Where are they now?"

With a nod of his head Dr. Lee indicated the next examining room where he had left the two young medics resting on tables. "They'd just had their breakfast when the call came. Between the blacktop where they collected the body and the infirmary, they puked up everything they'd eaten for the last three days."

"What rank or rate?" Lieutenant Evans asked, a damnable objectivity still coating his baby-smooth face.

"Lieutenant Evans, I don't think you understand," Dr. Lee said with tolerable patience, "this man has the evidence of having been . . ."

"I know, I know," Lieutenant Evans cut in. "I'll see for myself in a minute. What we must determine now is what we've got on our hands. Murder? Homicide? Suicide, possibly?"

"Sui . . ." Dr. Lee tried to repeat and couldn't. Incongruously he felt a giggle forming at the base of his throat. Never in a million years could a man commit suicide in the manner in which this body had been found. "No, no suicide, Lieutenant," he said, newly sober.

"Then what?"

"Come on, Lieutenant, I think you should take a look for yourself," Dr. Lee said with some dispatch, starting toward the closed door. Somehow he felt communication between them might go more successfully if both viewed the atrocity which rested in 4B Vault in the morgue below.

"In a minute, I said," Lieutenant Evans snapped and waved his hand, indicating he wasn't quite ready to move on. "Would this incident," he began, his voice low, "have anything to do with the ruckus at the Officers' Club last night?"

Now it was Dr. Lee's turn to appear puzzled. "I'm sure I don't know. What ruckus?" he asked.

Lieutenant Evans shrugged, as though now he'd brought it up he found it inconsequential. "Marital woes," he said patly. "The Mannings, who else?"

"Don't know," Dr. Lee muttered, momentarily disarmed by his own thoughts. He'd seen Rita Manning only once since the birth of her infant—girl, if he remembered correctly—at an Officers' Club dance. It was a fact of medical science that pregnancy upset most female figures. Rita Manning had blown that scientific fact sky-high.

"And I was wondering if they could be one and the same," Lieutenant Evans finished.

Belatedly Dr. Lee came back from his fantasy trip to face a very earnest Lieutenant Evans. "I'm sorry, Lieutenant. I'm afraid I was . . ."

"It would help if you paid attention," Lieutenant Evans snapped. "I said the commissary bartender was reported missing from his barracks this morning, the same one tending bar during the Manning ruckus. And I was wondering if they could be one and the same."

Caught up, at least for the time being, Dr. Lee shook his head. "I haven't the faintest idea, Lieutenant. There was no ID on the body. There was nothing on the body, not even . . ."

"Dental?"

"Haven't had time yet."

"There'd better be a full investigation."

"I agree, but what are we investigating?"

"Murder?"

Dr. Lee smiled with cool professional objectivity. "What else?"

"But who—and more important, how?"

"Not why?"

"Not in this case."

He saw a new bewilderment on Lieutenant Evans's face and knew that as long as he was going to have to make a full report to the captain, Evans better come and see for himself what the two medics had brought in a short time ago. "Will you come with me now?" Dr. Lee asked politely, considering their destination. "I think it's important."

"How long would positive identification take?" Lieutenant Evans asked.

"If you can give me a list of the men missing from the base this morning and their complete files, I can have it for you shortly after lunch, I think."

Lieutenant Evans approved and nodded. "Good. Then we will . . ." Apparently he wasn't certain what "we" would do then, for his voice drifted, as did his attention now focused through the window to the August morning where heat waves were already beginning to shimmer and dance off the treeless parade ground outside. "This is a hell of a place, isn't it, Doc?" he muttered.

"Perfect training ground for duty in the Sahara."

Lieutenant Evans looked back, an expression of barely concealed annoyance on his face.

Dr. Lee slid off the examining table. "I think now you should see the body so that you can make a full report to . . ."

"Not necessary," Lieutenant Evans said hurriedly and backed toward the door, stepping through it into the hall.

"What the hell do you mean by that?" snapped Dr. Lee, following after him, sick to death of shouldering the entire weight of what had been found on the blacktop road in no-man's-land. "Something happened last night that I think . . ."

"A death," Lieutenant Evans said patly. "Not an unusual occurrence for a base this size."

Dumbfounded, all Dr. Lee could do was gape.

"Of course I'll tell the captain the nature of . . ."

29

"You don't know the fucking nature of anything!" Dr. Lee exploded. "Get your head out of your ass and come look!"

Oh, hell. He saw the look of shock on Lieutenant Evans's face and knew he'd caused it and regretted it instantly. When he really got pissed he always got obscene.

"Look, I'm . . . sorry," he muttered, and felt the first drop of perspiration course down the small of his back. By midmorning his shirt would be drenched. "I do think you should see it," he said simply.

Lieutenant Evans was newly sobered. "What . . . is it . . . precisely? Some kind of . . . mutilation?"

All right, he couldn't fight Evans's instincts. Then he'd have to settle for a word description. "The body has been skinned entirely. There's nothing left."

Lieutenant Evans turned away and gazed out through the screen door at the end of the hall toward the shimmering parade ground. "That's not . . . possible."

"You want to come and see?"

No answer to that challenge.

"And what's more, the medics said there wasn't a trace of skin near the body, everything gone, clean as a whistle."

"That's not unusual, is it?"

Now it was Dr. Lee's turn to blink. "Not . . . un . . .?"

"Foraging animals down in that part of the base, not unusual. Skunk, possum, hungry night creatures. And, as far as that goes, the wildlife could be responsible for the death of the man. You know, something large. A wolf, a coyote, bobcat, they're all around."

Dr. Lee didn't concede anything. It was madness—or at best rationalization. "Unless the bobcat brought his own surgical kit, it's out of the question. The incisions where the skin had been loosened are precise and professional."

For several moments both men stared at each other.

"Well, file your report, Doctor," Lieutenant Evans said with dispatch, and was halfway out on the shaded front porch before Dr. Lee caught up with him.

"Wait!" he called out. "What about the Manning ruckus last night?" he asked out of the blue, though he then realized he was detaining the man in any way he could—at least until he got some sort of direction from him concerning the body in 4B Vault.

Even Lieutenant Evans looked bewildered. "I don't follow you," he said.

"The Mannings," Dr. Lee repeated, coming all the way to the

door and passing through it as though Evans had been holding it open for him. "You said, didn't you, there was a ruckus last night at the OC. What kind?"

"I wasn't there," he said, and Dr. Lee thought he detected a note of relief, "but the commissary bartender filed a report last night . . ."

"I thought you said he was missing from his barracks."

"The other one. There were two."

"Of course."

"The man said a domestic quarrel took place between Lieutenant Manning and his wife, that the nature of the argument was not clear, though at one point Lieutenant Manning hurled a glass through the window that looks out over the woods."

"Must have been shattering, to say the least," quipped Dr. Lee.

"Glass everywhere," said Lieutenant Evans soberly, oblivious to the humor. "Mrs. Manning's father called this morning to say that she hasn't come home yet. I have no idea what I'm supposed to do about that."

Now both men stared, unspeaking, out at the dusty parade ground filled with marching men. Someplace in the distance Dr. Lee heard the rumble of earthmovers starting work again on the drainage ditch in the place where the body had been found.

"Look, Evans," he began, trying again, no longer interested in the Mannings or detaining the man. "What in the hell am I supposed to do? Just tell me."

Apparently Lieutenant Evans heard, showing a new soberness, and drew a slightly shuddering breath but did not alter his gaze out over the dusty parade ground. "What would you do, Dr. Lee, if it were just an . . . ordinary death?"

"Well . . . I'd . . ." Dr. Lee hesitated and then pushed on. "I'd identify cause of death first and then I'd file a death certificate with the Navy Department in Washington. I'd have the chaplain write a letter to his folks and I'd have the body shipped home, wherever that was."

"Then do it."

Dr. Lee gaped. "What do you mean, do it?"

"You just outlined your own course of action. Now do it."

"But this man didn't drop dead of heat stroke or a heart attack . . ."

"Would it make any difference?"

Dr. Lee followed after him to the top of the steps, mad as hell and knowing full well he'd better not show it. "What about my own ass that gets singed for falsifying records?"

"We'll cover you. We won't let anybody challenge you. I promise. Do it. Put this one to bed."

"You can't be serious?"

Dr. Lee never found out if he was serious or not. At that moment a young boot running helter-skelter around the perimeter of the parade ground caught Lieutenant Evans's eye, that one small sliver of undisciplined movement so close to the hundreds of cutout men. Apparently Lieutenant Evans had recognized him, had known all along he was headed for the porch of the sick bay, a message clutched in his hand.

"Who is . . .?" Dr. Lee began.

"Captain's aide," replied Lieutenant Evans. Then softer he spoke a single word: "Trouble."

At that moment the young sailor rounded the corner of the parade ground and spied them on the front porch. The young man broke speed quickly, his head hanging loose for a moment as he gasped for breath. "Message, sir, from Captain." Now he stood at the bottom of the steps and extended a slightly crumpled manila folder, a single paper clip holding something secure inside.

Lieutenant Evans reached for it, couldn't get it and descended two steps in deference to the man's obvious breathlessness. Without a word he opened the folder and squinted down on a single piece of paper on which—as well as Dr. Lee could tell without appearing to pry—were half a dozen crudely scrawled lines.

Dr. Lee stepped back and settled for watching Lieutenant Evans's face. The young sailor had withdrawn a discreet ten feet away, clearly taking himself out of the officers' circle.

"Bad news?" Dr. Lee asked, confident Lieutenant Evans had had ample time to read the brief message.

"Shit!" It was softly spoken, though filled with annoyance more than anything else, perhaps a tinge of disgust.

"What is . . .?"

"Rita Manning's father is outside the captain's office raising hell," Lieutenant Evans said wearily, still reading the message—or more accurately rereading it. "I have to go," he announced, apparently sensing his boss was being held captive by the irate old man.

"Hey, wait!" Dr. Lee shouted after him, seeing the young sailor take the lead at a trot, as though to set the pace for both of them back to the Exec Offices in Administration.

"Can't!" Lieutenant Evans called out. "You know what to do. I've told you. Now take care of it!"

Dr. Lee was about to object again when Lieutenant Evans called out with great force and full voice, "Captain's orders!"

Dr. Lee started to call out again, then changed his mind. Futile, all of it. What the shit? So Rita Manning was missing. News flash. My God, Navy wives turned up missing every day from this base—bored, looking for greener grass, sick to death of Navy bullshit. On occasion Dr. Lee didn't blame them. Why this one particular broad should upset the whole base—Okay, he'd been given orders. The skinned man in 4B Vault died of a heart attack. Pray God no one opened the casket. What the hell, he'd have it sealed. Not that that would prevent anyone from—

Suddenly, with stiffened arms he leaned heavily against the creaking railing. This was going to be his last duty. On to private practice and some greenbacks. Enough of this bullshit circus that was the Navy. Falsifying records. It could be his ass. Abruptly he looked up from his bowed position.

What the—

It was the silence that had caught his attention. The parade ground, which only moments before had been covered with hundreds of marching men, was now empty. No one in sight, though whirlwinds of dust spiraled upward under the duress of the August breeze.

Startled, he looked beyond the parade ground toward the classroom buildings where normally there was endless coming and going. Nothing. No one in sight; nor did he see the faintest glimpse of life or movement in any direction, only the heat rising from the hot earth and the rapidly climbing sun and the persistent flap overhead which was the flag bouncing lethargically in the heat of morning.

Dr. Lee continued to stare slowly in all directions, feeling a peculiar and bizarre aloneness. Suddenly he shivered in the heat of the morning and turned abruptly back into the cool shadows of the sick bay, heading reluctantly toward 4B Vault and the man who had died of a "heart attack."

What the hell? For all Dr. Lee knew his heart probably had stopped in shock as the first strip of his skin had been ripped from his body.

Pray God it had, he breathed, and closed the screen door firmly on the peculiar emptiness of the morning and tried to close his mind as well and hoped the dead man's mother did not want to see her boy for one last time.

September 27, 1963

The Base

Generally it was his favorite time to run, the exact hour the first tentative light of day split the mystery of night and the world became visible, if nothing else.

But now something was wrong, had been wrong all night and yesterday and the day before that and the day before that, a sense of surprise and disappointment. Tension? Perhaps. Mark Simpson shook his head once in a scolding mood. Nerves, that was all. And transition. He increased his walking pace and plunged his hands deep into the pockets of his warm-up suit and felt lint and—

His pace slowed as his fingers examined a small, round, hard object which nestled in his left pocket. Still mystified, he withdrew a perfect deep-purple seashell, its interior like finely grained and highly polished marble. Though it was a small and simple object, it brought him to a complete halt. His head slumped forward as he tried to deal with the recurring waves of homesickness.

He'd pocketed the seashell just last week as he'd taken a final run down Miramar, the little gem of a beach just four blocks from his home on the outskirts of Balboa. Miramar's sand was packed as hard as a cinder track, and the gulls in the hour of dawn always ran with him. As treat for a good four-mile run, he'd return in

34

the lapping surf, breaking speed to chase the waves, the salt sweat stinging his face despite the coolness of the morning breeze, a profound sense of deriving energy from breaking day, night once again defeated.

He stood for a moment, head down and eyes fixed on the eroded, sunbaked red-clay road at his feet. Somewhere along the rim of his consciousness he heard a blackbird crying. Instead of sea breeze and salt spray, he smelled the landlocked fields of the farm community.

What was he doing here?

The question entered his mind stealthily with a degree of calm politeness, as though it knew if it presented itself often enough, sooner or later an answer would have to be forthcoming.

Slowly he raised his head and drew a shuddering breath and rubbed his thumb lovingly over the satin surface of the seashell and gently pocketed it again as though it were a jewel and looked ahead and saw his running destination. No flat, smooth cinder track of Miramar's beach now but rather the unlikely gates of an abandoned Navy base, the best place, he'd been assured by Coach Herbert, for track and field men at the university to train.

Pay no attention to the snakes and skunks and the assorted wildlife. The track is marked by green arrows. Four miles to Coffin Pond and four miles back to the gate. Run it all.

Mark looked up at the late September haze and tried with conscious effort to put Miramar and his home out of his mind and concentrate first and foremost on the run. He was stiff, out of shape. He knew that. Out of condition after the lost time of preparation and travel. He was here, so he should make the best of it. It was his decision; his senior year and the scholarship had been so large that only an idiot could have turned it down. By accepting it he'd eased the financial burden on his mother and that was the important thing.

He looked up and saw it—just as Coach Herbert had said he would—the half-fallen, weathered and cockeyed sign—

NAVAL AIR TECHNICAL TRAINING CENTER.

He stopped again, amused by the incongruity, and thought of the shared bewilderment of those seventy-six thousand men who twenty years ago had passed in and out of these same gates, many having joined the Navy hoping to see an ocean and seeing instead only oceans of wheat fields which surrounded the base.

"One of the largest," his mother had told him. She had been pleased with his scholarship and his chance to see the last place she and his father had lived before he had shipped out to the

Pacific and his death aboard the *Lexington*. Well, maybe she hadn't been completely pleased. As he had approached the time to leave, her pleasure had turned suddenly to something morose, melancholy, and when she'd taken him to the plane, she'd pleaded with him not to go. He still didn't understand that.

Less than twenty feet from the dilapidated gates, Mark tested his emotional reflexes to see if he felt anything yet about thinking of his dead father.

Nothing. But then he'd been only an infant at the time. In truth, he remembered his father's friends better than—

Run.

Time was passing. Quickly he increased his speed, the gates drawing nearer, a crumbling sentry box in the middle, road parting.

Let's see your ID, sailor.

As he passed by the sentry box, Mark looked carefully through the broken glass. Beyond, on the desk itself, he saw a rusted clipboard with several sheets of yellowed, curled paper rustling in the slight, early-morning breeze.

Like a ghost town, the place was. From where he stood just beyond the gate, he saw only abandoned and crumbling structures, ragged with peeling, Navy-gray paint, weed-infested foundations, steps and walks and driveways which led nowhere. It was a rank and neglected, overgrown vista, a modern ghost town of waste and death and silence and sun.

According to Coach Herbert the base had been vacated by the Navy shortly after the war and given to the university, which thus far had put it to absolutely no purpose except as a place for track-and-field men to train on its deserted streets. Also, according to Coach Herbert, a handful of walkers and joggers from town used the base for daily exercise, and these few, along with the vast assortment of wildlife—hawks, rabbits, skunks, snakes and birds—were the only inhabitants of the base now—

—along with the ghosts of the past.

It had been Coach Herbert's poor joke as Mark had left his office.

Mark began his knee flexes and wondered what self-respecting ghost would be caught in this disreputable place. For a moment he suffered another throbbing ache of homesickness and reached in his pocket for his seashell and decided to keep it close for comfort, pass his year's sentence here and try very hard to justify the school's confidence in him.

There it was again, like the homesickness that wouldn't leave

36

him alone, a disquieting sense of being on the verge of something—a brink, a transition. Something was going to happen. He could feel it.

He looked quickly over his shoulder, thinking he'd heard something. Nothing but the abandoned sentry box and the yellowed pages rustling in the breeze. From where he stood the sun's direct rays struck the twin shattered windows which resembled monstrous broken eyeglasses.

Run.

After his layoff, four miles was going to seem like forty. He knew that, and he suspected he was merely postponing the delicious agony. Start slow. No dash techniques this morning. You have to build to that. Just slow.

Run.

He ignored the impatient voice, and with the discipline of a professional commenced his slow and systematic warm-up, legs spread now, hands on hips, slowly rotating the trunk of his body, stretching the ligaments and tendons that had grown stiff during the idle days.

Overhead a hawk glided silently by in the silent morning, catching Mark's attention only as its shadow passed over his face, intersecting the sun. Startled, he looked up in time to see it silhouetted by the rising sun, wingspan enormous, graceful, sliding.

My new running companion? Mark wondered ruefully. Quite a change from the little sea gulls. Nothing puny about this specimen. Fascinated, Mark briefly abandoned his warm-up and watched the primitive grace of the hawk, gliding so at ease in complete defiance of gravity, failing for long seconds to use its wings for any purpose other than gliding.

Looking up, squinting, Mark turned in a slow circle, following the bird, suffering the peculiar illusion that the hawk was looking back at him, gliding closer, each graceful ring a descent closer, still closer, until Mark could see clearly the tawny and dark brown geometric design of the coat and wings, could see the crook of the beak, the talons tucked neatly up against the underside, like wheels on an airborne plane.

Suddenly the rays of the sun cleared the horizon rim and struck Mark directly in the eyes with a blinding radiance. At the same time he heard a close and frantic flapping of wings, and, as he ducked his head in defense against the sun, he felt the sudden displacement of air upon his face, felt as well the sweeping contact of a wing. With spasticlike defenses he lifted both arms in a

37

flailing motion, while at the same time keeping his head down, eyes closed. He jerked rapidly in several erratic circles, all the while moving back toward the sentry box, not daring to lift his head until he felt the constancy of wood behind him.

Only then did he lower an arm and squint up into the sun, fully expecting to see the hawk launching itself for another attack.

"Son-of-a . . ." he muttered, only then aware of his rapid pulse. The limited patch of blue sky which he saw between his blinderlike hands revealed nothing. Slowly he lowered both hands and made a survey of the full field of dawn sky.

Nothing. Not a sign of the daredevil hawk.

He stepped away from the overhang of the sentry box, thinking the bird had drifted off in another direction. Still nothing. The sky was a rose-and-yellow streaked dome with an aggressive purple tint forming along the edges.

Run.

What earlier had been an imprudent voice now struck him as being wise, for the longer he stood here at this crumbling gate, the more pronounced became his distaste for this modern ghost town and the more profound became his confusion.

He ran loosely in place about a minute and then commenced two slow circles of the sentry box. Then forward motion at last, his arms hanging loose and disjointed as a rag doll, his face lifting directly overhead, then falling forward, the neck tendons stretching, giving, finding the rhythm of the slow jog.

There. It felt great. Slowly pick up just a tad of speed. Keep your eyes open for green arrows, Coach said. Ah, there was the first. Okay, hang a left.

As he did, he felt a sudden blast of heat as though it were ripening around him, the sun still climbing and promising to be one hell of a day. New torrents of perspiration gathered on his brow and joined forces and dripped down into the corners of his eyes, and he stumbled slightly as the road ahead blurred. He made two hasty swipes at his eyes and wished he'd brought a sweatband, but who'd have thought he would have needed it anywhere in September? He certainly hadn't needed it at home.

The stinging spread and he ran blind for a moment and felt the ribbed soles of his running shoes catch on irregularities in the buckling pavement and decided prudently to halt and clear his vision before he fell flat and did painful damage. A dozen steps later he trotted to a halt and felt the warm surge of blood that was always the result of a sudden stop and thought with black humor that in the last ten minutes he'd managed to shatter just about every rule of good running.

So be it. First priority of any run is vision. Accordingly, he lifted his arm to his face and, using his sleeve, made two massive swipes at his forehead. Suddenly, out of the corner of his eye, he saw a flash of white against one of the gray barracks. He turned rapidly on the movement, focusing on the exact place it had registered on his peripheral vision.

Nothing, though the whole place was spooky as hell. Raising his head, he scanned the front of the enormous barracks and saw on the third floor what appeared to be a mattress hanging half in, half out, its stuffing spilling a gray trail like vomit on the window ledge below.

Rat heaven, he thought, and, weary of interruption and needing a scapegoat, he added mentally, *health hazard. University's fault. The whole thing should be bulldozed to the ground and something should start fresh.*

Slowly, feeling a diminution of energy, he squatted in the middle of the street, thinking to do knee bends, but lacked the energy or the desire to rise immediately, and settled almost comfortably into a grasshopper position, straddling the faded yellow line in the center of the road and wondering—with no great need for an answer—if his father had ever walked down this particular street.

He had been stationed here for three years, the Episcopal chaplain. According to Mark's mother his father shouldn't have been shipped out at all. The training center was to have been his permanent duty station, but one day orders had come inexplicably. His father hadn't challenged them and found himself in the Coral Sea on the doomed carrier *Lexington.*

The September sun made a shimmering mirage on the deserted pavement. Mark pushed up and started forward, scarcely breathing. He had no clear memories of his father. Of course during the years he'd managed to put together a fantasylike collage of photographs and brittle letters and what little he could coax out of his mother. To this day she seemed loath to talk about Gerald Simpson.

Also mixed in with Mark's "memory" of his father were peculiarly vivid "memories" of a man named Alec Manning, his father's best friend. Shortly after the *Lexington* went down, Manning was killed on the *Yorktown* at the Battle of Midway. There were almost as many photographs of Alec and Rita Manning in that old Navy album as there were of his father—four very attractive faces, two women posing, a bit stiff, and the two men slightly more sober, as though the discipline from the training of the Navy could not be wholly shaken even in domestic moments.

Without warning, a sense of loneliness pressed down on Mark, along with the heat of the rising sun, a condition he thought he'd grown accustomed to after twenty-two years. "A natural-born loner," his California coach had called him, one prerequisite for a good runner.

Yet sometimes he ached with physical pain for a hand, an understanding voice, a love, a father who hadn't been killed at sea, a mother who did not measure out her life in miniature gavels and dog-eared engagement books. Just a hand. Was it asking so much?

As new anger joined forces with old repressed angers, he pushed up out of the squatting position and started off again in a slow trot, aware of the sun climbing higher and hotter. Along with his sweatband he'd forgotten the small bottle of salt pills which Coach Herbert had given him yesterday.

Contained. Something was contained here. The disquieting feelings he'd experienced at the gate were growing stronger, as though he'd entered a quarantined area, something isolated from the rest of the world.

Suddenly a simple question occurred. Where were the other runners? Herbert said quite a few of the team ran out here, though each had his favorite spot, some preferring the track which encircled the football field, others the variety of rural roads on the outskirts of town.

Of course. It was too damned early. It had still been dark when Mark had left the dorm. They'd show up probably just as he was leaving.

All right, green arrow straight ahead and to the right. No more stops for anything, he vowed, and trotted down the center of the street, toeing the faded yellow line, drawing several deep breaths and once lifting his face up to the dazzling morning sky which was turning a radiant blue with lingering streaks of red and gold.

His hawk friend was no place in sight. Good riddance. And the mysteries of the past seemed less urgent as well, as though there had been an invisible barrier he'd had to cross and once past he was safe. Though these deserted streets and weed-choked grounds had once been a major cog in the greatest war machine the world had ever seen, now they proved a threat to no one—and certainly not to him.

40

Ah, it was beginning to feel good, the run, but then it always did once he started—the pulse picking up, the leg muscles adjusting, nerves, tendons stretching and—most pleasant of all—the unique sensation, part pleasure, part pain, of extreme vibration, muscles all set into movement by his purposeful, bone-jarring speed and stride.

Beginning to lag. Pick it up. Not too fast. Not too slow. A good, steady pace. One, two. One, two. One—

Swimming pool, the third he'd passed. This part of the base must have been the recreational area, movie houses and pools interspersed with low gray structures fronted with aprons of cementlike terraces. Warm summer evenings. Coke floats. Girls from town in summer dresses.

Abruptly he broke speed and came to a sudden halt, mystified by the powerful evocation of a past he had not known. He trotted breathlessly, hands on hips for a few minutes, and gazed to his left at the terrace fifty yards away.

He looked at his watch. Not seven yet and his first class wasn't until nine, so explore. If you have to start again, you have to start again.

On that note of resolve, slightly tinged with guilt, he broke speed to a rapid, loose-limbed walk, hands still on his hips, head hanging down, breathing heavier than usual. God, but he missed the ocean breeze, that uniquely California scent of water and flowers. He missed it so much standing in the middle of this cracked and crumbling street.

Great fissures spread out on either side of the street, as though a minor earthquake had struck the area at some time. In the scorched, scraggly, weed-infested ditches on each side, he heard a faint rustling.

What was he doing here? A single bead of perspiration ran down the bridge of his nose, gaining momentum with the help of gravity, veered to the left and slipped with stinging accuracy into his left eye. Quickly he brought up the palm of his left hand and commenced a brief, vigorous rubbing in an attempt to ease the stinging.

As the stinging increased, he saw a brief mind's-eye glimpse of his mother, still attractive in her forties, slim, erect, light blond with slight help from her hairdresser, the only minor key being a permanent expression of abandonment in her left eye—only the left. He'd observed it in countless photos—around the Christmas tree, in front of the pool, at his high-school graduation. The right eye always appeared laughing and happy, but it was as though all

41

the monstrous grief she'd felt when his father had gone down had taken up permanent residence in her left eye: all the sad memories, the endless nights, the tragedy compounded by the death of Alec Manning less than a month later, the bewilderment of being left alone to raise a child.

He missed her terribly and recalled how helpful and cheerful she'd been despite the fact of her bewilderment at his leaving.

Abruptly he let his head fall backward until he looked straight up into the highest, bluest sky he'd ever seen. There were usually clouds of some kind over Balboa, either low-lying ones promising rain, or high, white and fluffy ones promising the respite of shade. But here there wasn't a cloud in sight, just an endless blue bowl clamped tightly in an arc over the world—or at least this section of it.

Slowly he lowered his head from the taut backward angle and in the process caught a glimpse of something flying low through the lush green foliage. But it wasn't the hawk. He could see that clearly now. Some other bird. Large, but not the size of the hawk.

Nervously he scanned the blue overhead and thought, out of sequence and irrationally, of the large portrait of his father which had hung over the mantel in the family room, an enormous rendering taken from the last photo before his death and then painted over in oils, a technique which flourished on the West Coast and in all fleet towns—or so he imagined—filled as they were with families on the verge of separation. "Better have a large oil photo in case memories become everything." And his mother had had one, and Mark had grown up with it in more ways than one. Every childhood crisis, every flare-up of teenage angst, every minor rebellion, every major self-assertion, had been talked out, fought out, prayed out, dealt with, corrected in the family room before that massive countenance.

Not that Mark was hostile to him. It was impossible to be hostile to a ghost—and that's all his father had ever been to him.

He started walking slowly down the street, cutting a middle path in the event the rustling in the ditch did prove to be something hostile. He walked a bit more easily now, looking up once when he thought he sensed movement ahead, thinking another runner, perhaps. Company would be nice in this place. He'd remember that tomorrow and see if some of the others ran here, see if they minded if he tagged along.

Nothing up ahead but more of the same, each corner containing large, crumbling buildings or barracks with gray, peeling paint.

There was something about that enormous oil painting of his father that always caused him trouble. When his father had posed for it he was wearing not his Navy uniform but rather his priest's garb, complete with a large silver crucifix which hung over his black vestments in the vicinity of his heart. When Mark was very little he used to think it was God in the oil photo.

His mother had never remarried, and if a well-meaning friend tried to fix her up, the friend—well meaning or not—was forever dropped.

He stopped again at the approach to the intersection. In the silent, hot morning he heard a curious sound, soft, low, rhythmical, as though—

He looked straight ahead to the large barracks on the southeast corner and saw a flagpole and ran his eye quickly up, expecting to see a flag. That was the sound he'd heard, a flapping of heavy canvas against metal.

But there was nothing there.

As he squinted up at the vacuum, he heard a single shout— male, or so it seemed—a single word. "Man!" was what it sounded like, but when he reflexively turned rapidly in all directions, his eyes frantically searching everywhere—down the long, deserted avenues, across the gray peeling facade of each barracks, straight ahead to that distant stand of trees and high blue water tower which marked the end of the base—he saw nothing.

Someone playing games? Some sort of dumb-ass initiation of the new kid on the block? He opened his mouth, ready to call back something brilliant and appropriate, then changed his mind. He'd thought he heard a flag flapping in the breeze as well, yet there was nothing there.

What was the matter with him?

He picked up speed and eyed carefully all four of the large barracks at this intersection and walked directly through the intersection, looking straight ahead to that very distant and dark green stand of trees, his ultimate destination, the finish line by what was called Coffin Pond—a grim name for a friendly oasis. According to Coach Herbert it was the one spot on the base where it was safe to drink the water. Already he looked forward to the cool overflow from the water tower.

Then move it on out.

Without warning, without warm-ups, as much to leave behind the million unanswered questions of the past, Mark shot forward, approaching top speed in less than sixty seconds, breaking all rules of good running, remembering only at the last minute the

43

shoelace nature of the running course as explained by Coach Herbert. "Lace east and west and move one block at a time due south to no-man's-land, the drainage ditch and Coffin Pond."

With the first burst of speed, he felt an objecting knot in the back of his left leg, the calf muscle refusing to cooperate. But instead of stopping and negotiating the objection, he merely increased his speed and tried at the same time to shift his weight from the balls of his feet to the outer rim.

It was a dumb thing to do and he knew it was a dumb thing to do but he did it anyway and took the next intersection at breakneck speed and saw on his right a large, blocklike, cavernous building and decided another movie theater, what else? Now the awkward angle at which he was gaping back at the old movie theater began to affect the gait of his run. Though he was tempted a second time to blow off the run altogether, he persisted, knowing himself well enough to know that it was always easier to go ahead and get it over with—anything than to suffer the tidal waves of guilt which he was capable of inflicting upon himself. So run now and come back this afternoon.

Thus resolved, he looked back around and checked his footing for the length of the block. The ruptures and fissures in the asphalt sometimes could make for hazardous terrain. As well as he could tell, it was clear sailing to the green-foliage fringe about three blocks ahead, the eastern perimeter of the base. There he'd drop down a block and lace his way back, always moving closer to the blue water tower and the drainage ditch and the promised cool water from Coffin Pond. Again the name struck him as being melodramatic and bizarre.

He tried to anchor his speed now, not dropping back, not accelerating, just holding steady, giving his left calf muscle time to accept the fact that, like it or not, this body was going to run— now!

To his left, opposite the parade ground, he saw a low, rambling, frame building with decrepit wooden railing skirting an equally decrepit wooden porch. Mess hall? Didn't seem big enough for a base this size. Sick bay. Infirmary probably. Almost the right size for a base like this.

Now, without breaking speed and continuing to ignore the ever-tightening knot in his left calf, he studied the building from one end to the other as he ran, suffering more and more the bizarre impression that he was alone in this modern ghost town save for wildlife.

At that moment, as he passed by the sagging screen door which

44

led into the sick bay, he felt the minor objection of his left calf turn into a major revolt with a wrenching, cutting sensation, as though a tourniquet had been twisted too tightly, cutting off circulation.

"Damn!" he gasped, and vowed not to break speed; he lifted his head, thinking foolishly that more air in his lungs would ease the pain in his calf.

As his eyes moved in a blur past the front door of the sick bay, he saw a man, standing in the shadows of the portico, watching him. Shocked by the unexpected appearance of another human being, doubly shocked by the increasing discomfort in his left calf, he tried to channel instant concentration on both the man and his leg, but his pain won out over curiosity.

His left hand shot instinctively down to the trouble spot, and as the sudden shift in balance threw him off his gait, he stumbled on absolutely nothing, the toe of his track shoe catching on the asphalt, rendering him momentarily airborne. In that split second he knew what was going to happen, knew more—how long and tedious it takes a sidewalk burn to heal, endless crackings and bleedings, a real pain in the—

As the gray asphalt rose up before him, in an attempt to spare his knees, he sent both palms out in advance and let them take the brunt of his weight and fall. His elbows formed the second point of a three-point landing and finally his knees, though at that point the momentum had been broken and his skin had remained remarkably intact, though his right wrist throbbed for several seconds immediately following the impact.

"You all right?" he heard a male voice call out.

For a moment, under the duress of the fall itself, he saw nothing except the skittering, early-morning shadows on the portico. Still sprawled on the hot pavement, uncertain of the damage, he squinted in all directions up and down the porch in search of the owner of the voice.

He raised up from his sprawled position, thinking a new line of vision would help. But it didn't. No matter where or how hard he stared, he saw nothing but the shifting shadows themselves, that and the still, hot morning and the banging of the one-hinged screen door which led into the sick bay.

"Hey!" he called out, thinking if the owner of the voice was within earshot he would answer. "Anyone there?"

His voice echoed over the quiet morning with abnormal amplification. He looked sharply over his shoulder, thinking he'd heard something coming from the vast, empty parade ground.

45

Nothing. The morning was a vacuum in all directions. Slowly, gingerly, he lifted his left hand, feeling something cool and sticky creep around his wrist and track down his arm.

He gave the hand one loose-wristed and vigorous shake and saw drops of his own blood speckle the pavement in an abstract pattern, red on gray.

"Keep going," he muttered aloud, and took two or three tentative steps forward, stealing one last glance at the sagging front porch of the sick bay.

All right, what could it have been? A wind that sounded like a voice? A shadow that resembled a man? No wind to speak of. Something sounding like the screen door? He listened closely and determined it wasn't forming syllables now. Then only one logical explanation remained—his own slightly overworked, highly homesick state of distorted consciousness.

So, then, that was it, right?

Right.

Good, no problem. Maybe the fall had straightened something. Whatever, it felt easier now, and this time he wouldn't push so hard, establish and maintain an easy pace, build up slowly to peak.

He kept his head down, studying the pavement for unseen hazards, and ultimately became bored with blurred and grainy gray and lifted his head. To his surprise he saw the east edge of the base rapidly approaching, a thick stand of dust-covered and parched native trees, dense enough in most places to obscure the golf course on the other side, once a green jewel in officers' country, now—according to Coach Herbert—abandoned and overgrown and neglected as everything else in this godforsaken place.

He took a turn to the right and maintained a good, steady sensible pace along the eastern fringe road and glanced continuously toward the trees, as though the hazard of the unidentified voice might at any moment revisit him. Heading west up a barely discernible incline, he spied a series of low, rambling, frame buildings much smaller than the barracks, certainly smaller than the movie theaters and sick bay. This nest of buildings, though as dilapidated as the others, looked as though they had served a different purpose. He topped the slight hill and looked down on the rambling gray complex and thought, *Officers' Club? Dining room, perhaps?*

Take a look. Won't hurt. Time out. The run left a lot to be desired, anyway. He'd try to get back out after his last class this afternoon and do it again and do it right. He'd better start doing something right.

He came to an abrupt halt in the middle of the intersection and looked carefully at the sprawling gray complex. It did appear different in several ways. One-story for one thing. All the other buildings had been multistoried. And there appeared to have been at one time an attempt at landscaping, though everything now was rank and overgrown. Still—

Should he take a look or stay on course and make himself complete the run—at least to the pond? He lifted his head in search of air, baffled by the vacillation. He loved to run. He lived to run. In many ways he only felt whole and free when he was running. Then why the hell was he acting this way? He wanted to make a good showing here, and it wasn't the hayseed university he'd thought it would be. In the way of talent and facilities it had been limited but impressive—with the exception, of course, of this particular track. But what the hell? It was as good a place as any for rudimentary workouts.

Then the thought occurred. Simple. It was the past. The past was draining him, sapping his strength, altering his direction. His father had been here, he knew, as well as his mother. And he had been here. They all had left something behind and that was the distraction he was suffering.

Maybe that's why he'd come here, to discover some of the missing pieces of that absolutely nonsensical childhood he'd managed to muddle through.

Then take five. He sure as hell couldn't find those pieces while running top speed back and forth on the shoelace course. How would it hurt to explore for a while?

Slowly he started toward the edge of the pavement and cut a direct path across the overgrown grounds, heading toward the large, arched front door. Somehow the place reminded him of movies he'd seen of 1930s speakeasies.

Once having reached the torturous decision not to be disciplined, he found himself falling rather easily and pleasantly into the small revolution. Besides, maybe he'd done enough, considering his recent layoff. Certainly all aspects of his body reminded him of the half-assed morning run. His left palm throbbed and the blood had now blotted and dried and caked on the back of his wrist. The muscle in his left calf was beginning to come to life again, a kind of delayed reaction to earlier abuse. Then there was the matter of the heat itself. Coach had said it would probably take some getting used to.

He continued slowly down across the dusty carpet of the "lawn," feeling thorns accumulating in his thick socks.

Officers' Club. He was convinced of it now. In fact if he remembered correctly his mother had told him when pressed—normally she didn't like to talk about the past at all—that the "officers' country" was at the far south end of the base.

Less than twenty yards now from the front door, he saw matching lampposts on either side of the cracked sidewalk. Slowly he passed between them and felt a sudden compulsion to return to the street and the running course. He had no business here. Wasting his time was what he was doing. Worse—

But at that moment he reached for the one remaining knob attached to the door, which served one half of the arch, and pulled, expecting to find it locked, surprised to feel it give, and he determined that this building was in far better condition than the others, as though it had been used for some purpose after the rest of the base had been shut down.

Still, the door was unlocked and he saw no sign speaking of trespassing and as the whole base was deserted now—according to Coach Herbert—why not take a look at the place where his father and mother had undoubtedly spent many evenings?

He drew the door open six inches and waited in the event there was objection coming from any source. Nothing. The world had gone silent. No sound at all, either inside or out. Not even any distant sounds—no diesel trucks or joyriding teenagers, no bird screeches. Nothing.

Feeling timid, he propped the door open with his foot and peered around the edge of the other door into a spacious interior designed, as far as he could tell, on several levels. The entry level formed a kind of apron stage with the remains of contoured, padded-velvet seats skirting the arena of the entrance hall, obviously a place where officers and their guests could wait for service or a table.

The remains of a once elegant, black-and-white tile entrance hall showed clearly in the dust and sun-filtered light of early morning. Many of the tiles had been ripped up, leaving a snaggle-toothed effect.

It wasn't the missing tiles that caught his attention but the destroyed and yet tangible elegance of the club itself. Beyond the first-apron entrance hall was a larger, fan-shaped room, low-ceilinged, with several dozen tables still arranged facing a small dance floor and band shell. To the left was a handsome and quite large mahogany bar. The mirror behind it had been removed, leaving a clear glimpse of the unfinished wall's surface.

48

Slowly now and quite softly, as though he were on the verge of interrupting something, he closed the door behind him and heard the knob catch smoothly after all these years.

Once inside he paused again, having spied for the first time on the far side of the large dining room what appeared to be a sun porch. At least the glow of the morning sun seemed to be a lot brighter coming from that direction.

Well, first things first. As long as he was goofing off anyway, he might as well undertake his "adventure" in a systematic way. Slowly and quite stealthily, as though he were afraid of being discovered, he walked carefully into a small room off the large entrance hall, clearly a cloakroom with its line of wooden shelves and bars. The door was cut in half, the lower half forming a shelf for transactions.

It's that one, the mink cape.

It's lovely, sir.

Thank you very much.

Shit, his imagination was beginning to ease into dialogue. He smiled at his own foolishness, though at the same time saw the high shelves lined with white hats, some with more gold braid than others, yet all boasting some form of gold.

Even as he perceived the image, it faded, leaving him staring at emptiness, the shelves clean, though refuse seemed to have collected in the corners of the small room, as well as old and wadded newspapers.

Then in the silence he heard a sound. Instinctively he turned. Had someone just come in the door? Beneath his ribs he heard his heart beating with a sudden and erratic rhythm. He stared at the closed door for a moment and was amazed to see that it held, no twisting of the knob on the other side.

Besides, that hadn't been the sound he'd heard. Not a door-knob, something else. Something more like someone whispering, then falling silent. He held still for a moment longer, slowly searching the immediate vicinity for threats and hazards.

Nothing. His imagination again, and the spooky nature of the time and this place.

Now he moved into position at the center of the aproned foyer, the place where all the Navy wives could best see and be seen.

Who's that with Doug?

Can't tell. She's a knockout.

And where, pray tell, is Miriam?

Home. Ohio.

Oh, dear!

Again he smiled at his own foolishness. Too many old movies.

49

He'd grown up on them. Those voices inside his head belonged to June Allyson and Gloria DeHaven.

Still it was a hell of an impressive entrance. This point was highly visible from every other point in the room, save the sun porch—if that's what it was.

He took the small step down and felt a brief objecting ache in his left calf, residual discomfort from earlier abuse. Then he looked up and found himself staring at the large mahogany bar, a bit dusty now and abused, like everything else. Running the length of the mahogany front were several large and very deep scratches, as though something equally large and jagged had been dragged past it.

Still it was in good condition, all of a piece—or so it appeared—and capable of accommodating at least a dozen barstools. He approached it slowly, studying the configuration of raw plaster left where the large mirror had been taken down. In the dusty light it looked like a woman with spread wings. If they had valued the mirror and taken it down, why had they left the bar itself?

He was in the process of shoving his hands into his pockets when his left palm issued a throbbing reminder of his recent fall—sprawl more accurately.

You all right?

In memory he heard that voice again—or had he heard it the first time?

Belly up, mates.

What's your pleasure?

That's not a plastic palm over there, is it? My cousin was at the Coconut Grove—

Mark blinked. The dialogue that ran through his head was as stupid as ever, courtesy of M-G-M or Universal, but what in hell—that stuff about "a plastic palm" and the "Coconut Grove," what was that? For several moments he tried to figure out the mystery which had come from inside his own head and, at last, as though to avoid the voices that he did not recognize or understand, he moved to a position directly in front of the bar and peered over and to the right at a large empty tub, the sort that might contain—

—a plastic palm!

He stared at it and shortened his vision and concentrated instead on the millions of spiraling specks of dust caught in the microcosm of one direct ray of sun which apparently spilled in from a crack in the ceiling. Abruptly he looked up, as though it were suddenly imperative that he find the source.

Thank you, God, for Rita Manning!

50

While looking up he heard another voice, and, as he was not concocting them with conscious effort, he shook his head vigorously once, then twice, and squinted into the discomfort of voices, turned rapidly once in a single circle and felt again curiously breathless.

He stopped dead still. Come on, get out of here!

But the thought was canceled before he could act upon it. He glanced back at the ceiling, the mystery registering on the second glance. There was no crack in the ceiling, not that he could see. Then where was the light source coming from?

Now he tried to trace the shaft of light upward and discovered it disappeared into what seemed from ground angle to be a solid and unbroken surface. But what it was and what it appeared to be were two different things.

Hairline crack?

Had his father ever been in here in the past? His mother? Of course. Those grainy black-and-white photos revealed an amazingly young-looking couple, the woman fair, trim and pretty, the man in his backward collar, and between them—both holding on as though to their most treasured possession—a blue blanket bundle which contained an infant.

He grinned at this first image of himself. Then carefully, almost gingerly, he reached out with his right hand and felt the fine layer of grit and dust that lightly coated the surface of the mahogany bar. The spread-winged image behind the bar appeared flat and dull, smeared plaster with four-corner screwed indentations where obviously the mirror had been held into place reflecting rows of bottles and polished glasses—more often than not the vain, rouged and coiffured officers' wives trying to maintain enough self-confidence to make it through the evening.

Now he commenced to hum an old blues number under his breath and walked slowly down the bar, carefully dragging the third finger of his right hand after him, creating a single, clearly defined path in the process. At the end of the bar he dragged his finger across the seat of his shorts and looked closely down upon the large stone tub which might have contained a—

—plastic palm.

Nothing plastic here, sir. It's a genuine plant, is what it is.

What the hell! He looked sharply up as though the voices were outside his head. Was he flipping out? The place got to you if you let it.

Suddenly he felt an overwhelming desire, mounting almost to a need, to call his mother. For some reason he wanted her to know

51

he'd been here, had seen not only the base in general but this place in particular.

Abruptly he looked up from the stone tub and recalled the little phone table in the corner of the study at home, the place where the phone would ring if he called—and his mother would hurry to answer it. From there the eyes in his mind moved nonstop, as though the phone table were the natural extension to the sun-filled porch which he could barely see just beyond the large dining room.

Enclosed, glassed in, as well as he could determine, though from where he stood the plate glass was dust-smeared almost to the point of being completely obscured. Still, cleaned and polished, it would have been a pleasant place for dinner on a hot summer evening. Probably always reserved for the big boys, the brass, visiting admirals and other assorted flapdoodles and VIPs. If the big boys didn't want it, it was probably up for grabs.

What's Admiral Blake doing on base?

Strategic planning. Or so I hear.

For what?

Some big maneuver in the Pacific.

This time Mark stood quite still and listened with interest to the voices coming from inside his head, as though they were emerging from an independent source disconnected from him in all ways. Admiral Blake? Who in the hell was Admiral Blake?

Slowly he started forward, newly aware with movement of his scraped hand.

Dance floor. Small. Eight couples would be a crowd. Maybe naval officers didn't dance in those days.

Twenty more feet. Damn, the sun was blinding! Nothing to obstruct it. Full-length glass all around, overgrown, and rank nature forming the irregular green walls. Nothing plastic here. In fact while still a distance away he could see no break in the thick, almost junglelike density beyond the windows. Yet there was a door, which he could just now see beyond the arch which led to the sun porch, an exit through which couples could stroll on warm spring and summer evenings, drinks in hand while awaiting their filets or prime ribs.

No strolling now, unless you had a machete in hand. Curious. All the other local flora which he'd briefly observed in the few days since he'd been here had appeared brown and parched, wilted, burnt to a cinder, but this beyond the window was unbelievable. Somehow it even looked damp and humid, though he knew better, having just stepped out of the dry heat.

Hurriedly he looked about, surveying the rest of the limited area. There was nothing else, just the one table. No chairs, no empty decorative tubs, which might have contained plastic palms. Only that single table, stripped of everything, including paint, which apparently had chipped and peeled over the years.

He must call his mother this evening. He hadn't talked with her since the first night of his arrival. Not that she'd be worried. He suspected she'd ceased to worry about him years ago, maybe the year his father had died.

Suddenly, to his embarrassment, he felt a burning behind his eyes, and he lifted his head sharply to dispel both the hurt and the burning, and simultaneously felt a hatred for something so powerful he turned once in an erratic circle to escape the strong emotion—and couldn't. He walked quickly to the single table and felt the hatred build, continue to build within him, accompanied now by a soul-deep resentment. Abruptly he stopped before the table and leaned heavily on it with braced arms as though in fear of falling.

Her blasted calm!

Leave! Go! Run!

It was this last imperative that got him moving, the sport and pastime which was his only true passion, running as though if he ran hard enough and fast enough and long enough, nothing else would matter except the trial of the run itself.

Run!

On the second internal command he pushed away from the table and at that instant heard a sudden, loud splintering, a shattering of glass, as though something had been hurled at the large plate-glass window which now rained down on him in pointed shards, a crystal torrent from which he stepped back. Since he was in the position and had the impulse, he ran, his arms lifted in crossed defense of his face against the resounding collapse which seemed to continue endlessly. Though his face was averted now, he ran behind the long mahogany bar in an attempt to take cover and wait out the terrifying and totally unexpected collapse of the large glass wall.

Crouched behind the bar, he continued for several moments to hear the shattering of glass, as smaller falling pieces struck larger ones, reducing all to millions of fragmented and shattered pieces.

Still crouching, he checked both arms, the only part of his anatomy directly bared to the cascading glass. Nothing. Lucky.

What had caused it? Could he have caused it? This thought gave pause and in a curious way comforted him. He'd been the cause. When he'd turned around he'd done so with such force he'd unwittingly pushed the table into the glass which, weakened by age and climate, needed only that one small jar to come crashing down about his head.

As the last of the glass fell with an almost musical tinkle, he rubbed both arms again for telltale moisture, pleased to feel nothing except the palm of his left hand.

It seemed to be over. Feeling like a soldier peering over a wall, he slowly pulled himself to his feet, recording the damage as he rose.

My God! The whole wall was gone except for the jagged edges, an irregular saw-toothed design which served as a unique frame for the green jungle beyond.

Completely up now, he clung to the edge of the bar and felt for the first time the raw, hot feeling of the morning air itself, filled with humidity here for some reason. He tried to breathe deeply in an attempt to relieve the tension, but the air seemed only to clog his lungs like a solid and for a moment left him gasping. He tried once more and the gasping seemed to ease and he ventured slowly out for a closer look at the collapse.

Had one shove of a small table done all this? Carefully he drew closer, studying the shimmering floor which, under the flattering spotlight of a fully risen morning sun, appeared to be covered with snow, a glittering, reflecting surface like millions of spilled diamonds.

As he approached the periphery of the destruction he stopped. Should he report it? The gaping saw-toothed wall was now open completely to the outside. Big deal. It'd been open before, hadn't it? The front door had been his for a mere push, and besides what was here that anybody could want? Obviously local vandals had stripped the place years ago. The mahogany bar was of value, to be sure, but who could cart it off? It probably weighed a ton.

As he stood surveying the ruin, movement just beyond the window caught his eye. Quickly he looked up. Something had stirred in the greenery. He'd seen it, had heard it. Something not of the foliage.

There. He saw it again and thought it a bird. Bright red it was, but only visible in dots and flashes through the brilliant green. Then he saw an expanse of red larger than a wingspan, saw what appeared to be, from this distance and through the obstacle of trees, a human figure, a woman's back—as though she'd started toward the club, then changed her mind and turned quickly about.

"Hey!" he called out, both alarmed and pleased to find someone alive and human and so near.

54

"Hey! Wait!" he called again, briefly losing sight of that inter-mittent flash of red. He started forward unthinking, directly across the broad field of shattered glass, still searching for the red that he'd thought at first had been a bird but was a woman.

"Anybody out there?" he called full voice as he approached the door and pushed it open. He certainly hadn't seen her clearly, but had seen enough to know that there was someone out there and it was a woman. Why hadn't she come when he'd called? She'd heard. She hadn't been that far away. Maybe he'd frightened her.

There she was again.

"Don't be afraid," he called out in what he hoped was a soothing and conciliatory voice, having spied her full length at the end of the overgrown path.

Great God, who was she?

No runner, that. Not a student, though she looked young despite the distance, and looked gorgeous, something of a red and clinging dress outlining a perfect figure, her hair thick and long, possibly auburn, though he might have been wrong, for he'd seen her for less than a second. She'd appeared to see him and darted deeper into the woods.

"Hey, come back! Don't be . . ." He'd started to say "afraid." Then he bolted after her, taking care to avoid the naked roots, jagged holes where an overgrown tree had splintered the side-walk. Here and there a few concrete blocks had been pushed entirely upward, then had cracked as though under the duress of an earthquake, while others seemed to have collapsed inward as though the solid ground beneath them had given way, leaving nothing of substance.

It was like running an obstacle course. Not wanting to fall flat on his face twice in one morning, he was forced to keep a large portion of his attention on the treacherous underfooting. Thus when he reached the end of the path and the place where he'd last seen the visitor, she was gone, and he was left with the blazing sun pounding down on him and a shrill decibel level of ringing in his ears, and not anything red in that continuous and unalterable green.

"Damn!" he cursed softly beneath his breath, his head swiveling in one direction, then another. He hadn't imagined this one. He was certain of it. Maybe the voice back at the sick bay when he'd fallen, but there had been a woman here so recently that in the heavy air there still hung a floral fragrance, and there were no flowers blooming anywhere.

He closed his eyes and breathed deeply of the pleasant scent and was amazed it seemed to be getting stronger instead of dissipating.

Abruptly he opened his eyes and heard a tiny crack not too far away. Close by. Where? Again he turned in an almost spastic circle, searching, searching, for that one familiar flash of red. There. My God, how had she managed to get so far? At the end of the woods now, clear on the other side near the road that flanked the blue water tower.

This time he did not call or speak, not certain he could project his voice over that distance, thinking, too, that maybe simply a friendly gesture like a wave would do more than the sound of his voice. Slowly he lifted his hand, feeling certain her attention was his—at least for the moment. Her stance, her head, all seemed to be turned in his direction.

He raised his arm and held it for a moment, trying to discern if there was any reaction at all coming from her. But as far as he could see, there was nothing. She appeared to be standing at an angle close to a large, overgrown cedar, part of her body concealed behind the shrub, part of her face as well—half a woman.

All right, then start slowly. Saunter, don't run. Don't frighten her. Let her see you're coming, but quietly and disinterestedly. He walked as casually as he knew how, though not once did he take his eyes off that slim column of red standing partially concealed a distance away.

Something very different about her, something mildly dated, her hair drawn up on both sides resembling those old pinups of Betty Grable. And there was something else about her, the dress itself. Not a sports dress or a poking-around-old-places dress, but a dressy dress—a church dress, even a party dress. Why would she wear something like that out here?

Still she held her position, half concealed by the rank cedar, still apparently focused closely on him, the taut angle of her head not altering, as though to do so would break the invisible force which stretched between them.

He felt it, an intensity of focus and concentration. He couldn't have broken it if he'd wanted to. But he didn't want to, although he couldn't quite say why he didn't. It had been nice to discover someone else alive out here, not a ghost. Maybe that was all there was to it.

Though he had started out at a good speed, within twenty feet he had to slow again for countless obstacles—fallen trees which barricaded what remained of the path, parasitic creepers which had crept off the fallen trees and formed a network of tentacles in search of something else to live off and the disruptive walkway itself, a pitted stretch of holes and gullies and crumbling concrete. The closest attention had to be paid to each step.

To his surprise he looked up after several torturous and graceless moments to see the end of the woods, the gray-concrete street flanking the extreme south edge of the base, and about a block farther west the blue water tower. Of greater interest was the thick rank cedar behind which she'd hidden but which now bore no trace of her.

Panting and sweating, he stopped three feet from the cedar, still searching foolishly for that specific red that had first caught his eye. No red. Something else. A faint and familiar and irresistible scent—like hyacinths or something from early spring—

Where was she? Who was she? Why was she poking around in this godforsaken place?

Lacking an answer to any of these questions, he looked up slowly and felt a last bead of sweat roll slyly into the corner of his left eye. Again momentarily blinded, he rubbed the eye with his right fist and shook his head, hoping to shake loose the dripping perspiration. Through the blur of movement he saw a liquid scene of blue sky, parched trees, the distant globe of the water tower and—

—one slim slash of red near the tower a block away. Just standing there at the base of the six enormous steel legs.

He grinned and started out across the last stretch of parched grass and weeds down into a small gully and up again on the other side—on pavement now—the expanse between here and there unbroken, no thick and concealing foliage to obscure her from him and no need to keep a hawk's eye on the terrain underfoot and no place for her to hide, for he could see her now just the other side of a leafy grove of trees, which even from this distance seemed richer, greener, more luxuriant than the rest.

The pond, of course. Coach Herbert had told him about the pond. Less than half a block now, so close he could hear the water splashing as it spilled out of the underground pipe from the overflow of the water tower.

Twin treats coming up: a closehand look at Miss Elusive in red and a sip of clear, cool water. He hadn't exactly accomplished the run he'd started out to do, but he'd already reconciled that guilt. He'd come back after his class this afternoon and do it again. There was no meeting this afternoon. Coach Herbert had told him that.

Free to explore on your own, Mark.

The coach's very words, and although he hadn't planned it, as it had turned out that was precisely what he'd done. Now he was close enough for a friendly greeting.

"Hello!"

No response. Well, perhaps she hadn't heard.

"It's a hot one, isn't it?" he called out idiotically. Less than ten feet from her now, though he still couldn't see her clearly. Not her face at any rate, concealed as it was behind the thick, leafy fronds of willows which grew luxuriously so close to the water's edge.

But she was there, for he could clearly see the red dress from the waist down, the nipped, almost childlike waist comfortably cinched by a slim belt of the same material. And there was more— the way in which the remarkable fabric clung to the exact contour of her leg, a single curving angle worthy of a sculpture, unbroken by anything until he saw, dim through the barrier of green, those white, ankle-strapped platform shoes.

He stopped now, still on the edge of the pavement, something warning him. Her shyness was becoming too obvious, mildly painful. The last thing he wanted to do was contribute in any way to her discomfort. She might bolt again as she had done twice already.

"Are you . . . from town?" he asked, trying to make his voice gentle.

No response. Not even a shifting of angle. Where were her hands? He could see one red sleeve which appeared to disappear behind her back, a curiously relaxed and open posture for someone shy.

"I'm from California," he announced bluntly, and heard the echo of the stupid comment and thought it would never end, that resounding proof of his own taut nerves.

Well, what the hell? Maybe she was a local freak. Every town had them. Maybe they let her loose out here because she could hurt no one. So be it.

Suddenly he heard the splashing of the fresh, cold water, as though for the first time, and he felt the lining of his mouth go dry and hoped she didn't object to his approaching, at least as close as the edge of the pond.

"Thirsty," he mumbled, and smiled apologetically, hoping that the word sufficed as an explanation or as a warning that now he was going to move so she'd better be on guard.

A thought occurred. Maybe she couldn't speak. He took several steps toward the edge of the pond and saw that it was indeed in

58

the shape of a coffin, the force of the water coming through the underground pipe from the water tower literally carving the contours into shape.

Suddenly, coming from the embankment behind him, he heard a rustle, a twig crack, as though from the pressure of a single footstep. Less than five feet from the edge of the pond, he temporarily postponed his need for water and turned abruptly toward the high embankment.

He saw nothing—

He scolded himself for his own foolishness, confident she'd seen.

"Spooky place," he said in a tone of self-derision. "Could have sworn I heard . . ." he said, aware of the fragments which were passing for sentences. "Did you hear . . .?" he began, thinking to involve her in the minor mystery.

But the place on the opposite side of the pond, where he'd carefully charted the female contours attractively clad in red, was now empty.

He stared forward at the vacuum for several seconds. *Gone?* How was that possible? He'd looked away for less than ten seconds. Then the stunned paralysis was over and he ran back up onto the pavement and searched frantically in one direction and then the other, seeing nothing but the narrowing ribbon of gray and cracked asphalt. No telltale red in either direction. Nothing due north either, except the tide of abandoned and crumbling structures stretching into the distance, and certainly nothing behind him but the embankment itself.

For several seconds he stared across at the tree bough and felt stupidly accusatory. Was it the tree's fault? It had served as protector for her face, which he had yet to see clearly. Then why hadn't it protected her?

Only at that moment did he realize the stupidity of his thoughts. What in hell was happening to him?

It was the bough's fault, the tree's fault.

"Shit!"

This single, though satisfying word came out in the form of an obscene benediction. Bend over and get your fucking drink of water and get out of here.

You don't understand the fucking nature of anything.

He turned suddenly on the hot pavement.

Get your drink of water and hurry.

This thought came in the manner of an imperative command. But before he started back to the edge of Coffin Pond and the

59

seductive sound of cool, clean, splashing water, he looked again up the embankment to see if he could find a clue to the sound which had distracted him from the color red in the first place.

Nothing.

"Mark?"

He whirled at the sound of the voice so near, his name spoken as he'd never heard it before, as though it were merely a continuing part of breathing music. He looked in what he thought was the direction—across Coffin Pond—and saw nothing, then commenced turning in sharp circles, his head going in all directions in search of the one who'd spoken his name.

"Mark?"

There it was again, less wind, more of a voice, a delicate, almost childlike voice coming from—

There.

He stopped, turning, and wished he could stop the equally erratic beating of his heart as well. There was something. Not the red, though something. The something was white. No clear contours, but clearly white and situated near the top of the embankment, a white, perched something knotted in on itself.

Stymied but relieved to have found something that in a way confirmed his own reason, he ducked his head and tried to squint upward through the thick foliage to the top of the embankment. "Anyone there?" he called out, and heard a shyness in his voice, a trembling, the natural condition of someone who thought he was alone only to find out otherwise.

The perched, white something did not move or speak.

He stepped nearer to the edge of the embankment and again ducked his head, lower this time, and found a fairly unobstructed avenue up through the green foliage and saw what appeared to be two extremely tanned legs drawn up, arms locked about them, and even an added bonus of what appeared to be a blond head, hair cut short.

Mark froze, refusing to advance, unable to withdraw. There was something about the human figure—if it was a human figure—that seemed too fixed. And where was the face?

"Hello?" he called now and bent lower, thinking if only he could get a clear glimpse, all mysteries would be solved. Though he received no answer, he did manage a closer vision and saw that it was a human figure—male or female he could not say—human in that he saw two recognizable legs, small, almost childlike, the entire body curved in on itself.

Asleep?

Not possible, for who had called to him, called his name? He knew no one here except Coach Herbert.

Then leave. Whoever the sprite was dozing in the hot, still September morning, leave it be. Slowly now he backed away from the edge of the embankment. His shoe loosened particles of the dry, red, sandy loam and caused a miniavalanche. He looked quickly up toward the figure to see if the slight whisper of rushing earth had altered anything.

It hadn't. Someone had partied late or arisen early and now had found the perfect place to snooze it off.

Again he stepped backward and turned toward an angle which would enable him to get a drink from Coffin Pond and leave all life—wild and otherwise—undisturbed. Thirsty as hell, mouth dry. He approached slowly, looking for the easiest way down. Muddy, unsure footing. Damn! He felt his left foot slide ominously, a rim of red mud collecting on its left side.

Still thirst was insistent, and he reached blindly out for support which wasn't there, flailed at empty air, and at last slipped all the way down to his knees and found himself staring straight down into the clear, still reflection of himself, flawless, mirrorlike, though only a short distance away was the turbulence of the overflow from the high blue water tower which cast a huge, round, though shifting, shadow across the road. It moved with the sun.

A remarkable reflection. The texture of still water appeared to age him mysteriously, his sun-bleached blond hair resembling gray in the green-black depths of Coffin Pond. As he bent lower in a combination of narcissistic fascination and repulsion, he saw the shape and outline of his face alter slightly, the jaw fill and swell, the eyes submerge into deep pooled shadows, a curious bizarre hallucination of instant aging, until the closer he looked, the more clearly he saw not his face, but that of the man in the portrait which hung over the mantel at home.

His father. His face. Older.

He blinked once, then twice, seeing something that was not a part of the water, green-black scene, seeing a fragment of—

—red, just entering the liquid reflection, coming from—

—*where?*

He looked up as though an invisible cord had snapped his neck, trying to think coherently, trying to understand the source and nature of the red fragment which was not at all visible across the pond, the place where he'd last seen her.

Reflexively he tried to back away from the pond, but the muddy loam provided no secure footing. At the same time he felt his knees slide farther down toward water's edge, he pitched forward toward the edge of the pond. Frantically he reached out for support and came up with two handsful of mud, which held him for the moment and forced his vision back down into the water beyond the hallucination of his father's face, farther down to some depth beyond the surface where he saw with indisputable clarity the woman in red as though she were just emerging from some underwater chamber, her image as clear as his. She smiled at him now from her watery horizon, a smile more dazzling and gentle than he'd ever seen in his life, something childlike and vulnerable and terribly compelling.

Only once did he quickly lift his head again, thinking with a last shred of rationality that what he was seeing in the water had its counterpart of substance somewhere beyond the edge of the pond.

When a quick glance revealed nothing before him but green branches of the thicket itself, he looked longingly back down into the water for a more satisfying glimpse, and found her, found as well the smile, the wide-set eyes, the most magnificent and compelling female face he'd ever seen, so compelling that he reached one hand out and down and penetrated the surface of the water and did not find it unusual that the mirror image held no ripples, no surface disturbance, as though he had merely reached through glass toward that most admirable face, the red dress becoming clearly visible now, floating delicately about her like an aura, revealing now and then a glimpse of white flesh like marble against the contrasting green-black depths.

She laughed like a child at play and lifted her arms up to him.

He had thought first simply to reach in to her and draw her out to him on the embankment, but as he touched her hand through the surface of the water, he felt a tension in the fingers which suggested she was at home and did not want to emerge. Her hand, which had wrapped itself around his with all the grace and tenderness of gently lapping water, had commenced to pull him forward, her eyes holding him as fast as her hand.

In the reflection of the pond, their images briefly blended, his canceling hers, hers, his. He slid all the way down to the water's edge, now impervious to the muddy condition of his clothes, legs, shoes, only one goal in mind—his unobstructed meeting with that face which floated so close before him, so close to the surface, beckoning, always leading him forward until he lost his balance on muddy earth and fell slowly forward like slow motion, not even aware when he penetrated the water, because he felt nothing, none of the cold or wetness, the clinging clothes or heavy shoes.

Nothing mattered but the release he felt as he sank deeper and deeper toward her arms, which were now raised and open to him, an embrace which he ached to join—and which he would shortly, as soon as he fell deep enough, for she always appeared to be just beyond his reach.

For a few eternities he was having trouble breathing, something foreign catching in his lungs, causing an unpleasant sensation, as though a pillow were being held over his face. But the unpleasantness could be endured considering what was waiting at the end.

So he ignored the sensation of suffocation and pushed himself farther into the depths of the pond and was amazed it had appeared so shallow from the bank, for it was not shallow at all, was indeed bottomless.

He saw her now just below him in a shaft of filtered sunlight which caught the shimmer of her auburn hair and turned it into a halo of jewels. He tried to speak to her, but suddenly without warning she lifted a hand to his lips and pressed them gently closed, her eyes very near now, their depths even deeper than the pond, helping him past the diminishing sense of suffocation, her hands leaving his lips now and sliding around his neck, dragging his face down closer to hers. He suddenly felt such a surge of joy that he relaxed and slipped deeper into the water, always thinking that with each descent he would come within full range of that embrace.

Just once did he look back and that was at the sound which did not belong to this world but to that other one of which he had grown strangely weary. There was nothing in that world as enticing or as soothing as the face that was now directly before him.

What was that voice shouting from the other world? Like all his bad memories and bad dreams, why didn't it go away and leave him alone? No matter. He could and would ignore it. Nothing made sense up there on the surface. No need to respond. Here in that compelling face was the only destination for him that mattered.

They would explore the lower level together. Always together. Never again to be alone—

With the professional calm and expertise of a coach who'd worked all his adult life forcing young men to develop their bodies to maximum capacities, Dick Herbert knelt over the still figure, quickly positioned the arms and head at the proper angle for resuscitation, bent over, pried open the mouth and inhaled, exhaled deeply.

Again. In, out. Three, four. Wait. In, out. Three, four. Wait.

"Christ!"

All right, let's go with artificial respiration.

What if he hadn't decided to jog the new five-mile course on the base at this particular time on this particular morning?

Coach Herbert raised up with all the speed of a man who knew the dangers and potential tragedy of this moment and again bent the boy's arms at an angle beneath his head, sat slightly on his buttocks and searched for and found the base of the rib cage.

Lean forward, push down. Count three, sit back.

Lean forward, push down. Count three, sit back.

He saw two small streams of muddy water escape the boy's lips and trickle down out of sight beneath his head. Again and again the coach leaned forward and thought distractedly, what waste! for this body beneath him was in its prime, muscles taut, firm, not one square ounce of useless and destructive fat, damned near a perfect specimen and built for running.

Coach Herbert stopped for breath. He'd been pumping steadily for several minutes and had produced nothing more than those two thin streams of muddy pond water from the still figure.

Why had someone of Mark Simpson's caliber fallen carelessly into this shallow pond and apparently made no effort to reach out to the nearest embankment on either side and pull himself to safety? Yet there was the fact of it, and the second—more alarming—fact was that several minutes of nonstop resuscitation had passed and the prime specimen beneath had yet to draw a breath on his own.

Herbert looked up out of an emotion he'd rarely felt in his life—fear—and searched the horizon for help. Brain damage. It couldn't go on for too long. Where the hell were all of his hotshot runners who were supposed to do the course this morning? As he could see no one, he decided to try mouth to mouth again.

He'd first found the body floating spread eagle beneath the water. How long he'd been there Herbert really had no idea. Still, hang onto calm and reason. It couldn't have been too long. His color wasn't good, but it wasn't that bad either. Too much time was passing and he'd damned well better do something.

As he leaned forward for one last chance at resuscitation, he looked up and saw something white at the top of the embankment, squinted up out of his sweat and fear and saw what appeared to be a young girl standing there shyly, half concealed by the foliage.

"Hey!" he shouted up, and immediately fell forward and forced the boy's mouth open, knowing better than to waste a minute on just talking. Talking and working simultaneously, he shouted again, "Hey, you!" and felt again that most alarming of all emotions—fear—and recognized that its cause was the lifeless student beneath him. The tanned skin under the direct impact of high morning sun revealed a darkening blue tinge.

What the hell was the matter with her?

"You, up there! I need help. Can you . . .?"

Still she appeared to hang back among the foliage.

"Hey, please! I really need . . ."

At last she moved, though it seemed at a snail's pace.

What the hell was—

Then she descended from the top of the embankment, her slight weight braced against the downward slope. A pretty girl, fair hair cut short, bobbed, somehow old-fashioned in appearance. She held a twig in her hand, which she stripped of leaves in a deliberate, almost systematic fashion, all the while not really looking at what he was doing but focusing instead on the boy, her smooth, round face not revealing fear exactly, rather a knit brow which spoke more of curiosity.

"What's the matter with him?" she asked in a strangely low and musical tone, her voice much older sounding than her appearance.

Lacking the time and energy for an explanation, Coach Herbert felt himself growing dangerously frightened and consequently incoherent. "An ambulance . . . could you . . . needs respira . . ." All the time he splintered the air with fragments, he persisted with his attempts to resuscitate the boy, who continued to lie limp beneath him, the face turned to one side, mouth open and slack, while that damnable blue tinge became more and more pronounced.

Suddenly it hit him, the foolishness of their exchange, the dangerous amount of time that was passing. There was something on her face—or more accurately the vacuum on her face—the almost apathetic manner in which she gaped down, hands on hips, a shiny patina of sweat causing her smooth, unlined brow to glisten. She looked so young, so damned young and so—out of it.

"Look," he began, and started up from his squatting position over the boy. It wasn't until he was halfway up that he realized the only chance the boy stood for survival was his repeated efforts to revive him. Obviously he could not count on the young girl for help. It was a good twenty minutes run to the North Gate and another five or ten to the nearest house and telephone—and God alone knew how long for the local ambulance service to stir themselves.

"Christ!" he murmured, suddenly moved by the impending tragedy and his belated and really benign part in it. He straddled the boy again and turned his head in the opposite direction and again commenced the slow, rhythmic movements of artificial respiration. One, two, three, push. One, two, three—

Damn!

He'd worked too long to build a team that perhaps with luck might be considered Olympic material only to have—this. Breathless, he sat back on his heels and again studied the face and saw—nothing. Waste. What a waste! Nothing for the future here, no—

"Sir?"

He looked up out of the bleakness of his thoughts, surprised to see the young girl standing directly before him. Up close he saw red clay smudges on her white shorts and again wondered what the hell she was doing out here.

"Sir, do you want him to wake up? He's just asleep, you know."

For a moment he gaped up at the pretty young face. "No, I'm afraid he's . . ."

"Asleep, sir. That's all."

He tried to be patient. "He's not breathing."

"He's having trouble breathing, that's true, but that's because you're sitting on him."

He almost laughed, and under less tragic circumstances he might have. He started to speak, but decided again he lacked both the will and the energy. Instead he reached back and down for the boy's wrist, found the pulse spot and felt nothing.

Hell confirmed. He was dead.

Needing additional proof, he reached for the boy's neck, searching for that long vein that was always capable of recording the degree of life still remaining.

"Sir, let me do . . ."

"Sssh." For a moment he thought he felt something.

The girl's innocence and naïveté were beginning to be a nuisance. Best dispatch her for, if not help, at least the authorities—though now he wondered if she were capable even of that.

"Miss . . ." he began, feeling for the first time the awful weight of reality. The boy was dead. Even the word struck with an unreal echo against his brain. "Could you . . . would you go and find a telephone and call . . ." He hesitated, staring down on the lifeless profile, trying not to see it, not believe it. Call whom? The police? *Oh, dear God!*

"Would you go and find a telephone and call . . .?" Out of the depths of his own regret and remorse, he felt a gentle nudging against his shoulder.

"If you want him to wake up, get off him," she scolded.

"He's dead," he said bluntly. "Just go for help."

"No need," she persisted, still nudging him with one hand, a curious smile on her face. "Just get off him," she said, a mild, pleading quality in her voice.

Then, lacking the will to argue scientific fact with her, he shifted his weight to the right and swung his left leg up and over the boy's body and felt both knees sink in the soft mud, under added pressure.

At the same time the girl moved forward and squatted near the boy's head. "Wake up."

Though this was a command, it was not in any sense delivered with the imperative of a command. Rather he found himself listening with pleasure to the low, lyrical tone of the almost unbearable innocence of the young girl trying to resurrect a dead boy.

"Come on, open your eyes. Nap's over for both of us. I saw you coming. I did," she was saying now, and again it was the subtle beauty of her voice, combined with the grisly nature of the scene itself, that caused the coach to steal merely a glance again in that direction.

"Miss, you must . . ."

"Hello. See, it wasn't so bad. It isn't so bad, is it? Being awake, I mean, and in this world?"

It was hell, that's what it was, and he had to put a stop to this madness as soon as he could. "All right, that's enough," Coach Herbert managed at last, and stepped sideways toward the aberration that he felt must be stopped, and without looking simply entreated, "Please . . ."

Then he looked down, and in that single instant of fear and incoherency saw something that made no sense. Coach Herbert had left the boy with his cheek resting on his left arm crooked beneath his head, his right arm lying limp at his side. Only now—

Not possible. Not possible. Not possible—

67

The boy's eyes were open, staring in a curiously underdeveloped way, looking at the pond and the thicket of trees on the opposite side.

The girl continued to talk. "Do you feel rested? I always do. My mother can never understand the joys of a morning nap. I've tried to explain but it's hopeless." She laughed, a sound like music.

Coach Herbert felt his incredulity stretch to the breaking point. *Alive?*

Not possible. Though he wanted scientific and irrefutable confirmation, he again found himself peculiarly drained of energy. Then there was no need for confirmation anyway because the boy's eyes blinked once, a slow, almost drugged open and close.

Their eyes met in a brief moment of nonrecognition. At least Mark Simpson appeared not to know or recognize him. Then he did and slowly came up from his flattened position on the earth.

"Sir," he began, and had just successfully raised himself to his knees when he was overcome by a brief coughing paroxysm.

As the coughing and sputtering persisted, the girl moved back and watched with real concern.

Finally the boy looked up through tearing eyes, an expression of complete bewilderment on his face. "Where in the . . .?"

"Better?" This calm inquiry came from the girl, who was standing now, briskly brushing leaves and clinging things from her knees.

For a moment Coach Herbert saw the boy turn on the voice, as though only now aware that there were three of them present. Seeing that the person with the voice was female and clearly a stranger to Mark, his apparent embarrassment only increased until at last the face, which only moments before had been blue-tinged due to a lack of oxygen, now blushed crimson, indicating an emotional distress and a healthy circulation.

"I'm . . . sorry," Mark Simpson apologized, and coughed again in an attempt to clear his lungs. Looking a moment longer at the girl, he tried to struggle to his feet and still disguise his obvious weakness.

"Here, let me help you. . . ."

The music of the girl's voice brought Coach Herbert back to the moment. He looked up out of his stunned disbelief to see the young girl stooped over the boy, trying gently to urge him to his feet again.

He had been dead!

"Come on, stand up. You'd better. My mother always . . ."

She broke off, denying him the pleasure of her voice, a most

68

marvelous voice coming from that small frame. To Coach Herbert's increasing amazement, he saw Mark Simpson stand, wobbly at first, accepting without objection the girl's offer of a hand, and then at last testing his legs with a quick shake of each.

Finding them apparently reliable, the boy appeared to notice for the first time the disreputable condition of his clothes. "What . . . ?"

Coach Herbert assigned the mystery to a lesser part of his mind and came up with a solution he felt certain they all could live with. "You slipped," he said, too easily, too patly. But what the hell, he'd almost slipped himself on the slick underfooting.

Mark looked at him sharply, and for a moment Coach Herbert saw a protest forming on that young and clearly embarrassed face.

"Well, I almost did it myself," Coach Herbert went on, forcing a smile. The moment seemed to need one. "I'll have to see what we can do about that." He pointed back down to the mud-slimed descent that led to the edge of the pond. "Either that or ask the university to put in a drinking fountain for us out here." He forced a laugh at his own small attempt at humor.

"I didn't . . . slip. I don't think . . ." The hesitancy and the voice were Mark's, still protesting the solution. "Did I?" he asked, looking puzzled at Coach Herbert, all the while fidgeting with his soiled garments.

Coach Herbert noticed that in the meantime the girl had withdrawn a short distance, her back to both now, head down as though she were listening carefully and purposefully, keeping her distance and staying out of it. For that Coach Herbert felt a peculiar gratitude. Her presence only seemed to complicate things.

"Well," Coach Herbert smiled and moved the rest of the way up to where the boy was standing, "you're all right. That's the important thing. You gave me a scare."

Mark stepped away, though now he glanced briefly over his shoulder at the girl, who continued to maintain both distance and silence. Still looking at her, he spoke: "I don't remember slipping, Coach. I really don't."

Coach Herbert shrugged, momentarily bereft of reasonable explanations for the boy. He shoved his hands into his pockets, felt his stopwatch and pedometer and remembered the curious urge he'd suffered earlier that morning to leave the hot and suffocating confines of his office in the Athletic Department and jog the new running course.

"Well, whatever," Herbert concluded vaguely, and looked at the two who stood in frozen positions, their faces and bodies wearing a peculiar dappled coat of sun and shadow. "I think you slipped and hit your head as you fell. At any rate you were in dire straits when I came along."

All at once something occurred to him. If the girl had seen Mark running as she claimed to have done earlier, why hadn't she also seen him fall into the pond? In the quiet of the morning, the question which remained inside his head seemed to reverberate with embarrassing loudness.

At that moment she turned and looked directly at him.

Coach Herbert stepped up onto the pavement, still moving away, wanting only a distance between himself and the mystery. "Well, all that matters—as I said—is that you seem to be okay." He added a hopeful, "You're sure you're all right, aren't you? I mean . . ."

The boy nodded with reassuring speed. "I'm fine," he said, and for the first time managed what appeared to be almost a grin. "Though if you ask me, this place . . ." He broke off and looked around—not just at the pond, but an all-encompassing glance that seemed to include the water tower, the road, the dilapidated Officers' Club and the rest of the base as well.

Coach Herbert waited a moment to see if Mark would complete his opinion of "this place," but he didn't. "You want to come back with me now?" Herbert called, still walking backward on the hot pavement, not wanting to intrude and yet wanting to be of service if he could.

Again Mark hesitated. He glanced over his shoulder at the young girl, who was maintaining an admirable silence and distance, staying well out of it, as though she knew her presence was a complicating factor, yet did not know how to extricate herself.

"Well?" Coach Herbert prodded, still walking backward, waiting for a response. When an embarrassing length of time had passed and the boy seemed incapable of reaching a decision or delivering an answer, Herbert answered for him. "Well, take your time coming back. No running. Not in this heat. Certainly not after your . . ." He'd started to say "near fatal accident." What the hell, near fatal? There had been no pulse.

Finally the boy nodded.

"Then I'll see you later. Let me know if you need . . ."

"No, I'm fine." At last the boy moved of his own volition toward the edge of the pavement, as though he were aware that his response had been less than satisfactory.

Coach Herbert felt the reassurance he needed in order to turn about-face, and with a final wave of his hand start off down the straight, hot pavement. With his head down, the heat which struck his face seemed to come from a blast furnace.

He had been dead.

As Herbert turned the corner heading into the long street which led directly to the North Gate some six blocks ahead, he looked back and caught only a fleeting glimpse of the boy standing precisely as he'd left him at the edge of the pavement, and that patch of white just barely visible through the thickness of foliage.

And the other? He rubbed his eyes, looked away and then looked back. Nothing, just his impaired vision and the two young people standing with their backs to each other.

Though Herbert wasn't cold, he walked with his shoulders lifted and hunched, as though against a bracing wind, and he closed his hands securely about his stopwatch and the pedometer, grateful for those small instruments which could accurately and objectively measure time and distance.

Twice Mark started to call after Coach Herbert and ask him to wait. Twice he had changed his mind. For one thing, it seemed rude just to leave the girl standing there, though who she was and what she was doing here he had no idea.

The inevitable thoughts of the girl led him back to the mystery of the morning itself.

What had happened?

Slowly he bowed his head, as though the question itself were a thing of weight, and, with a curious residual physical weakness, he went slowly down in a squatting position. Finding that uncomfortable and difficult to maintain, he sat flat down on the earth with a comic suddenness, trying with great discipline and greater effort to find in his rather fractured memory the last coherent recall before—

—before what?

You slipped and hit your head.

Bull!

Then what did happen? Why was he able to remember nothing clearly except that he'd come here to run, had taken time to explore here and there and—

Officers' Club.

There was one clear memory. The Officers' Club, the broken window, the—

71

"If you're sure you're okay and wide awake, I'll be going."

He looked up sharply at the sound of the voice and saw tanned and pretty legs approaching him, then passing him by. "Wait." His request was soft-spoken, and he was on the verge of calling again.

But suddenly she turned and inquired for the second time: "Are you sure you're okay?"

He almost laughed. Her insistence that he'd merely fallen asleep was as crazy as Coach Herbert's that he'd slipped and hit his head. "I'm awake," he nodded, a touch of sarcasm in his voice. He continued to stare after her and began to concentrate on finding a way to make her stay, at least for a few more minutes.

He remembered something else now. Patch of white. Approaching Coffin Pond in need of water and seeing through the thick foliage a patch of white—like shorts or a tennis shirt.

"Were you here when I . . .?" He couldn't quite bring himself to say either "fell asleep" or "slipped," so he lightly shrugged and let her fill in the blank.

Waiting for an answer, he took advantage of her "full-length portrait," as it were, amazed at how small she was, almost child-like, though he knew better, for the white knit shirt revealed the appealing curves and angles of a young woman. The frame, though small, was firm, not a spare ounce of fat anywhere.

"What's your name?" he asked bluntly, pleased at the facility with which he was dismissing the unpleasant morning.

Still she didn't look up, so he had yet to record a clear glimpse of her face. Instead of providing him with an answer, she stepped backward all the way up off the pavement and turned and looked in the direction of the distant North Gate. "I have to go now," she said, her face turned away, her voice scarcely audible.

Nonetheless he heard and vigorously protested. "Hey, wait! You can't just wander off. I want to thank you and in order to do that I need a name."

"No thanks are necessary."

"I think they are."

"You just fell asleep, that's all."

"Please wait. Don't go."

During this rapid-fire exchange he scrambled up, amazed and annoyed that his legs still felt like partially cooked spaghetti. "My name is Mark Simpson," he said, at last catching up with her, though she'd started off at a fast pace, as though she had wanted to put as much distance between them as possible.

"Hey, come on, wait up!" Mark called out good-naturedly, and felt his heart quickening at the sight of her pulling ahead, recognizing within himself a genuine anxiety that she would simply walk away from him and that would be that. Without conscious thought, instinct told him to change his tactics.

"All right," he said in a tone of mock resignation, "I'll go back and fall in the pond again and then maybe . . ."

"No! Don't say that!" she murmured, and suddenly lifted her right hand and pressed it into service as a shield for her eyes.

"I was . . . teasing," he apologized lamely.

She looked puzzled, as though the transition had been too rapid.

"My name is Mark Simpson. What's yours?"

At first he saw the concern on her face turn to blankness and then at last a most becoming softness. "Cass," she said. "Cassie." Simultaneously she ducked her head as though embarrassed.

Though he heard the name and it was at least half the information he desired at the moment, he found himself fascinated by the manner in which her short-cut blond hair lay plastered by sweat on her brow, giving her a period look, like the Charleston bobs of the twenties and thirties.

"Cassie." He enjoyed speaking the name. "I don't know about you, but this heat's beginning to get to me. I'm a California boy accustomed to finding an ocean breeze around every corner. Do you suppose we could . . .?" He let his voice drift and merely glanced toward the Officers' Club half hidden behind its natural fortress of overgrown trees and shrubs.

At first she didn't appear to understand his suggestion. Then he saw a peculiar light of understanding, intersected immediately by rejection. "We can't go over there," she said, almost as though it were something he should have known.

"Why?" he asked, daring a step or two which shortened the distance between them.

"Because they're having a party there tonight and are getting ready for it. We'd only be in the way now."

This was said with such forthrightness, such certainty, that at first he felt no impulse even to challenge it. It wasn't until a second later, when the dusty, crumbling interior presented itself to him in crystal-clear memory, that it occurred to him to challenge her.

"Party?" he smiled. "Over there?"

She followed the direction of his hand aimed without question at the Officers' Club, and again nodded with absolute certainty.

He wanted to question her further as soon as he could gather together all the shattered fragments of his mind, but by the time he'd managed to do that she was off again in the opposite direction, walking away from him as she had the first time as though he didn't even exist.

"Hey!" he called after her a second time, and then a third, and felt a surge of anger at her stubborn and insistent departure. "Thanks, Cassie," he called out at the last minute, an impulse like reflexive good manners, though he wasn't absolutely certain what he was thanking her for.

Then, when he least expected it, when he had no more hope in successfully detaining her or calling her back, she appeared to stop of her own volition, hands on hips, her unusual face glistening with perspiration, a flattering patina which made her smooth, tanned skinned resemble rose marble.

"Would you like to come?" she asked, and the childlike image persisted and was enhanced.

"Where?" he managed.

"To the party," she insisted with childlike impatience, for the first time a smile adorning her face. "Well?" she prompted, and laughed at his hesitancy. Obviously it appeared to her as something comical.

Party? Yes, of course. Over there in that place which was good only to be bulldozed—

"Why not?" he said, now beginning to suspect that in all her innocence she was doing a pretty good job of making a fool of him. "Shall I pick you up?"

"No. I'll meet you at the North Gate."

Don't let her off the hook. See how far she intends to play her little game.

"What time?" he called out.

"Eight," she said without hesitation and commenced walking backward again. "I'm not ever really invited, you know, but I always go. No one seems to mind, so I'm sure it's okay if you come too. . . ." She paused for a moment as though expecting some sort of response from him.

At the moment he was incapable of response. The weakness in his legs was yet increasing and everything in the sun-drenched horizon commenced to spin.

"I wouldn't stay there too much longer if I were you." It was the girl again. At least he assumed it was the girl. The voice was female and several yards removed, but when he turned in that direction, he couldn't even manage to bring her into clear focus. She appeared as though underwater before him, a poorly defined, slim white column with wavering edges and floating substance.

74

"Did you hear me?" It was her again with her oblique and cryptic warning.

What the hell? It matched everything else that had happened to him this morning. He started to call her back but found he lacked the energy to do so. It was as though something had recently sapped his strength.

Mark ran his hand across the top of his head, massaging his skull as if it were a globe on the verge of cracking. A splitting headache. Small wonder. Get out of this heat. A comforting thought loomed before him now—his room on the third floor of the dorm. No roommate. His specific request had been granted, his things hastily arranged, but it was nonetheless familiar and private and cool.

It was that ultimate goal toward which he now hurried after a moment's final indecision. He'd had enough of everything this morning, and for all his effort he'd accomplished nothing except to allow one of the locals to make a complete ass of him.

He increased his speed, pretending that someone was chasing him. In California he used to get his best times on a run that way. Someone behind him—and gaining on him.

Run!

As always, Cassie used her key and let herself into the two-story Victorian frame house at the corner of Sorrento and Capri. She closed the door behind her as quietly as possible and heard only the sound of her breathing and heard her fear as well, but heard nothing else. Still she knew from experience that silence in this house was not to be trusted.

"Mother?"

Her voice sounded small and echoing in the cool, dark, wood-paneled foyer that still smelled of her grandfather's tobacco. Her Grandfather Butes had died years ago—how many years she'd lost track.

"Mother, are you here?"

Her breath quickened and she glanced hurriedly at the dark mahogany staircase to her left and could just barely see the top of the double doors which led to her mother's room. For several minutes Cassie held her position, waiting for telltale signals, subtle ones, the floorboards creaking behind those always closed double doors, her mother's unique scent understandably strong.

"Mother?" she called again, softer this time, though still the echo seemed to reverberate around her as though the foyer were an empty cavern. She waited, head down, for the echo to die, then looked up again.

She closed her eyes. It was not that unusual for her mother to be gone. Then why the apprehension? Slowly she ran the palm of her hand across her forehead where the residue of sweat clung.

Suddenly she heard a noise in the kitchen and looked sharply in that direction, trying to see through the high-noon contrast of sun and shadow down the long hallway that led to the study and dining room.

"Mother?" Her voice this time was low and did not seem to reverberate so much. Still there was no response, and for a few moments she was tempted to ignore the noise. A mouse, most likely.

Soothed by the thought of this possibility, she started slowly across the worn and frayed Oriental runner. Her grandfather had once wanted to replace it. "Must keep up appearances in a town like this, so important." But her mother had said no. At the recall of the ancient argument, she looked down on the runner. If it had looked bad several years ago, it looked worse now.

At that moment, quite unexpectedly, she suffered a curious juxtaposition of thought, seeing the boy in her mind's eye as he looked when the man dragged him up from the bottom of the pond. He would have to be more careful in the future.

What's your name?

Cassie.

She stood perfectly still on the runner, the toe of her shoe playing mindlessly with the frayed threads. Dangerous. One could trip so easily and fall.

What was his name?

The toe stopped its play and her mind moved into deeper concentration.

Get on your mark!

Mark.

In that instant she saw his face again in memory and found it incredibly pleasing and paradoxically wished she'd stayed hidden and out of sight this morning. She should have. She really should have.

"Mother?" Another call. Louder this time. She had grown weary of not knowing, and at the same time she increased her steps and started down the long, shaded interior hall at a quick pace, looking neither to the right nor to the left at the series of sepia-colored lithographs—all of Italian landscapes, the prized possessions of her grandfather. Cassie knew them by heart.

She kept her eyes focused on the slit of light coming from beneath the heavy, closed kitchen door. Not artificial light but sunlight coming from the large bay window, the breakfast nook, the place where she used to keep all her plants—until they died.

Grandpa. How she missed him. He'd been merely everything to her—grandfather, grandmother, father, mother, sister, brother. For some reason everyone had managed to die when Cassie had come along.

Now she noticed that the strip of sunlight coming from beneath the door seemed to elongate as she drew nearer. Just an optical illusion, the effect of shifting light on darkness? Three feet from the door she stopped.

"Mother?"

Her voice was little more than a whisper now. Again she held her breath, trying to detect the smallest sound. At the same time she saw the strip of spreading sunlight beneath the door darken, as though something had passed in front of it. For several moments she stood still, watching the shifting pattern. Surely it wouldn't be her mother. Not in the kitchen, not at this hour. Upstairs in her bedroom, maybe, but not down here. Not unless—

She shouldn't have stayed with the boy.

Suddenly the light beneath the door was clear again. She took one step closer and felt a strong surge of anger that she should be afraid in her own house. And it was her house. Her grandfather had told her so before he'd died.

The angry thought gave her strength and she went all the way to the door and pushed it open, her eyes in confrontation of—

Nothing.

The large room sat still and shimmering in the midday heat. The small window over the sink was open a crack, but she remembered leaving it that way after she'd finished her breakfast earlier that morning. The ruffled, faded, blue gingham window curtains hung limp and still, though outside the screeching cicadas filled the noon air with the sort of noise that ultimately no one hears.

Partially relieved, she moved slowly across the uneven linoleum floor—as ancient and as in need of replacement as everything else in the house, but her mother had always said no to everything, as though it were her house, while it was Cassie's house.

At the double sink she stopped and looked down and spied her cereal bowl where she'd left it soaking but unwashed.

It was her house.

Beyond the window she saw the weed-infested back garden,

blocked from view of the neighbors by a tall, unpainted board fence, individual slats tilted at angles like a snaggletoothed mouth, while rank and untrimmed trees cast thick shade everyplace and prohibited the growing of any ground cover save weeds.

Standing on tiptoe to gain a full, uncluttered view of the yard, she looked out of the window. From the overgrown earth she forced her vision into a slow upward climb, inspecting the thick overgrown branches of the native trees.

Mark.

In the dense, thick, upper foliage of the native trees, she saw the boy's face again and knew her mother would be angry and thought again of the need to find her and establish her mood and see if punishment was due. With renewed purpose, Cass searched every shadowed place in the limited yard, saw nothing out of the ordinary and turned slowly back to the kitchen, hearing again that slight disturbance in the pantry, a rustling like foraging. She stared at the closed door across the room.

"Mother?"

But the sound came again, and she knew it was merely the mouse family feasting on her spilled cereal from the morning. Leave them alone. With a sigh she abandoned her image of small, brown nibbling creatures and looked carefully about the kitchen, only at the last moment feeling cautious and foolish.

Still she continued to search for a few minutes longer, then realized she was hungry, but not so much as to go to the trouble of fixing anything. Later. After certain other things had been resolved.

Well, her mother wasn't here. But then Cassie had known that when she'd come in, hadn't she? Then look elsewhere and resolve the dilemma, because for some reason Cassie wanted to go to her room, close the door, sit and just think about the morning and the boy and what had happened.

It had been a good morning in many ways. Something had happened and she hadn't had to make it happen or imagine that it happened. That was her worst habit, really—regardless of what her mother always said. She could fantasize so easily, creations which existed no place except in the theater of her mind. The only trouble was the vast distance between the fantasies and this real world. The distance was painful.

She walked slowly across the uneven linoleum and saw the faded, dark blue triangle design in endless and ancient repetition. She remembered the day they'd put this linoleum down. She must

78

have been five or six. Her mother had given her three cellophane-wrapped pieces of pink saltwater taffy under the condition that she go out into the backyard and amuse herself until the workmen said she could come back inside. She'd never tasted saltwater taffy before, and always somehow still associated it with this cracking, fading linoleum and its endless blue triangles.

He had not slipped into the pond.

"Mother?"

At the sound of her own voice, she increased her speed and took the large, dark kitchen door at a fair clip, turned the knob with a force that felt strangely like anger and slammed the door behind her with a strength that confirmed her suspicion. She was angry.

Breathless from this brief dash, she stopped about halfway down the dim inner corridor and looked back, an accusatory expression on her face. She didn't like to get angry with anything or anyone. It always seemed such a waste of energy and time. Yet she was angry, could still feel it, like something turned sideways inside her with jagged edges—cutting, baffling, hurting.

Staring at the closed kitchen door, still trying to find her way out of this curious anger, she saw it again, that clear alteration in the light coming beneath the closed door. Anger forgotten, she stared forward and down at this new shadow which started on the right side of the slit of light and moved slowly from right to left, disappearing finally, the light slit restored, unobstructed.

She was here. Cassie knew it now. She couldn't say how she knew it but her mother was in the house. Slowly now, with an air of resignation, she started down the corridor again, trying very hard to get inside the theater of her mind. She needed to be there. It was by far the safest place for her to be.

So great were her skills and her needs that by the time she reached the bottom of the staircase, she saw before her not the staircase but a large room with brightly colored paper streamers laced back and forth from corner thumbtacks and at intervals large clusters of colored balloons which hung down like exotic, oversized grapes. There was music coming from someplace. Not very good music, but music all the same. And she was wearing a dress—soft beige—which floated, kind of like Rita Hayworth had worn in *You Were Never Lovelier* with Fred Astaire. She even looked a little bit like Rita Hayworth, her dark red hair smoothed down over one eye, but it was still Cassie. Black-and-white room, everything black and white and filled with pretty people all dressed in black and white. She wore the only color in the whole, big room, and that was only soft beige with a pink tinge, but still everybody looked admiringly as this beautiful Cassie started down the black-and-white marble staircase.

Slowly Cassie pulled herself up the stairs, one laborious step at a time, as though she were a hundred years old, keeping her eyes fixed on those closed double doors. One step, two step, three step, four. Five step, six step, seven potato more—

Where's my father?

He did not slip.

Oh, look at Cassie! Look how beautiful she is. That dress, Cass, wherever did you find it? It is you.

They loved her because she was so beautiful. Now from the massed crowd who stared admiringly, a young man came forward. He was more beautiful than she. Though she'd never seen his face before, she found him remarkable, and felt the most peculiar ache in the pit of her stomach as he looked up at her, as though he were capable of controlling her with a glance.

Almost to the top. Still hearing no sound, no voice, the double doors still closed and silent—

May I have this dance?

Of course.

Might I say how beautiful you are?

Thank you.

There were a hundred violins someplace close by, and the pretty black and white people were parting, making room on the highly polished black-and-white-marble dance floor. In the moment before the waltz commenced, Cassie lifted her hands and placed them on his shoulders and saw that his hair was still damp from the pond and felt compelled to ask—

Are you all right?

He nodded.

You mustn't go to sleep so near the edge of the water. It's dangerous.

"Cassie?"

The scene in her mind vanished as rapidly as a candle snuffed out. This voice did not belong in her private theater. This voice was here, coming from behind the closed doors. This voice sounded weak, as though it were ill or exhausted or disappointed.

"Cassie, is that you?"

She bowed her head and tried with incredible effort to retain the lovely scene in her mind. She wanted to dance with him, needed to see—

"Cassie, please answer if it's you. I thought I heard someone in the kitchen. Don't play games with me. It's too cruel."

80

Cassie shut her eyes tightly and concentrated with massive effort and could re-create—nothing.

"It's me, Mother," she called out, and heard the tone of resignation in her voice and was sorry for it because she knew her mother had heard it as well.

And she had. "Never mind, Cassie. I don't want to be a bother. Go on with what you were doing. I heard music. You don't have the radio on, do you?"

"No, Mother."

"Then go on with you. I don't need you. I really don't. I don't want you either. I'm sorry I bothered you."

"I'm alone, Mother."

Silence. No response. No need to play the game. Then go on in and get it over with.

Cassie shut her eyes and leaned against the closed doors for a moment as though she were on the verge of collapse. Carefully she wiped her forehead with the back of her hand, wiped her hand on her dirt-soiled shorts, tried to draw a deep breath but failed—

—and went in.

"Hey, Simpson, you okay? Coach wants to know. Meeting's at two. He says you went swimming in the pond. What sort of a dumb-ass thing is that to do?" The voice, heavily accented with the drawl of the region, cut through his thick afternoon sleep. "Hey, Simpson, you in there?"

For the first time came the courtesy of a knock, and Mark was grateful that the owner of the voice hadn't just burst into the room, though he was surprised he hadn't. There was an awkward, almost phony sense of hospitality to this place. Why it struck him as phony he didn't know. Maybe he'd just been so accustomed to California distance.

"Simpson, let me hear your voice or I'm comin' through." Even in a mild threat, the flattened diphthong of the regional dialect didn't sound like anything to be taken seriously.

"Present and accounted for," he called out, trying to give his voice a sense of high though sleepy spirits.

"Well, it's about time. Hey, can I come in? You haven't got a female in there now, have you?"

Mark smiled at the suggestion and was pleased to hear that they had the open-door system. Someone—he couldn't remember who—had warned him about the Fundamentalism in these Bible-Belt towns.

"Sure. Come on in."

At that moment the door at the foot of his bed opened a crack and a bright red head of hair appeared before him as though decapitated. There was thick red hair above a face with freckles and a wide-set grin which seemed permanently to split the all-American face that by rights belonged on a tractor.

"Terry Crawford," the flat Southwestern voice grinned and the face along with it.

Mark found both too infectious either to ignore or condemn. "Terry . . ." he repeated, and began laboriously to drag himself up from his stiffened and confining position of sleep.

"Wow! You look like somethin' the cat drug in."

The cliché was said with soft sympathy, Terry himself coming around the end of the bed, one hand outreaching as though he'd be more than glad to help if he just knew how.

The initial resistance to movement in Mark's body was incredible. Every bone, nerve and muscle seemed to be saying, Forget it. Another time, perhaps, but not now.

"I feel like . . ."

"Shit, I can tell that."

Still there was only warm concern in Terry's voice, and, as Mark tested each muscle tentatively for condition and reliability, Terry sat slowly on the edge of the opposite bed.

"Man, what happened to you?" he asked.

"You tell me," Mark muttered, feeling a new pain low in his back as though someone had hit him with a board. He managed to gain an upright position on the side of his bed and only at that moment noticed he'd not even bothered to change his clothes before he'd flaked out. He looked down with renewed bewilderment at the disreputable clothing that had seen him through the morning. Stiff and filthy beyond description, it had dried from his morning dip in the pond.

He was aware of Terry watching him closely, something else now added to that look of concern. A quick glance up told Mark what it was.

"Look," he began, apologetic. He shrugged, then instantly regretted it as a sharp pain ricocheted across his shoulders and settled in the vicinity of his neck. "I don't know what happened." Embarrassed, he studied the palms of his hands and saw the rough, raw place where he'd tripped and sprawled on the street in front of sick bay. A booby trap, that's what that whole base was.

In the ensuing silence he felt his embarrassment vault and

82

wondered what precisely Coach Herbert had told this guy—and how many others had he told, and now did Mark have a new stigma to live down in addition to the one which labeled him as being the new guy from Cal?

"What time is it?" Mark asked suddenly, as much to squelch his own thoughts as anything.

For a moment Terry didn't move but continued to sit on the edge of the bed. "What did happen?" he asked again bluntly.

Though Mark had known it was coming, still he was unprepared for it. Idiotically he shrugged and began to feel dual discomforts: those coming from his stiff body and Terry Crawford's relentless focus.

"Don't you remember anything?" Crawford pressed further, his wide-open, all-American face wearing an expression of mild offense.

"I said I didn't," Mark snapped, then stood abruptly and felt every vertebra in his spine object. He ignored the objection and walked to the washbasin, with what he hoped would resemble purpose, turned the cold knob on full force and hoped it would be enough to drown out any further questions.

Terry apologized. "Sure didn't mean to poke," he drawled. "I just thought maybe I could help."

Mark tried to drown his remorse beneath several violent splashes of cold water. "You didn't," he replied at last, his voice muffled behind the towel as he vigorously rubbed, then massaged his face. It felt good. "That's one weird place out there," he added lightly, dragging the towel down his neck, then tossing it back into the washbasin.

A look of relief crossed Terry's face. He leaned back on the bare bed. "The base?" Terry grinned now. "It's great. I love it," he added. "Nobody bothers us out there. We can do anything we damned well please."

For some reason the "damned" sounded stiff on his tongue, as though it were a new word, one he'd never used at home. But the most arresting part of what he'd said was his expression of fondness for the base. By the time Mark had reached the athletic dorm after the walk back this morning, he'd privately vowed never to return. With Coach Herbert's permission he would scout the town for a new course. It wasn't a large town or a busy one. Surely someplace there were four or five quiet miles that he could run at varying speeds. Training was all; he didn't need to be told that. It was just that where he trained was important and the base wasn't conducive to—

"Besides that, it's always fun when you're just doing the repetitive work," Terry went on, still talking, "to look at the old buildings and try to guess what went on inside them." He stopped talking and stretched out completely on the bed.

With mixed feelings Mark watched and listened, still standing by the washbasin and wanting very much to change clothes but postponing it for a while.

"So I think you'll come to like it," Terry grinned up at him. "It ain't much but, as Coach Herbert says, it's all ours. Mainly because no one else wants it." He laughed and laced his arms behind his head and made a pillow. "I'll go with you next time," he offered with new thoughtfulness in his voice. "I don't know what you tangled with this morning because there ain't nothin' out there but a shrill old hawk and ghosts."

For a few seconds Mark stared down on him, only then remembering the swooping hawk who'd greeted him at the North Gate. He nodded slowly, broadly. "I met the hawk."

He reached for the straight-backed chair at the desk, lifted it around and sat backward, feeling the muscles in the insides of his legs object.

"Of course you did," Terry laughed. "She's a mascot. Some of us take table scraps out for her and leave them at the gate. When we finish the course and come back, they're always gone and she's circling slow and easy overhead." For several moments he seemed relaxed, staring straight up at the ceiling, as though not seeing the ceiling at all, apparently seeing the hawk instead.

"Hell, man, she's probably just pissed because you hadn't brought her anything," he exclaimed in a new burst of energy. At the same time he sat up and swung his legs off the bed, as though sitting too long didn't suit him. "Well, what do you say?" he asked broadly. "Tomorrow morning at five? That's my best hour. When's yours?"

First light of dawn, his, too. Still, Mark hadn't planned on going back. His hesitancy registered, and Terry slumped on the edge of the bed, his long body resembling a deflated accordion.

"Hey, what did happen out there?"

There was something so sincere and concerned in the invitation to speak that for a moment Mark was tempted to oblige. Only at the last minute did good sense and better judgment intervene. As he replied, he felt the need to conceal his face and rested his forehead on the back of the chair and spoke to the scuffed, worn brown carpet.

"It was . . . just different, that's all. I'm used to a track."

"Who isn't?" Terry cut in acidly. "We're the very poor cousins of the Athletic Department, slightly lower than the dust under that rug. The hotshot footballers get first bite of every pie, basketball next, baseball next, wrestling next, swim team next . . ."

Mark understood the image of an empty pie plate. Things had been exactly opposite at Cal. Track-and-field athletics meant Olympic exposure, worldwide exposure. "Give them what they want," someone high up had said, and their training facilities were the envy of those from every school who came to their invitational meets.

Why the hell had he left all that to come here? The question, still unanswered and growing more persistent, plagued him for a few seconds, then passed.

"Hey, man, you really don't look so good," Terry said, disarming him with what sounded like real concern.

Reluctantly Mark brushed it aside. He didn't know anyone here well enough to tell him what had happened at the base this morning.

"Tell me something," Mark asked, choosing his words carefully, not wanting to reveal anything even obliquely.

"Sure. What? Anything," came the ready response.

"Does anybody else use the base now for any purpose besides us?"

Without hesitation Terry shook his head roughly. "Who'd use it?" he asked. "And for what purpose? It'll all be bulldozed over one day. As the university grows they may press it into some kind of service."

"But what about student groups?" Mark persisted, trying to ignore the puzzled look on Terry's face.

"What for?" he asked, his expression distorted with bewilderment.

"I don't know," Mark said. "I was hoping you could tell me."

For a few seconds the two stared at each other. Finally Terry shrugged and stood up and reached for the ceiling in a long stretch. "Hell, I'm not sure I know what you mean," he announced at the end of a yawn. "Maybe they do. I don't know everything that goes on at this place. God knows what the Greeks do on Friday and Saturday nights. I guess sometimes the pretty boys take their girls out to no-man's-land. We have one guy who likes to run on Monday morning just so he can count the rubbers."

Mark listened, not hearing what he really wanted to hear but asking other questions anyway. "Girls. Does the female team . . . would they be working out at the same . . .?" He broke off because the look of broad incredulity on Terry's face could just barely be endured.

"Are you crazy, man?" Terry asked, his blunt superior manner beginning to get tedious. "This here," he grinned, "is the Bible Belt and nowhere in the Bible does it say the female of the species is permitted to put on skintight shorts and run like hell, causing their boobs to bounce—and everything else they've got that ain't anchored down, for that matter." He did an imitation of a girl supporting heavy breasts.

"No, no female team, Simpson," Terry concluded, a slight tone of weariness in his voice. "Women in these parts are taught to stay barefoot, pregnant and in the kitchen."

At last Mark had heard enough. He stood up as well, very grateful now he hadn't revealed more of himself. "Well, I was just curious, that's all," he smiled, still safely noncommittal, and stepped to the door, his hand on the knob, ready to open it and clear his room.

Terry saw the gesture and apparently understood it. "Hey, look, man, I'm sorry I couldn't tell you . . ."

"That's all right. I was just curious."

"Did you see someone out there this morning? Is that . . .?"

"Naw."

"Coach Herbert said you almost drowned."

Mark forced a laugh. "I was just cooling off, that's all."

For several moments Terry seemed to study him, as though he wasn't buying a word he'd heard but didn't know Mark quite well enough to challenge him. As though stalling for a few moments, now he asked, "Are we on for tomorrow morning?"

"Why not?" Mark smiled, knowing that such a run would never take place.

The lie seemed to evade Terry. He grinned, pleased. "I'll grab some steak scraps tonight for our feathered friend. You'll see. She's practically a pet."

Mark nodded.

"Speaking of food," Terry went on, passing in front of Mark and gaining the hall, "smell that? We've got a cook here that won't quit. You name it and that old hag works her special magic and all you have to fear is the weekly scales and old Doc Robbins."

The name was familiar, though Mark couldn't put a face with it. The team doctor, of course, and sometime trainer.

"Well?" Terry asked, the question clearly an invitation along with his extended right hand which pointed in the direction of the dining hall and the admittedly good food odors.

Mark smiled at the invitation but declined. "I need to . . ." he began, and let the fragment drift into a gesture toward his clothes, smudged and filthy from his bizarre morning.

Terry understood and obliged. "I'll wait."

"No, you go ahead. I'll catch up."

"You sure?"

Mark nodded, beginning to feel suffocated. Why the ungodly interest of this watchdog? His thoughts broke off as he realized. Coach Herbert had set a watchdog on him. *We paid too much for the kid to have him going around falling into ponds; keep an eye on him.*

"Hey, you still with me?" It was Terry again, looking worried and suspicious.

"Sure," Mark smiled and stepped back into his room.

"I'll save you a place in line," Terry offered now, clearly feeling the weight of his responsibility.

"You do that," Mark nodded.

"And after lunch we can go to the track-and-field meeting. Then I'll show you the campus haunts."

"I'll be along," Mark called out to Terry, who was still walking backward down the corridor, now rapidly filling with guys on the way to the dining hall. Several looked with curious familiarity at Terry and then back at Mark with less familiarity and greater curiosity.

My God, had Coach Herbert told the whole damned dorm? And what precisely had he told them?

Everyone keep your eye on the kid from Cal. He's a real—
Shit!

With a feeling of paranoia and embarrassment he stepped quickly back into his room and closed the door. He shut his eyes and wished like hell that he wasn't here. Maybe it wasn't too late to go home. He could call his mother tonight.

The absurd and childish thought lasted only a moment, then died. He couldn't do that. He wouldn't do that. Burned his bridges, something like that.

Slowly he opened his eyes and stared about the Spartan room. Only the necessities. His suitcases were not fully unpacked yet. Still he was here and here he would stay until the end of the year, the end of his scholarship.

This morning there had been something he'd been following, trying to find. He continued to stare forward at the floor, seeing neither the floor nor the worn brown carpet, seeing instead the welcoming shade and the cool pond, the splash of water from the overflow drainage ditch—

Then it was gone and he was back in his cramped dorm room, hearing shouts in the hallway, perfectly normal sounds of this life and this world. Then why in the hell did they depress him?

Quickly he glanced at his travel clock on the edge of the desk. A few minutes after twelve. Meeting at two. He'd be back for it. For now he wanted only to get out of here, to walk a normal street filled with normal people and sounds. As for lunch—he'd pick something up along the way.

The direct plan of action helped spur him into movement. He pushed away from the door, stripping off the soiled shirt. At the same time he fished through an opened but as yet unpacked suitcase propped up against the wall and withdrew his bathrobe and a clean change of clothes. No towel. Maybe there would be one in the shower. If not, he'd use his bathrobe.

He started toward the door, then stopped, still hearing a parade of laughing, chattering voices on the other side. He leaned his forehead against the closed door and again shut his eyes, giving the parade a chance to pass.

Mark flung open the door, kept his head down and ran in the direction of the showers at the far end of the hall.

"Hey, watch out!"

"He's the Cal wonder."

"We run on the track, Simpson, not in the dorm."

The laughing, jeering voices followed him all the way down the hall and into the stalls and were finally drowned in the direct and stinging spray of a cold shower.

Balboa, California

Twice Brett Simpson had figured out the time difference between the West Coast and the Southwest, thinking that might be why she hadn't been able to reach Mark. Now at midafternoon— three-fifteen to be exact—she quickly figured out the difference again. Five-fifteen. He should be in the dorm for dinner. Then why didn't anyone answer the phone?

She tried to control her annoyance and anchored the phone between her jaw and shoulder, then reached for the card which Mark had given her with the address and phone number of the dorm. Ignoring the repetitious buzzing in her ear, somehow knowing that the receiver wouldn't be picked up, she focused on the heavy black printing and saw a vivid image of her son, an exact duplicate of his father, of the father he had never known in all ways but one.

Gerald Simpson had been the most focused, single-minded man she'd ever known, all his energies devoted without pretense, without show, to the service of God and others.

After so many years her loneliness only occasionally hurt deeply. Most of the time it was something she was almost proud of, the fact that after all these years she still ached for that fair-haired man. Despite his backward collar and gentle ways, he could always make her feel as though she'd been lovingly ravaged.

Something in her upbringing caused her to blush at the thought, but the source of pride was too great. She measured specific memories for a moment longer—his scent, the feel of his skin, the almost frightening abandonment of a man who during the day preached moderation in all things.

On a slight surge of anger she put the receiver back on the hook and told herself it was only a matter of trying again. Her normal

89

feelings of regret that Mark had made this silly decision had been complicated this day by feelings of worry.

She stood up and straightened the waistband on her shorts, tucked in her shirt and found herself consciously trying to plot out a course of action. There were several alternatives. Her favorite was the garden, a postage-stamp-sized showplace of color and conformation.

She could start the baking for the Navy Wives Auxiliary bake sale at Balboa this weekend. She'd volunteered for her specialty, brownies. She'd better start them today or she'd never get them finished.

But for several additional moments she stood unmoving before the phone desk, endlessly smoothing the beige fringe on the runner at her feet with her bare toes.

Without consciously choosing a direction or a destination, she wandered, head down, back through the small corridor which led to the living room, that perfectly decorated room where no one ever went. When Mark had been small she'd kept the door closed. Now she kept it open.

She stopped in the doorway, finding the soft rose and beige pleasing in much the same way that she would admire a model or a display room in a magazine. Then her eyes moved from the back of the rose-satin brocade sofa to the focal point in the room—the large, oil-painted photograph in the gilt frame of Gerald Simpson which hung over the mantel.

Slowly, never taking her eyes off her husband's face, she started around the end of the sofa and sat on the middle cushion, continuing to study that youthful face. At times she resented his youth as if by dying he'd managed to outwit the ravages of age and—to make the offense worse—he'd left a carbon copy of himself, an exact duplicate.

Reverend and Mrs. Gerald Simpson.

How proud she'd been, despite her unbelieving father who'd condemned them both to a hat-in-hand existence. In the beginning it had been like that, but Gerald Simpson had risen far and fast—until Pearl Harbor.

For several moments she studied her clasped hands resting on bare legs, and in a curious little rocking motion curled them close to her body. It seemed to comfort her.

I can't understand it, either, Brett, but there they are. Orders. Coral Sea, the Lexington.

For twenty years her anger still had not abated. They'd been told the base would be a permanent duty station for Chaplain Simpson.

At that moment she saw in her mind's eye a vivid image of Alec Manning, Gerald's best friend. Tall, dark as Gerald was fair. More of a rogue, yet down deep—

It had been Alec who, despite his own grief, had taken her in hand. Alec dead now. And Rita.

Slowly she sat back down on the edge of the sofa, feeling the awesome weight of the survivor. It had happened so fast, the three deaths within six months of each other.

Hurriedly she moved away from the sofa, coming back once compulsively to smooth the cushion so the room would look picture-perfect.

It was over, all of it. And in a way, with Mark's departure, for the first time in all the intervening years it was mandatory that Brett find a new life for herself. The absurdity of such a prospect struck her as she reached the door. Mark was always scolding her for living in the past.

She retraced her steps back down the hall, past the phone desk and the sun-room toward the French doors which gave a perfect, uncluttered and dazzling view of her garden. There was a kind of healing in the first glance, as she knew there would be.

So much for the unfathomable past. Good riddance.

She'd seen the red dress in the Officers' Club long before Alec had and had tried to warn him.

Watch out.

She almost stumbled going down the three shallow garden steps that were as familiar to her as any in the world.

Mark would be hard pressed to account for the whole day, but there it was, gone. Though it was seven o'clock according to the Union clock, the September sun seemed loath to set and cast over everything unreal and lengthening shadows. On top of the wasted afternoon and evening was a goodly portion of guilt.

He'd missed Coach Herbert's meeting. At exactly two he'd been wandering about on the far side of the campus in a lush, shaded, older residential neighborhood with old-fashioned and well-preserved houses on streets which oddly bore names of European towns—Canterbury, Dover, Versailles, Sorrento. Someone affluent and influential had done the grand tour, then returned to create his own town.

Now, at a few minutes after seven, Mark ambled lazily and without direction across the green which fronted the university library and boasted a pleasant arrangement of fountains and flowers and gray stone benches. There were very few flowers left after the heat of the summer. A few parched and bedraggled marigolds and wilted zinnias. Even the grass was straw-colored and brittle.

Abruptly he stopped and stared directly down on a flower bed which had been partially turned, one half cluttered with dried and dying marigolds, the other half moist and dark, rich looking, the entire bed being made ready for new fall plantings. With his head down he stood at a relaxed angle which denied the inner turmoil.

His mother. Her garden. How she loved it and the hours she put into it. And, as there was no single growing season in California, she was at it literally all year round and loved it. Suddenly his sense of homesickness became almost insupportable. As though without warning his body weight had become too much for him, he squatted slowly, then sat heavily on the grass, continuing to stare blankly at the partially dead, partially resurrected flower bed.

Not off to a very good start, was he? Made a fool of himself this morning and let a freaky girl finish the job for him. Was rude to a teammate and missed Coach Herbert's first meeting. As the list of offenses grew, he propped his knees up and rested his head on them, closed his eyes and smelled the peculiar perfume of freshly turned earth and fertilizer.

My God, he'd grown up with it in his mother's garden.

Call her.

This imperative command was so out of step with the rest of this still-warm, slightly indolent evening that he looked sharply up as though someone had called to him. Across the haze of dying sun he saw from his ground angle a slow stream of students making their way to the various dorms, toward the library and classrooms for evening studies.

There was another thing for his guilt list. Already he had homework assignments—English, European history and aesthetics—and here he sat, homesick. Slowly he shook his head. He'd been all right until this morning. The first part of the week had gone smoothly enough. He'd met all his classes and found them satisfactory if not scintillating. What the hell, it was his last year. He was getting a degree in business which he had no intention of ever using. To run was all that mattered.

First he had to find Coach Herbert and offer some sort of lame excuse for missing the team meeting. Then he had to call his mother.

Perhaps it would help if he could just hear her voice, hear that terrific where's-your-backbone tone that got him through grade school, junior and senior high school, and which on occasion had helped him to understand that most painful of all ordeals—losing.

Across the green about fifteen yards away he saw a laughing, chattering mixed group, about twenty in all. Their raucous voices and too-loud laughter spoke of early boozing. Obviously a few others felt no compunction to crack the books.

Still his primary concern wasn't for them but for himself. He'd thought once, melodramatically, that he'd work hard and distinguish himself in this last year. A berth on the Olympic team, qualify for the eight-eighty—and it would be all the sweeter to do it here where his father had spent so much time.

His mother. Call her.

He stretched again and watched the tag end of the laughing, jostling parade, all headed in the opposite direction from the main flow of students. The jolly band was headed away from the campus and library. Wryly he considered joining them. He was sure he would be invited. They looked that sort.

For several moments he stared at the empty sidewalk. Truly empty now. Not even any students heading toward the library, a peculiar vacuum, as if the entire population had reached its destination and had left the world to him.

Meet me at eight o'clock at the North Gate. I'm never invited but they always let me come.

He continued to stare at the brilliant rays of the dying sun. What was happening to him? He couldn't go back to the base tonight. The place was unpredictable in daylight. He'd be a fool to—

Even the thought was something to be avoided, and in an attempt to evade it he started trying to organize a plan of action in his splintered mind.

All right. First, go to the Athletic Department and see whether Coach Herbert was still around. Probably not. Then go to the dorm and ask Terry Crawford for his phone number and call him—privately, if possible—and try to explain his absence at the team meeting. He'd think of something, hopefully.

Then call his mother and tell her—what? What the hell, he'd never had any trouble in the past talking to his mother. Why should he now?

The slight scolding served its purpose, and for several minutes he steadily increased his speed, walking easily along the west

93

perimeter of the campus, still amazed at how much heat the evening sun was capable of producing even at this late hour. He lifted his left arm and glanced down at his watch.

What in the—

He stopped and gaped forward at the watch, saw the crystal cracked, both hands missing, just the face itself. In a mixture of shock and anger, he tore off the watch and felt the silver expansion band pull at his arm hair. He held it up for closer inspection and thus confirmed the damage, bewildered by it.

When had that happened? Not this morning, surely. He'd looked at the watch several times since then. Hadn't he? Now he examined it closely and wondered if it could even be repaired. The entire glass face was shattered, a frozen spiderweb effect. The greatest mystery of all was the missing hands. Sharply he tilted the watch on its side, thinking perhaps the two small pieces of metal had slipped loose from their anchoring sockets and fallen to the frame itself.

But there was nothing there. Not even the rattling of something caught. They were gone, both hands, rendering the face useless.

He stared at the damage, torn between worry it could not be repaired at all and how such massive damage had been done to it without his awareness of it. He looked up, newly discouraged. The hands could have fallen out through the shattered glass. He could have done it this morning. He'd taken a bad fall—several, come to think of it. Still, you'd think he'd know when he'd done this much damage.

Now, although he knew it was a foolish gesture, he carefully slipped the watch back onto his left wrist. Tomorrow he'd look for a watch repairman and see what could be done. In the meantime he'd say nothing to his mother about—anything.

Thus resolved, he started across the busy intersection which boasted a handful of small campus businesses on the opposite side. The early-evening foot traffic on the sidewalk was considerably thinned, most of the students apparently having reached their early-evening destinations. As he reached the opposite side and as the front door to a hamburger joint was pushed open, the indescribably delicious smell of meat and onions cooking greeted him.

Starved. A good sign. He'd missed lunch and dinner. Not exactly training-table food, but what the hell? It might be a good idea to just toss this day into the trash can in all respects and start fresh tomorrow. No need to heap guilt upon guilt—although his mother wouldn't agree.

Call her.

Later. First food and then hopefully the head would clear, the pieces of this insane and fragmented day would fall into place and in the process make sense, and next week, next month, next year he would blame it on the moon or the tides.

As he drew nearer to the fragrant aroma, he looked into the dark cool cavern of the hamburger place and heard a jukebox coming from the recesses, a nice song, a ballad which he'd heard a couple of times out in Cal, something about wine and roses. For a few seconds he just stood on the hot pavement in the reluctantly dying sun and listened. Good mood music, bad mood.

"Hey, you going in or coming out?"

The voice was female and strident. He looked up to see a surprisingly attractive girl in a clinging red dress. Long, thick, slightly curling auburn hair. A student, no doubt.

"I'm . . . sorry," he mumbled, and stepped quickly out of the door, only then aware that he'd been blocking it.

"That's all right," she grinned. Her voice was softened by a becoming smile. "You alone?" she asked now, halfway through the door, looking back at him over her shoulder in a provocative, almost flirting manner.

"Temporarily," he smiled.

"You new on campus?"

"Temporarily."

"Where are you from? And don't say 'temporarily.' "

There was something about her, not precisely masculine, but aggressive, sure of herself.

He started to walk away and say nothing, then changed his mind. "Temporarily," he said broadly and grinned, "I'm from the athletic dorm. Permanently from California."

A pleased look crossed her pretty face, along with the most becoming smile. "I knew it!" she exclaimed. "You're a jock. You walk like one. You even stand like one."

"Guilty," he nodded, though secretly he was proud.

"Not football," she said, and it was partially a question. At least it required either affirmation or denial.

"No."

"Not basketball."

She was really quite attractive, well built, almost as tall as he, with more than her share of female curves, all in the right places.

"I give up," she said. The voice which first had seemed strident had suddenly become musical and beautiful.

"Track," he confessed at last, finding the harmless exchange enjoyable, finding it difficult now even to take his eyes off her.

"But of course," she said, and lightly slapped the side of her

95

head, as though for some reason she should have known all along. "Well, happy running," she added, and stepped farther into the dark cavity of the open door. The wine and roses song was still on and from someplace in the dark he heard laughter.

"Thanks," he said in response to her wish for luck and was on the verge of following her in when suddenly from the recesses of the café he heard her voice, quite a distance removed now, as though once inside the door she'd moved rapidly toward the back.

"Hey, no!" she called out, her voice stern, insistent and aggressive. "Not in here. You can't come in here."

He stopped as though he'd run into an invisible barrier. Was she speaking to him? There was something so inhospitable in the voice, the same one that only moments earlier had laughed and joked with him—

"I don't . . . understand," he faltered, calling into the darkness, squinting, trying to see.

"Of course you do," came the voice again. "You're due someplace else, aren't you?"

Abruptly the jukebox record came to an end and left only a muddled silence. No music, no laughing voices, not even any street sounds.

"I . . . don't understand," he repeated.

"Go on, now. You know where you have to be. Close the door, Harry. You're just letting the heat in and the cool out."

He heard footsteps then—not female footsteps with the appealing clicking heels on the hard surface. This stride was male and coming from the dark interior of the restaurant.

Knowing what was going to happen, Mark stepped out of the doorway, and at the last minute a large, beefy black hand reached out, grabbed the edge of the door and slammed it shut, leaving Mark standing on the pavement, staring foolishly at the closed door, suddenly struggling mightily to control new panic.

I'll meet you at the North Gate at eight.

Cass.

You fell asleep.

Had she told him her last name? If so, he couldn't remember.

Still it made no sense—and yet the girl in the red dress might know Cass. Cass could have told her—but how could she have known him?

His head pounded as he walked on down the empty sidewalk. Only once did he look back at the closed door. Maybe it was a private club. Maybe he didn't qualify for membership. Maybe—

Suddenly he was tired of speculation. If any of it made any

96

sense at all, it was beyond him. For now he was left with certain basic and very understandable needs. He was hungry to the point of weakness, and he was suffering from the kind of mental and emotional constipation that always plagued him on days when he didn't run.

Then the order of business for the evening should be food first, then a brief, lung-splitting, head-clearing sprint. For the rest of it, let it go. Let it all go. He'd been born to it, all aspects of life appearing to him like a gigantic jigsaw puzzle with several pieces missing. He'd never really understood any of it. Why should he be granted the gift of understanding now?

Strangely he found a degree of comfort in that small excursion into weary cynicism.

Up ahead, brilliantly spotlighted by the last rays of sun, he saw a sign boasting square block letters which read HOUSE OF GREEK. An unexpected bonus. He saw in his mind's eye gyros dripping with meat and dressing. Even his taste buds were working over-time.

I'll meet you at eight at the North Gate.

At this moment, focusing on the forthcoming gyros, he approached the front door of the Greek restaurant. Through the broad front windows he saw a small arrangement of tables, a long counter at the rear and nothing else. Closed? No sign that said so. Slowly he pushed open the door. Not a sight or sound of human life.

Then suddenly a booming voice with a broken accent invited, "Come in, come in. I've been waiting for you."

It was curiosity, nothing else—though maybe a bit of loneliness and the more urgent need to postpone his return to the dorm and the wrath of Coach Herbert—that led Mark at five to eight to the long avenue that culminated at the North Gate of the base. That and the fact that he'd eaten three gyros and had gone in about thirty minutes from a distressing hollowness to an equally distressing fullness.

Also, he'd had a most enjoyable chat with the old Greek who owned the restaurant. The old man, with his broken accent and gentle ways, had made him feel most welcome and at home and quite normal. Zelius was his name. Apollo Zelius. And he wasn't so old really; he'd served about twenty years ago as one of the civilian cooks on the base. After the war when the base had been deactivated, he'd stayed in the community. He'd never married, though he'd gone to classes at the university and ultimately taken a law degree—or so he'd said. Mark wasn't so sure he should believe that part, but he had chosen to believe his warmth and kindness and his incredible perception.

You homesick? Let me tell you about homesick. Twenty-four, just off the boat, no English, family back in Athens.

Mark broke his halfhearted jog, still too full to move effectively, still enjoying—even in memory—the warm, easy, hospitable and relaxed atmosphere of Mr. Zelius's place. All the time Mark had been in there no one else had come in, so in essence he'd had the garrulous old man to himself.

Old? If he'd been twenty-four before the war, that would only make him someplace in his forties. My God, he looked much older. Maybe he'd lied about his age.

What matter?

Mark felt better, despite his gluttony, than he'd felt all day. A curious bonus to the evening was simply the knowledge that now he had someplace to go, an ear to listen—a colorful personality who asked no questions and who accepted him for what he was.

All right, let's try again, he counseled himself, stretching up in an attempt to accommodate his gluttony, at last drawing a deep breath and breaking into a slow, jaw-jarring jog. It felt good. For several minutes he kept up this peculiar gait, not looking up from the cracked sidewalk which was deserted—as was the street. He'd left the last of the houses about two blocks behind.

I'll meet you at the North Gate at eight.

Her voice was still so clear and so near. Had she been trying to make a fool of him?

Failing to concentrate on his stride, he broke it and looked up, amazed to see the light at last fading. The North Gate should be about a block up ahead. He couldn't see it yet, obscured as it was by the fast falling night. Abruptly he broke speed and abandoned all pretense at running and walked easily through the warm September evening, hands on hips, breathing hard. Too much food, too gluttonous. He'd have to watch his trips to Mr. Zelius's in the future.

He stared ahead in the vast, sprawled direction of the base and saw nothing but the black pit of night growing blacker and deeper. Where were the lights of a party, the music, the noise and for that matter where were the cars, the traffic—and the girls?

Less than fifty yards now from the North Gate, he stopped trying to make out certain forms—the large sentry box, the center island dividing the road. No one in sight.

For a moment he suffered an unexpected disappointment, as

98

though deep down, through all the layers of doubt and disbelief, there'd always been one small flicker of hope.

Stupid!

On this sharp self-condemnation, he walked slowly on a few steps closer to the sentry box and, out of habit, lifted his wrist to check his watch and belatedly remembered it was broken.

Abruptly Mark came to a halt before the deserted sentry box. He saw movement out of the corner of his eye—or thought he did. Reflexively he turned toward it, only to find nothing there. He was getting as spooky as an old woman. Go back to Appollo's for a quick cup of coffee, then to the dorm and the phone

He saw it again. Something white and floating just beyond the concrete standard. Over there. He turned toward it again, and again it was gone. But now he was in no mood to wait for it to reappear. The day had been too long and tedious for games of cat and mouse.

"Cass?" he called out softly.

The black border of night which clung to the concrete standard remained a solid black. A few yards beyond in that curious last light of day he saw the empty flagpole, and he remembered hearing a flag flapping this morning in the heat of a windless day.

"Anybody there?" he called out, grateful now that he was alone and there was no one close by to hear and record his apparent insanity. For several moments he kept his eye on the black vacuum but nothing responded. He was in the process of turning back, looking forward to the jog back to campus, when softly—so softly at first he thought he'd imagined it—like nothing more than a breeze he heard—

"Is it you?"

Shocked, he looked back. Still he saw nothing but deepening night and the deserted sentry box. "Who's there?" he called out, lowering his voice. He started forward toward the sentry box, on the verge of calling out again.

Out of the blackness he saw the door on the left side of the box open slowly and a small, curiously garbed figure emerge. Most predominant in the darkness was a large field of white, like an oversized shirt that extended well below her hips and seemed like the cut of an apron. So startled was he by this curious apparition that when it started toward him, he instinctively took a step back, as though to maintain a safe distance until the specter could be identified.

Then all at once the figure giggled. "Hey, it's just me," a soft female voice confessed. "Cass. Remember?"

Of course he remembered. He'd known all along who it was. It was just her curious garb that now puzzled him—that and the equally curious sensation of ease which he felt, as though in her presence all mysteries were made tolerable.

"Cass," he called out, wanting a definite confirmation, still trying to see precisely what it was she was wearing.

She drew as near to him as the top step of the sentry platform and stood hands on hips, almost a playful posture as though she, too, were relieved and glad to see him.

As he had drawn nearer the step at the same time, he saw clearly what she was wearing. A large, oversized man's white shirt—it appeared to swallow her whole—and rolled-up blue jeans with, he suspected, loafers and socks, although he couldn't clearly see her feet. She looked boyish and strangely dated.

"Hi," she said. "I didn't think you'd come."

"I didn't think *you'd* come," he parroted.

For a moment the impasse held, each studying the other as though neither was plagued by the self-imposed blindness of night.

"Oh, I forgot to tell you," she murmured. "It's a costume party. I'm sorry. Well, I'm sure it won't make any difference."

"Costume?" he repeated, still fascinated by her and by the attractive shyness which could alter and become playful, almost flirtatious.

"The forties, you know," she nodded. "You were supposed to wear stuff from the forties. Junk like this." She pulled out the sides of the oversized white shirt and executed an exaggerated and comic curtsy.

"Party?" he repeated idiotically, then stepped closer, amused and intrigued by her clowning. He'd not observed that particular characteristic this morning.

"Of course, party," she said, with a tinge of mild impatience in her voice. "Good heavens, you *were* out of it this morning!" She drew very near to him now, less than three feet separating them.

He didn't remember her being so small, either. She scarcely came up to his shoulder. Tonight she looked for all the world like a small boy.

"Don't you really remember, Mark, or are you just kidding?" she asked, as though she truly wanted to know.

"I remember. I just didn't know whether or not to believe you." In the dark it was impossible to read her expression. All he knew for certain was that she was standing very still before him. Had he hurt her? Impossible. He shouldn't have said that about not believing her. He was on the verge of apologizing when suddenly she stirred herself to life and dismissed everything.

100

"Well, no matter. We're late as it is."

As she grabbed his hand, he started to follow her, unprotesting, but at the last moment he hesitated.

"Hey, wait," he laughed, and pulled free of her hand—and instantly regretted it. "A party?" he demanded.

She stood a moment as though gathering all her available patience. "The one I told you about this morning," she said, something maternal about her now, a loving patience like a mother with a favorite child.

He appreciated her patience. For some reason he was deeply appreciative of the fact that she'd even appeared at all. Still—

"Where is this party, Cass?" he asked, displaying a patience of his own, truly not wanting to offend her.

"Well, not here. It's down there." He saw her point in a vague southerly direction deep inside the base.

"Where?" he asked again, peering out into the blackness of night, seeing literally nothing.

"Well, you can't see it from here," she protested, a little less patiently. "We have to go." Again she started off through the broad front gates and had taken half a dozen steps before she stopped and looked back. "You are coming, aren't you?" she asked, neither patience nor impatience in her voice now, but rather a kind of quiet pleading that he not make her life any more complicated or difficult than it was already.

He started to protest again. One did not start off into an already-suspect no-man's-land in the darkness and in the company of a slightly fey, slightly kooky girl on the way to a nonexistent party without at least token resistance.

But as she waited patiently for him in the dark in her oversized white shirt and rolled-up blue jeans, he found himself feeling merely grateful that she was here. He grinned back at her and started forward, remembering an old piece of unfinished business.

"What's your last name?"

Apparently she didn't hear, so pleased was she that the debate was at an end and they were at last on the way. She quickly took the lead, setting a fast pace past the sentry box, talking all the time but never answering his question.

"I really was afraid you wouldn't come, you know. And I almost came back this morning to see if I could find you. But I didn't because I was late getting home and my mother . . ." Abruptly she broke off.

He kept pace with her and now walked beside her, his fascination growing. She seemed so mercurial, impossible to predict.

"Your mother . . . what?" he asked, trying to prod her into speaking further.

Apparently she had said all she wanted to for the time being and seemed more than satisfied to walk beside him, her head lifting now and then as though she loved the still, warm evening and loved in particular this evening in this place.

"Where do you live?" he asked.

"Near campus," she replied quickly.

Again he let it slide and looked ahead in an attempt to chart the direction. Straight down to the west side of the base, as well as he could tell. Followed to the base's natural conclusion, they would end up at Coffin Pond in the vicinity of the Officers' Club, the scene of his early-morning fiasco.

"Where precisely is this party?" he asked again. Maybe if he asked it often enough she might give him an answer.

"Not far," she said. Her voice indicated a resumption of high spirits as she looked back at him.

He could just barely see her features in that peculiar light of night, but what he saw he found more than pleasing. As the silence between them persisted and became good, he tried to determine the nature of her attraction. She wasn't pretty—not in any sense of the word. Certainly not California pretty—tall, leggy, sun-bleached blond hair, aggressive without inhibition or apology. Generally he liked California women. They made it easy for a man to be a man.

But with this one there was something different. She was physically small—in fact this morning when he'd first seen her he'd mistaken her for a child—but she was no child. Close observation of her firm taut body confirmed that. An athlete's body—a real athlete, not just someone who rode the waves on Saturday and Sunday. Her short, wavy, close-cropped hair continued the overall impression of a child, but again there was a style and a specific cut which enhanced the natural wave and was most becoming.

"Are you feeling all right now?" The question came from her and was not addressed directly to him but rather to the night in front of her.

It took him a moment to comprehend. "Yes. Fine," he replied quickly, hoping he did understand. "You mean this morning, don't you?"

"Yes," she nodded. "Coach Herbert was very worried about you."

"You know Coach Herbert?" he asked. They were walking together now and he found it pleasing.

"Oh, yes." She nodded vigorously. "In a town like this everybody knows everybody, particularly in the university community."

"Do you go to school?"

"Off and on. Mostly off."

"Where do you live?"

Abruptly she laughed, as though amused by his single-mindedness. "I told you. Near campus."

"It's a big place."

"I live with my mother."

"Where?"

"It's my grandfather's house. I loved him. I told you that, didn't I? He's dead."

Suddenly something in her voice had gone so sober and desolate that though he was tempted to push further for specifics, he couldn't quite bring himself to do so. All he could muster was a muttered, "I'm sorry."

For a few moments the silence deepened, like a newly filled well. They had passed two intersections, going deeper into the abandoned base. On either side of the street the large, empty, collapsing structures stood like crouching dinosaurs, shadows only in the moonless night, which nonetheless boasted a faint illumination from some unknown source.

He started to ask her to identify certain buildings, some of which he remembered from the morning, but there seemed more now, the street on both sides lined with them, a veritable city, though he could have sworn this morning this particular stretch leading down to Coffin Pond from the North Gate had been mostly empty on both sides, stripped of structures of any kind. Had they taken a turn when he hadn't noticed?

"Where are we?"

"Not far now. I think you were there earlier this morning."

"Where?"

"The Officers' Club near no-man's-land, not too far from the pond."

Abruptly he stopped walking and waited for her to realize it and turn back.

"What's the matter?" she asked, standing ten feet in front of him, far enough for night to obliterate all of her except the field of her long, oversized white shirt.

"How did you know that I was in the Officers' Club this morning?" he asked, and heard a new seriousness in his voice, as though the time had come for answers, no more games on either side.

Apparently she heard the tone and responded to it and stepped

103

closer in the process. "I saw you," she said flatly, as though it were something he should have known.

"Where?"

"From the top of the embankment. I'll show you. It's the best vantage point on the whole base. You can see ever so far." There was a light, almost lyrical quality to her voice that seduced him for a moment into forgetting his question and—more important— the implications in her response.

If she'd seen him at the Officers' Club from her "vantage point," then she must have seen everything—his pursuit of the woman—

The thought struck him like a blow from behind. The woman! He had seen the woman, the color red. He'd seen her twice.

Apparently she saw his expression and was alarmed by it. "Are you . . . ?"

"How . . . long did you watch me?"

When at first she didn't answer, he repeated the question with greater urgency. "How long? Did you see me go into the Officers' Club?"

"No, I . . ."

"I thought you said . . ."

"I saw you come out," she laughed, a nervous sound, as though she felt tension building and did not like it. "I can't see through the building, you know." Her voice drifted and, as though impervious, she drifted along with it, moving ahead of him a few feet, head down, apparently concentrating on the pavement. Suddenly impatient, she looked back at him.

"Let's not ruin the night. What difference does the morning make? Come on, it's not far now." Without giving him a chance to respond, she started forward, disappearing into the night with such suddenness that he didn't know whether to run after her or not.

"Hey, wait!" he called.

"Keep up. It's not far."

Obviously it was her way of signaling no more talk. While he had another thousand questions, he tabled them for the time being and increased his speed until he was able to see the white of her long-tailed shirt. He thought again how bizarre she looked and wondered curiously if he looked bizarre enough to get into the party.

"Hey, do you think they'll let me in dressed like this?"

At last she stopped and waited for him to catch up with her. In her tone and manner he heard her apology and conciliation. "Of course. Why shouldn't they?"

"You said it was costume . . ."

104

"If you want to," she added with almost childlike emphasis. "You know. It's like any of those things. If you want to dress up and look dumb you can. If not . . ."

"I don't think you look dumb."

"Sure I do."

"No. I . . ."

"Well, I don't dress like this all the time," she laughed and again they started off, walking side by side, relaxed.

"What did you do this afternoon?" Her direct and unexpected question caught him off guard.

At the same time he heard a sudden rustling in the dusty brush to the left of the road. He looked in that direction and continued walking for several steps, still keeping an eye on the rustling bushes, which persisted and seemed to grow louder.

Apparently she saw his tension but had failed to hear the movement.

"I heard something," he said vaguely, though at that instant the rustling fell silent.

She laughed, a curious counterpoint to the darkness of the night. "Of course you heard something. Anything. Everything." With each word her voice expanded until at last it seemed to encompass all of the night. "Lots of things live out here all the time."

He dragged his focus away from the side of the road. "Like what?"

"Snakes, for one. Lots of snakes. They love the nooks and crannies of the abandoned buildings. Cool, you know."

No, he didn't know. Snakes hadn't really been a problem in Balboa.

"Lots of other things as well," she went on, and abruptly turned the corner, heading east.

Again he had to hurry to catch up. "Poisonous snakes?" he asked with mock concern.

"Some."

"Some?"

"Most aren't, though. Just rattlers."

"Do you know the difference?"

"Of course!" she exclaimed, with just a tinge of resentment that he'd asked such a question.

For several moments they walked in silence. In the dark he thought he heard something else. Music, this time. Either quite distant or well muffled. He lifted his head and listened and heard it again. A jazzy tune as well as he could make out. "Do you hear?"

"Once out here I found an entire family of abandoned kittens."

This solemn announcement overrode his question, and he felt such a profound drop in her spirits that for a moment he couldn't think of what to say.

"Eight altogether!" she exclaimed. "Can you imagine? They could hardly walk and they'd been taken away from their mother and just dropped off."

He knew that sound well enough—breaking emotion—and felt helpless. "What did you . . .?"

"Why, I took them home, of course," she said, and the sorrow instantly diminished. "I wrapped them in my sweater and lined my bicycle basket with leaves and grass—you know, to make it soft—and put them in the basket and took them home."

"Did you keep them?"

"For a while. My mother adored them but my grandfather said we couldn't keep them all, so I chose homes for them very carefully. Some went to neighbors, some to friends of my grandfather's. I kept three—but they're all dead now."

There'd been something so plaintive, so sorrowful in this recitation that for a few moments he'd been unable to think of anything to say. Also his mind had snapped to attention on her mentioning her homelife. Grandfather. Mother. Never a mention of a father.

"I take it your father approved as well. Of the kittens, I mean."

As she turned another corner she said something very low, almost under her breath.

"I didn't hear you."

"Father's dead," she said, and her voice went as flat and as dark as the night.

He started to pursue it further, but something in her attitude and manner warned him against it. Also at that moment she pointed straight ahead.

"There it is!" she exclaimed. Her mood had changed from black night to one of high and rare anticipation.

Again he caught her mood, as though it were a contagion to which he was highly susceptible, and he looked eagerly ahead in the direction in which she was pointing and saw nothing but the pit of night, which seemed blacker and darker at this far end of the base. "I . . . don't . . ."

"There, silly. See the Officers' Club?"

Despite her mild scolding and despite the fact he was looking very hard in that direction, he still saw nothing. Ultimately he stopped, frustrated, curiously breathless again, as though he'd run instead of walked.

106

She in turn stopped as well and looked back at him, her features strangely clear and perceptible.

He laughed to cover his embarrassment. Was she trying to make a fool of him again? "I don't see anything. I'm sorry."

"Well, of course, you don't. Not from here." Without warning, she came all the way back and took his arm and leaned very close, a pleasant sensation. When she spoke, her voice was low, playful, as though she knew very well the effect she was having on him. "It's off limits, you see," she whispered, as though listening ears were close by.

"I don't understand," he confessed, telling the truth in all respects, though what he really didn't understand was the pleasurable sensation of the skin on his chest tightening as she leaned yet closer.

She had to stand on tiptoe even to get in the vicinity of his ear. "The university, you know," she whispered, "made the base off limits to all except the track guys. They say it's not safe—and it really isn't." She stood back and seemed to survey the shadowy outlines of decrepit buildings. "I've been in some of those where, if you weren't careful, you'd go right through the floor. Not safe at all," she repeated somberly. "So," she went on with new energy, "the kids who party out here have to do it on the QT, if you know what I mean." She took his hand this time and he felt a delicate pressure. "Come on. I'll show you everything."

He allowed her to pull him forward, his attention torn between the curious attraction he felt for her and the dread of finding out that again he'd allowed her to make a jackass of him.

"Listen!" The hushed, whispered command was hers, and he obeyed.

The music he'd first heard several yards back was clearer now, though the tune was antique.

"Hear it?" Her grin was wide and infectious.

He scarcely had time to nod before she was guiding him forward again, running toward the low, squat silhouette of the Officers' Club, the place where the jukebox tune was coming from. But nothing else—no lights, no cars, no couples strolling the cracked and weed-infested sidewalks.

"Cass, are you sure?" he whispered.

"Come on," she whispered back. Then, apparently feeling resistance she didn't want to deal with, she drew free of him and made a funny little sound of pure glee and started off down the sidewalk, a comical, disjointed gait.

He stood for a moment and watched her. All he could really see

107

was the white of her long shirt. Lost in the darkness, it resembled the disjointed cavorting of a scarecrow. At last he started off after her, despite the foreboding which was still plaguing him, but which he ignored with the rationalization that he was only remembering the spooky morning when he had let his imagination run rampant.

It might be good to see the shadowy place again in her company and if there truly was a party going on inside—

He heard a sharp rap and looked ahead to see the long white shirt standing at the door, which was as dark as ever and as closed.

The music was loud and clear, though a little flat. He remembered the disemboweled and silent jukebox he'd seen this morning. Surely another one—not the same.

Now he heard her knock again and saw her steal a glance back at him as she eagerly waved him forward.

"Come on!" she whispered loudly. "When they open the door we'll have to slip in quickly. No one must see the lights."

The music seemed to be growing louder, as did her pounding. He was on the verge of retreating, unable to understand any of it, when suddenly a small box in the top of the door opened a crack, speakeasy fashion, and he saw the lower quarter section of a male face and the light-flooded opening.

At first the mouth appeared merely slack, without recognition. Then—

"Cass, where in the hell have you . . .?"

"I've got someone with me," she interrupted hurriedly, standing on tiptoe in order to reach the small square opening.

Strange, Mark hadn't noticed it there this morning.

"Who?" the male voice demanded, suspicious.

"Oh, you know him," Cass chided, a slight tone of flirtation in her voice.

Mark maintained his distance ten feet back on the sidewalk. From where he stood, beyond the fragment of the male face, he saw a flood of colored lights, equally distorted fragments of shoulders, faces, arms—male and female blending—a laughing and incoherent jigsaw that caused him to wonder if it would make any more sense if he saw it whole.

"You remember," he heard Cass whisper to the face in the open square. "You said you saw him here this morning. His name is Mark. Track. California."

For a moment he was amused by the equally fragmented way in which she was introducing him. Then something else she'd said registered.

You saw him here this morning, remember?

He looked up sharply. The conversation at the door was still going on, though he suspected it no longer concerned him. The face was leaning closer, only its mouth and teeth and the distorted area round its lips visible. He was whispering something and Cass was listening, her right ear turned toward the talking mouth, a breaking smile on her face, as though she were anticipating the punch line of a joke and already enjoying it. Suddenly, as if on cue, she giggled, and immediately clamped both hands over her mouth as though she were on the verge of laughing too loudly and summoning attention.

"Mark, psst. Come on."

He saw her wave him forward. The small window in the top of the door had been closed. The area around it was dark as usual.

"Are you coming?" she whispered, and ran back to where he stood, grabbed his hand and tugged him forward with a gentle insistence. "It's all right. They know who you are. Amos was here this morning."

"Where?"

"Where what?"

"Where was he?"

She seemed taken aback by his harsh tone. "I don't know, Mark," she said, a mild tone of hurt in her voice, which provoked a tone of regret in his.

"Sorry," he muttered, and regretted his withdrawn hand. "It's just that I didn't see anybody here."

"Well, Amos didn't want you to see him. As I said, this is all very much off limits and the kids may get into trouble." She stopped speaking and stood beside him, apparently willing to answer any further questions.

When he could think of nothing further to say, he offered a smile and said, "Come on. Let's go find us a party."

His reward was more than gratifying, instantaneous and wholly unexpected. With childlike enthusiasm she grinned and, as though unable to resist some powerful impulse, stood on tiptoe, placed her hands lightly on his chest and delivered a feather-light kiss to the side of his face—a sensation which left him momentarily breathless, and left a lingering fragrance he found memorable and irresistible.

"Come on, then!" she smiled, and reached for his hand.

This time he followed after her without any resistance and heard the music change while the door was still closed. Another golden oldie. Something about being on a slow boat to China.

109

As they approached the door, it opened as she reached for the knob. Within the instant the area around the door where they stood was flooded with light, color and noise—voices raised in laughter and shouts and song. At the precise moment he was trying to take it all in, a spotlight flashed a blinding white light directly into his eyes, causing him to tear loose from her fingers to lift his hand into an immediate shield.

At the same time he ducked his head and stumbled blindly over the worn threshold, struggling against the watery, teary sensation and the peculiar optical illusion of seeing the crowded, fragmented room and smiling chaos even with his eyes closed.

"Hey, you all right?" The inquiry was close, the voice male.

He blinked his eyes in rapid succession, still unable to lift them, though he did manage to open one and saw standing directly before him a pair of scuffed brown loafers, a penny tucked in each flap, wildly checkered red-and-white socks below rolled-up blue jeans.

"The light . . ." he mumbled.

"Sorry about that. The boys kind of get carried away when someone new comes in. Well, Cass, see you later. Glad you could make it."

At last the watery blur began to clear. At the same time the noise around him rose. Though he still was not quite ready, he looked up anyway.

The empty, dust-filled, collapsing room which he'd first viewed this morning had disappeared. In its place was a swirling cosmos of color and movement. Lights had been mounted at various distant points in the large room, their shifting beams aimed at the large silver mirrored ball which twirled slowly from the center of the ceiling and caught and reflected every color which fell within its path.

The ceiling was crisscrossed with multicolored layers of crepe paper streamers, punctuated here and there with low hanging clusters of colored balloons. Dancers reached up now and then to puncture one, causing a slight explosion, which in turn triggered scales of laughter from the crowd below. A motley crowd, Mark noted now, of out-of-date fashion—there the curious aberration of a zoot suit, baggy trousers attached to suspenders and drawn up well above the waist, a key chain which dipped down to the top of black polished shoes before climbing up again to an exactly oversized and ill-fitting white jacket with an oversized bow tie.

"Bob, you look marvelous!" Cass called out admiringly to the zoot suiter. "Wherever did you find it?"

"My old man's. Would you believe it? This is the way they used to look." The reply was sent back on the run as the boy hurried toward the large mahogany bar—which only this morning had boasted nothing but dust and cobwebs and bad memories.

Not so now. Now at least three dozen people struggled to push closer to the two bartenders, who appeared to be wearing Navy whites beneath their long aprons. Both were working so hard that at moments the white of the uniforms blurred under the duress of speed. In the crush of people shouting for the bartenders' attention, Mark saw several naval uniforms, vintage World War II—officers' uniforms for the most part.

"A lot of closets have been raided, haven't they?" Cass murmured, and pressed close and clung to his arm, as though she, too, was slightly bewildered by it all.

For a moment he was distracted from the noise and the music and color. Looking down at her, he realized that he owed her an apology. Clearly there was a party—though he was still unable to figure out how.

"Cass, I . . ."

"Come on, let's get us a drink. Amos will wait on us first. We've known each other forever." Again she was off, dodging through the dancing couples who, consistent with the forties theme of the evening, were doing the jitterbug.

Mark followed a distance behind her, fascinated by the ease with which she moved through the group. Almost everyone spoke to her or waved. Then one guy grabbed her about the waist and hauled her to the center of the dance floor.

Mark came to a halt, wondering if he'd lost her for the evening. Suddenly he saw the laughing boy cease to laugh, saw Cass speaking to him in low, inaudible tones, saw the boy instantly remove his arm from her waist and back hesitantly away. He was saying something, shaking his head in an apologetic movement, both hands now upraised, as though—

Abruptly the boy turned and darted off through the crowd, gone—leaving Cass standing alone amid the dancing couples. Though her back was to Mark, he sensed anger, and the moment she turned he saw anger confirmed.

She drew even with Mark and muttered one word. "Jerk!" Then said it again low, under her breath. "Damned jerk!" All at once under the shifting lights from the whirling mirrored ball, she didn't look so young, but unbelievably old and tired.

Fascinated by this rapid transformation, Mark fell behind as she moved rapidly past him, heading for the long bar and the

111

crowd of people pushing against it who were clearly taxing the abilities of the two bartenders to fill all orders.

Undaunted, Cass moved to the extreme left side, sidestepping the large decorative pot which—

Despite the crowd jostling around him, Mark stopped again and stared down at the pot. He remembered that very clearly from this morning—empty then, cracked and filthy. Now the red clay ceramic exterior glistened as though it had been freshly washed. A rubber plant stood erect, leafy and green, boasting of good health.

"Come on, Mark. Please." The urgency in the voice came from Cass, beyond the plant—at the end of the bar where apparently one of the bartenders was an old friend and had just ignored a dozen others, focusing all of his attention on Cass.

Beneath the long bartender's apron Mark saw ill-fitting Navy whites. In fact he saw more—saw that the predominant uniform in the room was Navy white. Surely there weren't that many fathers with closets to raid.

"What do you want to drink?" Cass called out as he drew near.

"Can't," he called out. "Training, you know. A Coke." For a moment he thought he saw disappointment on her face and wondered what difference it made to her whether he drank or not.

"One Coke, Amos, and one rum and Coke. More rum than Coke," she said to the tall guy behind the bar who looked older than student age. "Come on, Mark. Come closer. I want you to meet Amos."

He obliged, though out of the corner of his eye he caught a glimpse of people about the bar no longer pushing or calling out orders. Now they were all standing silent, merely watching them with various expressions of curiosity and resentment.

"Mark, this is Amos Foster. He's an old friend and a good one."

Her introduction was sincere, and Mark reached across the end of the bar and grasped Foster's hand and found it like ice.

"Sorry," the man grinned as he quickly withdrew his hand. "I've just filled the ice drawer."

"It's okay," Mark said, feeling suddenly self-conscious, aware of all the waiting faces and staring eyes. "Looks like you've got a crowd here," he added idiotically.

He heard the jukebox go silent somewhere behind him. The entire club, which only moments before had been a din of noise and shouts and laughter, had gone suddenly mute, as though someone had turned down the communal volume.

He looked over his shoulder and saw nothing out of the ordinary. For a moment the dance had come to an end, and couples were drifting slowly off the dance floor, some heading for the fringe of tables and chairs around the periphery of the club.

"Here you go, Mark."

At the sound of the voice he looked back and saw Amos handing over a glass of Coke, the light, white foam spilling over the top through chipped ice. At the same time the jukebox took off again in a nonsensical golden oldie called "Mairzy Doats," and within the moment jitterbugging couples filled the limited dance floor to overflowing. The noise level rose and, having delivered Cass her drink, Amos turned back to the others who, having waited patiently, now commenced to shout out their requests and fill the air with obscene comments. Everyone laughed and, after the mysterious pause, the party commenced again.

Again Mark looked to Cass for direction. Without a word she lifted her drink and sipped it down to a level which would not spill when transported, then, with a glance in his direction, she started off toward the large arched doors which led to the sun-room—the place where this morning the massive window glass had shattered.

As they continued to dodge their way through the crowd, Mark wondered how the gaping hole had been obscured. While the night was not cold in any sense of the word, with the absence of sun there was a preautumn chill in the air. More importantly, how had they concealed the noise and lights from the authorities?

As he moved in close quarters between several couples—the guys, he noticed, were wearing officers' uniforms—one jostled his hand holding the Coke. As the cold liquid spilled, Mark quickly extended the glass in front of him until he was through the congestion and approaching the arched door.

He looked ahead to see Cass patiently waiting for him, her face partially obscured by the angle of the glass from which she was drinking, though her eyes were on him and seemed to reflect amusement as he gingerly shook his soaked left hand.

A moment later neither her eyes nor her amusement was of primary interest to him. Behind her in the sun-room he saw a large black drape which obviously had been hastily hung from the molding along the edge of the ceiling. As he drew closer he continued to look past Cass, carefully inspecting the obscuring drape, curious about what was being hidden.

"I was here this morning," he said, continuing to walk past her onto the sun terrace itself, noticing the three couples seated at the

113

far end. The only table that had been here this morning was still here—that small one situated directly in front of the broken glass window.

Was it broken?

"Mark, where are you go—"

He heard the bewilderment in her voice, chose temporarily to ignore it and proceeded in a straight line to the black drapes and jerked them up and back.

"What in the . . .? Have you gone. . . .?"

Her mystification encircled him, but he continued to ignore it for a moment longer, gazing up at a crudely crisscrossing, wooden-board patching. At least a dozen pieces of mismatched lengths were nailed together in no order, for no purpose than to obscure the jagged, shattered glass on the other side.

"Mark, are you all right?"

Cass's inquiry was small yet so practical that he allowed the black drape to slip back into place. In the same movement—with what he hoped would be a mildly comic touch—he drew out one of the chairs from the near table and held it for her.

Apparently both the comic touch as well as the invitation were lost on her, for she shook her head and walked back to the north wall. In a childlike gesture, she slid down the wall until she was seated flat on the floor, knees raised, her elbows resting on her knees, drink suspended loosely in her hands.

For a moment he stared down at her, not quite understanding what her simple rejection meant. Then quickly he scolded himself.

"May I join you?" he asked, standing over her, hoping it wasn't too late.

She smiled up at him. "Are you sure it's safe?"

He heard the pointed sarcasm in her voice and was sorry he'd given her cause. Without asking again, he followed her lead and slipped down the wall until he was seated in exactly the same position, drink suspended in his hands. "I'm sorry," he muttered. "As I told you . . ."

". . . you were here this morning. I know."

"It was different then," he went on, trying to keep the defensiveness in his voice to a minimum.

"Well, of course it was different!" she exclaimed. "They've been working out here all afternoon trying to get this place ready."

"They did a great job."

Someone laughed at the far end of the sun terrace and he glanced around her and saw two of the guys dressed in the popular Navy white. When he didn't speak immediately, she followed his gaze and looked closely at the six, then looked back, softly perplexed.

He smiled at her attitude, part play, part maternal, as though she were dealing with a high-strung child. "The uniforms," he shrugged. "Was everyone's father in the Navy?"

"No. But there's a warehouse two blocks from here with cartons piled to the ceiling and each carton is filled with whites—all sorts, all classes. I started to take you there. For a costume, I mean. But we were late as it was and . . ." Her voice drifted and she commenced to play with her glass, turning it slowly around and around, tilting it now and then, the rum and Coke coming near the edge but never spilling over.

For a few moments silence persisted between them, though the background din was as consistent as ever. The six at the opposite end were growing louder, their slurred tongues suggesting they were getting bombed out of their heads. Peculiar, but Mark had not seen them make any return trips to the bar. They must have their own bottles. Puzzled, he again leaned forward and glanced in their direction and immediately got his answer. Several large flasks were being passed back and forth.

One girl held up a full bottle of what appeared from Mark's distance to be bourbon. At the exact moment she raised it, one of the "sailors" made a grab for it and grabbed for her as well. First safely stashing the bottle behind, he then capitalized on the twin elements of surprise and superior strength, rose suddenly, pushed the girl on her back and straddled her.

A shriek of mock protestation filled the sun terrace and brought several people from the large room to the arched door to see what had been the cause of this distress signal. One glance and their alarm appeared to be relieved.

"Atta boy, Paul, go gettum!"

"Hang on, Patty. You've been there before."

As their comments dwindled along with their interest, the crowd quickly dispersed back into the large room, leaving the sun terrace strangely quiet, Paul still perched atop Patty, his hands moving slowly down the front of her oversized white shirt, paying no attention to her face, which had gone suddenly inert.

One of the nearby "sailors" reached back for the filled bottle of bourbon, twisted the cap off and—with surprising and sober gentleness—lifted the girl's head and tilted the bottle to her lips. She swallowed twice, made a face and turned her head in a thrashing movement toward the other two girls who had with-

115

drawn to the far corner and now sat in Cass's position, heads down as though embarrassed.

Oh, Lord, Mark brooded wearily, orgy time.

As far as he could tell, Cass wasn't even aware of the attack at the far end of the sun terrace. The "sailors" had now succeeded in removing the oversized white shirt, but the blue jeans were proving to be a bit more troublesome.

"Cass, come on, let's go," he muttered, and saw her still brooding down on her drink.

"Where?" She looked up sharply, as though he'd just made a completely insane suggestion.

"The other room?" he suggested, and made it a question. He had just started to his feet when again she objected.

"Let's stay," she said, tugging at his arm and drawing him back down to the floor.

He said nothing, but simply looked toward the far end where it now appeared the girl was being very cooperative. Her hips lifted as she slid the blue jeans down, while the "sailor" worked on his own confinement of clothes. The other four in the initial party had completely withdrawn to the far corner where they sat, curiously quiet, in a circle, heads down like children playing jacks.

Mark watched Cass as again she saw the direction of his gaze, followed it and looked back amused. "That's none of your concern," she said. "Leave them alone. After all, it is a party." Having spoken, she leaned back against the wall and closed her eyes and appeared to be listening to the music—which he couldn't identify, a soft, slow melancholy ballad he'd never heard before.

As he settled, not quite relaxed, next to her against the wall, he looked toward the one empty table, surprised to see it was no longer empty. At some point—possibly during his fascination with the rape just under way at the far end of the sun terrace— two had entered and taken the table by the black drape which now obscured the broken window.

For some reason he was initially startled by their presence. At the angle in which he sat on the floor next to Cass he couldn't see their faces. The man was dressed in the garb of a naval officer, the woman in red. The man's "costume" seemed better fitting than the others, the light khaki officer's jacket smooth across his broad shoulders. Upon closer scrutiny, Mark now noticed a fringe of slightly graying hair directly above the starched collar. This wasn't a student. If he were, he was an older one.

"Who . . .?" he began, looking back at Cass—only to find her gone. Where in the hell? All at once he was on his knees, looking first toward the fun and games at the far end. Christ!

The couple was fully under way now, the boy's bare ass fully exposed, the girl's legs seeming to object with a violent twitching now and then like a half-dead chicken. No sound, though, neither of pain nor delight. Just a silent rocking motion with no one paying the least attention.

He closed his eyes as he turned away and dragged himself forward to the arched door. Where in hell had Cass gone—and when? One minute she was here and the next—

As he looked out over the crowded scene, he tried to single out a long, oversized white shirt and close-cropped blond hair, but now the room appeared to be filled with long, oversized white shirts as well as Navy whites. Several times, just when he thought he'd found her, the girl would turn and it would be someone else.

He searched for several minutes and at last, with an irritation born out of the difficult day, he muttered, "To hell with it!"

He turned a final time to look down at the far end of the sunroom, fascinated, yet loathing his fascination. As he turned, his eye again caught the two by the window whom he could see clearly now, having improved his vantage point by standing.

Something stirred within him, some inexplicable twinge of recognition. The man's profile was as familiar as—

He felt his pulse accelerate. In defense against what he could not understand, he shifted his eyes to the seated woman who sat opposite the man, head down, hands folded demurely, passively, in her lap as though she'd been scolded or chastised in some way.

Red dress. Clinging.

Through the window this morning after the glass shattered. Her! He'd tried to follow her, had lost her, then found her, then lost—

He stepped back and collided with a body.

"Hey, watch where you're going, buster!"

He tried to apologize but his mouth was dry.

There were soft moans coming from someplace close by. He wished they would stop. They seemed to be provoking similar ones deep within him.

The man, familiar even in profile, moved close now to the woman, whispering something seriously. He looked angry. Mark had never seen that profile, angry or moving, had only seen it frozen and fixed for all time over the mantel.

Not possible—

Why was she crying? The girl was crying. The moans were growing as well, the soft protestation still increasing, as though someone were in pain close by.

Why didn't they turn down that blasted music blaring so close

117

to his ear? And the lights were blinding him again, as though all beams had focused on him.

"Cass!"

He tried again to tear his vision from the two by the window. *Don't cry. Please.*

Get back in the frame where you belong.

"What's the matter with you, fellow? A little early to be bombed, isn't it?"

Still he tried to move backward, wanting only to vacate the sun terrace as quickly as possible. But he kept colliding with bodies, dancing couples like human obstructions, almost as though they did not want him to leave the room.

"Please," he muttered, and tried to turn about, the better to make his way through the crowd, which seemed to have grown denser, a solid glut of flesh and balloons and upturned laughing faces—all except the two at the table in the sun terrace who appeared now to be locked and frozen on his vision as well as in their positions.

"No!" he protested, failing to understand. With a strength born out of fear and motivated by a need to survive, he suddenly gave one massive push at the packed bodies. At that exact moment a woman's ear-piercing scream escaped from the sun-room. A second after that the lights flickered and blinked off.

He found himself in a peculiar blue light which seemed to have no specific source yet which lasted a moment longer and clearly illuminated one face seated at the table by the window looking directly at him—

His father.

"Where in the hell did you meet this guy, Cass?"

"Around."

"Watch his arm there."

"Hurry. We've got to get him out of here before the police . . ."

"No problem. Just relax. They're still inside, will be for a while. Where to?"

"Uncle Polly's."

"He's closed."

"No, he isn't. Please, Amos. Just get us out of here fast."

"Close the door. You okay?"

"Hurry."

The voices reached Mark over a velvet blackness. He liked it hat way. Someone else was in charge for a while. He didn't know whom and he really didn't give a damn.

He felt a hand on his forehead, cool and small, felt a slow bounce and acceleration of a car, as though it were making its way carefully across an open field. It was his disinterested guess that he was in the backseat of a car with his head resting somewhat awkwardly in someone's lap, his legs and feet curled in a cramped position against plastic seat covers.

"Keep your lights off, Amos, please, until . . ."

"What the hell, Cass, I've gotta see!"

"They're all over the place. Where did they come from?"

"Just campus cops."

"Still, if they arrested him . . ."

"Big deal. What's so special about him?"

"Scholarship."

"Big fucking deal."

The heartwarming concern coming from the backseat was consistently punctured by the cynicism coming from the front. Suddenly the car and everyone in it took a bone-rattling bounce. He could feel the springs beneath him object.

"Amos, please be careful," she scolded, raising her voice over the rattle of the car.

"What the hell, Cass?" The cynicism was rapidly changing to anger. "You told me to keep my lights off and then you bitch when . . ."

"Over there. There's the road. Be careful, there's a gully."

"Gully, hell! Looks like the Grand Canyon. We can't make that."

"Sure you can. Take it slow and easy."

"Shit!"

Mark kept his eyes closed and concentrated on the lap beneath his head, the hand resting on his forehead, the sensation that—when he'd least expected it and needed it most—someone cared. The perception moved him and momentarily took his mind off the dipping, struggling car.

Only then, as he felt gravity tug him toward the edge of the seat as the car apparently took a sharp downward dip, did he begin to wonder what in the hell was the matter with him. Why was he struggling up from unknown depths of unconsciousness while others—at least these other two around him—sounded alert and functioning?

The undercarriage of the car struck something hard and he heard an ominous scrape, as well as a series of oaths and curses coming from the front seat.

119

"Keep going," Cass whispered at the first break in the curses.

"Keep going? How in the hell . . .?"

"Please, Amos. Go on. We've got to get out of here."

There was such urgency in her voice that Mark opened his eyes, expecting to find blackness, and found instead a distant flashing of red and blue lights altering the pattern of night at predictable intervals like police cars from a distance.

At that moment he heard the screech of shifting gears, heard a foot press down hard on the accelerator and felt gravity reverse itself, felt himself now roll back and press against the back of the seat, his head tossing as disembodied as a puppet with slack strings.

"Terrific, Amos! Good. Now left. You're doing fine."

Something continued to clank ominously beneath the car.

"If there's damage, Cass, I swear . . ."

"I'll cover it. Keep going. No lights until I tell you. Turn here, Amos. Right. Then go straight on to the North Gate."

"I know the way."

There was a silence as taut and as tense as their recent exchange, though in the silence and the sense of a successful escape, Mark dared to relax a moment, still enjoying her closeness if nothing else.

What had happened?

Sun porch, he remembered that. Couple at the far end. Black drapes covering the broken window.

He must have made a sound. Suddenly he was aware of her leaning close over him in concern.

"Amos, I think he's hurt."

"Bull!"

"No, really. His head's bleeding."

Mark groaned and moved his hand reflexively to his forehead and—finding it whole—slipped it down to his left temple and met her fingers through what felt like fabric which she was holding against his head.

"Easy," she murmured. Gently but firmly, she took his hand and replaced it at his side. Once again he felt her twisting beneath him, as though she'd felt compelled to check the rear window.

"Okay, Amos, I think we can turn on the lights now and go straight to Uncle Polly's."

"I told you he wouldn't be open. Not this late."

"He will be. Now please go."

Still trying to figure out the mystery of his injured head, Mark heard a tone of voice coming from Cass he'd never heard before.

"Hey, you shouldn't be doing that," Cass protested as he grabbed for the back of the seat with one hand, the edge of the seat with the other, and slowly, awkwardly, tried to drag himself up to a sitting position.

"It's all right," he muttered, not so certain that it was. Again his hand moved instinctively to his left temple. Now he felt a thick, sticky substance, still moist at the center though growing dried and crusty as he moved his fingertips down the side of his face.

Once up, he clung to the back of the seat for a moment, then at last opened both eyes—though the left did not seem to open as readily as the right—and looked out at the passing blackness. In the distance he could see an explosion of lights, like Christmas, multicolored and flashing.

"What happened?" he asked of no one in particular, fairly certain someone would respond. When no one did, he swung his legs down and sat upright in the seat and at the same time felt the small trickle of something wet roll down the left side of his face.

"Here." Quickly she extended what appeared to be a handkerchief.

Wordlessly he took it and applied it to the trickle on the side of his face, then examined the cloth. In the half-light he saw new splotches, new stains. "What in the hell happened?" he grumbled, as though he were asking the handkerchief.

"Please," she said simply, her voice low, as though there might be listening ears in the car. Then she added, "You remember Amos?"

No, he didn't remember Amos. It didn't seem important except that it was Amos who was driving the car, helping him to escape. "What happened?" he asked again, aware of the idiotlike repetition but at this point not giving a damn.

"Sometimes it happens. Usually once, twice a year. At the beginning of school and the end—isn't that right, Amos?—as though they want to inform us at the beginning that we're not here to have fun and remind us again at the end of the year of the same thing. Right, Amos?"

Mark looked toward the front seat and saw through the windshield that they were approaching the North Gate.

Amos slowed the car and carefully guided it to the right avenue, slowing even more as he approached the sentry box. As he drew even with it, he stopped altogether, rolled down the window and handed out a small white piece of paper of some sort.

"Commissary man Foster, sir, on twenty-four-hour pass."

The sentry box was black, empty, deserted, the narrow door off

its hinges and leaning at a distorted angle against the curb. Th
front glass was broken. There was no one inside.

"Thank you, sir," Amos smiled cordially, withdrew the paper
rolled up the window and guided the car through the North Gate

"Oh, Amos, you are so damned silly!" Cass laughed. She leaned
forward in the seat and pushed playfully against the back of
Amos's head.

"Can't be too careful." He grinned at her in the rearview
mirror. "How's our runner doing?" As he asked the question he
angled his vision backward in the mirror.

As there were streetlights now placed at intervals in ever
block, Mark caught a glimpse of his face. He had seen him
someplace, but he couldn't remember where. Obviously a clown
though, handing out passes to nonexistent marines.

"Feeling better now?"

The soft though insistent voice dragged his attention back from
the rearview mirror and the eyes staring steadily back at him
Unable to answer the question, Mark hoped that a bewildered
shake of his head would suffice. "It's been a hell of a day," he said
at last, his voice low. "Did I fall asleep again or slip like this
morning?"

"Neither," Cass replied patly, ignoring his sarcasm. "This time
you were pushed. When the police arrived at the front door, the
mob headed for the rear door of the sun terrace. Unfortunately
you were standing directly in their path."

"Should have moved," came the chant from the front seat.

"What'll happen?" Mark asked, ignoring the chant. "To the
others, I mean."

"Oh, the police will arrest a bunch of them. There'll be head
lines in all the state papers. STUDENT DEBAUCHERY and all that
Fathers will have to come up with a lot of bail money and a few
cases will make it to court and promptly be thrown out. This time
next month there'll be another party at the club, bigger and
better." Her voice became a drone, as though she were boring
herself with its predictable repetition. "We play games with the
authorities. I sometimes think they enjoy it as much as we do."

Suddenly she leaned up sharply. "Left here, Amos, remember
Uncle Polly's. I told you."

"And I told you he was closed."

"Not tonight."

Again Mark heard that tension in her voice, as though she
disliked intensely being argued with.

At that moment Amos cut a sharp left, so sharp that Mark
collided with the door handle and Cass collided with Mark

Apparently hearing the scrambling in the back, Amos again peered into the rearview mirror. "Well, you said left," he proclaimed.

Still Mark struggled to place him. Someone he'd met at the party, he was certain of that. As he tried halfheartedly to solve the mystery, Mark gazed out of the window, still dabbing now and then at his left temple. He recognized the scenery now—one of the main arteries which led to the campus corner. If he wasn't mistaken, behind him by about three blocks were the athletic dorms where he should have gone and stayed for the evening. What in the name of God had sent him back out there?

"Are you sure you're all right?" The soft, concerned voice was Cass's again, who leaned closer, bridging the distance between them. "Don't worry. We're going someplace where someone can help you. Uncle Polly's," she added brightly. "You know Uncle Polly. You were there this evening."

He looked down on her, puzzled, and wondered if the blow on the head had affected his mental processes. It had been several hours since anything had made any sense.

"Well, son of a bitch!" This soft exclamation came from the front seat.

Mark glanced up to see Amos guiding the car close to the curb on a darkened street—a completely darkened street with one exception, the bright spill of light which poured out from two large plate-glass windows. Mark stooped over the better to see and recognized the familiar, plain interior of the place where he'd consumed a massive and delicious dinner, the Greek place run by the old immigrant.

"Uncle Polly's. There he is!" Cass exclaimed, and scrambled easily to her side of the car, opened the door and crawled out, reaching back toward Mark.

Father.

The single word crept into Mark's consciousness like a thief and crept out again, stealing some of his sense of balance and equilibrium. As he reached up for the front seat he saw a figure standing in the door of the café. It was the Greek, although now he appeared to be clad in some sort of robe, as though he had closed, gone to bed and gotten out of bed for them.

"Help me, Amos. He's unsteady."

"So are we all," came the disinterested voice from the front seat, though now he rolled down his window and called out, "Uncle Polly, you should be in bed. You need your beauty sleep. You're not getting any younger."

The old man didn't respond, though he waved away the

123

comment with the back of his hand and continued to stand against the door, holding it open.

"Real excitement out there tonight, Uncle Polly," Amos went on, twisting about in his seat, resting his elbows on the open window. "You should have been there."

"You kids!" Uncle Polly replied, a good-natured scolding in his voice. "Not serious enough. It's a wonder you make it to adulthood."

"Screw adulthood!" Amos laughed back at him.

During this exchange Mark was doing his best to propel himself toward the open door where Cass stood as though underwater, one hand extended to him in the distance, though every time he placed any degree of weight on his arms they buckled. At the same time his vision was expanding to take in the sidewalk, the light spilling through the plate glass and even Uncle Polly, seeing the difficulty Mark was having, hurried toward the car and the open door.

"Here, grab on," he ordered with a reach that extended beyond Cass's.

Mark saw a large hand, the back and knuckles covered with tightly curled black hairs, the hand itself speckled with brown spots like large freckles. This hand seemed to hold steadier than the other, and he grasped it now, feeling strength propel him forward.

"But watch your head," a low, warm male voice commanded. It was the same voice he'd heard earlier in the evening, a trace of that accent—just a trace—more audible on certain words than on others. "Come forward. That's a good boy."

Without being able to say quite how he'd managed to make it from the cramped quarters of the backseat of the car to a more or less upright position on the sidewalk, Mark nonetheless found himself in the cool night air. The old Greek was on one side, supporting most of his weight, while Cass served on the other, a fragile support but a desirable one.

Where Amos had gone he had no idea. He considered turning about to see, but the new, upright position seemed to play havoc with his already questionable center of balance and Amos's presence was forgotten.

As the day's various insanities gathered into one absurd congregation, Mark felt a hot anger, as though he had suddenly perceived with perfect clarity the fact of his manipulation.

"Hey, wait, young fellow. Not by yourself, not just yet," the old Greek said, protesting Mark's useless bid to stand and walk alone

124

and sent Cass ahead for the door. "Open wide, dear," he instructed.

Mark felt the man's enormous hands renew their grip and he was amazed and impressed with the strength the old codger could muster.

"Through the door."

Mark was first greeted by the heavy, lovely smell of garlic—tons of garlic—and a rack of lamb roasting somewhere. It was a delicious odor and reminded him of his gluttony here earlier in the evening—three gyros, the need for a walk, which in turn had led him back out to the base and—

"Here we go." The singsong voice was the old man again, guiding him down into a chair near the back of the café close to the glass-doored refrigerator. Through the smoky doors Mark could see great blocks of féta and jars of black and green olives. "Easy down."

At last Mark felt all support leaving him save that of the chair beneath him. As he started bonelessly downward, he reached up and grabbed the edge of the table and hung on for several seconds, aware that he was being closely watched.

"A clean cloth, Uncle Polly. And some water," Cass murmured and stepped close.

Mark felt her hand on the side of his face. He was aware of Uncle Polly also drawing near, an equally close examination.

"What happened?" Uncle Polly asked.

From the downward angle of his vision, Mark could see wrinkled blue pajama bottoms protruding from beneath the equally wrinkled wine-colored robe. Now Mark listened closely, hoping her answer to the old man's question might reveal something that would answer a few of his own questions.

"Cops," was her brief reply.

In its brevity Mark closed his eyes. No solution there.

"Bad trouble?" Uncle Polly asked. They were both still hovering over Mark.

"I don't know. I didn't stay," Cass said. Mark still felt her hand on his forehead.

"Good girl!" Uncle Polly murmured. "This one was in earlier, you know."

"I know."

"He didn't talk much. Didn't tell me he was going out to the base."

"Probably didn't know he was."

"What happened to him?"

125

"He was standing in the wrong place when the sirens came."

Something about this entire, though brief, exchange struck Mark as bizarre—smaller points which he could not articulate and larger ones which he could. "I'm present and accounted for," he muttered, pulling away from her hand and maintaining his place in the seat, afraid to trust his legs as yet.

For several moments the silence about him was dense. For the first time Mark heard the scuffle of feet moving away, and he looked up to see Uncle Polly disappear behind the counter through the swinging doors that led into the kitchen, leaving him alone with Cass, who during the interim had seated herself on the edge of the table, her feet resting in the seat of the other chair.

"You feeling better?" she asked, apparently giving him all the room he needed.

He nodded, puzzled by the sensation in the air, feeling that by speaking on his own behalf he'd angered them in some way. "That seems to be the most pertinent question of the day," he mumbled, rubbing the back of his neck now, feeling for the first time an uncomfortable tightness there.

She laughed softly and he looked up to see her studying her hands, palms wide open, fingers extended. "Probably tomorrow it will be my turn."

The nicest aspect of what she'd said was the inference that they would see each other tomorrow. That possibility pleased him immensely. "Cass, I . . ." He leaned forward in his chair and was on the verge of thanking her directly and sincerely when the kitchen door opened and Uncle Polly appeared, clean cloths in one hand and a small stainless-steel basin in the other.

"Here, Florence Nightingale," he called out in a good-natured jab—which Cass either didn't hear or chose to ignore. "Do your best," he added, and placed the items on the table. "I have a better remedy," he went on expansively, and hurried back to the counter, reached down and brought forth a large bowl heaped with tjatjiki and a basket of wheat biscuits. He returned to the table and placed the delicacies next to the basin of water. "There. Eat heartily," he beamed.

As though to demonstrate, with one fluid motion Uncle Polly picked up a biscuit, aimed it like a kamikaze pilot down toward the mountain of white, creamy tjatjiki, scooped up an enormous amount and popped it all into his mouth. He chewed contentedly at the bulk for a few seconds before he could speak. "Double garlic, Cassie, just the way you like it."

She gave him a warm smile and thanked him.

126

Mark sensed a friendship of long standing. What was its basis and what was the secret of its success, this unlikely alliance between the old man and the young girl?

"Hold still." The command was hers, and Mark was aware of her standing close, guiding a warm, damp cloth gently over his left temple. There was a slight stinging and he shut his eyes again.

"It's not bad," Cass said quietly. "Scraped more than anything. Feeling steadier now?"

"Absolutely," Mark said with conscious effort, and sat upright. For the first time he saw the trail of dried blood that cut an uneven pattern on his knit shirt.

"Come on, eat, then," Uncle Polly commanded. "All he needs is food. A growing boy and all that."

Mark felt Cass retreat, looked up to see her place the basin of water and cloth on the counter and found himself staring straight into Uncle Polly's face, which just for a moment was distorted, his mouth bulging with yet another ladened biscuit.

"Come, eat!" he now commanded, and shoved the bowl toward Mark, who found the odor irresistible and with a grin dipped a biscuit into the soft creamy mixture. He guided it into his mouth where at first he felt the pleasurable sting of extra garlic and then the terrific combination of mixed yoghurt and cucumber.

Uncle Polly saw his delight and nodded. "Good, huh? Put hair on your chest." So saying, he reached again for a biscuit.

Mark chewed, swallowed and looked up to see Cass watching from behind the counter, a curious expression on her face, one of lostness, almost exclusion. Uncle Polly followed his gaze and clearly disliked what he saw.

"Come, come. Why do you stay there?"

Cass laughed. "I don't want hair on my chest."

Uncle Polly shook his fist at her in mock anger and again gestured more forcibly for her to come and join them. At last she did, drawing out the chair nearest the counter and sitting primly on its edge.

"Come. Eat!"

Apparently she found him as irresistible as Mark had and reached for a biscuit. For several moments each seemed content to dip and snack and avoid looking at each other. Finally it was Uncle Polly who broke the silence.

"Why did you two go back out to that place tonight? That place is no good. You know that. I told you many times, no good! Cops are right. It's dangerous. You should stay away."

Mark saw a curious look pass between the two which he could

127

not recognize. Then Cass looked sternly at the old man as though she didn't like what he was saying.

"All right, all right, Uncle Polly," she said in resignation, holding up her hand as though to stay his anger.

"I've warned you. I've warned you before. Let it go at that." Uncle Polly shook his head and repeated his command. "Now eat!"

But without warning Cass stood up and smoothed down her long white shirt, which looked considerably the worse for wear. "I'm tired. I'm going home." So saying, without a moment's hesitation she started around the table toward the front door.

Stunned by the rapid transition, Mark rallied just before she reached the door. "Wait, I . . ."

"No, you stay here and talk to Uncle Polly. He's a great bullshit artist, so be careful."

"No, I want to come with . . ."

"I'm going home."

"I'll walk you."

"It's out of the way. And there's no need. My mother . . ."

Mark had just started to his feet when the same large hand covered with tightly curled black hairs that had helped him out of the car planted itself again on his shoulder.

"Let her go," Uncle Polly warned soberly. "Don't argue. Not with her. Useless."

Mark considered shaking off the hand as well as the advice, but as he looked toward the door he saw that it was too late anyway. The door was swinging closed and he could see Cass moving quickly away from the light, disappearing into the darkness. For a moment he felt her absence like a deprivation and continued to gaze out at the darkened pavement, trying to figure out if she'd left in anger and if so, why.

While he was concentrating on those questions, he heard a chair scraping and knew that Uncle Polly had left the table. At that moment he didn't give a damn. All at once he glimpsed an unsettling pattern to this entire bizarre day—always reduced to a position of relative helplessness, always weak when everybody else around him was strong and in charge.

The perception—right or wrong—stunned him. That had never been the case in his life before. Up until now he'd either set the pace and led or else had made his own way.

His thoughts were interrupted by a loud noise, something set down before him with considerable strength, clattering against the Formica-topped table. Startled, he looked up to see Uncle

128

Polly grinning down on him, then gesturing toward the bottle and two glasses as though it were a brilliant solution to almost all his problems.

Mark looked closely at the bottle and saw that it was Nine Star Metaxa; he was familiar with it, though he didn't really care for it. It was strong as hell, and besides—training.

"No. No, thank you," he muttered, and again glanced toward the door and the blackness beyond and wondered if he could catch up with her. What in the hell had caused her to leave so suddenly?

"Oh, come on," Uncle Polly chided. "One glass, how will it hurt? Relax. Make you feel like a new man." As though to demonstrate, he took the already-opened bottle and filled a glass almost three-quarters full and quickly drained it himself. He made a face at the empty glass and breathlessly pronounced, "Good. From the gods. Come, you, too."

Again Mark shook his head and felt weary from the repeated need to resist the man. "Must go."

"Don't go after her. Useless."

Mark pushed all the way out of the chair and wavered a moment, hung onto the edge of the table and felt a new throbbing in the left side of his temple. "Damn!" he muttered, and resented the clear I-told-you-so look on Uncle Polly's face.

"You should sleep here tonight," Uncle Polly scolded. He reached across the table effortlessly and guided Mark back down into the chair.

"Can't," Mark muttered again. "Got to get to the dorm."

"Why?"

"Not supposed to stay out."

"Leave Cassie alone."

There it was again, that peculiar admonition. The old buzzard was overstepping his bounds. Still, Mark was curious. He'd been unable to learn a great deal about the girl on his own. Maybe Uncle Polly—

"Do you know her well?" Mark asked, trying to make the question sound offhand and casual.

"Well!" Uncle Polly repeated. "Her grandfather was my good friend and a brilliant teacher, professor at the university."

Mark listened carefully, as fascinated by the sudden and unexpected air of familiarity as by what the man was saying. The friendship with Cass's grandfather surprised Mark. This man seated opposite him, once again urging a drink on him, was old but didn't look that old. Again he saw Uncle Polly lift his glass, tip

129

his head sharply back and drain the glass, then hold a rapturous pose for a moment, staring straight up at the ceiling.

In an attempt to get him back on track, Mark said quietly, "Cass . . ."

The old man nodded broadly and at the same time made a circular motion with one finger in the vicinity of his ear, a classic gesture implying—

"Crazy," Uncle Polly pronounced flatly. "Old Karl always used to say the girl was crazy, but he loved her, he did, and on his deathbed he asked Uncle Polly to keep his eye on her and I've tried my best, but . . ."

"Where's her mother?"

Uncle Polly had just lifted his newly filled glass and now stared at Mark over the rim. "Home," he said quietly and tilted the glass and drained it.

As the once-filled bottle before him shrank with incredible speed to half full, Mark began to doubt the dependence and reliability of Uncle Polly as a source of information. Besides, he longed for the privacy of his room at the dorm. He needed time to try to understand the events of the day and night.

And he must call his mother.

Father.

He had to put that bit of foolishness out of his mind. All of the males at the party tonight had borne a startling resemblance to his mother's photo albums which were filled with yellowed and curling snapshots documenting her life as a Navy wife. Under the strain of the moment he'd simply thought that the man by the black-draped window had—

"Come, I command you." The mindless voice was indeed a command, and Mark was jolted back to the small café by the glowering Uncle Polly, who again extended a filled glass toward him. "Come! In Greece no man drinks alone. To do so is . . ."

"I said no," Mark repeated with as much force as he could muster and still be polite. "I'm in training, you see, and that's not allowed."

"To hell with training! Our Greek athletes drink this like mother's milk and they perform like gods."

A debatable point, but Mark lacked both the energy and the desire to debate it. "Maybe another time, Uncle Polly," he soothed, and was pleased to find that now he did not need the support of the table. He moved instantly toward the door and away from both the hand and the influence of the man who, mildly drunk, glared at him from the table.

"Be advised," Uncle Polly slurred after him. "Stay away from her. She is trouble, so sweet and helpless. You hear? All women . . ."

At the door and feeling safe, Mark stopped and looked back at the man issuing the curious indictment. "Thanks for the food," he said cordially. "I'll be back in again. I promise."

"You must listen to me!" Uncle Polly warned with new urgency and at the same time pushed up from the table with such force that his chair clattered backward. "Wait!" he called after Mark, who with mild alarm had already passed through the door and let it slam resoundingly behind him.

"Wait!" the old man shouted again, and his shout joined the slammed door, to echo mysteriously around the quiet sidewalk which was deserted, as was the street, as was the whole world as far as Mark could see. What the hour was, he had no idea, but was now convinced it was later than he'd thought.

"Listen!" Uncle Polly commanded. "Come back and drink with me. It would be the wisest thing you've done today. I promise. Come back! You hear me talking? Come back and I'll tell you stories you've never heard before. You there!"

As his voice pursued Mark down the darkened sidewalk, Mark considered returning—at least long enough to quiet the man. He had been decent and friendly and not like most in this peculiar town. But something—fatigue, confusion and an equally persistent need to be alone—prohibited him from turning back, and to his surprise he found himself searching the darker places close to the shop fronts and only then realized he was still hoping to find Cass.

But he found nothing except deeper shadows and heard nothing but the echoing of the slightly drunken rage of Uncle Polly, still yelling at him even though he'd managed to put a distance of about a hundred yards between them.

Then suddenly there was silence. Though Mark continued on down the darkened sidewalk, hands in pockets, head bowed, he was convinced that now the shouting was over. Uncle Polly would simply close up, lock his café, go to his bed and sleep it off.

All at once on the far side of the street, the darkness of the night was shattered by a sudden sparkling flare—like the striking of a match—in the front seat of a parked car. Startled by the alteration, Mark glanced in that direction and saw the car of ancient vintage and saw as well the face of the man briefly illuminated by the flaring match.

Amos?

131

Again he stopped and gaped in that direction and saw the small light of the match now extinguished, saw in its place the curving white paper of a cigarette, red tipped in the dark. Black night once again of a piece, the man's face was obscured.

Mark found himself gazing foolishly into an abyss. What if it wasn't Amos? But if it was, what was he doing parked alongside the darkened curb as though watching?

Without warning Mark felt his heart accelerate, felt as well an uncomfortable trembling that started across the back of his shoulders and spread instantly down his arms and affected his hands until he felt palsied with fear.

Why was he afraid?

Get out. Move on, a voice advised.

And this he did, turning away from the parked car and the small distant flare of a cigarette. He fought against looking back.

He increased his pace until he was briskly striding down the deserted sidewalk, hearing only the muffled tread of his own footsteps and the slightly erratic pounding of his own heart.

Coach Herbert stood at his open window, hands behind his back, dreading what he had to do, trying to ease that dread in brief enjoyment of the half-assed basketball game a few of his track boys were playing on the court below outside the dining hall.

Terry Crawford made a bounding leap for the airborne ball and came down hard at a twisted angle on his ankle.

Coach Herbert winced for him, threw open the casement wider and shouted down, "Be careful down there, you hear? Doc Robbins will have your hide if you sprain any of those ankles."

Suddenly he felt the weight of all those upturned faces. Most—perhaps all—hadn't even known he'd been watching. A few waved self-consciously and for a few minutes the earlier hilarity died. He saw them merely bouncing the ball in a dispirited way and was sorry he'd had to play the role of wet blanket. But what the hell? Most of them were scholarship boys. The university had paid handsomely for their well-disciplined machines with hopes riding high for the school's first Olympic team.

Coach Herbert's gaze grew even more fixed as he tried to deal with the great surge of feeling and emotion he experienced in merely thinking the words.

Olympic team.

His dream for as long as he could remember. First as a track star at Michigan State and later as a young coach, then a middle-aged coach and now—

Was it too late?

No, of course not. Never too late for a dream, and this year he had assembled the most gifted team that it had ever been his pleasure to coach. This year, perhaps.

He stood a moment longer, staring down on the deserted basketball court. He was sorry he'd spoiled their fun, but maybe a year from now with hunks of gold dangling around their necks they'd forgive him and thank him.

The glorious vision was rudely interrupted by a single knock at the door, jarring Coach Herbert back from the projected glories of the future to the unpleasant realities of the present. He looked sharply toward the door as though he were already in confrontation with the young man on the other side. A real disappointment, that one, though not too late yet to force him into line.

Since that unfortunate episode several days ago, Mark Simpson had been noticeable only in his absence from everything—from all workouts, from all runs, from all team meetings and, Coach Herbert assumed, from his classes as well. There was no doubt about it. He needed to talk to the boy now before it was too late.

On that note of grim resignation, Coach Herbert secured the casement window and called out, "Come."

At the same time the boy knocked again, thus obscuring the command. Coach Herbert called again, louder, and heard the edge in his voice.

He continued to stare at the still-closed door and was on the verge of calling out a third time when at last he saw the knob turn, and put himself in the shoes of the young man who'd just emerged from behind the closed door. The quick exercise in empathy helped. He felt his disappointment salved as he saw apprehension and concern on Mark's face.

At least he wasn't taking it lightly. If there were problems of any kind, Coach Herbert would be more than happy to help him solve them, for this boy was the primary gem in his talented new team, the one they'd paid a small fortune for in an attempt to lure him away from the razzle-dazzle of the Cal school. Even now Coach Herbert felt it difficult to believe in his own good luck.

"Mark," he called out, seeing the boy emerge from behind the door and quietly close it behind him as though he knew it was going to be "that kind of conference."

"Sir," the boy said with unerring politeness, which served only to soften Coach Herbert more.

In the bright sun of afternoon he observed again what he'd first observed last year when he'd flown out to California to see Mark Simpson, that God had blessed him with an almost perfect runner's body—tall, lean yet muscular, long arms and legs, compact torso—and all these natural gifts had been enhanced by years of good training and personal discipline.

What the hell had gone wrong these last few days?

"Come in, come in," Coach Herbert invited warmly, gesturing the boy from the area around the door and toward the easy chair opposite his desk.

With a nod, murmured thanks and only a moment's hesitation, Mark moved to the center of the room, then to the designated chair where he sat immediately, at first nervously on the edge, then at last sliding back. But the stiffness remained.

Coach Herbert considered sitting in the comfortable swivel chair behind his desk, then changed his mind. Don't put more barriers between them. Besides, only at that moment at this close range had he seen an ominous scabbed-over area on the boy's left temple. Something—or someone—had recently dealt him a teeth-rattling blow.

"What's this now?" Coach Herbert asked, trying to fill his voice with more concern than accusation. As he started toward the injured area, the boy's hand moved rapidly up, at first protecting the injury, then concealing it.

"Nothing," Mark said quickly, and drew back from Coach Herbert's inspection. "I'm afraid . . . Clumsy, that's what I am. I tripped over a throw rug in my room and banged into the side of the . . . dresser. . . ."

Coach Herbert did not need that revealing pause to know the boy was lying. He hadn't worked all his life with young men for nothing. God, how he hated falsehood! As he turned away in an attempt to digest his disappointment, an unsettling expression on the boy's face caught his attention, as though the greater disappointment in the room was Mark's.

"Dresser? The side of the dresser, you say?" Coach Herbert asked, moving back to his chair and feeling the desk to be a small barrier compared to the lie which stretched ponderously between them. He watched Mark closely, hoping, praying, he would smile, shake his head and correct his lie. But he didn't.

"You know, Simpson, that your scholarship is based on your active participation in all team activities and not breaking training

134

and following all the dictates of Doc Robbins and myself. And if that sounds a little like indentured slavedom, no one ever said that athletic scholarships represent the best in democratic action."

The edge had returned to his voice, along with a rising anger. Why the hell had the kid felt it necessary to lie? Try him with the truth. Coach Herbert was capable of understanding.

"Did you hear me, Simpson?"

"I did."

"I don't like to have meetings like this—but the year's still young. Whatever the trouble . . ."

"No trouble."

"Then where the hell have you been?"

At this the boy looked up for the first time, and Coach Herbert saw the splintering of emotions and took some encouragement from it. At least he hadn't totally misjudged the boy. Something was bothering him, something which he felt a strong compulsion to conceal.

"Mark, listen," Coach Herbert began, leaning closer to where the boy sat, "let's level with each other, shall we? Believe me, it's the best in the long run."

"I don't understand, Coach."

Now as he looked up, Coach Herbert saw a faint blankness on that smooth brow. Damn him, he still was playing the old hide-and-seek game.

"Well, let's see if I can't assist you to a degree of understanding," Coach Herbert snapped, and pushed away from the desk, anger vaulting, a great deal of it aimed at himself.

Had he misjudged him?

"Okay. We've had a team meeting every day this week. You've missed them all."

"I . . ."

"No, let me finish," Coach Herbert demanded. "You failed to report for workouts and you've not done the base course once since Monday. Now I could very easily find out about your class attendance—and will, if I have to—but prefer that you tell me. And it damned well better be the truth. Is that clear?"

Coach Herbert waited a few moments longer for the boy to say something, anything, in his own defense. But the boy said nothing and continued to sit, obviously feeling miserable, still studying the palms of his hands with relentless fascination. Just as Coach Herbert was on the verge of staging an explosion, he saw those hands tremble and a new redeeming thought entered his head.

"You're not sick, are you, Simpson?" he inquired. "Well, are

135

you? For God's sake, help me, Mark!" Coach Herbert pleaded with genuine feeling. "We need to work together, not against each other. Are you sick?" he prodded.

"No," Mark replied too quickly. "I mean not really. I just . . . I don't . . . I'm not sure . . ."

For a few seconds Coach Herbert found himself gazing down on his position of consummate despair. "Come on, now. It's not that bad," he comforted, again reassured by the boy's easy vulnerability. "Tell me. Let me help," Coach Herbert concluded simply.

Mark retreated to the window. "I . . . I don't know, Coach," came his stammer, which suggested another adventure into falsehood. "I've felt like hell since that day . . ."

"How?"

Mark looked over his shoulder almost fearfully at the direct and blunt interrogation. "I . . . don't know," he stammered again.

He might be one hell of a runner but he was also one hell of a liar.

"Dizzy, you know. Not much appetite. Light-headed. That's how I got this." He tapped gingerly at his left temple.

Coach Herbert listened closely, more than eager to give him the benefit of the doubt. For several minutes the two stared at each other across the expanse of the room. Then without a word Coach Herbert returned to his desk, stretched across the expanse for the telephone, lifted it over the clutter of papers and reports, anchored the receiver between chin and shoulder and punched extension 376.

Coach Herbert waited for the first dial tone and its familiar buzzing. Still willing to give the boy the benefit of the doubt, he asked further, "What else? What other symptoms, I mean. Can you tell me so I can . . .?"

Then he heard the familiar raspy voice of the team physician and trainer on the opposite end of the line.

"Doc Robbins here."

The voice and the speech pattern instantly conjured up the man himself, small, wizened, nearing retirement—that would be a hell of a painful day—semibald pate glistening with the perspiration of effort as he labored over tight muscles, pulled muscles, strained muscles. How many over the last quarter of a century Coach Herbert would hate to estimate.

"Robbins," he said, "Coach here. Listen, I need a med exam on one of our boys. I'm going to send him down right now."

Ah, that brought the frozen statue at the window to life! Mark

Simpson's head jerked around, his face a map of bewilderment and protest.

With a staying gesture, Coach Herbert tried to hold all objections coming from the boy for a few more minutes.

"Who's the boy and what are you looking for?" Doc Robbins asked, his voice now filled with a kind of weary professionalism.

"Mark Simpson and you tell me, okay? That's your job."

"Simpson? Why Simpson?"

"Will you do it? Can you do it now?"

"I said I would. You don't believe in making it easy on a guy, do you?"

Coach Herbert smiled. Robbins was a first-class doctor and trainer but a chronic complainer. "I'm sending him down right now. Check him out, will you? Thanks, Doc." Quickly he hung up, feeling a need to address the boy by the window, who apparently had swallowed his initial urge to protest and now seemed to have sunk to even new levels of despair.

"Hey, what's the matter?" Coach Herbert asked, suddenly feeling compassion for the boy despite his recent lies. "I should have had this done the other day, you know, the same day I dragged you from that pond. I'm sure you don't remember. We got about half of Coffin Pond out of your lungs—me and that girl. Hey, what *did* happen to that girl?" Coach Herbert inquired now with suspect ease. "You know, the one who . . .?"

"I don't know."

"I've seen her around. She seems very nice, very attracted to you—if you know what I mean." The tone was purposely light.

When he still didn't respond one way or the other, Coach Herbert abandoned the subject of the girl, though only temporarily. He'd ask the other boys later if they knew who she was and where she lived.

"Well, come on," he said on a note of dispatch. "I'll walk you down to Doc Robbins's inner sanctum. I have to go that way anyway."

"Coach, it really isn't necessary." These were the boy's first words in some time and not terribly encouraging ones, his voice was so low as to be scarcely discernible, and he sounded breathless, as though he'd run a great distance.

"Well, I'm the coach and I disagree," Coach Herbert said gently. "As I said, this should have been done the very day you . . ." He broke off, still as puzzled by that day as ever, still able to see Mark floating—apparently lifeless—facedown in Coffin Pond. As the

137

vision faded he reached for the boy's arm and urged them both into the comfort of action. "Come on, Mark. It won't take long. Robbins isn't a good enough doc for it to take too long."

"Coach, I . . ."

"Come on. Let's put our minds at ease over one problem, then we can tackle whatever else is . . ."

"I said that nothing is the matter." The objection was strong and accompanied by a gesture in which Mark drew away from Coach Herbert's hand on his arm.

"Mark, I know better."

"Then you tell me." Mark Simpson stood before the window, now openly confronting him. In a way his belligerence was easier to deal with than his quiet despair.

"I'd like to," Coach Herbert muttered broadly. "In fact that's what I'm trying to do, and let's start with a clean bill of health. Then we can proceed from there."

For several moments Mark looked as though he were on the verge of a response, but finally the belligerence was defeated and he gave a massive shrug which seemed to speak of despair and passivity. With a heavy sigh he started around the desk, walking directly past Coach Herbert and out the door.

Too docile, Coach Herbert thought, worried. Not the most desirable characteristic for a competitive runner.

"Hey, wait, Mark. I'll walk with you."

But as he accelerated his speed in an attempt to catch up with the boy, the phone rang on his desk with a suddenness that startled him. Standing in the exact center of the open door, he looked first in the direction of Mark Simpson and saw him just starting down the steps that led to the gym and training rooms below. "Mark, wait!" he called again and expected, hoped, the boy would look back and obey.

But he did not, and as he slipped from sight on his way down the stairs, Coach Herbert looked back, annoyed, toward the persistently ringing telephone. Damn! Talk about lousy timing!

Finally resigned, he abandoned the door and ran back toward his desk, stretched across the cluttered expanse again and lifted the receiver. "Hello? Hello?" Breathless from his sprint, all he heard for a few moments was the sound of his own labored breathing and an empty receiver.

"Hello? Anybody there?" he asked further, raising his voice over what now sounded like static. For a moment he thought he heard a small, distant voice.

"I can't hear you. I really can't. Can you speak up?" He was

138

practically shouting. When he received no answer, he turned and sat on the edge of the desk and saw several boys glance in from the hall. Quickly he motioned for one to come and close the door. After several seconds of exaggerated charades, one of the boys came hurriedly forward and with a self-conscious smile reached in and drew the door closed.

The door secured, Coach Herbert was on the verge of shouting again into the receiver, but at that precise moment the line went dead, filling his ear with a loud and persistent buzzing. He listened for a few additional seconds, then held out the receiver and looked at it as though it were the offender. Once more he put it to his ear and, hearing nothing, returned it to its cradle across the desk.

He wondered who it was and then dismissed it. The various extensions were always getting screwed up. He had heard a woman's voice—or so he thought.

He was still perched on the edge of his desk, his hand still on the receiver, when the phone rang again with a startling suddenness that caused him to withdraw his hand as though the phone were hot. It rang three times before he reached for it, and now he shouted angrily into the mouthpiece.

"Hello? Who the hell is this?"

There was a pause, then from the rasping voice: "Who put the burr under your saddle, damn it?"

He blinked at the familiar voice, the equally familiar clichéd humor. "Robbins, that you?"

"None other. I was going to be mad at you but you beat me to it."

"Why? What . . .?"

"I thought you were sending the Simpson kid down."

"I did. A few minutes ago."

There was another pause. "Then he got lost on the way somewhere."

"What do you mean?" Coach Herbert demanded, anger increasing at this turn of events.

"Can't make it much clearer, Coach. I was ready to close up shop—have to take Ellie to the doctor's—when the boss man calls and says . . ."

Coach Herbert tuned out what he'd said. He was sorry that Robbins had had to make other arrangements for his wife Ellie, a warm, once plump, gray-haired lady—lady in every sense of the word—who had been mother to every athlete in need of mothering for the past quarter of a century. Now, as a reward for a

139

lifetime of selfless and giving love, Fate had given her cancer and less than a year to live.

"I'm sorry, Doc," Coach Herbert muttered, wishing the apology was capable of covering everything. "I don't know where the kid is. I saw him start down the steps. I saw that much."

"Why didn't you come with him?"

"I started to. Phone rang."

"Well, he never made it. What was the trouble?"

"I don't know. He's the one I told you about Monday. Slipped and fell into the pond, remember?"

"Yeah." The pause before "Yeah" was significant. Robbins had been skeptical of the story when Coach Herbert had just related it to him. Apparently he still was. "Well, what do you want me to do now? Go look for him?"

"Oh, no. You go on home. I'll round him up. We'll set it up again for tomorrow."

"Whatever you say."

"He's obviously disturbed."

"Obviously."

"Give Ellie my love."

"She's doing fine."

"Good. Good." Coach Herbert stood abruptly, as though to move away from the grim subject. "Well, talk to you tomorrow, Doc. Again, thanks."

"Good luck with the kid. From what I hear he's one hell of a good runner."

"Yeah. Got to get his head straight first, though, don't we?"

There was a pause. He waited to see if Doc Robbins would say anything further. When he didn't, Coach Herbert called a cheery "So long" into the receiver, replaced it on the desk and sat a moment longer with his hand on it, as though to contain everything that had just been said—the boy with such promise who had first lied to him and then disobeyed his order, the dying Ellie, the whole mishmash of a crazy, mixed-up world.

Suddenly, weary of fruitless effort, he pushed himself up from the edge of the desk and walked slowly back to the window where earlier he'd watched the basketball game in the courtyard below, now empty except for blowing wind and dust and early dying leaves. A change in the weather, a change in time? He could hope. Indian summers were a drag on runners. They required a brisk, nippy climate to give them their edge.

What a disappointment Mark was proving to be. Still, he would have to try. The year was early yet. If he could exert a good positive influence soon enough, perhaps there was hope.

For starters, he would have to find him before he could help him. *If I were a lost, disturbed, homesick, possibly physically ill young man two thousand miles from home where would I go?*

For several moments Coach Herbert continued to stare down on the empty courtyard and the small blowing things of a transitional season and searched his head for a reasonable and satisfying answer.

—and found none.

"Mother?"

Cass waited outside her mother's closed bedroom doors, knocked once, called, and waited for a response. When none came she called out softly, "I'm going now."

She leaned up against the door, her ear pressed against it. She was certain her mother was inside. She'd heard her down in the kitchen about four, and an hour later had heard her double doors close—the ones against which Cass was now leaning and which she didn't dare open without an invitation.

"Can you hear me, Mother? Is there anything I can do before . . . ?" She broke off, thinking she'd heard something.

Nothing.

For a moment she closed her eyes and rested her forehead against the door. Should she apologize again? She'd apologized several times before, every day since the night of the party. She was sorry, but her mother had maintained a longer silence than usual.

"Mother, I said I was going now. I won't be late. Will you be all right? You want me to go, don't you?" With her eyes closed she continued to listen, hearing nothing.

"Good-bye, then," she called out cheerily.

Her grandfather always used to say, "Be cheerful around her."

Suddenly her thought was violently interrupted by the sensation that the Oriental rug beneath her feet, which led to the top of the steep staircase, had turned to ice. Within the instant she felt herself lose her center of balance, her right foot airborne above the slippery underfooting, her fall pitching her forward, where for one terrifying moment she found herself staring straight down the steps as though into an abyss.

Frantically, reflexively, her hands clawed at air in an attempt to break her fall. She felt her left shin come in scraping, painful contact with the top step, then found herself pitching forward.

If it had not been for one lucky grab at the banister, she would

141

have fallen headlong the length of the staircase. But her right hand, in its flailing, made fortunate contact with something of substance and she held on, throwing her entire weight against one wrist, which held fast.

When the momentum of the fall had played out, she found herself in a peculiarly crucified position, flattened against the wooden turnings of the staircase, half crouched, half seated, her dark blue cotton skirt pushed up, revealing a skinned shin which was just beginning to show blood.

For a moment longer she held onto the banister, looking down the remaining length of the staircase, then she closed her eyes, realizing that if she hadn't caught herself in time she would have reached bottom with more than a scraped shin.

She glanced up to the top of the landing and discovered herself at eye level with her mother's door. She saw light coming from beneath the slit, a shadow intersecting the light source, as though someone had been standing close to the door on the other side and was now moving away from it, going deeper into the room.

Suddenly angry, Cass started to call out again, then changed her mind. Anger served no purpose in any situation. Her grandfather had taught her that.

Then leave. She knew what she had to do and the best thing to do was to get it over with.

On that note of resolve she slowly pulled herself to her feet, bent over to examine the scraped shin, dabbed at the blood pricks with the tip of her finger and stood up. She restored her white blouse to her skirt band and, maintaining a death grip on the banister, started slowly down the stairs, checking everything—legs, ankles, arms, wrists—for hidden damage.

At the bottom she glanced back up the steps and saw the fringed end of the Oriental runner protruding out over the edge like the guilty culprit that it was. She thought it had been nailed down. Well, she'd check on that later. For now she longed for the quiet and peace of this autumn evening and the appointment she was bound to keep, the first since—

She felt a surge of unprecedented excitement as she hurried out the front door and closed it behind her. She used to lock it all the time, but it didn't matter now. It really didn't. Locked, unlocked, always the same.

From the top of the porch steps she watched the early-evening traffic for a few minutes. The once quiet residential street was now a secondary artery leading directly to the heart of the campus, and the sedate and respectable old Victorian houses

142

which lined both sides were beginning to show the stress of age. A few at the far end of the block had already been converted into multiple apartments. But not at this end. Here there were four holdouts. These four were still the main sentinels of Sorrento and Capri and likely to remain so, as none of the four owners were particularly interested in money or the future.

She bent over in brief examination of her shin and was pleased to find that the slight bleeding had stopped. Then hurry! She'd looked forward to tonight for several days—at least part of it, the good part. She'd deal with the rest later.

As she started down the half-dozen broad steps that led from the portico to the sidewalk, she instinctively reached for the hand railing for support and touched bottom safely, smelling that unique blue-smoke haze of late autumn. She considered going back for a sweater, then changed her mind. There would be other sources of warmth tonight.

She did miss her radio, though—she'd lost it sometime at the beginning of summer—the little gray portable her grandfather had given her. She had carried it everywhere. It brought as much of the world to her as she wanted, and when that was too much she could always flip it off.

As she unlatched the white gate she froze for a moment. Using all the self-control she could command, she successfully resisted the impulse to look back toward the house—specifically at the large, gabled, second-floor windows of her mother's room. Cass knew her mother was there watching, safely hidden from sight behind her dark green velour drapes.

Instead Cass waved across the street at the little blond-haired girl on the tricycle who stood behind the slats of the white fence as though imprisoned. The little girl waved back, and Cass resolved the next time the child's mother called to see if she could baby-sit she'd say yes.

Again she fought against the temptation to look back at her own house. She darted across the busy street through the traffic and increased her speed, foolishly thinking that distance might make a difference.

Hurry, hurry, don't look back. Step over, step over the sidewalk crack or else you'll break your mother's back.

The foolish rhythm of the childhood doggerel pursued her down the street until she broke into a run as though trying to escape it. She darted without looking into a busy intersection, ignoring the screech of brakes and the shouts of the angry driver, ignoring everything except the need to break free.

143

As he walked, painful questions kept resounding in Mark's head like the reflected cadence of his footsteps on the pavement. *What the hell was he doing? What the hell had he done?* Was it his conscious intention to blow everything? Was this his subtle method of putting an end to an intolerable situation? Because if his answer to any of these questions was yes, then he certainly was going about it in the right way.

Mark felt newly despondent, yet pleased that—unlike the last several days—at least now he was moving. Where, he had no idea. His first thought had been simply to leave behind the threat of a physical examination with Doc Robbins.

Why?

Wouldn't it have been easier to go through with it and apologize to Coach Herbert for a faltering beginning and then start again? Easier? Perhaps. Then why didn't he do it?

Shit, no answer.

Lacking as well a conscious destination, he lowered his head against the congestion of late-afternoon traffic and concentrated on his ancient tennis shoes protruding at regular intervals beneath the mussed khakis which he'd intended to change but which he'd never done for lack of energy and motivation. He had managed to slip off the white knit shirt he'd lived and slept in for three days and change it for a clean, though wrinkled, navy blue knit shirt which he'd fished out of his still unpacked luggage.

Curb. Step down. Sound of car on left. Look up. A distance removed, you can make it. No eye contact, please, with the giggling, chattering group just stepping down from the opposite curb. Without question he obeyed the robotlike voice in his head and allowed his arms to hang loosely at his sides. Step up. Hazard past. Proceed to next intersection, then turn south.

Abruptly he stopped, for the first time objecting to the robot voice inside his head. A car went by, radio blaring the title song from *Hello, Dolly.* His mother had gone up to LA to see it with a friend. Mark was supposed to have gone with them but—

Mother.

Damn! Had he called her—or did he merely think he'd called her? He couldn't remember. Once. When? Several days ago it had seemed so urgent. Now— He really couldn't remember.

Suddenly his strange behavior and lack of will and discipline frightened him. He stopped on the cracked sidewalk and felt the puzzled, slightly annoyed silence of several small groups behind him who had tried to accommodate their stride to the obstacle that was himself.

144

"Move it over, fellow," one muttered and brushed rudely against him.

He looked up, murmured an apology and searched as well for a safe harbor. Unable to find one, he started off again, still not fully recovered from his recent bout with fear and bewilderment over what had happened to him—what was happening still. He maintained a fairly steady pace for the next couple of blocks, taking care not to annoy pedestrian traffic. He did not by nature like to annoy anyone.

Why hadn't he just taken the damned physical and—

Maybe he should just go back. It probably wasn't too late to offer Coach Herbert an apology and go ahead and take the exam.

Then turn around. Now.

The mind was sending urgent commands fast and furious, but the nerves, bones, muscles, blood—all the various parts—were not responding. If anything, they were in open defiance. He felt his speed increasing until he was performing a kind of limp-limbed jog, the vibrations of impact feeling good and stimulating on his face and chest.

The pedestrian traffic was clearing now. He knew where this street led—and continued anyway. After all, there were at least four long blocks left before—

His anxiety was eased by the pungent smell of frying onions coming from one of the houses on his left, all modest though well-cared-for dwellings. Life proceeding in an orderly, unsurprising fashion.

For a moment he felt tempted to stop and breathe deeply of the perfume of frying onions but changed his mind. No time. One more intersection, then he'd turn about and head back toward campus, mend his fences there, then call his mother and mend those fences as well. With all fences mended and back on the straight and narrow, his own life could proceed as orderly and unsurprising as that fortunate family eating fried liver and onions.

For the first time he smiled at the bizarre nature of his thoughts. Someplace deep inside him was an idiot who had lain dormant for all these years and who only now had surfaced.

Idiot. Idiot. Fool. Fool. Cross now!

But still the brain's messages were being blocked and he ran directly past the third intersection—which left only one. Still time. No need to panic.

In a brief sprint he was amazed that with such halfhearted effort he'd managed to work up a sweat. Now he felt the beads run down the small of his back. There was a small waterfall, as well, coursing down the bridge of his nose and settling into the line that led down to his mouth. Once there, the salt water slipped into the corner of his mouth, and he tasted the salt and found it so pleasing he ran his tongue around his lips now in search of all he could find.

He wasn't sure why it tasted good, but it did. The ocean, that was it. He felt now a deep ache for it and wished, childlike, that he could close his eyes and open them on that familiar vista of white sand and lapping blue water—and the sound. The sound was as important as anything, that subtle and constant hum like an extension of one's own heart and pulse, like a force that was always with you, clarifying, reinforcing and sustaining.

Suddenly the pain of homesickness became so acute that he literally stopped in his tracks, bowed his head into his hands and supported the ache in that manner for several moments, not particularly worried about obstructing the traffic, for there was no traffic here, nothing except the soft reflected heat of early evening and the curious silence which he'd noticed before at the edge of the base. It was like a sleeping ghost town—too weary from its own past even to wake up and challenge the present, to say nothing of the future.

All right, so he was here again against his will. Now let's turn around and—

He lowered his hands and, looking straight ahead, saw the girl. He knew immediately who she was and was astounded at the pleasure the knowledge brought him.

Cass—in a becoming skirt and neatly fitted soft plaid shirt— stood on the pavement before the sentry box, extending something straight up in the air to an incredibly large hawk that was circling overhead. The hawk appeared to drop lower and lower with each circle.

He'd heard about this. From whom? Someone had told him of the great hawk that took food from human hands.

That's why she attacked you. She felt you should have brought her something.

Who? He couldn't remember.

It didn't matter, for Cass continued to stand, stock-still, her right arm extended straight up in the air, keeping her eye on the hawk only when it was convenient to do so. If the hawk circled beyond her range of vision, she apparently felt no compulsion to turn and follow it, but continued to stand, that right hand lifted at a rigid angle.

Cass's back was to him and, as she hadn't turned in any direction,

146

he was certain she was not aware of him. Watching with considerable fascination, he momentarily abandoned his pledge to return immediately to the campus and the dorm. He now found himself maintaining a posture as rigid as hers, with partially held breath, alternating his vision between her rigid back and the hawk, which seemed to be holding a constant elevation, not rising higher or dropping lower.

Still she stood, unmoving, and he tried to identify the nature of the food she was offering the hawk. From this distance he only saw a faint color of red, the object itself lumpy and soft. How patient she was—and something else—how knowledgeable, as though she'd done this many times before and knew precisely how long she'd have to wait before the hawk—

The distance between hawk and girl was shortened with that circle—less than twenty feet—and she looked up at that moment as though she knew the distance had been shortened between them.

Still lower the hawk continued to descend. Ten feet now, no more. A magnificent and graceful creature with an incredible wingspan. The closer the hawk flew to the girl, the smaller Cass appeared, the more gigantic the hawk. Yet, despite its size, that slim upraised arm had not altered its position, neither in fatigue nor fear, but continued to hold steady the proffered piece of meat, still waiting for it to be snatched up.

And then it was, in one dramatic swoop, which happened so quickly Mark wasn't sure the meat had been taken until at last he looked away from the graceful beauty of the soaring hawk and saw Cass's hand empty, slowly falling back down to her side. For a few seconds she stood in a strange mood and manner, as though wholly drained by the encounter. Not once did she look up to see whether or not the hawk had consumed the piece of meat, not once in either curiosity or pleasure did she lift her eyes to the soaring bird, which now had been diminished to dot size by the incredible height at which it was flying.

At this moment Mark's attention was still fixed on Cass, who continued to appear drained by the feat. Her left hand was quietly caressing her right arm, as though only now did she feel the natural fatigue which came from holding it upraised so long.

He was on the verge of stepping from the curb and making his presence known to her in the event she turned abruptly and thought he might be spying on her, but at the exact moment he stepped from the curb he heard her voice, subdued, confirming his suspicion of weariness.

"I don't know why I do that. I guess so that she'll leave us alone. Are you ready?"

147

So stunned was he by the sound of her voice, lifted as though she were speaking to someone, he didn't even hear the last of her command, a clear question, as though she'd been expecting him. She had yet to turn and confront him, and he thought foolishly for a moment there was someone else close by but out of sight to whom she was speaking. Caught in this moment of confusion, he saw her turn at last and face him with a smile, that one hand still rubbing the arm that had been upraised for some time.

"Well?" she demanded, still smiling, clearly not at all surprised to see him there.

As his bewilderment and confusion continued to mount, he did well to laugh and shrug his shoulders, and was then aware that he probably resembled an idiot.

"Come on," she invited again, and effortlessly bridged the gap between them, taking his hand. She either didn't see his confusion or chose to ignore it. "Tonight we'll explore on our own," she promised, standing so close. Her weariness seemed to lift and was replaced by an irresistible warmth.

"W-wait . . ." he stammered, affected by both her closeness and warmth. "How did you know that I . . .?"

"Oh, Mark!" she scolded and withdrew a few steps. "We talked about this at Uncle Polly's. Don't you remember? That awful night. You said you wanted to see more out here and I said I'd show you tonight."

There was something so confident and insistent in her manner that for a few moments he doubted that he would have the nerve to voice the thunderous rebuttal forming in his head. There had been no such talk, no such conversation and certainly no such arrangement. Had there? That night had been very confusing in and of itself, but still he would remember a prearranged date with her. In fact, as he recalled now, when she left early he'd been afraid he would never see her again.

He finally managed with a gentle insistence, "I really don't recall any . . ."

"Of course you don't," she agreed, took his hand and started to lead him toward the North Gate of the base. Once he saw her look up quickly, as though in search of something.

He followed her line of vision, but the hawk was gone, no place in sight.

"You really weren't doing too well that night." Now she stopped in an attitude of playful confrontation. "You do remember that much, don't you? The party at the Officers' Club? The police . . .?"

He nodded, fascinated as ever by her face, such a pleasant combina-

148

tion of very young girl and young woman, as though she were caught in a transition she herself didn't fully understand.

"All right," he smiled, surrendering to her claim that the meeting tonight had been prearranged. He really didn't want to argue the point, particularly since in her presence he felt better than he'd felt in several days. No deep nagging anxiety over how he'd goofed or screwed up the golden opportunity or alienated those people who were important to his career.

Apparently she saw the resolve as well as the surrender on his face and interpreted both correctly. "Good," she grinned, again reaching for his hand.

Together they started off toward the sentry box, heading directly for it when, in the new spirit of play, he broke from her hand and started around the left side, leaving her the right.

"No!" she cried out sternly and pushed close against him. He felt his arm go around her shoulders as though to protect her from something. "Bad luck," she murmured, nestling close under his arm.

He noticed that her head came only to his shoulder and she really was most appealing. "Don't tell me you're superstitious?" he asked.

"Aren't you? When you run, I mean in a race," she went on, "don't you do certain things, maybe say certain incantations, think certain things?"

He listened and walked easily beside her and was forced to deny all. "No, not really," he said, head down, studying the pavement beneath their feet. "I've known guys who did all those things—and worse. One guy I knew in Cal quit running when his, quote, lucky, unquote, shoes wore out. Just quit altogether." He laughed. He could see the face in his mind's eye but couldn't dredge up a name to go with it. "You see, in the final analysis there's not really a great deal of luck in running," he said, stating his belief, and then conceded, "Oh, there's some, sure. Just as there's some in everything you do. But when you run you're either prepared or you're not prepared, well trained or not."

He fell silent, trying to organize his thoughts for further elucidation, when he heard something and looked up. In the dying light he saw a car about two blocks ahead, the motor laboring up the simple grade. He squinted into the distance, surprised to see a car out here— and what appeared to be, from this distance, a vintage car at that. "What do you suppose . . .?" he began, referring to the car, but she interrupted, apparently unaware of the car.

"So you're not superstitious at all? I can't believe that. Everybody is to . . ."

"I didn't say that," he replied, somewhat absentmindedly, still

149

focusing on the car, which seemed now to be moving at a snail's pace, the engine puffing and chugging. "Look," he invited very succinctly, pointing with his left hand, the one not wrapped about her shoulders.

At last she followed the direction of his hand toward the car, which had made it to the next intersection and appeared to be merely waiting, as though for dense traffic where none existed.

"Car," she said simply and once again launched into the subject of superstition. "What about ladders? Do you willingly walk under ladders? Or black cats? I've known people who consider black cats lucky."

He continued to listen to her, but at the moment was unable to respond, focusing on the aged car, which appeared to be merely idling at the intersection less than fifty yards ahead of them.

A Chevy? It looked like an old Chevy twenty to twenty-five years old. It was in mint condition; its patina of wax glistened in the brilliance of the late-afternoon sun.

"What are they doing?" he asked, his voice lowered as though the occupants of the car half a block away could hear.

"A car," she repeated broadly as though to a child. "It's just a car."

"Why are they parked there?"

Now it was her turn to squint into the distance. "Who says they're parked?"

"Well, they're not moving," he insisted, pursuing the silly argument. "And it's not just a car. It's an antique car."

Readily she obliged but seemed bored by both the car and his persistent interest in it. "Oh, it isn't an antique at all. Lots of people here have cars like that. Some even older. There's a car club here, and once a year they hold a convention out at the Holiday Inn and have a big parade down Main and all that stuff."

As she launched into a childlike description of the car parade, Mark listened, continuing to concentrate on the car parked at the intersection now less than twenty-five yards away. A Chevy, no doubt about that. Early forties vintage was his guess. A light turquoise blue in color, its front windshield curiously darkened, as though blacked out by some substance and yet—

"Oh, come on, Mark. It's just a car. Let's cut across here to the barracks. They're fascinating. Have you ever seen inside? The barracks, I mean."

Abruptly Mark stopped, not hearing what she was saying, all his attention on the still-idling car with its curiously darkened front windshield, no sign of life nor movement coming from without or within. What the hell? He shivered suddenly in the warm evening. For some reason he didn't want to go any closer to the strange car, and what he found most curious now was Cass's total lack of interest in it.

150

"Come on, Mark," she called, and left the street to run down a small culvert, then up the other side, heading toward a large gray barracks. On the second floor he saw a frayed piece of fabric hanging outside the open window, lifting now and then in the slight evening breeze.

But for the moment his interest was not on the abandoned, crumbling barracks. Coming from inside the car he heard the rough scraping of gears being shifted. The sound suggested either an inept driver or ancient gears or both—and yet, despite the sound of impending movement, the old car didn't move but continued to vibrate in stalled inactivity.

"Mark, why are you so interested in that old heap?" Her voice came from the other side of the culvert and contained just a hint of irritation blended with amazement. "Don't tell me you're into cars. You don't strike me as . . ."

"I'm not."

"Then why are . . ."

"Why isn't it moving?" Then he heard the low, accusatory tone in his own voice, and the next moment felt idiotic again, engaged as he was in a battle of wits with a car.

"Probably a beginning driver," Cass called out across the small distance. "My grandfather taught me to drive out here. It's a perfect place. You can't hit anything that isn't already falling down."

Beginning driver? That was a possibility, the car pausing while someone instructed someone. Still, why the darkened front windshield? How long would it be before—

"Do you like old cars, Mark?"

The inquiry came from his left, and he glanced in that direction to see her squatted down on the crest of the ravine, her elbows resting on her knees, a comic position, partly bored child, partly seductive young woman. The pose caught his attention and held it.

At the same time he heard the ancient motor turning behind him and looked in time to see the Chevy of ancient vintage rattle across the intersection, moving very slowly, but moving nonetheless, though still no sign of life or movement coming from within.

"Do you? Like old cars. Can you hear me, Mark?" Obviously she was beginning to lose patience.

Mark was still watching the slow progress of the old car up the street which led to the North Gate. "Yes. Yes, I do," he answered distractedly.

"Then sometime you must come and see the old car my grandfather left locked in the garage. You'd like it."

Just as the Chevy topped the slight hill and slowly disappeared over it, it dawned on him that she had issued a direct invitation, one which ensured that he'd not only see her again but that he'd see her on her own ground at home, perhaps even meet her mother.

"I'd like that," he replied eagerly, and took a last look at the crest of the hill. The car was gone; there wasn't even the echo of the rattling motor.

"Mark, please come on."

He shook his head and started down the small culvert and mounted the other side, talking most of the way. "Didn't you find anything strange about that car?"

"No," she replied flatly. "A lot of people keep their old cars around here. This isn't hot-rod California, you know. People are a bit more conservative."

He drew even with her and nodded in agreement to everything she was saying, finding something so appealing in her small, urgent face, beautifully colored in the last warm rays of evening sun, a double golden glow accenting her tan. "Tell me about your grandfather's car," he asked, standing close, looking down.

"No need," she replied, and moved away, leading him steadily toward the large, two-story barracks. "I said you could come by and see it sometime."

"When?" he asked, pursuing her in more ways than one.

She shrugged. "Sometime."

"Come on, Cass. When?"

She looked back at him over her shoulder, as though puzzled by his insistence. "Are you interested in old cars?"

Perhaps the invitation depended on such an interest. "Sure," he lied. "Isn't everyone?"

She looked at him briefly, as though he'd said the most stupid thing possible. "Well, come on. Let's have an adventure! Have you ever been inside one of these things? If you listen closely you can hear . . ." Unfortunately she ran so far ahead that the last of her words were lost in the distance.

He called out, "Wait!"

She had already darted up the half-dozen or so steps which led into the barracks. Her first exaggerated step up suggested a missing stair, and, sure enough, as he drew near he saw that the bottom step was gone. Catching up with her so that they might start their "adventure" together, he, too, took the necessary leap to clear the first broken step and bounded the rest of the way up and through the door to find himself in a small entrance room slightly larger than a hall, with a wooden partition like an old hotel on his left. Behind it was a "bar," he noticed. A pegboard— or what was left of it—was covered with countless hooks. Keys?

152

"Cass, where the hell are . . .?"

At that moment, through the door straight ahead, he saw her, poised at what appeared to be the beginning of a narrow wooden staircase. On her head was a white sailor's hat arranged at a jaunty sideward angle. He noticed she was carrying a second hat, which she extended to him in a get-into-the-spirit-of-things manner. Only then did it occur to him that this bizarre place, this base, had probably been her playground, the place of her growing up. Undoubtedly she knew every inch of every building.

"Come on," she called, the delight and excitement clear in her voice. "I found one for you. These are clean. Look! Usually you have to put up with the hair oil of the guy who wore it before you a hundred years ago."

He took another quick look around this "outer office" area and saw in the corner behind the counter a wadded crush of yellow newspapers plus several stiffened sheets of what appeared to be a calendar. Might be interesting reading. Souvenirs of the past.

As he walked deeper into the barracks he found himself in a large area which most likely had been a recreation room or a common room. Pushed against the far walls he saw several moth-eaten, nondescript sofas. Also contributing to the sense of disarray were several card tables, all tilted at distorted angles due to missing legs. He noticed many ringed and rotten water spots on the bare hardwood floor. On the ceiling directly above where he stood, he saw several ominous protrusions, part of the structure already weakened and collapsing.

Safe? He doubted it, but what the hell? The grin on her face, the jaunty angle of the sailor's cap, the beckoning way she offered the other cap to him—all this conspired to make such judgments as "safe" and "unsafe" totally immaterial.

"Where did you come by these?" he asked, returning her grin and feeling the responsibility and guilts of that other world roll off his back like so much excess baggage.

"Around," she replied. "I know where everything is. Here, put it on and we'll go try to find the guys who wore these before us."

Before he could respond, he felt the sailor's stiffened hat thrust into his hands and looked up to see her scamper up the steps toward what appeared to be the second-floor landing—and disappear at the top to the right.

"Wait up!" he called out with mock weariness. It seemed to be the command he was constantly shouting after her. She'd obviously done all this before, but it was brand-new territory to him. "Cass, please wait!"

At last he followed after, climbing the steep, too-narrow stairs

153

with greater care, testing each step at first and deciding to hell with it and plodding straight up after her. As he emerged onto the second-floor landing, he glanced to his right in the direction he'd seen her take. With only his head and shoulders cleared, he looked down what appeared to be an endless hall lined on both sides by doors—a glut of doors—suggesting cell-sized rooms behind them.

About halfway down in the shadowy hall, the only light came from the far window and even that was limited to the half-light of day's end, so the shadows were considerable. Still he saw what appeared to be a large wicker basket halfway down the corridor. Laundry? Linens, perhaps? It appeared to be on its side, lid askew, held by one tenuous wicker hinge. Clustered around it as though blown there was another scattering of wadded, yellowed newsprint.

He took careful note of all this minutiae and only belatedly realized why. What he was really looking for was no place in sight.

He pulled himself up to the landing and heard an ominous crack in the banister and let go as though it were hot, then looked in the opposite direction down a long corridor identical to the one on his right. He could have sworn she had gone right, but maybe he was mistaken. Perhaps there was a way round behind the stairwell that he didn't know about.

But a glance in that direction revealed nothing except another obstacle—larger than the wicker basket. Something black and square totally occluding the passage. He stared at it for a moment and thought it resembled an old-fashioned safe—that square, that solid and that black.

At the top of the landing he found himself looking straight into a curious alcove, a three-sided affair which might have contained candy-bar, Coke and cigarette machines. All gone now, though lighter shades of gray paint indicated the size of the machines that had protected the wall, like the silhouette of a squat skyline. Still hanging over the sillhouettes was a bulletin board, securely anchored despite the passing years, and still bearing large silver thumbtacks with curled, yellowed pieces of paper of various sizes still attached. He stared at the board and felt a compulsion to read the ancient notices, and felt an equally strong compulsion to locate Cass.

"Hey, where are you?" he called out, full voice, and heard that peculiar ghostly resonance of a flat, dead surface. His voice had come out strangely amplified.

154

He waited a moment, feeling oddly self-conscious, and listened to the spiraling echo of his own voice.

"Cass, can you hear me?"

Of course she could hear him. The second floor of the barracks was large, but not that large. She couldn't have gone back down unless there was more than one staircase. At the top of the steps he stood, fingering the white sailor hat, turning it around and around in his hands.

Let's go find the guys who wore these—

"Cass? Come on. If we're to have an adventure, you've got to help me. Come on, you hear?" He broke off, certain he'd heard something.

He had. His own voice in echo again. "Hell!" he muttered, and looked nervously back down the stairs, thinking he'd heard something down there as well

"Cass, come on! Enough is enough. Let's just get the . . ."

Suddenly he broke off. Music? Was that what he heard? Couldn't be. And yet—

He walked slowly toward his left, determining that was the direction. And it was music. Distant, flat, of poor quality. On an old phonograph, maybe. A tune instantly recognizable but he couldn't name it. Blues something.

As suddenly as the music had started it stopped. He'd taken less than half a dozen steps down the corridor and now he stood still, as though his momentum were controlled by the invisible and distant music. For a few moments he stood motionless, staring past the large, up-ended wicker basket toward the far window at the end of the corridor, listening. But he heard nothing. No sound inside or out, except for the muted thunder of his own pulse.

"Okay, Cass, have it your way," he called out, and rubbed the twitching nerve on the left side of his face, both annoyed and captivated by her propensity to play games. "Cass, where the hell are you?"

He glanced back over his shoulder, for the first time noticing the diminishing light entering the window at the far end of the corridor. The great black square block still occluded the passage—but for someone like Cass that would present no obstacle.

"To hell with it!" he muttered aloud, and started to yell one more time, then changed his mind. He'd go back down and wait for her outside. If she didn't come soon, he'd go on back to the dorm.

His thought was intersected by a second distant sound of music. He turned sharply to the right again, his mouth reflexively open, his eyes wide, searching the increasing shadows beyond the wicker

155

basket for an explanation. Failing to see anything out of the ordinary, he listened and could not identify the music, although it sounded childlike and Western, a sharp, clear cadence with some handclapping, a flat male voice belting out something about the heart of Texas.

"Cass, is it you?"

He was confident that it was, for within the realm of reason it couldn't be anyone else—

"Cass?"

When he still received no answer, he took a final look behind him to check his rear flank, then started slowly down the corridor toward the upturned wicker basket and the direction from which the music seemed to come. He vaguely recognized that tune now. He'd heard it someplace on a novelty record, that same tune coming through the shadowy silence of the evening. . . .

About ten steps down the hall he stopped listening to the catchy repetition of the song. "Cass, can you find something else on that thing? Anything." He'd made a poor attempt at ease and humor and waited to see if she'd respond.

She didn't. Instead, all he heard was the mindless repetition of an equally mindless song—for now the volume seemed to increase as though someone had turned it up.

When he least expected it, he felt sudden anger surface. What was she trying to do? Make a fool of him again? Apparently it took no great effort to do that.

All right, push ahead. Open every single damned door until she was found out, along with whatever it was making that racket.

"Cass, I'm coming, you hear?" He shouted this at the top of his voice. By way of response he heard the stupid song increase in volume as well, a blaring, childishly simple tune boasting altogether no more than thirty or forty notes. Now, as he drew even with the first door, he reached out to push it open—and the rusted doorknob fell off in his hands. It so startled him that he dropped it suddenly and jumped back as it rattled noisily about the rotting floor. Then he looked back at the door and, with the toe of his shoe, gave it a push. To his surprise it opened.

Startled, he held his position in the corridor for a few seconds and tried to peer in and around the door and saw nothing of substance in the small, cell-like room with its window glass broken and the light beyond fading fast. There was no furniture in the room, just the corners filled with what appeared to be debris that had blown in—old, wadded newsprint, faded candy wrappers and empty cigarette packages.

The awful music increased. It was beginning to get on his nerves—

the repetition as much as anything, though the increasing volume wasn't helping.

He backed out of the cell-like room and began in an almost spastic fashion to practically hurl himself at every door, throwing them open with such force that they bounced back against the wall and many swung shut again. From his brief glimpses he saw all of them were basically the same—a small, barren, cell-like room with broken windows, devoid of all furniture save for the occasional tattered window curtain like a flag of surrender, nothing anywhere capable of producing music—if that's what one could call the raucous, by now almost earsplitting, tune.

"Cass, for God's sake turn it down!" he shouted. Yet he could scarcely hear himself over the shrill high notes. Neither could he hear the doors as he hurled them back against the walls, searching, searching, finding nothing.

Directly in front of him now was the upended wicker basket. As he drew near he saw it was blocking one of the doors on the left side of the corridor. Why bother moving it? More of the same. Empty, debris-strewn cells, nothing more.

Thus resolved, he eased past it and threw open the door on the opposite wall, finding a slight variation, a very soiled mattress resting against the wall, the gray ticking slashed, the entire thing covered with a pale yellow stain as though it had been urinated on repeatedly. He could smell it, the strong acrid odor of human waste.

"Christ!" he cursed, and quickly closed the door and thought that the best thing that could happen to this place would be to burn it to the ground.

"Cass, for God's sake turn that down!"

Useless. She couldn't hear him. No one could hear him as now static joined the stupid tune, as though, due to the increased volume, something was on the verge of burning itself out. Hurriedly he counted three doors that remained to the end of the corridor.

4B Vault. He was in the wrong place.

4B Vault. He was in the wrong place.

4B Vault—

Above the din of the music and his own rapidly accelerating pulse he heard and recorded the number.

4B Vault.

What the hell did that mean? It meant nothing, of course. Open the remaining three doors and get out of here with or without her. The smell of human waste seemed to be growing stronger as the music grew louder still.

Oh, to hell with the last two doors, he decided, feeling only an

157

increased need to flee this place which had gone within the last few minutes from something silent and benign to something unspeakable and frightening.

"I'm taking off now, Cass," he tried to shout over the earsplitting music which was so loud the rhythmical and predictable handclapping caused his ears to ring. Now abandoning his search of the last two doors, he turned hurriedly back to the central staircase, thinking only he had to escape into the quiet night outside and the early-evening air, unpolluted by the ancient odors of excrement. Not so ancient apparently. Someone had—

As he approached the large wicker basket, he lifted his hands to his ears in an attempt to muffle the raucous noise. Something about the way the basket was positioned caught his attention. It looked as though it had been dragged into position purposefully to obscure this door, as though—

He stared for a moment at both the basket and the closed door. Why hadn't it occurred to him the first time?

"All right, Cass. Game's up!"

He bent over and gave the large basket a shove and jumped back as he heard something rustling inside, sudden and furtive movement, and instantly thought, *Snake!*

Instead he saw several large rats dart out into the shadows of the hall—three or four, he couldn't tell—saw them collide heavily with the baseboard as though they sought escape from him. Ultimately they all disappeared into the shadows at the end of the hall.

Struggling to maintain a degree of equilibrium from his own fright, he tried to draw several deep, shuddering breaths in an attempt to still his heart, which was beating too fast.

Then a thought intersected, born of persistent reason. Rats would not be comfortably and securely nesting in a place that had only recently been dragged into position. At the intrusion of this troublesome thought, he looked back toward the door.

Leave it alone.

Open it.

"Cass?"

Then suddenly, personally challenged in some way by this last mystery, he stepped around the one protruding end of the basket and—carefully this time—pushed open the door. He kept his hand on the doorknob, ready at any moment to close the door again, though he fully expected to see Cass grinning up at him, sitting cross-legged—her favorite position—on the floor.

But he didn't see her. Saw nothing human. Saw something—

158

A small, gunmetal-gray, rolled-top portable radio, a telltale light visible behind its control panel, sat exactly in the center of the room, a curious white towel folded neatly and resting to one side, as though the floor in this immediate area had been cleansed. For several moments he stared transfixed at the bizarre and unexpected sight of a portable radio playing all by itself, the tune still as thunderous and as mindless and as annoying as ever—and that single folded white towel resting to one side.

Stealthily he leaned farther in, thinking she might be hiding behind the door. But the room was empty of everything and anything—save for the portable radio and the towel. Then all at once he could not bear the shrill music any longer. At some point—either due to the tension, the odor, the noise or perhaps all three—he reached down quickly and twisted the three knobs atop the radio. Only when he turned the controls did the noise subside.

While the new silence was a relief, it was taut as well. For several moments he continued to hear the same tinny rendition of the same stupid tune. Grasping the doorknob, he found that he was unable to drag his eyes away from the radio. Of course there were questions inside his head: Where had it come from? Though old, it seemed in good condition. Who had turned it on? And where had Cass gone?

He turned to retreat to the corridor, and looked back and down on the radio, only now determining it was still on. No sound, thank God. No thunderous insanity, but he could still see the dim glow of a light through the control panel.

In the new silence he dared to relax for the first time in several minutes. Still grasping the door, he leaned against it and closed his eyes to rest them.

4B Vault— CRYPT

He opened his eyes at the curious repetition. Weary of no answers, he pushed away from the door and would have passed through without hesitation, but at that moment he heard a single crackle of static electricity coming from the radio, a curious sound as though it were trying to attract his attention.

Without conscious thought of why he was doing it, he stepped back into the room only far enough to retrieve the radio and the folded towel, then, moving with all the speed and stealth of a thief, he hurried from the room, not bothering to close the door, almost colliding with the large wicker basket but sidestepping it in time, clutching the radio to him as though the basket were a threat. As he ran on down the corridor to the central staircase, he heard a continuous stream of static, the tuner apparently caught between signals.

As he started down the stairs, he threw a quick glance to his left and saw the large, black, squat object still blocking the whole passage in that direction. Now he secured the portable radio and the towel under his left arm and, using his right hand to steady himself, moved eagerly down the steps, hearing an ominous creaking now and then, amazed the building hadn't already collapsed.

He hit bottom and gingerly stepped around some broken glass and hurried on across the large expanse of the common room, looking neither to the right nor left. The radio tucked under his arm crackled again with static. Though he was tempted to stop and examine it, he vowed not to stop until he was safely out in the night away from this place.

"Hey, what's your hurry?"

At the sound of the familiar voice, he swiveled his head in all directions, unable to locate her in the vast, dim interior of the large room. Apparently she saw his confusion and sent him a hint.

"Over here. Beneath the window."

Now able to follow the direction of her voice, Mark looked sharply toward the south window and saw her. She had relaxed into an oversized brown leather couch. On either side of her, framing her in a bizarre way, were jagged ripped places in the brown leather, almost symmetrical white slashes, as though a surgeon rather than a vandal had attacked the sofa.

Initially pleased to see her, he remembered how only a few moments earlier he'd yelled his head off for her upstairs and she'd been down here all the time. He started toward her, still brooding, though fascinated and pleased, as always, by her appearance. About twenty feet from her, he sent ahead a mild accusation.

"I called you. Did you hear?"

At that moment the radio beneath his arm crackled again. The sound caught her attention and she leaned sharply up from her relaxed position on the old couch, trying to peer beneath the concealment of his arm.

"What the . . .?" she began, and apparently saw more clearly. All at once she was on her feet, a delighted eureka! expression on her face. "Where did you find it?" she grinned, bridging the distance between them, her hands moving immediately toward the radio.

"Upstairs," he said, momentarily postponing his accusation.

160

"And this as well." He produced the towel and held it and the radio up for her inspection.

"Well, my . . ." she began, and eagerly reached for both.

He relinquished them, put off briefly by her joy and surprise.

For a few seconds she turned the radio over in her hands, as though examining it for damage. "It's mine, you know," she grinned up at him. "It is," she repeated, as though he'd challenged her.

"Yours?" he repeated.

She nodded. "Early this summer—sometime in June, maybe earlier—I came out to Coffin Pond to cool off." She looked up, as though aware that what she'd said required an explication. "I do it all the time in summer. I hate the campus swimming pools. They're so crowded and I'm not the world's best swimmer and I don't have the best figure. So Coffin Pond suits me fine. I just splash around and cool off and nobody bothers me and I don't bother anybody."

There it was again, that captivating quality, something to do with the extraordinary light and animation which covered her face when she spoke on almost any subject. Now she apparently saw the intensity of his focus and blushed.

"What are you . . . looking at?" she faltered, lowering her head and falling into a close, self-conscious examination of the towel. "Look!" she exclaimed, not waiting for his reply but holding up the hem of the towel where he saw a small, slightly curled name tag, one of those that are pressed on with an iron.

"How did it get on the second floor of this barracks?" he asked.

She shrugged. "I don't know. I remember I put the radio and the towel at the edge of the pond and I splashed around for a few minutes and when I reached for the towel it was gone, as was the radio."

"You didn't see anyone, anyone at all?"

She shook her head and began to examine the dials of the radio, turning the controls rapidly while a discordant babble filled the silence of the night—part music, part talk, part static.

"It was on when I found it," he commented quietly.

At this she looked up. "On? You mean it was playing?"

He nodded, and recalled how the volume had seemed to increase of its own volition, recalled the tune, the mindless refrain of handclapping. "Have you ever heard the song called 'Deep in the Heart of Texas'?"

For a moment she looked puzzled, then grinned. "A golden oldie?"

161

"I'd say so."

"There's a station here that plays only . . ."

"But why was it on?"

At his persistent questioning she shrugged again and looked down at the radio as though it were withholding a vital clue. "It's never worked right," she murmured, "all the time I've had it. Shorts out and all, you know."

As she fiddled with the dial, he heard again that curious nonsensical trail of part song, part human voice, part static, nothing clear or discernible. At last she settled on a heavy orchestral rendition of "What Kind of Fool Am I?" For a moment the harmony—strings—seemed to have a soothing effect on both of them.

The large room in which they stood was cast totally in shadows now, as was the limited view of the world beyond the shattered windows. As the music continued to weave its own special magic, she said, "Thank you for finding my radio," said it softly and walked back to the sofa and sat to the left of the ripped leather cushion, apparently leaving the intact center for him.

"Come on," she invited with a smile. "Let's just sit for a minute." As she scooped up her sailor's hat from the couch, apparently it occurred to her that he wasn't carrying or wearing his own. "Hey, where's your sailor hat? Did you lose it?"

For the first time he, too, realized the hat was missing. "I must have put it down upstairs someplace," he said vaguely.

"No matter," she smiled, and again patted the center cushion where she wanted him to sit. "Well, what do you think of it?" she asked, seated beside him, her feet and legs curled to one side, that continuous and enchanting aura of little-girl excitement dominating everything.

He found her disarming. "What do you mean?" he asked.

"This place. This old building, isn't it marvelous? And they're all over the base, just like this one. Alive once, terribly alive. Like in limbo now, you know."

In the shadows he watched her closely and listened. The Anthony Newley tune was over, the station—wherever it was— now coming in quite clear. No static. The announcer sounded very young, a telltale crack in his voice giving him away. When he finished plugging a place called Hamburger Heaven, an equally melancholy tune filled the quiet night air—heavy on violins—a song he vaguely recognized as being from the musical *West Side Story*.

"I love that song, don't you?" she said softly. "I can't tell you how glad I am that you found my radio. That makes you special."

162

"Where were you? Earlier, I mean."

"I . . . don't understand."

"Upstairs I called you several times. I thought you'd gone up ahead of me."

She laughed. "I had."

Puzzled, he looked at her. "Then how did you . . .?"

"The fire escape, silly," she chided, and pushed against his shoulder in a playful movement. "In each of the last two rooms there are metal fire escapes which lead down."

He hadn't gone in the last two rooms. He'd started to but changed his mind. "Didn't you hear the radio?"

She shook her head. "I wanted to come back down here."

"Why?"

Again she laughed. "I've seen upstairs several times. I used to play up there when I was a kid, and my grandfather . . ." She broke off.

He started to pursue the subject, but suddenly, coming from the top of the stairs, he heard a faint disturbance, like footsteps. He looked immediately in that direction, as did she. Only now did he notice that from the angle at which they sat the second-floor landing was obscured. Not until someone was on the fourth or fifth step down could he or she be identified.

"Turn it down," he whispered, trying to warn her.

But apparently she didn't hear and it was too late anyway, for at that moment two boys started down the steps, identically clad in Navy bell-bottoms and white T-shirts which fit like second skin. They took the stairs in a jaunty manner, both talking rapidly, though apparently neither was listening to the other.

Alarmed, Mark was on his feet, baffled by their sudden appearance and equally baffled by her equally sudden relaxation. Speechless, he found that for several seconds all he was capable of was gaping at the two who had appeared like twin apparitions out of the darkness and who now were moving straight ahead toward the front door as though they did not hear the blaring radio.

At that moment Cass turned down the volume and called out quite cheerily through the new, heavy, ominous silence: "Did you find them?"

Both boys stopped a few feet short of the outside door. One stepped forward, grinning. "Sure did. What do you think?" He turned about in an awkward, "modeling" circle, exaggerating certain female movements of the trade. The boy behind him whistled.

"Terrific!" Cass grinned, and sat up on the edge of the couch, placing the radio in her lap. "Is that all you need?" she asked.

The boys shook their heads. "Hell, no, but the others can come out and get their own," one replied. "That trunk weighs a ton!"

"When's the show?"

"Next month. We'll see you get a comp." They both looked at Mark. "Maybe two."

"Thanks."

"Bye, now." With cheery waves both boys hurried on through the front door and without warning broke into an exaggerated version of "Some Enchanted Evening," trying for the deeper baritone registers and failing.

Still smiling, perched on the edge of the couch, Cass listened and winced at each sour note. "Hope they're safely hidden in the chorus," she murmured, and immediately turned up the volume on her radio.

For the moment he was still trying to quiet his pulse from the apparitions which had just descended the stairs like ghosts who belonged. "What the . . .?" he stammered, and pointed toward the front door.

She looked up from the radio as though surprised by his attitude. "Oh, them," she said lightly. "When I went down the fire escape, I saw them and they told me they'd heard there were trunks of Navy stuff up here. I just sent them on up."

"Navy . . . stuff?"

"High-school kids," she concluded. "They're doing *South Pacific* at school next month. You heard them," she added, as though baffled as to why she was having to explain all this twice. "And I'm sure you know what high school budgets are like. This stuff's just rotting out here. Someone might as well . . ." Her voice drifted as she broke off, apparently to listen to her radio.

Mark repeatedly tried to find something to quarrel with, to object to, to argue with. He even walked back to the staircase and stared up, as though to see if there were other apparitions lurking about on their way down.

Behind him, now he heard the music coming closer, and found it difficult, if not impossible, to question her further. Everything she'd said sounded valid and made sense. It was just that he hadn't been expecting—

"Are you ready?" she asked, coming up beside him. She'd turned the volume down so low he couldn't distinguish the song or the singer.

It didn't matter. He believed her now. It was just—

"Come on," she urged, and tucked radio and towel under one arm and took his hand in an endearing gesture as though to reassure him that everything was all right. "I want to show you

164

something else," she said, and warned him on the way through the front door, "Watch your step." She jumped to the ground, the radio clutched in both arms as though it were a prized possession. "Thank you so much for finding this," she whispered after he'd jumped down beside her. "I knew you were good luck from the very beginning."

She was standing so close, her voice so compelling, that for a moment all mysteries, all failures, even the weight of the past seemed to slip from Mark. Slowly he took the radio from her and, without breaking the connection with her eyes, he leaned over and placed it carefully on the cracked sidewalk. When he straightened up, he noticed she'd dropped the towel as well. He took her by the shoulders and found a child's shoulders, so small and frail, and yet it wasn't a child's face that looked intensely up at him.

"I know so little about you," he said, and felt her eyes hold him fast.

"There's nothing to know."

"Everything."

"Nothing matters but . . ."

Without being able to say exactly how it happened, he felt his arms close about her, felt her straining up to bridge the distance between them, felt the softness of her breasts pressed against him and felt sudden tidal waves of desire as he found her mouth, found her lips open.

It was only with the greatest of reluctance that he brought the kiss to an end and enfolded her in his arms and felt the reassuring strength of her arms as they tightened about his neck and held on, as though suffering the same frightening pleasure as he, recognition of mysterious and mutual feelings.

He lost track of how long they stood thus. It didn't matter. With her in his arms, all the splintered emotions of the last few days and weeks vanished. In their place he felt harmony unlike any he'd ever felt before.

She spoke first, so close to his ear he felt the warmth of her breath. "It's late."

"You said you wanted to show me . . ."

"Not now. You must get back to the dorm." She moved away first, looking small in the darkness of the night.

"Why?" he objected. "There's no need."

"There's every need," she said with surprising urgency. "You're not off to a good start and if you lose your scholarship you'll have to leave, and then what will we do?"

There was something so plaintive in her voice—yet how did she know?

165

"All athletes have to toe the mark," she smiled, retrieving the radio and towel. "I know you haven't been doing that and I don't want to be responsible."

He nodded, still amazed at her perception. "Coach called me in right before I came out here."

"What did he want?"

Mark walked a few feet away, sorry that the mood had been shattered. "He thinks I ought to have a physical."

She laughed softly behind him. "That's always their first solution. It's the body who is the betrayer, only the body."

She paused, and he found himself listening as closely to her silence as he'd listened to her strange words.

"Well, we must keep them happy. We both must," she said, "though sometimes I wish . . ."

He looked back over his shoulder at her. She hadn't moved and continued to stand on the crumbling walk, radio and towel clutched in her arms with the same force and intensity she'd held him.

He couldn't deny the rightness of what she'd said nor did he want to. He didn't enjoy walking out of step with everybody. He would have to try to make his peace with the authorities and then try his best to deliver the cooperative, quality athlete they'd paid so handsomely for. Still, the thought of not seeing her again as soon as possible was almost unsupportable.

"Cass, I . . ."

"It's all right," she said, and stepped toward him, effortlessly bridging the distance between them. "I have things as well. We'll set a date—say a week from tonight. That way we'll have something to look forward to and it will make the tedium of the days at least moderately bearable."

Her fingers intertwined with his, and, as he considered her proposal, he felt her pressing closer to him and knew the deprivation would be as hard on her. Then her words dawned.

"Cass, why a week? Surely . . ."

"No. We must be careful. We don't want to destroy anything."

Destroy? It seemed a harsh word to describe a budding and very promising relationship. Now he repeated with bleak incredulity, "But a week!"

"It will pass rapidly," she soothed, her voice firm.

Suddenly nothing would do but to take her in his arms again—radio, towel and all—and their lips found their way together effortlessly. Though the kiss commenced with even greater passion than the first one, abruptly she ended it by pulling away and gazing up at him for a moment with what appeared to be hurt and frightened eyes.

Then she was walking away from him, walking in a brisk pace down the sidewalk, diminishing into the night.

"Hey, wait!" he called after her, baffled by her quick change of mood.

"A week from tonight, Mark, at the front gate. Please be there." She was increasing the distance between them.

"Cass, wait! Where are you going?"

"Home."

"Let me walk you."

"No, you mustn't."

"Cass!"

He called again when he reached the end of the walk, looking in the direction she'd taken, and thought he saw her about half a block away—not moving north toward the gate or even south toward no-man's-land, but east toward the collapsing, high, barbed-wire fence which separated the edge of the university property from the Navy property.

Still mystified by her abrupt change of mood and rapid departure, he shouted again into the now-silent black fabric of night. "Cass, I can't wait a week! I must see you!"

He stopped walking to stand in the exact center of the street and listen. If he was unable to see her now, maybe he could hear her, gain a clue as to her direction and intent.

Had he in some way offended her? Had he moved too fast? Had she been frightened of—

As all the possibilities of the abrupt conclusion cartwheeled through his mind, he continued to stand and stare foolishly into the black night. Discouraged and disheartened at facing another week without her, he turned slowly and started back toward the street which led to the North Gate. Unfortunately he didn't know the twists and turns of the base as well as she did. Where the road was leading eastward he had no idea and now was in no mood to find out.

She was as elusive as the night. A week! Seven days!

As the perception continued to beat against him, he walked more slowly, head down, trying to organize his thoughts and—more important—his emotions. Both seemed to be completely haywire. He looked up from his brooding and stopped again, hearing something.

167

The silence was less than complete, marred by crickets and frogs and other unidentifiable night creatures—and something else. Was he hearing it in memory or was—

He glanced to the right in an attempt to get his bearings as well as trace this new sound. Not new, he'd heard it earlier. A bit tinny, now and then punctuated with static but nonetheless clear, the jinglelike nature of the song, a mindless repetition of words and handclappings. It was so distant, so faint. Surely it was coming from inside his own head like a prerecorded echo.

He did not move from the spot and again inspected the darkness in all directions. He was imagining it, that was all. She probably was halfway home by now, while he stood, turning in a slow, demented circle, looking for—

What?

Now he froze, his attention fixed on the large barracks which they had explored earlier more or less together. On the second floor in the window near the south end, shattering the darkened facade, he saw a light, a single light, coming from behind a brown shade. For several moments he stared at it as though it were an unearthly phenomenon. Then he saw a shadow pass on the other side, a single dark form which moved slowly across the illuminated shade and then back again and then disappeared.

He felt his eyes grow fixed on the patch of light as though it were vital to keep it in sight while the brain worked out a reasonable solution.

As the light and shadow remained unsolved, he saw the dark form pass back and forth before the closed shade again. At the same time he felt a peculiar breathlessness within his lungs, felt a slight telltale trembling creep across the back of his shoulders and start down into both arms.

Suddenly the solution of the mystery was no longer important. There was a threat in the night and in this place. Something was stirring that he couldn't understand and for which he possibly had no defense.

Hurry! Leave!

He obeyed these twin commands, though as he started off at a jog toward the North Gate he heard it again—or thought he heard it—that tinny, jukebox rendition about the stars at night being big and bright deep in the heart of Texas.

Hurry!

And he did, though even as he ran the volume seemed to increase and join the increased rhythm of his heart—

168

When you ask one man to spy on another you have to choose a safe setting for the report. It was despicable, approaching a kind of immorality as far as Coach Herbert was concerned, yet that's what he'd done—was doing now.

As he looked around his comfortable den lined with trophies and photos of glistening, sweaty young men, he settled back into his recliner chair, feet up. He hoped this was the right setting as well as the proper moment.

Opposite him, perched uncomfortably on the brown corduroy ottoman, was Terry Crawford.

With a calm which belied his inner turmoil, Coach Herbert leaned back farther into his recliner and asked quickly, "Can I get you something, Terry? Food?"

"No, sir. Coach, I'm fine," Terry said too rapidly. He was nervous, if nothing else. That made two of them.

At this awkward moment Coach Herbert recalled the clear look of disappointment on Terry's face when he'd asked him to keep close accounts on everything Mark Simpson said and did, every place he went. Terry hadn't approved then and he still didn't approve.

But what alternative did Coach Herbert have? A prime athlete failing to live up to his potential in the first month of training. Drastic steps were called for.

"Are you sure? Lemonade?"

"No. No, I'm fine, sir. I really am. Really, I'm okay." The boy clasped and unclasped his hands, sat upright on the ottoman and looked perfectly miserable.

Maybe if Coach Herbert explained it would help both of them. He liked Terry, liked his openness and honesty and, in a way, even liked his disappointment at what he'd been asked to do. Now Coach Herbert leaned forward in the recliner, straddling it, both hands palm down on the dark green velvet.

"You know, I've never done anything like this before, Terry," he confessed quietly, and waited a moment for the good feeling that accompanied all confessionals. Maybe he hadn't said enough. "All I really wanted you to do, you know, was keep an eye on him. You know what I mean."

"And report back to you."

"Well, of course," Coach Herbert agreed readily. "What good would it do for you to keep an eye on him if you . . ."

"He didn't do nothing, Coach." There was an edge and accompanying it was a sudden movement as Terry abandoned the ottoman and paced rapidly as far as the fireplace, which he now stared down into as though in utter fascination.

169

Laboriously, Coach Herbert pulled himself up out of his recliner, stretched a tight kink out of his lower back and took a step toward the dead fireplace and the boy who stood with his back to him.

"Look, Terry, I don't bring boys here just as athletes. Of course if they can help our program, that's an important bonus. But there are other factors, other considerations." He paused a moment to see if these "other factors" could provoke a hint of curiosity from Terry. Apparently they didn't. "It's the whole boy we're interested in here," Coach Herbert intoned, aware of the cliché. "I've suspected from the beginning that Mark Simpson had problems, has problems, big ones."

"He's okay," Terry muttered, mildly defensive, as if he, too, had had one or two complaints but they were too small to waste breath on.

"I didn't say he wasn't okay," Coach Herbert agreed gently, and completed the distance to the fireplace, his eye falling on the Coach of the Year award he'd won in '59. "Mark Simpson is more than okay," he agreed now with Terry, who had yet to look up from the fireplace. "He has the potential of being one of this country's great runners. I mean world class. Olympic material, no doubt about it."

At last Terry looked up, a peculiar expression on his face, one of sudden ambivalence, as though to say, "Is he that good?"

Seeing the expression, Coach Herbert nodded. "He is . . . that good," he said quietly, and rested one arm on the mantel. "That's why I asked you to keep an eye on him."

"I did," Terry nodded. "Like I said. Nothing to tell. He did everything he was supposed to do—as least as far as I could see."

"Make his classes?"

"Every single one of them. At least he got through the door. What he did after that, I don't know."

"What about training sessions?"

"Same thing. First one there, last to leave."

"The runs?"

"I stuck with him like glue."

Coach Herbert nodded, pleased in a way that Mark Simpson's delinquency was over. Apparently he was back on track. Doc Robbins had pronounced him physically fit, a fine specimen. Now Terry had just reassured Mark that he'd met all his obligations, academic as well as athletic. Then why the nagging doubt? Was it something he saw in Terry's face, something Terry was withholding?

170

"Is there something else?" Coach Herbert prodded, following after the boy where he'd collapsed in the corner of the slightly worn brown tweed sofa.

At the direct question Terry looked up and quickly looked back down at the palms of his hands. He shrugged once lightly, opened his mouth once, as though to speak, then quickly closed it, as though to imprison the words before they slipped out.

"Come on, Terry. What is it?" Coach Herbert prodded again. "Tell me everything, whether you understand it or not, whether you think it's important or not."

"Oh, hell, I think I understand it, Coach. I just . . ."

"What?"

"Well, several of us have tried to, you know, include Simpson in stuff other than training. I've asked him to the movies. Chuck thought he might like to go bowling. And others, too, and he don't go no place with no one."

For several moments Coach Herbert stared at the boy, as though if he could just comprehend his face he'd understand his words. "I . . . don't understand."

"He keeps to himself, I mean. Day and night. It's like he's all locked up, and the reason I mention it is because he wasn't like that at the beginning. This is something that's happened since . . ."

Coach Herbert waited to see if he'd complete the thought on his own. When he didn't, Herbert leaned forward on the edge of the sofa and asked, "Can you be more specific?"

Now Terry shrugged massively and looked as if he might stand but didn't. "What's to say? The guys are, you know, trying to make him feel at home, knowing he's a long way from home, but every time anyone says anything to him he just clams up and looks at you like you've committed a sin or something. And his running . . ."

"What about it?"

"Well, my God, Coach, most of us are here because it's what we want more than anything else in the world. Simpson looks like he's serving a prison sentence. And it's worse on the base. Did you know he won't go near Coffin Pond? Won't go within a block of it. He adds Nimitz Boulevard to the course to make up for what he loses in no-man's-land."

"But he does run the prescribed time?"

"Oh, yeah, never misses. At least not this week—or last. What is it with him and Coffin Pond?"

"Well, he did have trouble there, you know," Coach Herbert

171

nodded slowly, rose from the sofa, shoved his hands into his pockets and walked back to his recliner chair.

"What kind of trouble, Coach?"

"I don't . . . really know," he answered vaguely but honestly. "He . . . slipped, struck his head that first week. If I hadn't happened along . . ."

"You told me then he was drowning."

Coach Herbert started to correct him. "Drowned" was what he started to say, because even now he was prepared to swear that Mark Simpson had been dead when he'd pulled him out of Coffin Pond. If it hadn't been for that girl—

Suddenly he looked directly across at Terry. "Is he seeing anyone? I mean female. You know, is there . . .?"

"If there is I don't know about her," Terry said, and now stood as though weary of sitting. "He just don't go out at night, at least not when I've been following him. Do I have to do the same thing some more, Coach?" he asked now almost plaintively. "I mean it's really a drag at times."

For a moment Coach Herbert brooded on all the implications. Finally, with Terry watching him closely, he let him off the hook.

"No."

The relief on Terry's face was massive.

"But . . ." And with the "but" Coach Herbert slipped the hook at least halfway back in. "Don't spy on him, as you put it," he smiled. "Just kind of keep your eye on him. Not in a vindictive way. Certainly not in a conspiratorial way, but more out of concern for a fellow teammate."

"Why?"

The direct, almost challenging, question momentarily took Coach Herbert off guard. "You see, Terry, I recruited Mark Simpson. I spent considerable time in California talking with his coaches, to his teammates, to his mother, to him. That kid I recruited out in California was open, outgoing, enthusiastic, a leader with more hangers-on than you could shake a stick at."

As he talked, the look of incredulity on Terry's face grew to almost comic proportions. "You're kidding!"

"No."

"Well, what happened?"

Now Coach Herbert shrugged and shook his head. "My point, Terry. I don't know, but I'd like to find out."

With this simple declaration, the two men stared at each other for several moments, as though each waited for the other to speak and thus clear the mystery.

When the silence stretched on, Terry's face brightened, as

172

though he'd just remembered something. "He does go to one place on campus, the Greek place. You know, old Uncle Polly's café."

Coach Herbert looked up, surprised. "You mean he doesn't eat at the training table?"

"No. No, he eats there, but he usually walks down to Uncle Polly's right after dinner. Usually he'll have an orange juice and sit in the front window and look out and he doesn't say nothing to nobody. If Uncle Polly isn't busy, he'll talk to him for a while and then leave and go right back to the dorm and hit the books."

Coach Herbert looked bewildered. "Why Uncle Polly's?" he asked softly, not particularly addressing the question to Terry but more to himself, thinking aloud.

"A lot of kids go there."

"To eat, yes."

"And to talk. Uncle Polly, he's interesting, you know. He's easy to talk to."

"Okay, but you say they don't talk."

Terry shook his head. "No, not much. Simpson just sits there and . . ." Abruptly, he broke off. "If that's all, Coach, I've got to be going. Test tomorrow in history."

It had been an unsavory job for the boy. For that Coach Herbert was sorry. "Are you hungry?" he asked quickly. "I bet I could scare up some of that roast we had for dinner. I make a great sandwich."

"No, don't bother."

"No bother."

"I'm not hungry." Terry made a move toward the hall that led to the front of the house and the door. The exit was so abrupt that by the time Coach Herbert realized it was happening and followed after, the boy was almost to the front door.

There appeared to be just enough time to thank him. "Terry" he called out, still flustered by the boy's rapid departure, "I am grateful."

"No need. Didn't do nothin'."

"Do you understand?"

"Sure."

"Sometimes periods of adjustment can be very difficult, particularly . . ."

"I know."

"Will you continue to kind of keep half an eye on him for me?"

At last the boy stopped and looked back, as though annoyed by the request.

"No spying," Coach Herbert reassured him, catching up at last

173

and helping him with the door. "You see him every day. You train with him. Just try to be nice to him and see if you can get him to talk, find out what's on his mind, you know."

"Fat chance, that. What the hell, coach, I have a girl. She . . ."

"Please, Terry. I'm not asking for any more reporting—unless you see or hear something worth reporting."

"I know."

"Thanks, Terry."

"Didn't know I was going to have to be some kind of damned baby-sitter my senior year."

"You're not."

Terry was out of the door now and halfway down the steps.

"I do appreciate it, Terry," he called after the boy, who was already disappearing into the night at the end of the sidewalk.

"Night, Coach."

Back in the house, Coach Herbert closed the door behind him. He did know one thing: Unless Mark Simpson solved his own problems now—or allowed him to solve them for him—he might as well kiss his running career good-bye.

To run well required many things. The obvious ones, of course—God given talent and man-given training—and the third more intangible quality—will. In this last category Mark Simpson was failing miserably.

Hell!

As his discouragement vaulted, Coach Herbert felt it fall down on him. He'd had such hopes for the boy and had paid a fortune for him. What had happened—was still happening—and was it too late to stop it?

Lacking answers and in real need of relief, Coach Herbert rubbed his eyes and thought of the pot roast, still warm from dinner. Maybe a slice or two would help, wedged between rye and plain old French's mustard and a slice of onion.

What the hell, it wouldn't hurt to try—

Terry Crawford hurried through the middle-class residential neighborhood, wishing the meeting had never taken place, wishing Coach had chosen someone else to do his dirty work and hoping earnestly that this was the end of it. Because if it wasn't—

With this inconclusive threat he broke speed and thrust both hands into his pockets, walking more slowly. What really bothered Terry Crawford was that he'd failed to tell the coach everything.

As he proceeded on down the quiet, dark residential street heading back toward campus, he thought of the evening when he'd tried to bridge the gap that was developing between Mark Simpson and the rest of the world. Once his door had been opened to him and what Terry had found hunched over the desk in the dim light of a gooseneck lamp appeared zombielike, a ghost.

He'd been polite, answering Terry's stupid questions of "You hungry?" "What you studying?" Politeness, that's all Terry had gotten in return.

As he'd left Mark's room after an embarrassing silence, he'd looked back. In the instant before he'd closed the door, Terry had seen something that caused the hair to stand up on his arms, had seen Mark Simpson not as he'd appeared moments earlier—a guy about Terry's age—but in that split second as Terry had looked back toward the door, he had seen an old man. It was as though before his very eyes Mark Simpson had gone from twenty to—

Terry shivered in the cool autumn evening, recalling not only the physical changes of thinning, graying hair and the deep-cut lines, but the look on the stranger's face, one of almost dispassionate calm and that maddening politeness as if nothing were wrong.

The only trouble—then as now—was that for just a moment it hadn't been Mark Simpson sitting there. It was someone else, someone who looked like him but it wasn't him. Terry was prepared to swear to that grim fact.

As the sidewalks here were deserted, he covered the next three blocks fairly rapidly and looked eagerly ahead to the bright lights of the campus shops, the general Friday-night glut of students wandering in and out of Hamburger Heaven and Piggy Heaven and the Greek place.

As he drew near to the first commercial shop, he broke speed, encountering reassuring knots of laughing, chattering students. Aware he was breathing far too heavily for a harmless three-block sprint, he halted a moment, hands on hips, and allowed his head to fall back while he filled his lungs with the food-scented night air.

God, he was hungry!

Across the street he saw the Greek place where he'd followed Mark Simpson on several occasions this week. Terry didn't like the food. He was all-American in his appetites. Anything you had to eat off a stick was questionable from the start. Too much garlic as well. Strong.

Still, he felt drawn to the broad plate-glass windows—not in any

175

open manner but using the trees on the opposite side of the street for concealment as he'd done before this week, many times before.

As he drew even with the shop, he stopped directly behind a tree, one of many planted at intervals the length of the block, fully aware of how dumb he must look to those passing behind him. He tried to modify his position—less peering out and more simply leaning against—and belatedly realized that most of the kids were too involved in their own melodramas to pay much attention to his.

Thus reassured, he leaned against the tree and gaped across the street, his eyes moving first to the small table by the window, the place in the past where he'd seen Mark Simpson just sitting there along with an orange juice, staring out at the sidewalk as though searching for someone or waiting.

Now the table was empty, as was the entire café as far as he could tell. In surprise he started forward, not particularly concerned with concealment now, for there was nothing and no one to hide from. Strange. He moved slowly toward the curb, searching each corner of the brightly lit, though apparently deserted, café. At the edge of the curb on the opposite side he stopped, unable to comprehend this unprecedented sight. Someone was always in Uncle Polly's place—moving around, playing the jukebox. In fact Terry had passed by as early as seven in the morning and on occasion seen sleepy-eyed Uncle Polly talking with a couple of agitated students. He knew no hours, Uncle Polly was fond of saying. He just knew the needs of the students.

Slowly Terry started to cross the street. If Uncle Polly had wanted to close up early, wouldn't he have just turned out all the lights, put out his sign CLOSED and called it a day?

Halfway across the street, Terry looked at the other bustling fast-food emporiums. Nothing slow about them, kids passing in and out of the doors as though they were giving stuff away. But not here.

As he approached the front door, Terry veered suddenly past it, as though coming to his good senses at the last minute. He didn't want to go in there, didn't care for it even when it was packed and jumping. Now there was something wrong, something he couldn't see from the street, something he really didn't want to see.

He walked past the broad, plate-glass window, past Mark Simpson's usual table, and stole a backward glance through the

176

swinging doors which led to the kitchen. At that instant he saw a shadow move across the two small smudged windows in the tops of the doors. Uncle Polly was in his kitchen putting together some new garlic horror.

With this explanation came a degree of relief, and he stopped on the sidewalk, reversed his position and started walking slowly back across the pavement in front of the café, still gaping in at the deserted room. As he drew even with the kitchen doors on the back wall he stopped and peered in again.

A Coke wouldn't hurt, and on the way back to the dorm he'd stop off for a pizza. Just a Coke now.

In this state of indecision, he walked past the café, heading in the opposite direction, and fell eagerly into the shadows on the other side. Cleaning shop, closed for the night and casting only convenient black on the sidewalk.

Wait! A stroke of luck. Terry pressed back against the cleaning shop and watched a couple drawing near, arm in arm, the girl bowing her head into the boy's shoulder, laughing at something he'd said, both veering toward the door of the Greek place, reaching for the knob and drawing it open.

Or trying to. Locked?

From his concealment in shadows, Terry watched first the boy, then the girl, then the boy tug at the door, their initial expressions at the obstacle one of offense, as though someone had personally challenged them. Ultimately both shrugged and peered into the well-lit café, then looked at each other and shrugged again, and without a word entwined arms and started off down the street.

Terry watched them until they slipped effortlessly into the Coney Island place.

Locked? Lit up but locked? Made no sense.

For the second time Terry shifted the mystery and started across the broad spill of light coming from the two large windows. Again, midway across, he looked back in toward the kitchen doors.

Wait! There was Uncle Polly himself, half in, half out of the swinging doors, a large white apron wrapped around his protruding middle, talking backward into the kitchen, obviously to someone out of sight, talking quite volubly and excitedly—at least as far as Terry could tell. Angry, too.

Terry started to move back to some position of safety and concealment but realized there was no time and no point. Whatever the nature of the conversation or argument going on inside, it seemed to be growing more heated, as now Uncle Polly propped open one side of the swinging doors and angrily motioned for someone to exit. Several times he made a broad, angry, sweeping gesture, as though to assist whoever it was on his or her way.

By way of concealment Terry did draw back as far as the curb, to the extreme edge of the light spill, and held his position, beginning to hear faintly the man's voice raised in what sounded like rage.

"I told you, I told you, I told you! Leave me alone!" he heard Uncle Polly shout. "How many times do I have to tell you? Leave me alone!"

Another knot of kids passed by on the sidewalk and intersected his vision. He wondered if they could hear the male voice raised in outrage and looked in their direction. Apparently not. But then they were giggling among themselves so loudly they probably could't hear anything or anyone. Now Terry found himself reluctantly waiting for them to clear his line of vision. In a few seconds they were gone, leaving him with an unobstructed view of the café and the large man, the doors still propped open.

"I've listened to you for too long! I listened to you against my better judgment!" Uncle Polly bellowed now.

And it was a bellow, the tone and pitch clear, something driving the normally placid man into a dangerous rage.

"Now I listen no more! You wrong! You wrong!"

As he yelled he started back through the kitchen doors. As they were swinging shut behind him, suddenly Terry saw a blinding flash of red fill the black vacuum of the kitchen, saw the old Greek fall forward—first onto his hands and knees—and then struggle backward as out of the red and orange explosion smoke began to billow—enormous clouds of it enveloping the fallen man and fast spreading into the café itself.

My God! Terry continued to gape at the awesome sight. Clearly an explosion of some sort—

But he'd heard nothing! Explosions make noise. And there had been no noise—only that sudden red flash, like those awful newsreels of atomic explosions. First the sight and seconds later the sound. So he knew the sound would come.

But, yet there still had been no sound, only the fierce red light, which seemed to be growing brighter even as Terry watched. It was increasing as well, seeming now to follow the old man as he crawled on hands and knees away from the kitchen doors, clutching his arm. Even from this distance Terry could see it was bleeding, as though he'd been cut by flying glass.

Reflexively Terry looked around on the sidewalks to see if anyone else had witnessed the explosion. Finding himself totally alone, he rushed toward the door to help the old man.

Locked. Now he commenced to pound frantically, trying to signal Uncle Polly, who was still crawling away from the explosion and spreading smoke.

"Uncle Polly, here! Over here! Unlock the door! Quick!"

Though he was pounding with such force he was afraid he'd break the glass, the old man had yet to look up at him. Was he deaf?

"Unlock the door!" Terry shouted again, wondering if maybe he shouldn't stop wasting valuable time and call the fire department. There was a phone booth on the corner. If only he could get someone to—

"Uncle Polly, can you hear me? The door. Unlock the door!"

Though the smoke appeared to be growing thicker, the old man seemed to be staying just ahead of it, maneuvering his way around the counter, still on all fours. Through the two small glass windows that opened back into the kitchen, Terry saw a hot, red glow which, like the smoke, seemed to be increasing. Whoever had been back there didn't stand a chance.

"Uncle Polly, this way!" He pounded even harder. If the man didn't hear him in the next attempt, he'd be forced to break the window glass, reach through and unlock the door himself. He couldn't just leave the two of them in there. Suddenly an awful thought occurred. Whoever had been in the kitchen was probably beyond help, or else he would be on his way out now as was Uncle Polly. Who had it been, the person who had provoked Uncle Polly to this unexpected rage? Whoever it was, he was at present in the exact center of that red glow and in what condition Terry had no idea, didn't want to even think about.

As his terror increased, he backed away from the door and the billowing smoke which was still increasing. Now he could smell it as it slipped through cracks around doors and windows. He looked frantically up and down both sides of the street. Still no one.

Then run! Find the phone. Try the pizza place across the street. Get help—quick!

On this fearful note he started off in one direction, then suddenly changed his mind and quickly reversed his steps. At first

179

not certain why he'd reversed direction, he remembered the nearest phone booth was at the opposite end of the block. As he passed by the café again he paused long enough to peer in. At first he couldn't see anything for the smoke, which was like a solid.

"Hey!" he shouted, realizing for the first time maybe he didn't have time to go for help. "You, in there!" he called again idiotically. At last he bent over, stripped off his heavy cowboy boot, angled it down until he was holding it by the toe and took aim at the glass nearest the inside knob. With the first blow he heard the glass shatter and saw the confined smoke come billowing out the small jagged opening.

Covering mouth and nose with one hand, he reached carefully through the new opening in search of a latch or bolt. For several moments he fumbled, fighting back the aggressive and acrid fumes that smelled like chemicals burning.

"Uncle Polly, can you hear me? Please!"

Then he had to fall back for a moment, withdrawing his hand which thus far had not been able to locate the latch still holding the door fast. Three feet back on the sidewalk, he peeked through the gray smoke to an occasional, darting finger of red. The fire was spreading fast; it had started in the area of the kitchen but was now moving out.

Suddenly he heard something behind him. Music—at least that's what it sounded like. He turned on it with an expression of breathless desperation.

Across the street he saw—poised in the night shadows and half concealed behind one of the trees—a girl, fairly young looking, straddling a bicycle, both hands gripping the handlebars. She seemed to be wearing a long, white, oversized shirt. In the shadowy distance that large, white field was the first and most predominant item he noticed.

No matter. Help had arrived. Accordingly he waved off the smoke that seemed to be pursuing him and shouted, "Would you go for help? The phone . . ." He pointed to the phone box at the end of the street. "Call the Fire . . ." He realized she had yet to move and he broke off.

"Can you hear me?" he cried again, moving to the edge of the curb, looking back frantically once into the café that now appeared to be inundated with smoke, nothing clearly visible through the plate-glass window—not even Uncle Polly himself.

"Listen, there's people in there! I need help. I can't leave. Please call the Fire Department!" Again he broke off.

She had yet to move in any way. In fact now there was

180

something spooky in her passivity, as though she knew very well what was happening and simply didn't give a damn. As the exigency of the moment pressed down upon him, again he heard that tinny music and saw in the basket of her bicycle what appeared to be a small portable radio.

"Can't you hear me?" he called directly. "If you can . . ."

But suddenly he saw her climb back up on the seat of the bicycle, one foot lifted to a pedal, her face still turned toward him but—as far as he could tell—not a sign of expression, neither understanding nor comprehension nor apprehension, just a blank, young-girl face who might have been staring into an empty shop window. Slowly now she pressed down on the pedal, and started moving down the sidewalk. She glanced back at him once, though still there was not a sign of human emotion on her face.

He started to call a final time but changed his mind. There was something about her that caused his better judgment to advise him to let her go.

It was up to him. At that he ran back to the door and reached carefully through the jagged glass, again feeling in all directions for whatever it was that was holding the door fast. He closed his eyes, turned his head away and tried not to breathe as he searched.

His mind, independent of his hands, saw the girl again, poised over her bike, gazing across at him with calm, level, unperturbed eyes. Despite the smoke and increasing heat he felt a shiver. He'd seen her someplace before—where he couldn't remember—but this was no time to stop and search his memory.

Why the hell couldn't he find the bolt? What was it that was holding the door firmly closed?

Suddenly behind him he heard a screech of tires and looked over his shoulder to see a most reassuring sight—a black-and-white police car, one officer already hurrying toward him, the other, he saw through the windshield, talking into a mike. Probably calling for more help.

As the first officer ran toward him, Terry stepped back from the door and tried to wave away the smoke, which was growing thicker, in an attempt to draw one deep breath, the better to answer questions. Turning his head away, he saw—standing just on the edge of the light—the girl again, straddling the bike, her long, oversized white shirt, a steady stream of tinny, vintage music coming from someplace close by.

Then the officer was even with him. "Come on, kid, give me a hand!" he shouted.

181

Terry saw his intent was to break down the door and he turned his back on the shadowy figure and the tinny music and rushed to where he was needed.

All day long Mark had felt a kind of irritability. The walls of his room had become like bars. He felt caged and cut off, as though life were going on all about him but had come to a halt here.

Irritability increasing, he stopped pacing in that same limited circle in which he'd walked off most of the afternoon and listened. Sirens. Fire? Ambulance? Police? It was hard to tell.

He glanced at his watch. He could start now, couldn't he? He'd been a good boy, made every class, every training session. He'd even put up with the big-brother tactics of Terry Crawford, though he resented them like hell. Never in his life had he been spied on and he hated it.

He continued to stand before his closed door like a prisoner. He was not quite certain of the conditions of his release. Could he go now? Did he have to stay some more? He'd waited for this evening, the very evening she'd set, and he knew where he could meet her and how she would look at him when she first saw him and what her hand would feel like in his and how she would lean lightly against him when he put his arms around her shoulders.

Slowly he leaned forward against the closed door. The sirens were getting louder. Maybe the dorm was on fire. What a bit of luck that would be! This past week had approached the unbearable on several occasions—the godawful routine, the mediocre classes, the worse than mediocre training facilities, the spying, the isolation, the sense that there was a very good possibility he'd screwed up in a way he'd never screwed up before.

He closed his eyes under the remembered tedium of the week. The sirens were growing yet louder, coming closer—

No matter. He'd served his penance. In a few minutes he'd leave the stench of this place for the clear air and deserted streets of the base. The thought alone soothed, and he recalled now a phenomenon which he'd only noticed this week. During workout sessions with other members of the team, when they jogged or ran the base courses, that bizarre and mildly ghostly geography was empty, meaningless, bland, no drama whatsoever. It was only with Cass in the early evening hours that he felt something he'd never felt at any other time.

What the hell? He was growing spooky.

As the sirens grew to deafening pitch, he went to the window and peered out and saw several excited knots of people doing the same, saw a thin curl of gray smoke rising into the evening sky from the vicinity of the campus shops. Someone was burning the pizza.

With a smile he leaned forward on the windowsill, beginning to feel the tension of the difficult week ease despite the distant smoke and sirens. Two floors below he saw more guys spilling out of the dorm, all pointing excitedly toward the smoke and sirens, most now hurrying in that direction like kids.

He was about to turn back into his room when he caught sight of a girl on a bicycle just turning the corner of the intersection. It was what she was wearing that caught his eye more than anything, that very familiar oversized man's white shirt, tail out, rolled-up blue jeans. He returned to the window and looked more closely. From this third-story angle it was difficult to tell. Was it—

Then, as the bicycle turned the corner heading down to the avenue which in turn led to the base, he saw in the basket an equally familiar gunmetal gray portable radio with a rolled top and at that moment recognized as well the short-cropped blond hair, the compactly shaped body despite the "costume" she was wearing.

He leaned farther out, feeling the first warming excitement and anticipation that he'd felt all week.

"Cass!" He called her name but doubted if she'd heard over the confusion of sirens and shouts. He started to call again, then changed his mind. No need to waste time. Hurry instead. Catch up with her. Along with the glorious sense of seeing her again was the equally glorious realization that she, too, had remembered their date—if it could be called that. He was never quite sure whether, when he saw her, it would be the last time he would ever see her again.

But there she was, just turning into the intersection, pedaling against the tide of people and cars, all of whom were now hurrying toward the increasing smoke and the ever-increasing sirens of every fire truck in town, or so it seemed. Seeing her, he felt an almost unbearable compulsion to call again but knew now it was useless over the confusion below.

Instead he hurried away from the window, caught for a moment in indecision. It had been his plan to change shirts, run the razor over stubble. Did he have time? Did he want to take time? He wanted to catch up with her now, didn't want her to get out of his sight.

183

And she was early. He looked at the desk clock. Seven-ten. Hadn't she said eight, their customary time? Oh, what the hell? He couldn't remember and somehow it didn't matter. None of the customary rules of decorum seemed to matter where Cass was concerned, as though someone had given her permission to pass through this world perfectly free to apply her own rules.

As his thoughts cut a jagged path through his consciousness, his fingers had been moving by rote down the buttons on the front of his shirt. Now they stopped, fixed at midpoint down the shirt.

What had happened to him? When exactly had the passion of his lifetime—running—become a drag and a bore? The answer was immediately available, though totally puzzling and mystifying. Since he'd arrived here. That had been the beginning of his disenchantment. Since he'd first explored the base on his own, that first hot September morning, since his "accident" at Coffin Pond, since—

Hurry. Cass was probably there by now. He unbuckled his belt, slid the shirttail in all around, smoothed it down, adjusted the waistband of his jeans and buckled the belt, then threw a long quick glance into the mirror. The face staring back at him was a little weird.

The man there looked tired, circles under his eyes. Where had those come from? He was the original early-to-bed, early-to-rise kid, had been all his life.

White chapel. Mourning. Baby carriage.

Still gazing at the face in the mirror, he saw the scene superimposed as though it were on his own face. Probably remembrance of the photo album of his mother's. Strangely he felt a strong urge to flip through those musty-smelling pages again, like a passport to himself.

He'd call her tonight. The last two times they'd talked had been most unsatisfactory, however. Bad connections. Static. On both occasions he'd lost her voice entirely and been forced to hang up.

Go now. Hurry. Everything else could and would wait.

Joyfully following this inner voice, he flung open the door, surprised to see the corridor deserted. He took the two flights of steps downward running, skipping several, and landing on the first-floor corridor with a bounce. He pushed open the near exit door and felt the first refreshing breath of cool evening air, mingled with smoke coming from someplace.

He looked toward the direction of the campus shops three blocks away and saw the column of gray smoke, still rising in the air. Even though the sirens were quiet, the deserted feeling around the dorm and in the parking lot made him suspect that everyone had chased the fire. What was burning? he wondered, and stood for several seconds staring in that direction, as though, if he stared long enough, he'd be able to see over the distance.

No matter. He'd hear all about it later. He was certain about that. For now, Cass was probably waiting. She'd had a good head start and the bike had given her yet another advantage. As far as he was concerned, he'd earned this evening, had already paid for it, and all he wanted was to spend a few hours in her sweet, mysterious presence and forget all about training schedules and homework and responsibility to dead fathers.

He broke into a careless run to cover as much ground as quickly as possible. In a remarkably short time he looked up to see the North Gate of the base coming into view and thought of the last time he'd met her, the curious ritual he'd witnessed as she'd fed the large hawk.

No hawk, not a sign of her. Just a high evening sky of late Indian summer and the good smell of something burning.

"Cass?" He called her name and found it pleasing and, still approaching the sentry box, proceeded to search every shadow for a glimpse of blond hair. "Cass, are you here?"

For some reason he glanced over his shoulder, as though somehow she might have fallen back and come up from behind. But there was nothing there but the emptiness of the street itself. For several moments he stood in the middle of the pavement facing the sentry box and the forked avenue that led into the base.

But still he saw nothing except the street itself leading to the remains of the Officers' Club and on down to the end of the base known as no-man's-land and Coffin Pond. For a few moments he stared fixedly in that direction. There was still apprehension. He knew the rest of the team always snickered at him when he stopped short of going to the extreme south edge of the base and took instead an alternate route but one of the same mileage, the one which veered safely away from the area once called no-man's-land.

Abruptly he turned away, as though even now he found the direction offensive and gazed toward his left to the east and the direction on the base that he'd not yet explored. The street that ran east and west beyond the sentry box appeared to be wider than the others, a boulevard with a small green island down the center. For some reason that direction attracted him, as roads never taken always attract.

185

He started walking slowly past the sentry box, keeping to the left or east, noticing now a high fence with a slanted, barbed-wire top which rose up from the ground in a curiously graceful spiral about seventy-five feet away. As his eyes traveled down the fence, they veered to the right at the first intersection. There was something in the exact center of the intersection, though he couldn't see what. A poised something.

"Cass?" Although he couldn't be certain, he thought he saw the outline of two wheels, a bike, and straddling it—

"Cass?" he called again, continuously squinting into the distance. Then he broke into a trot and increased his speed until he had crossed the distance between them by half, still searching for some familiar sign and at last saw it in her upraised hand, the energetic wave cheery, as though she wanted to attract his attention. It was her. He could see clearly now. A long, oversized, white shirt, rolled-up blue jeans. No "costume" this time; apparently she simply enjoyed wearing the fashions of several years ago.

Then he thought he heard her call out something. As though speed impaired his hearing, he slowed to a walk and called back, "What? I didn't hear you."

"I said I didn't think you'd come. I'm so happy you did."

The sentiment, so sweetly and faintly spoken, moved him. Was she as uncertain and insecure as he? "I didn't think you'd come either," he called by way of reply, and again broke into a trot, wanting to bridge the entire distance between them as quickly as possible, and drew close enough until he could see her plainly.

"Well," she grinned, "you've worked hard and kept everyone reasonably happy and now the rest of the day and the night belongs to us. My grandfather always used to say . . ."

As she turned her bike about in an attempt to change directions, he lost part of what she was saying and concentrated instead on her first curious comment. How had she known he'd done well? And had he?

Then she was directly beside him, the bike pointed straight down the boulevard in an easterly direction, past several buildings he'd never seen before. "Are you ready?" she smiled. "How shall we do it? Do you want to hop on the bike or shall I go slow and you walk?"

"I see you've brought the radio," he interrupted, pointing toward the gunmetal gray portable which he'd found.

"Oh, I never go anyplace without it. I felt so lost and I was so grateful when you found it. Shall I turn it on?"

"Did you hear a siren?"

She stopped abruptly, halfway in her reach for the radio dial.

When she didn't respond for several seconds, he said, "Something was on fire. Near the shops. Campus shops, I guess. I couldn't see. I was wondering if . . ."

Suddenly, without warning, she pulled herself up on the bike seat and started slowly pedaling away from him.

"Hey!"

"Come on if you're coming."

Given no choice, he broke into a trot. She was so unpredictable, so capricious. But then he observed she was going very, very slowly, barely able to balance the bike in an attempt to allow him to catch up. So he did, and when the pace of the bike was so slow he could manage to keep up with it, he asked the first question that came to mind, the most logical one.

"Did I say something wrong? For a minute there you looked . . . angry."

"Not angry," she smiled, wobbling with the bike, moving in erratic circles. "It's just that . . ." She broke off and encircled him, slowly emerging on the opposite side.

When she still seemed disinclined to finish what she had started to say, he stopped walking and allowed her to encircle him again, then prompted, "It's just what?"

She stopped the bike directly in front of him, a mild though clear stance of confrontation. "Well, you always want to bring that world," and she bobbed her head toward town, "out here and ruin this one. The only way you can really have any fun out here is to listen closely for the ghosts and hear what they're saying and forget all about what's going on back there. That's not important. That's not real. This is the only place that matters."

Near the end her voice had grown softly rhapsodic. Feeling almost mesmerized by her tone and the fluid nature of her movements, Mark watched transfixed as she looked carefully, lovingly in all directions, gazing out over the deteriorating and decaying buildings as if it were some sort of promised land.

"It's so beautiful, don't you think?"

At first he didn't respond. Beauty was present, not in the collapsing structures of the base but rather in her face, the soft diffuse light in her eyes and in the constant, though mysterious, devotion she felt to this rusty cog in the Great War machine. He came up beside her and lightly reached out for the handlebars of her bike to prevent any future escape.

"Did you know someone here? On the base during the war?"

At first her face registered only surprise, then she smiled, then

187

laughed outright. "Of course I did, silly! I swear, Mark, you do say the . . ."

"Who?"

Despite his hold on her handlebars, she backed effortlessly away from him, turned the bike around and, still smiling, called out, "You, silly. You were here and so was I. Don't you remember? Don't you really remember?"

Before he could answer she once again commenced to pedal slowly away from him. "This isn't the first time we've met, you know. Come on, I'll show you everything. Are you game?"

This challenge was hurled over her shoulder without looking at him, and all he saw was a small, compact, determined figure pedaling slowly away from him, music coming from the portable.

He smiled after her retreating figure. If she said so, he'd string along. He'd been a baby here in his crib. Of course he didn't remember her or anyone else.

"Hey, wait!" he called after her, wishing she'd drop the bike and just walk beside him. He wanted to talk and disliked the freedom the bike gave her. He was about to suggest this when suddenly she pointed toward a very impressive large building on the right, a curved, rounded driveway leading in behind a large stand of trees, culminating in a front door and the tattered remains of a dark green canopy. Six standards were still in place, suggesting that once the canopy had been extended out to the drive. Certain VIPs were given full protection from the wind and elements all the way inside the building.

"The Administration Building," she called back. "Isn't it immense?"

Again he saw her straddle her bike, gazing up at the structure, which was indeed the largest he'd seen on the base. Three stories, it rambled off in all directions, almost covering the entire block on which it sat. He observed several wings connected by covered walkways to the core of the building. As with all of the other structures, all that was left of the exterior was now a peeling, faded Navy gray, though in the upper windows he noticed what appeared to be lined drapes. Undoubtedly officers' dining rooms of some sort—for those not able to make it the distance to the club.

"Are you all right?"

He looked up sharply at the sound of the voice. Male, clearly not hers. What in—

"Did you hear that?"

She looked back at him, an expression of surprise on her face. "What? The music?"

"No, a voice. A man's voice."

"What did it say?" She was looking at him closely, her interest intense.

Suddenly he felt foolish. "Come on. Are we going into this monstrosity or not?" He started off toward the long, rambling driveway, trying to remember where he'd heard that voice before.

"Mark, wait. What did the voice say, the voice you heard?"

He looked back at her, amused that at last her attention was his. He'd have to remember that in the future. Just mention spooks and—

"We did know each other, you know," she repeated, quite serious now, a touch of defense in her tone as though he'd challenged her.

He turned about, confronting her. Maybe he'd imagined the voice or heard it somewhere and was now hearing it in memory. "If you say so," he smiled, and started off again down the rounded driveway toward the large Administration Building.

He thought he'd hear her at any moment slowly pedaling after him, then leading the way on their "adventure." When he didn't he looked back to see her exactly where he'd left her on the boulevard, staring after him. "Aren't you coming?" he called back.

"We did know each other!" she exclaimed. "I have proof if you want to see."

He smiled at her claim. "If you say so. Was your dad stationed here?"

She nodded. "For a while. Before he was killed."

He blinked at this announcement. She'd never told him this before. He held his position. "I'm sorry."

"Why? Your dad was killed too."

Stunned he moved toward her. "I never told you that."

"It's true, though, isn't it?"

"Did . . . I tell you?"

"It doesn't matter. Come on, Mark, let's go."

To his surprise she wheeled the bike around and headed back down the boulevard. "I thought we were . . ." he called after her and gestured back over his shoulder toward the Administration Building.

"There's nothing in there but about five hundred rusty typewriters in the basement. I'll show you one day. Right now there's something else more important."

As he struggled with the transition and looked almost longingly back at the Administration Building, he heard the radio's tune change to a real golden oldie, a melancholy tune, something about the white cliffs of Dover. As she pedaled away from him, the music swelled as though she'd leaned forward and adjusted the volume dial. Again he felt that awesome splintering of emotions—part of them fed up with her whimsy and her capriciousness, the other half finding it inconceivable that he should be anyplace else but here with her.

Thus torn, he started forward, not ~~as~~ AS rapid ~~a pace~~ LY as before. Let her do the waiting while he caught up. But a few minutes later, when he saw her drawing farther and farther away, he at last broke into a reluctant trot, then a halfhearted run, seeing her a mere speck at least two blocks ahead of him.

Then suddenly she disappeared. One minute there, the next gone.

He broke speed, breathing heavily, and stared forward into the vacuum of empty pavement. To the right up ahead there was a stand of enormous cottonwood trees just turning yellow under the threat of coming winter. Now the gold of an early evening light seemed to be emanating from these enormous cottonwoods.

The rather dramatic and beautiful optical illusion captured his attention while he waited to catch his breath. Then she reappeared, closer now, apparently having retraced the street for a short distance.

"Aren't you coming?"

At first he nodded, pleased he'd found her again. Then he was jogging toward her where she stood even with the dazzling cottonwoods. Still fifty yards away, he called out, "Ever seen anything like that?" and pointed in the general vicinity of the trees which, as he drew closer, seemed to radiate more and more light, all golden.

"What?" she called back, apparently not understanding.

"That," he said with strong, though mock, emphasis, still pointing toward the enormous and now almost blindingly bright cottonwoods.

"Oh, that!" She smiled as he drew near. "That's the chapel."

He blinked, first at her for her apparent misunderstanding, then back to the golden trees. Only at that moment did he see it, the first break in rank of typical naval architecture, which had been almost totally concealed by the stand of native trees.

For the first time truly oblivious to her movements, Mark left the street and tried to find the remains of a walk which had led from the street to the chapel. Finding none, he took the small, weed-filled ravine at a trot and climbed up the other side.

In a state of nostalgic awe he started toward the small church that somehow seemed to belong to New England landscapes, a

190

smaller version of churches he'd seen on calendars of snow-covered Vermont scenes, remarkably intact and remarkably beautiful and—most important of all—his father's domain.

Only now did it strike him as strange that in all those voluminous albums spilling three-by-five pieces of the past into any lap that held them, out of all those thousands of snapshots, he was unable to remember one of this chapel, and yet it seemed the most natural place to pose for photos.

"Mark?" The voice was soft and respectful and came from the street, as though she wanted him to come away and continue on with her.

But this was too important. "I would like to stay here for a few minutes. Do you mind? If so, you can go ahead." Of course he hoped she didn't want to go ahead. Only a few minutes, that was all he needed here. Then a thought occurred. "Was this the only chapel on the base?"

As he turned back with the question he saw her place her bike gently on the shoulder of the street, retrieve the portable radio and start down the ravine, following the same path he'd just taken.

"This is it," she called out, picking her way carefully through the long, stickery, dried underbrush. "It's pretty, isn't it?"

Pleased that she was in the process of joining him, he again felt the peculiar tug of twin forces—one dragging him closer to the chapel, the other seeming to come from her and dragging him away from it. His curiosity about the building was sharp, and he started eagerly ahead, head uplifted, eyes searching the façade, still amazed at its mint condition. A thought occurred.

"Has it been used since . . .?"

"Not that I know of. There was an old organ in there once a long time ago, but someone sold it and took it out. I think the university sold some of the pews to a local church. Beyond that . . ."

All the time she talked, behind him he heard that curious tinny, old-time music. Vintage. God knew when. This one familiar and jaunty.

Double doors, heavy, Gothic in design, peeling slightly. Locked? Open, please let them be open. Tentatively he grasped the ornate blackened brass knob and wondered why vandals hadn't ripped it off over the years. It appeared to be solid brass.

At first the door held fast and—half in disappointment, half in anger—he pulled with all his weight and felt the rusty, creaking hinges give and felt a draft of cold air as from a tomb. Peering

191

through the crack in the nearly opened door, he saw a dazzling sight—light coming from some unknown source, the golden glow of evening sun on golden cottonwoods streaming through the riotous colors of stained glass in a hundred light paths cascading through royal blues and greens and purples, refracting the light and sharpening it. It was as though every rainbow in the world had spilled there.

Astonished by the unexpected beauty, he pulled the door all the way open and felt it secure against its own weight and found himself in a small vestibule—eight-sided in shape, waist-high shelves running around all eight sides, a convenient place obviously for stacking literature and brochures.

To the left he saw three large posters, two curling up from the bottom, having peeled free of the securing thumbtacks. He drew nearer, fascinated by the third, a large red one, still intact from the day it had been attached to the bulletin board. The word WAR printed in bold black letters across the top and then the top view of a burly male hand. On the ring finger was a ring with the Nazi swastika imposed at its center. The bottom line read simply FOR CARELESS TALK.

Mark stared up at it for several minutes. Truly a museum piece which would fetch several hundred dollars in the trendy California flea markets. The other two posters were carrying basically the same message, one a black, murky ocean with a man's terrified face and hand only visible before it went down. On this one in solid black letters it read SOMEONE TALKED.

"That's my favorite." It was Cass, standing directly behind him, cradling her portable radio, pointing to the lowest poster curled up on itself.

With a smile he acknowledged her presence, glad she was with him, and stepped forward and carefully uncurled the poster to find a Norman Rockwell cocker spaniel with enormously sad brown eyes resting his head on the back of a chair, his muzzle resting atop a sailor's middy. Behind, on the wall, was a red-edged gold star.

Mark stood back and surveyed all three relics from the past, grim reminders of those conflict-ridden days, then walked past Cass into the chapel itself where the dazzling multicolored sunbeams were streaming in countless variations through the windows. "It's in almost perfect condition," he marveled, walking slowly down the long center aisle. Hymnals were still stuffed in pockets on the back of each pew, and now he spied a stack of what appeared to be programs or bulletins near the end of one of the back pews, as though an usher had handed them out only yesterday and had placed the excess on that bench.

Curious, he started toward them, then suddenly changed his mind and continued to stand at the edge of the long center aisle and look at them at the far end. A few had spilled over from the neat stack. Again he felt a compulsion to retrieve one and felt something else as well, a deep and powerful instinct which suggested he would do better to stay away from them.

What the hell? They were just abandoned programs, that's all. What difference did it make?"

"Mark, you all right?"

Apparently his private battlefield had become visible to Cass. He was aware of her coming up on his left side, bringing the music closer. He couldn't identify the song now. It didn't matter. He was beginning to feel a curious lassitude, which commenced somewhere low on the back of his head and moved steadily down his neck and out over his shoulders. The creeping numbness was not unpleasant, like the threshold to oblivion following a couple of good stiff vodka sours.

"Mark, did you hear me?"

Quickly he reached out and grasped the back of the near pew and leaned against it for a moment and felt the polished smooth wood grow cold beneath his hands as though he were grasping a cake of ice.

"Come on, sit down for a moment," Cass urged in soft consideration that moved him greatly. She seemed so concerned, so worried.

"I'm . . . sorry," he gasped, feeling peculiarly breathless. He sat heavily on the edge of the pew.

Abruptly he turned about, despite the pounding in his head, and saw Cass just exiting through the vestibule at the rear of the chapel. "Hey, where are you going?" he called after her.

Curiously, she put a finger to her lips, as though to indicate he didn't have to shout, then stepped back in the direction where Mark sat, just a step, no more. "Water," she whispered in a massive stage whisper. "There's water around here someplace, fresh water. I'll get you some."

"Don't. It's not . . ."

But she was gone before he could stop her. With strange reluctance he turned back around to confront the empty chapel, the weakness still with him but not as pronounced. Seated or standing, just a few minutes to catch his breath, that's all.

Yet in a curious way he was glad she'd given him these few

193

moments. A few, that was all he'd wanted. This place had belonged to his father. It might be fun to call his mom tonight and tell her that he'd visited the chapel on the base.

He closed his eyes briefly to rest them and thought now he heard something at the back of the chapel. Cass returning? As he glanced eagerly in that direction he started to his feet, using the back of the pew in front of him for leverage, wanting to demonstrate to her that he was fully restored, ready to push on.

But at the exact time he commenced his forward movement, he simultaneously looked up and saw what appeared to be a woman seated in the front pew, a prim black hat perched on her head. The hat appeared to be veiled but he couldn't be certain. Seeing her, Mark felt his pulse accelerate, then mysteriously stop. Even as he stared at her, she seemed to slip in and out of focus, her bowed head and slim shoulders blending liquidly with the shadows.

Mark blinked again, still more than willing to believe it was an optical illusion of some sort. But she was real, for now he saw her bend over as though tired or grieving.

Slowly, carefully, he sat back down, feeling strangely like an interloper. For God's sake, was the chapel still used? By a local church, perhaps, or as a private place of worship for people from the town? Could he slip out without the woman seeing him? Her mood was growing clearer every moment. She was quietly distraught and there was something else different about her. Her hat. Few women wore hats now, even to church, but no one wore hats like that, the kind that perched forward. Pillboxes, his mother had called them. She'd worn them.

Along with this interior warning came a brief, though potent, surge of anger. Was it Cass again up to her tricks? Was she playing games? She'd slipped out several minutes ago—more than enough time to have put on the hat and the black suit coat and God knows what else. Cass, of course. With the realization came relief, though neither had done much to ease the mystery. Why was she so insistent on playing with the ghosts of the base?

He started to lean back in the pew when suddenly the old wood creaked. He froze, not really wanting to seek her attention just yet. At that moment of intense scrutiny of the back of the woman's head, it occurred to him that Cass must have slipped on a wig, along with the hat. The hair that was spilling out beneath the pill box from a high pompadour was auburn, thick and wavy, a luxuriant head of hair that bore no resemblance to Cass's short, fair, close-cropped hair.

Though his eyes burned from his intense scrutiny and though

194

he would have loved to have closed them momentarily, now he didn't dare, for fear some new mystery would appear.

The sound—so faint—sent new tremors across the back of his shoulders. He looked sharply up toward the plain square pulpit, though such a sound did not belong in a pulpit. It could not possibly have originated there. There, he heard it again, unmistakable this time. A baby! A baby's fretful cry.

He leaned slowly out into the center aisle and saw near the front pew—a mere arm's reach from the grieving woman in black—a large, deep blue and white baby carriage. At that exact moment the woman's arm reached for the side of the carriage, and, though her head was still bowed, indicating she was concentrating on something in her lap or on her private grief, her hand commenced gently to rock the baby carriage, a soothing vibration which ultimately calmed the fretful infant concealed inside.

Where had they come from?

That thought persisted over all others. They had not been here when he'd first entered the chapel. He could swear to it. He'd seen the woman only shortly after Cass had left.

"Cass?"

To his own surprise he called out the name and heard the echoing vibration of his own voice and wondered why it sounded so loud. He had not intended to speak that loudly. He looked up toward the front of the chapel to see if the woman had heard him and, if so, if she would respond. From where he sat he was unable to discern any change in the slant of the downward angle of her head. In fact, even that one hand did not miss a beat in rocking the baby carriage.

As his apprehension increased, he began to lose confidence in his theory that the woman was Cass in a different "costume." He supposed there was always a possibility that people from town occasionally came out here.

He turned restlessly in the pew and glanced back toward the vestibule. He wanted very much to leave, but for some reason was reluctant to do so. For one thing, he didn't want to call attention to himself.

At that moment he heard the door open and close softly behind him, heard steps move several feet across the wooden floor, then heard—

Nothing.

Again he looked sharply over his shoulder, and his eyes focused on the large archway which separated the vestibule from the body of the chapel. If it wasn't Cass—

But then he saw her, that field of a white shirt, her marvelous

195

and unique face looking back at him with a bland, almost passive look, and of course the ever-present radio was still clutched in her left arm, though it was silent now.

When she saw him, a rewarding expression of pleasure crossed her face. "I couldn't find any water," she called out, full voice. "Not nearby. But I know where . . ." Her voice, like his earlier, seemed to reverberate endlessly about the chapel.

He lifted a finger to his lips and then pointed quickly toward the front of the chapel. He looked back toward the arched doorway to see if Cass had seen them yet, the black-veiled woman and the baby carriage. She had. He'd not seen such an expression on her face before. Usually jaunty and filled with a kind of inner aplomb, now it was her turn to gape. Her face seemed to lose its color. One hand moved slowly to cover her mouth, and over that barrier he saw her eyes grow wide. It lasted only a moment, as though, despite her strong emotion, she didn't want him to see it and interpret it.

She turned and, without a word, ran from the vestibule.

He started to call after her but changed his mind and instead left the pew from the right, circled back by the stack of abandoned programs, snagged one and stuffed it in his back pocket, then took the vestibule running. Outside he noticed the golden glow from the cottonwood grove had faded, leaving only a rim of light around everything.

"Cass?"

From the top step he looked in all directions for the white shirt and detected it through the grove of trees; she was poised on her bike in the street, he assumed.

As he started down the steps he took a final backward look into the chapel as though he were capable of seeing around the angle of the vestibule and into the church itself. Who was she? He had no idea, but it was at the top of the list of questions to ask Cass. She had seen something.

"Cass, are you all right?" he called ahead, hurrying around the cottonwoods, keeping his eyes fixed on that small figure in the oversized white shirt straddling her bike. She didn't respond—but he didn't really expect her to. Not yet. She might not even have heard him, though now he was almost even with her, only a few feet separating them.

"Are you all right, Cass? She scared hell out of me as well. You know what I thought? I thought it was you playing games. You know, in a costume. Where did she come from? Who was she and how did she get in without . . . ?"

196

Cass appeared to look at him during this excited tirade, then, while he was still talking, she reached over to the basket of the bike and flipped on the radio. Without offering a response of any kind, she hoisted herself up on the bike's seat and started a slow, wobbly pedaling—which nonetheless separated them instantly—putting distance between them.

"Cass? Did I say something?" He broke off when he saw her circling back to where he still stood on the pavement. As she disappeared behind him, he asked, "Why were you afraid? Did you know who it was?"

"I wasn't afraid." This defiant response was delivered directly in front of him and the bike stopped. She touched her feet to the ground, though she still clutched the handlebars.

"You could have fooled me," he chided gently, recalling the wide, fixed eyes, her hand covering her mouth, as though to stifle a scream before it left her throat.

"Yes, I know her," she announced defiantly. "And you should, too."

Puzzled, he looked down at her and was on the verge of asking for clarification when she added, her voice low, as though someone might be listening, without inflection or tone, "She is my mother."

Then she was pedaling again, circling him once while she found her center of balance, then slowly disappearing into the night.

Still too stunned to respond, he tried to call after her and couldn't.

"Cass, where are you? Please come back! I can't see . . ."

But she was gone into the night, leaving him alone on the dark road. Through the cottonwood trees he could see the mysterious light coming from the chapel, a multicolored light, as if some illumination were spilling through the stained glass. Then he heard music, organ music. It was very close and loud and growing louder.

He looked back through the trees toward the chapel. The light spilling from all of the windows seemed to have increased, as though someone had turned up all the lights inside. At the same time the organ swelled, filling the quiet night where he stood.

He found himself trembling and thought first that he was cold, but the seizure had nothing to do with body temperature, rather it was in the music, a stately version of "Rock of Ages."

He took a few steps back in the direction from which he'd come and halted, staring through the trees toward the chapel. Al-

197

though good sense told him not to, he started back down the rounded drive, trying to see through the trees to the chapel itself, where now he saw the large front doors open, the spill of light even brighter, though he still could not see movement.

And then he could. Not directly, but in the passing shadows which disappeared and reappeared on the nearest rectangle of light, as though there were a great deal of shifting about inside the chapel.

He continued on around the curved drive, breaking his pace as he saw something else which arrested his attention. Now, standing in the open front door of the chapel, he saw a man, his arms braced on either side of the door, his visibility enhanced by the fact that he was wearing Navy dress whites. He appeared to stand there for a moment, arms braced, head slumped forward in a bizarre crucified position, as though he weren't feeling well or suffering from some deep and internal grief. Then abruptly he dropped the pose and turned slowly back into the chapel. At the last minute he closed the double doors behind him, a gesture which left the front of the chapel in darkness, only the light spills on either side alternating in the solid fabric of night.

Mark held back on the edge of the open space which led to the front of the chapel. What exactly was going on inside he had no idea, but it scared him.

Then he heard something behind him and turned on it.

It hadn't been footsteps. Something else. Like a sudden breeze rippling the cottonwoods. Or wings. That was it. It sounded more like wings, something swooping in from behind and suddenly changing its mind and darting skyward again.

He looked up at a sharp angle and saw low-hanging, boiling clouds—a night storm was imminent—but saw nothing else, nothing that might have made that sound.

Now he drew back into the grove of cottonwoods. From this vantage point he glanced back toward the chapel, hearing nothing but watching those curious spills of light on either side, four identical rectangles resting on the ground, as though the chapel inside was completely illuminated.

Weary of this splintered evening and his cartwheeling emotions, for several moments he wanted very much to throw open those double doors and confront the light source and the people who'd mysteriously gathered. For what purpose he had no idea.

Then he heard it again, that nonhuman sound. Something behind him. He could feel the displacement of air, like a small window fan. If he moved into the grove of trees, he'd diminish his visibility to zero.

Then get out. Move out.

This voice was insistent and seemed to be quite agitated. At the moment he considered heeding it, something swooped so close to him he was forced to dodge back. In the process his shoe caught on a root. In the split second before he fell, he reached frantically out on either side in a futile attempt to restore his center of balance—and failed—falling backward with such force that his head struck something hard and unyielding and for several seconds all he heard was a high-pitched, persistent siren joining the organ music, and saw nothing save the darkness which was brilliantly outlined in vivid reds and blues and greens.

Reflexively he groaned and rolled to one side, his arms and hands moving to the throb on the back of his head. At that moment he heard the sound again. Like a low rush of wind, starting a distance away and picking up speed and sound as it drew nearer. From the rush of wind he now heard something else as well, like someone whimpering. Not human, he'd never heard a human make that sound. This was something else. And he smelled something as well, something acrid and rancid.

Still alert despite his throbbing head, he heard the curious sound growing louder. Sensing its approach, he rolled quickly to the left, and as he did he felt the tip of something brush against his arm. Though still incapacitated by the fall, his instincts suggested that he get out. Immediately!

As he pulled himself to his knees he looked up at the boiling night sky beyond the grove of trees, thinking whatever had approached him with such force would have to cross that part of the sky. But he saw nothing except for the low-hanging and fast-moving clouds themselves.

Leave!

The advice was strong and persistent. Though he felt an equally strong compulsion to stay and confront whatever it was in the night sky that seemed to object to his presence here, nonetheless he rose unsteadily to his feet and was just attempting the first step when he heard it returning. It seemed to be coming faster this time.

Frightened now by what he could not see, let alone understand, he moved deeper into the trees, thinking the dense foliage would afford him a degree of protection. As he turned back toward the street which led in front of the grove of trees, he saw something. The white shirt was familiar and highly visible, as was the straddled position on the bike.

"Mark, are you still in there?"

Never had he been so happy to hear her voice nor to see her.

199

"Here!" he called out, and increased his steps through the trees, cutting a straight path through the shadows to the road beyond. "Cass, I'm here!" he called again.

In the echo of his own voice he listened carefully for the sound of whatever it was that had—

"Where did you go?" Cass asked now. "I got clear to the infirmary, to the sick bay, thinking you were right behind me, talking all the way, when I looked back and couldn't find you. Mark!"

Something—the fall backward striking his head, the recent heavy fear, the sense of events conspiring, of unexplained mysteries—all these took a toll, and he stumbled forward out of the edge of the trees and went heavily down on his knees and found he could not immediately rise. Something had drained him of all vitality.

This had prompted her cry of alarm. With secret pleasure he saw her drop her bike in the center of the road and hurry toward him, her voice, face and manner rewarding and caring. "Mark, are you alright? Where have you been? I thought you were right behind me. I really did. I kept talking but you . . . Are you ill? You don't look so good."

Still on his knees, Mark reached one hand back to the place where his head had struck something hard in his backward fall. In the cool, chill light of a moon sliver he saw a dark substance coating the tips of his fingers.

She saw it as well. "Mark, what did you do?"

At first he didn't reply, occupied as he was with listening for that curious rush which had recently terrorized him. All he heard now was the deep silence of night itself. Even the organ inside the chapel had fallen silent. The chapel.

"Cass, look." Still on his knees he pointed back to the place where only a few moments before he'd seen windows brightly lit and shadows crossing in front of them. "Do you see it?"

Then he hung his head over, still occupied with that damp, sticky stain on his fingers and the corresponding stickiness on the back of his head. Through his hair he felt the goose egg slowly rising, split at the exact center from the collision with what must have been a rock.

He waited patiently for her astonishment, giving her all the time she needed to deal with the mystery. As his fear receded, cool, comforting reason rushed in. Perhaps there was no mystery to it at all. Perhaps groups from town came out here from time to time, people who at some point in their lives had been connected with the Navy in general and this base in particular.

"Do you see?" he repeated when she still had not responded.

"W-what?" she stammered softly, her focus rapidly shifting between the place where he knelt and the abyss of blackness beyond as though she wasn't looking in the right direction.

"The chapel. Don't you see the lights? There's someone inside. Lots of people. I saw them." He broke off as she rose slowly to her feet, gratified that at last she'd seen and understood. He started to go with her but changed his mind and now wished that she would return as well. Whatever it was that had attacked him might attack her. "Cass, come on. Let's . . ."

As he looked over his shoulder he was startled to discover that he couldn't see her. He whirled about quickly, ignoring the rising bump on his head. Then he saw her about thirty feet into the grove, that blessed beacon of her white shirt still serving him well.

But something else now caught and held his attention—the total darkness coming from the chapel, that direction as yawning and black as every other. No light coming from any source, within or without.

Stunned, he dragged himself slowly to his feet and was aware of her coming back, drawing near on his left. With all his attention now focused on the absence of light, the absence of movement, of everything which earlier he had seen clearly, he said,

"I don't . . . understand."

"It's nothing, Mark."

"Nothing, hell!" he exploded and felt the goose egg explode as well and quickly clamped his hand atop his head as though he were trying to hold the lid on a volcano. "I swear, Cass, not ten minutes ago there were lights inside, so bright as to cast shadows all around, and I saw someone standing in the door, and you saw . . ."

"I told you who you saw."

Had she? Then he remembered that bit of idiocy. "How could it be your mother?" he demanded, suddenly angry.

"She comes out here quite often," Cass said softly, something in her voice that suggested she was trying to deal rationally and calmly with a madman.

"Why?" he demanded, confronting her at the edge of the trees. He saw something white in her hand now, like a folded piece of paper. But it wasn't the paper he was quarreling with and it really wasn't her. It was just the conspiracy of mysteries which had to stop—and soon. Something had to be logically explained, the matter closed.

"Why?" he repeated more forcefully. "Why does she come out here? And why didn't you speak to her? 'Hi, Mom,' something like

201

that. And who's the baby? And what was the baby carriage all about?"

It wasn't that he'd completed his tirade. It was just that temporarily he'd run out of breath. Then, too, he didn't really want to take it out on Cass. Still, if she couldn't answer his questions, maybe she could answer a few that pertained to her own mother. Was that asking too much?

She stepped closer to him until less than three feet were separating them. She was so small, so vulnerable and now so sad, as though someone had just delivered a death message from which she had not yet recovered. She continued to finger the white paper in her hand. Where it had come from, he had no idea.

"Mark, I'm sorry," she said softly—and answered nothing.

"For what?"

"For what happened."

What did she mean?

"My mother was here because . . . of this." Slowly she extended the piece of paper.

He looked at it, foolishly trying to determine its nature without touching it. For some reason he didn't want to take it.

"It's yours," she added. "You picked it up when you left the chapel. I saw it in your back pocket before we got separated. It must have fallen out when you fell."

Her voice was so soft and extraordinarily musical and so filled with concern that after a few moments he felt strong enough to take the paper, whatever its nature. He couldn't recall picking it up.

"My mother was very fond of him, too, though no one believed it at the time."

Nothing she was saying was making sense. At last he reached for the paper, thinking it would help.

She continued speaking, moving closer, bringing her unique and welcome comfort with her. "They were so close, you know. All of them. Surely your mother told you. My mother didn't tell me much, but my grandfather did before he died."

He felt the thickness of the folded paper—program of some sort—and started to examine it immediately, but couldn't quite bring himself to take his eyes off her face. She was so close and in the light of the moon extraordinarily beautiful. Besides, he still hadn't understood a word she was saying.

"Cass, I'm . . . afraid I . . ."

"Our parents," she said at last with a hint of mock scolding, as though he should have known all along. "They were good friends, the best of friends. Our fathers particularly. When your father was killed, mine . . ." She broke off, as though suffering a momentary embarrassment or else afraid she'd said too much.

Mark stared down on her, his attention torn between her closeness itself and the fact of what she had said.

"Did your mother ever . . .?" Cass began, and apparently felt no compunction to finish. "If you saw anything in the chapel tonight it was probably caused by . . . that."

Mark lifted the folded progam and held it up and discovered it was too dark to read it. For several seconds he tried to catch a suitable angle in the moonlight, but the program remained a gray blur. All at once a small, limited eye of light shone on him from the street and he looked up, startled, to see Cass straddling her bike again, the light coming from the front of the bike, obviously for night riding.

"This may help," she called out.

He felt strangely sheepish, so involved with minor mysteries that he hadn't even heard her walk away. Again he glanced down at the program which remained gray and liquid-appearing. He took a final look over his shoulder at the darkened and quiet chapel, feeling somehow that if he left the trees he'd have to leave that mystery forever unsolved.

"Come to the light, Mark." The soft, compelling voice was Cass's.

He started moving toward the limited light and the girl behind it.

"Here, hold it down. Then you can see."

As he drew near the light, Cass angled it lower, the better to focus on the program. Mark obliged and held it in the direct path of the light, seeing the U.S. Navy insignia embossed in blue and gold on the cover. There was printing along the bottom of the cover, but it was too small to read, despite the light.

"Inside," Cass prompted.

Again he obliged and opened the curling, yellowed pages and saw a printed order of worship, saw a listing of hymns and Scriptures. The service conducted by the Right Reverend some-one and dedicated to the memory of—

He blinked down on the name, thinking the dancing shadows and light had played tricks. He looked up at Cass, who in the limited light looked suddenly and mysteriously old, like a woman twice her age.

"It's your father's," she said simply, and incongruously smiled, as though struggling and failing to conceal a secret delight.

And that was the name he'd seen. Gerald Simpson. In that

instant Mark saw again, as he'd seen several times every day for a period which merely encompassed his whole life, the oil painting over the small terra-cotta mantel at home, those level eyes, that brow, that entire countenance which—rightly or wrongly—somehow suggested that the man behind it had never faltered under any condition.

"I am . . . sorry, Mark." It was Cass again, her voice filled with compelling sympathy. The secret delight—if it had ever been there at all—was gone now. Perhaps he'd imagined it. "It's the memorial service for your father. That's probably what you saw in the chapel."

He looked up at the insane suggestion. "I don't understand. How could I have seen something that happened twenty years ago?"

In response to his perfectly logical question, she laughed as though he'd said the most stupid thing possible. "Oh, Mark, really! Surely you know better than that. Of course you can see what happened twenty years ago. Thirty years ago, for that matter. One hundred and thirty. Everyone can. Nothing ever gets permanently lost, just buried under the false challenges of every day."

As she spoke he looked back down on the program, feeling very strange about holding this important part of his father's life and death in his hands, yet feeling—nothing.

"And what do you think it is that you're supposed to feel?" she asked quietly, uncannily keeping pace with his thoughts. "My father's memorial service was held in this exact same place a few months later. Same program, as a matter of fact. Only the name was changed." Only on the last sentence had her voice grown hard and bitter.

Again Mark looked up from reading, feeling a need for a break from the events of the evening, from her, and yet dreading when she would leave him and say good night.

By way of reply to his close scrutiny, she nodded, slightly defensive, as though he'd challenged her. "Alec Manning," she announced simply. "Surely your mother has mentioned his name?"

Mark nodded. He'd seen the name in one of the old photo albums—four poised people standing before someone else's camera in front of a low, squat bungalow, a trellis in front and assorted lawn furniture behind them. All four looked uneasy and sober. For some reason they had looked uncomfortable with each other. Though he felt stupid asking, he asked anyway. "Then you are . . . ?"

204

"Cass Manning." She smiled in the most captivating manner. "Our fathers were . . ."

". . . the best of friends." Her grin was infectious and he caught it. For a moment, despite the grim twists the evening had taken—dead fathers and dead wars—all was forgotten in their smiles, their closeness, with only the small bike light between them. "Cass Manning," he repeated, growing more and more mesmerized by who she was and by her beauty, at the same time afraid to recognize it or move on it in any way. Like the interior warfare he'd suffered all his life, some powerful force deep within him simultaneously cursed and rejoiced, loved and hated, praised and condemned.

"Is anything wrong?" she asked, apparently seeing the conflict on his face.

For want of an honest answer, he backed away from the light and held up the memorial program. "It's so . . . coincidental."

She shook her head and at the same time wheeled her bike over to the side of the road and laid it down carefully. The limited eye of light hung suspended only inches above the earth.

"Nothing's truly coincidental," she suggested, walking slowly back toward him. "Not that someone grand and divine sits above us and plots our lives and sees to it that we execute them according to that plot. *We* plot them, all aspects of our lives, all aspects of us. We are the grand and divine thing that sits above us."

He listened closely, aware of her drawing near, but aware, too, of what she was saying and, in a way, surprised to hear it coming from that inexperienced face. "Who told you all of that?" he challenged directly, smiling.

She hesitated only a moment before answering. "My grandfather." Gently she removed the memorial program from his hand and placed it on the ground. "Come on," she invited, and commenced to pull him back into the thick grove of cottonwoods, now dark. "Did you know these trees were here long before the Navy came? In fact my grandfather told me that probably they were close to two hundred years old. Can you imagine that?"

At some point, as though confident he would follow after her, she drew free of his hand and walked ahead, but this time by only a few feet, making certain that they more or less kept pace, and continued to talk in a nostalgic way of the times her grandfather had brought her out here and told her this and that.

"I thought your mother . . . ?" Mark interrupted.

"No," she answered quickly. "She was always too busy or not feeling well. She's been ill off and on since my father died."

205

"My mother told me that she'd disappeared."

"Not disappeared. Just went away. She was . . . in mourning."

Mark understood that, recalling that curious and grieving left eye of his mother's. For a brief and poignant moment he saw the two tragedies of war compounded, not just in the waste of death itself, but in all those peripheral lives—wives, daughters, sons—forever altered, changed.

"I did love him," Cass mourned.

Mark assumed she was speaking of her father, Alec Manning. "Did you . . . know him? Really know him, I mean. I can't even remember mine, except for photos and what my mother has . . ."

"I didn't mean my father," she broke in, suddenly stern. "No, of course not. I didn't even have photographs. My mother destroyed them all. I was talking about my grandfather."

"Why? I mean why did she . . . ?"

"Come on, let's sit." She patted a place beside her where she had relaxed against the trunk of a gigantic cottonwood.

Still remembering past hazards of this grove of trees, he looked about and listened for whatever it was he'd heard earlier and searched through the thick foliage for lights—ghostly or otherwise—coming from the chapel and saw and heard nothing. But he still felt it, a warning as strong as he'd ever felt, all nerve endings on the alert.

"Come on, Mark. Let's sit. Just for a minute. I've waited all week to see you and it will be another week before . . ."

"Why?" he objected, easing down beside her, pleased that the waiting had been as unpleasant for her as it had been for him, distressed they both would have to serve that bizarre penance again.

In answer to his urgent "Why?" she leaned back against the trunk and closed her eyes. In the cold light of the moon she looked—dead. Eyes closed, face too relaxed.

"Why, Cass?" he repeated. "How would it hurt? Have coffee in the afternoon. A quick lunch, a sandwich at Uncle Polly's. How would it hurt?"

"Uncle Polly's caught on fire tonight." She smiled softly, her eyes still closed.

Stunned, he raised up to his knees. "Was that the . . . sirens I heard earlier?"

To his question she nodded, head back, and did not open her eyes.

"Was it bad? The fire, I mean."

She shrugged. "I don't know. I didn't hang around."

"Was Uncle Polly all right?"

She nodded. "Oh, I'm sure he was. You'd be surprised at Uncle Polly's ability to survive."

It seemed a curious thing to say, and Mark started to ask questions, but he really didn't want to. She seemed disinclined to answer them and he was beginning to fall under the spell of her face, bathed in cool-marble moonlight.

"My mother had been to see him earlier," she murmured. "They're old friends, you know."

"Was that before she came out here?"

Again she nodded. There was a moment of silence and then she said, "She's angry, you know. With me."

"Why?"

Cass laughed softly. "Because this wasn't part of her plan."

"What plan?"

Suddenly the relaxed expression was gone. In its place he saw wide-eyed terror, as though he'd just spoken the most unimaginable threat.

"What's the matter, Cass? Don't be afraid of her. I'd like to meet her. Could I?"

"No," she whispered, as though the trees had listening ears. "No, you must never!"

"Why?" he challenged, trying to talk her out of her fear or at least try to find its cause. The transition had been incredibly fast. One minute relaxed, almost sleepy, the next—

"No, Mark. I beg you, don't try. Don't ever try. She . . . No, please!" As her fear increased she became incoherent.

He reached for her hands and felt them cold and trembling. She was on her knees now, as though she were ready to bolt from the grove of trees as well as the horrible suggestion. In his attempt to ease her fear, he reached out quickly and enclosed her in his arms, drew her close and shut his eyes against the sensation of her body pressed against his.

"Don't, Cass, please," he begged as he heard tears. He was completely baffled by her strange reaction to his simple request.

At some point the tears abated but she continued to cling to him, as though she'd not known so much love and closeness in her life that she could go about turning her back on it.

Nor had he. As he felt the first objecting ache in his knees to the rough terrain and knew that hers must be objecting in the same manner, he eased down onto earth and took her with him until they were lying sideways in each other's arms, no objection at all coming from her. In fact, quite the contrary. She moved closer,

207

nestling into his arms, her breathing growing more relaxed, though he could still feel tension in her body, a rigidity which suggested that she still was trying to deal with the residue of the deep and abiding fear that had overtaken her.

As he relaxed he felt soft grasses beneath his head and considered asking further questions but changed his mind. No need to upset her further—not now. There would be time for questions— if they were still important. For now he could feel her so close to him, could hear the shuddering residue of her sobs. She seemed so frail, so vulnerable and, compounding this, he realized how similar both their childhoods must have been—brought up by a wounded mother, a ghost of a father, an almost constant funereal atmosphere and a grief that was never quite understood or assuaged.

"Mark, I'm sorry." This delicate apology came from the hollow next to him into which she had wedged herself.

"For what?" he challenged softly. "It was none of your doing. Nor mine."

She seemed to think on this for a moment. Then, in a voice that was scarcely more than a whisper, she asked, "Do you like me?" The inquiry was simple, childlike and moving.

"You know I do," he replied with equal simplicity.

"No, I don't. I never know," she murmured.

He heard despair and a degree of weariness belonging to middle or old years.

"Well, I do," he said, and enclosed her more tightly and felt her return the favor, felt as well a pleasurable pain inside his groin. *Move carefully,* an interior voice advised him. The need was there for him. Did hers match it? "Cass . . ."

At the exact moment he decided to practice patience and self-restraint, he felt her hand pull loose from his embrace and press lightly on down against his stomach, a singular sensation that did far more than a mere tightening of skin. Did she know what she was doing? She seemed at times so young, so inexperienced.

Slowly she raised up on one elbow and looked down on him. In the half-light of the fully risen moon he could see her clearly, on her face not a sign of her recent tears. "The first time I saw you I thought you were the most handsome man I'd ever seen."

As she leaned across him, he could feel her breasts on his chest and felt as well a gentle pressure of her hip against his thigh. In an attempt to ease his increasing discomfort—or at least postpone it until he could make sure he was reading the right signals—he laughed. "That's quite a compliment, considering the first time you saw me I'd just been dragged half drowned from . . ."

"Oh, no. I saw you long before that," she smiled down on him.

"When?"

She hesitated for a moment as though aware she was on the verge of saying the wrong thing. At last she spoke. "When you first entered the base. I mean that's when I first saw you. Before you started that crazy run."

He had had no idea she'd been watching him. Now he wondered if she'd seen everything—obviously she had—the numerous stops and starts, the sprawl in front of sick bay when he'd thought he'd heard a voice call out—

"Did you . . . ?"

"No. I saw you come onto the base and I watched you for about ten minutes. Then I split and went on down to Coffin Pond. That's where I go almost every morning."

"Why?"

She shrugged, and her fingers commenced to trace a line across his forehead and down the left side of his face. "Why what?"

"Why do you go to Coffin Pond?"

"Why do you run?"

"I enjoy it."

"Well?" She smiled down on him, leaned farther over him, and now her finger was moving across his lips.

The soft sensation on his face was beginning to affect regions below. He still had to know. Was she teasing him? There was something childlike in her face, her manner, her gestures.

"Cass . . .?"

Before he could speak, she leaned over and kissed him, very chastely and sweetly, her lips tightly closed, just resting on his, a child's kiss.

Reflexively—for the sensation had been too sweet for it to end—he lifted his hand to the back of her head and held her fast and raised up to meet her lips again. This time he did not find them chastely closed, found them open and warm and moist. This kiss differed vastly from the first, and he pulled her atop him, felt her legs separate over him, felt her straddle him and felt a threatening explosion in his groin.

Apparently she was feeling the same discomfort, for she raised up, though she never took her eyes off his face—nor he hers. As each fumbled with buttons and zippers, the moon slid behind a cloud and for a moment he lost the blessed specifics of her face.

But when she returned to him and brought the moon with her, it wasn't her face that held him enthralled. Along with the rolled-up jeans she'd also discarded her oversized white shirt. For a brief moment in the ivory patina of moonlight, she resembled a statue come to life and standing directly over him.

Stunned by her beauty and suffering now more than ever that enviable discomfort that precedes sexual release, he ceased to wonder if this was "the time" or if she knew what she was doing. He was certain that she did. There was nothing naive or uncomprehending about the woman standing over him. Where the child had gone, he had no idea, and at this moment didn't care.

Slowly pushing himself up as though to greet such beauty halfway, he found himself on his knees before her, an appropriate position considering the awe he felt for such flawless artistry. Only in passing did it occur to him that it would be almost impossible to conceal this body in jeans and shapeless white shirts.

But she had, for though her face was obscured in the shadows, he knew this to be Cass, sweet Cass who'd saved his life, who had grown up and somehow survived the funeral parlor of her childhood, and who now knelt before him, her face a flawless cameo of love and need and mutual desire.

No words were spoken. Their hands reached out as if by mutual consent and commenced a savory and delicious expedition, both starting the pleasurable journey on the face, a gentle touching of lips once more, as though their instincts had warned them to pace themselves, lest they mar the journey. So in twin gestures, as though in some past life this mutual seduction had been choreographed and was now simply being reenacted, both their hands reached out, their fingers tracing the lines of the jaw where it broke to accommodate the mouth.

He saw her smile, a delighted smile of full pleasure, as though only in this kind of worship could the splintered present and grief-ridden past and mysterious future be made whole and at all palatable.

"You are so . . . beautiful," he whispered, his hands moving ahead of hers on the slim white column of her neck now. As he stroked it he felt a curious and momentarily disarming image. He thought for an instant he saw the skeleton structure of the neck, the smooth ivory flesh fallen away, only the bleached white bones of vertebrae visible. Yet to his touch it was smooth and soft as velvet.

Then she was keeping pace as well. As her hands glided liquidly down his throat and pressed against his chest, he felt the tension continue to build. He'd never enjoyed such pain before. The lighthearted sexual encounters which had taken place on the still-warm night sand of Miramar Beach had been, for the most part, exercises in fumbling, always a degree of embarrassment, seldom more than the release of a brief orgasm. What he sensed was about to happen here bore no relationship to those earlier experiences.

While he was still concentrating on the playful manner in which her hands encircled his nipples, the index finger of both hands moving in a merry-go-round gesture, causing skin to tighten and grow hard all the way up the back of his neck, and, still enjoying these unique sensations, his hands made the staggering discovery of her breasts.

For several moments he was fearful that the playful and deliberate seduction was over. Need as hot and as pressing as any he'd ever felt in his life exploded within. He was only partially aware of his hands rapidly covering her breasts, not quite able to cover such fullness, so firm yet soft to the touch, rippling beneath his palms, seeming to press back as though they were created for the sole purpose of being touched and fondled and suckled. Now emerging beneath the palms of his hands he felt the small soft cores growing hard and erect. His fingers brushed against each nipple to confirm their erection and at the same time he heard a soft intake of breath and was delighted to know her suffering was keeping pace with his own.

Unable to resist, sorry if it was premature, he bent over, took her right breast and closed his lips around that small hardness. At the same time her hands, as though as weary as he of deliberation and pause, moved nonstop to the area of his greatest discomfort. As both her hands closed about him, he abandoned her breast— not through any desire for abandonment, but because her touch had ignited a heat within him so powerful that he could feel it spread in all directions.

Then she was falling gently backward, taking him with her, still holding on, guiding him down on top of her. As her hands fanned out over his back, he slipped into that dark warmth and kept going and only regretted the limitation of physiology, for while he had penetrated as deeply as the contour of her body would permit, still he tried for several thrusts to alter the nature of bone and muscle. Not until he heard her soft gasp did he realize he must be causing discomfort.

But as he raised himself up over her and looked down on her face, it wasn't discomfort he saw there. Her features, though

211

distorted, bore a sublime cast to them, as though she too wanted a deeper penetration. Supple and ingenious, she lifted her legs and wrapped them about his waist and arched. He discovered he could go deeper and deeper still, until his hot release came, as though someone were pulling all of gravity out of the world through the organs of their bodies.

The outcry was hers. He muffled his in her breasts. Just when he thought he could not endure the rushing waves of pain a moment longer, they commenced subsiding.

Slowly she lowered her legs and was content to wrap them around his buttocks, still anchoring him inside her. Her arms, which had been outflung at the height of orgasm, remained outflung. Her head turned once from right to left and then she lay still, as though dead.

But he could feel her heart beneath his cheek keeping pace with his own. He considered words but found his head empty, his tongue useless. Perhaps later.

For now, still inside her, he tried simultaneously to relish the comfort, yet did not want to put all his weight on her. In a few moments he would speak, would tell her of his love for her, would tell her that he had no intention of waiting a week before seeing her again. It really wasn't a matter for discussion. Nothing in the world mattered to him now but her, her presence, her face, her voice, this body.

"Cass?"

She said nothing, but tightly drew in one hand from its position and placed it on his lips and simultaneously lifted her thighs beneath him.

As he felt himself shift inside her, he also felt the tension begin to crest again. There were two more explosions, cries followed by a series of shudders which—like everything else—matched his, until at last it subsided. For several minutes he was limp atop her, until it occurred to him again that his weight was causing discomfort.

As he started to roll to one side, she reached out for his face, her hands clasped on either side to hold him fast and close. He could see her forehead, damp and shiny from the recent exertion. When at first she didn't speak but continued to gaze up at him with an expression he couldn't clearly read, he felt well content just to lie atop her, still coupled. What a unique sensation—to be buried so deeply inside her.

"Are you all right?" he inquired gently, finding her face even more beautiful than ever.

"I was about to ask the same of you," she smiled up at him. Her right hand was caressing his brow.

The sensation was such that he closed his eyes. "I love you," he whispered and gathered her to him. In the process he rolled to one side and took her with him and again felt her nestle in close beneath his arm. In this new position Mark found himself staring up into the limitless night sky covered with stars.

It reminded him of an old movie palace in Santa Monica; the artificial ceiling effect was the same, though in the case of the movie theater some of the stars had fallen.

"What are you thinking about?" she asked, almost sleepily, her voice drifting like liquid.

"Home," he answered honestly.

"The athletic dorm?"

"No," he laughed, "California. Have you ever been there?"

She shook her head. "I haven't been anyplace. My mother has, but . . ."

He found that an unusual claim for a Navy brat, but as she started to explain he remembered and understood. "Your mother was from town, wasn't she?"

Cass nodded and said nothing further, pushing closer against him. He could feel her shiver.

"You'd better get something on," he suggested, feeling very protective.

She scrambled up, retrieved her garments where she'd dropped them and, in the process, handed his over as well.

As he slowly commenced to pull on socks, he was still baffled by her refusal to talk about her family. She seemed to be more than willing to talk about her grandfather, but her mother and father were apparently nonpersons. He looked up with a question, and immediately canceled it in the beauty of watching her dress. Under the cold spotlight of the moon she still resembled a statue come to life, gracefully bending and stooping, the entire, normally mundane process rendered as beautiful as a ballet under her particular artistry.

"Is anything wrong?" she asked, suddenly noticing his attention, one arm just extending into the oversized arm of the white shirt.

As he had not yet commenced to dress, he continued to sit, feeling foolish, but still mesmerized to the point that nothing really mattered. "Nothing's wrong, I assure you," he smiled. "Nothing at all."

Apparently she sensed the fervor of his reply and, moving

more slowly now, drew on her shirt and began carefully to button it, something studied and childlike about her. He thought she would speak, but when she didn't, he did.

"I hope you don't think I plan to wait another full week before seeing you again."

Though the declaration was gently spoken, he filled his voice with enough edge and determination so she wouldn't mistake his vow for harmless chatter.

Dressed at last, she stood before him and ran her hands through her hair, using her fingers like a comb. Then she moved closer, less than two feet from him, and stood, hands on hips. "I think you'd better put your clothes on. That's what I think."

Slowly he obliged, regretful that she hadn't responded directly to his challenge. No matter. He'd pose it again in a minute. It was important for her to realize how important she was to him.

"Mark?"

He looked up as he drew on his slacks and saw her standing at the edge of the trees, staring toward the now darkened chapel.

"Were you . . . frightened by what you saw in the chapel?"

As he buckled his belt he thought her question unusual, particularly since her consistent role had been to reassure and make light of the unusual incidents that had happened to them out here. "Not frightened," he said, and realized in part it was a lie. He had been alarmed when, without warning, he'd seen the woman in the front pew. One minute the chapel had been empty, the next—

"Your mother," he said, drawing on his shirt, "she took me by surprise."

Even as he said it, it sounded strange, that "antique" lady who'd materialized in the front pew—who couldn't have been anybody's mother. He looked up from dressing to see Cass still standing at the edge of the trees, gazing toward the chapel and saying nothing.

"Why do you ask?" he said, sitting long enough to put on his shoes, then starting toward her.

She shrugged, though not once did she lift her eyes from the chapel, as though she were watching for something.

"What is it, Cass?" he asked, concerned about this change in her mood, although he knew now he should be getting used to it.

For several seconds she said nothing, but from where he stood he could see her as she glanced beyond to the chapel, her expression dark, as though everything she viewed was seen with a strange degree of contempt. "Sometimes I hate this place," she

214

murmured. "I really do. You asked me if I'd ever been to California. I've never been anyplace but here. This was my playground, my school, my bedroom. My grandfather used to bring me out here in my stroller and we'd . . ." Abruptly she broke off, as though unable or unwilling to speak further.

Moved by her indisposition, her vulnerability and her recent gift of herself to him, he put his arms around her shoulder and drew her close. To his delight she didn't object.

"Let me take you home," he whispered, close to her ear, wanting to get her out of the night chill, wanting a warm place for both of them to sit and talk.

But the words had no more than left his lips until she drew away from him and his suggestion. Without a word of explanation or apology, she started back through the trees in the opposite direction, moving toward the road and her abandoned bike and radio.

"Cass?"

But there was no response. For a moment he even lost track of her as she passed through the darkest part of the grove, then reappeared on the street side, moving with what appeared to be rapid and stoical determination.

"Cass, please . . ."

All at once his voice was drowned in a sudden blare coming from the radio. Apparently in an attempt to cancel his voice she'd simply flipped it on, uncaring what station. For a few seconds the once silent night was filled with the sounds of static and babble.

Frustrated by her mercurial moods—one minute receptive and vulnerable and the next angry and distant—he gave up trying to call to her and started after her, merely wanting her not to get too far ahead of him, as she'd done on occasions in the past, and then suddenly disappear.

The music first seemed to increase to a decibel level—much louder than he would have thought the old portable capable of achieving—then, without warning, it seemed to diminish gradually, as though—

"Cass, wait!" He'd just caught sight of the spokes of the wheel and knew she was pedaling away from him. "Cass, I must talk to you!" But now he could see her clearly, pedaling for all her might, as though she wanted nothing so much in the world as to escape from him, his presence, his voice. This had a devastating effect on him, the realization that, despite their recent closeness, he still could say things that could drive her away.

"Cass! Please!" he called again, but to no avail. The dark

215

vacuum that was the night road was as empty as though she'd never been there. Even the once blaring music was gone, silence covering everything as well as blackness, giving him the impression that he was utterly alone, had been all evening.

But he knew better than that, for he could still feel her, warm and receptive, and still longed for her. He started to call again and knew it would be futile. Finally, half in pursuit of her and partially just feeling the need to move, he started off down the darkened road in the direction of the North Gate. Only once did he look back toward the chapel to try once again to understand what had happened.

He *had* seen lights and movement and he *had* seen the woman seated on the front pew, her right hand gently rocking the baby carriage. He'd seen a man appear in the doorway and he'd seen lights. He had seen them all, and yet where had they gone?

The memorial program! Where was that? He wanted to keep it.

For a few seconds he felt in his pockets and looked about on the darkened pavement to see if it had dropped out of his pockets. Once he considered retracing his steps back into the trees to search for it there, but he changed his mind. For one thing, he didn't want to go back into the grove of trees. Not now. For another, he wanted very much to follow after Cass.

Of course he knew he didn't stand a chance of catching up with her—not with her on the bike and him on foot. He'd said something—what he had no idea—witlessly pushed too hard and too fast and he'd frightened her away. Slowly he started walking down the road, forgetting the lost memorial program in the new mystery of her totally unpredictable personality.

Suddenly he heard a loud report, a muffled, popping sound—like an exhaust or a gunshot. He froze, stopped by the unexpected sound which continued to reverberate endlessly through the still night.

He looked in all directions and saw varying degrees of blackness, the only clear light source that soft, diffuse and remote halo of light which sat in an arch in the northwestern sky which, of course, would be the lights of the town.

What had it been? Where had it come from? Again he searched the road ahead, behind and on either side and saw nothing and waited a moment to see if it would come again. When it didn't, he started on down the street, newly alert, trying to keep his mind off the recent and most gratifying closeness and on the various hazards of this night and this place.

Though he had been walking in a semi-relaxed state, now he

216

took his hands from his pockets and increased his speed and wondered if there was any other way off the base than through the North Gate. If not, then that meant that she was still up ahead someplace.

He increased his speed to a trot and thought how foolish this effort was. On her bike, she probably was off the base halfway back to the campus by now—or home. Wherever home was.

Breaking his recent vow to keep his mind off certain events and on the night, he almost stumbled before he saw it, the blown-out tire lying on the road, the rest of the bike dropped unceremoniously on the side of the road. As he hopped almost spastically on one foot in an attempt to avoid sprawling over the unexpected obstacle, he quickly regained his balance and looked down and back and saw it clearly.

Cass's bike abandoned. And there was the obvious explanation of what he'd just heard—the blown-out back tire, bits and shreds of rubber still hanging loose from the tire casing. As the fact of the damaged bike soaked in, a new thought amounting to an instant fear occurred.

Cass! Had she been hurt in the blowout? If she'd been traveling at any rate of speed she would have lost control and—

Quickly he hurried to the near ravine and looked down, holding his breath, half afraid of what he'd find and half afraid of what he wouldn't find.

But there was nothing in sight. Certainly not the oversized white shirt and rolled-up jeans—the peculiar mark and signature of the most appealing and fascinating girl he'd ever known. With the reaffirmation of love came a reaffirmation of urgency.

If she were on foot now—and maybe hurt—there was a possibility he could catch up with her, and on the walk back to the campus perhaps he could apologize for whatever it was he'd said that had frightened her or put her off—or whatever. He knew nothing for certain except the piercing need to see her again, to be with her, to touch her. It was as though their separation—instead of being one of approximately twenty minutes—seemed like twenty years.

Enough. Go after her. Find her and never let her out of your sight again.

So involved was he in this new and appealing emotion, he failed to hear the irrationality of his own words. All he wanted was to find her and hold her and keep her safe.

"Cass?" he called aloud, confident she still might be close enough to hear. "Cass, are you hurt?"

217

But there was no response, although once he thought he heard a very distant radio, growing fainter, as though it was being carried off into the night at a fast rate of speed.

Then he was running, hoping that if he could just overtake her they could recapture the perfect moments they had had earlier. Though the mysteries still plagued him, they now seemed less important than regaining the presence and love of Cass Manning. To that end, he increased his speed and raced off into the night, not knowing where he was going or where he would find her or if he would find her, but running anyway, like a man who had absolutely no choice.

Rafael's Shrimp Bar
Balboa, California

Brett Simpson sat alone at a window table for two and looked out over the Pacific Ocean, visible only in the cresting, crashing white foam which seemed to accelerate as the tide approached the shoreline, then, having spent itself on the sandy beach, drifted out again to rebuild its strength and regain momentum.

Despite the cheery jukebox playing a Cole Porter melody and the small but appealing fire crackling in the firewell, she felt twin tensions. One was the predominant and compelling one that had followed her all day, the one she'd awakened with this morning which—regardless of what she'd done—was with her still. What it was, she had no idea, this breathlessness, this pacing, this tension.

As though mesmerized, she continued to stare at the crashing waves and at the same time lifted her old-fashioned and sipped and kept her eyes averted from the rest of the small restaurant in the event she saw someone she knew. Which wasn't likely; she'd chosen Rafael's because she'd come here only once with Mark and enjoyed the privacy and quiet atmosphere.

She sipped again at the old-fashioned and briefly scolded herself. What was she in the process of becoming? One of those pathetic, nameless, faceless, middle-aged widows who frequented bars alone in search of—

Suddenly she blushed at her own thoughts and privately admitted she had thought of such a thing. A simple, uncomplicated sexual partner. An encounter, no commitments. No nothing. Just mutual gratification and, hopefully, satisfaction.

As she sipped again at her drink, she felt a raw heat move up her jawline over her cheekbones, hopefully to disappear into her hairline.

219

Yet she knew it hadn't been that need that had driven her here. Not that her loneliness wasn't painful and insistent, but she'd learned to accommodate it over the years in her club meetings and charitable work and, of course, in Mark himself. She looked down at her drink, amazed to see that it was almost gone.

Mark.

There was the cause. She'd awakened this morning with a terrible oppressive sense, the same she'd suffered at various intervals throughout his childhood and youth—when he'd gone off to Boy Scout camp the first time, and when he'd stayed to see that John Wayne Western over again and Brett feared he'd gotten lost or—worse—been kidnapped. As she foolishly resurrected old fears to join her new one, she again scolded herself and looked nervously about, afraid people were staring at her or capable of seeing her foolishness and commenting on the fact of her presence here, unescorted, drinking alone.

She momentarily closed her eyes and fondled her empty glass, wishing briefly that she'd stayed home. What had she hoped to accomplish sitting in a strange restauraunt? Actually, if she remembered correctly, she hadn't hoped to accomplish anything except the cessation of the tension she'd felt all day.

That had been what she'd wanted to escape from. Heaven only knew she'd tried to work it off during the course of the day. She'd done an early-morning, two-mile jog around the neighborhood—which hadn't helped her at all but, instead, had only served to remind her of Mark. They'd done the same jog together countless times.

It had been right after the jog that she'd tried to call him the first time. No answer.

Then she'd weeded the large back flower bed, pulled out all of the dead summer plantings, fed the soil and prepared the bed for autumn mums. Before she'd showered, she'd tried to call the dorm again. Still no answer.

A luncheon meeting of the Tuesday Book Review Club. She didn't even remember the book review now. She did remember Sally. She'd gone with Sally, who'd talked endlessly about her recent cruise in the Mediterranean and the lovely man she'd met from Indiana who had promised to call her when he was next in California.

The luncheon, instead of distracting, had merely compounded her depression. Midafternoon and she'd tried to call Mark at the dorm again. Still no answer. She'd checked the number with local information. The number had been right.

220

"Another cocktail, ma'am?"

She looked up, startled at the near voice, and saw a young waiter in a short white jacket lifting her empty old-fashioned glass.

"Yes," she said. Then with a caution that had marked her entire life, she added, "And a shrimp salad, please. No bread. Extra sauce."

"Sure," he grinned, and wrote nothing down but held up the empty glass. "Same thing here?"

She nodded and looked away, not wanting to get too friendly. One more drink and the salad and she'd return home and try to call Mark again. Someone would have to be there now around dinnertime.

The Cole Porter melody was over and someone punched up a mournful ballad—unrecognizable as far as Brett was concerned. When Mark had been home she'd more or less kept up with the rock scene, the new singers and their songs. Now she never even played the stereo and seldom turned on the radio, except for news and weather.

"Here you go. Here's your drink and the salad's on the way."

The voice, so near and sudden, startled her. She looked up to see the young waiter grinning down on her again, a fresh old-fashioned in his hand.

"Sorry," he murmured, apparently aware that he'd startled her.

She nodded and took the drink and saw no need for further conversation. Obviously he did.

"Are you . . . waiting for someone?" the boy asked.

"No," she replied, and heard the edge in her voice and did nothing to alter it.

"Just asking," the boy grinned.

She sensed an impudence, as if he knew that his question had caused discomfort. Baffled by his intentions, she looked out the window at the night beach. A few people were strolling across the sand and beyond, at the very edge of the water, now and then she saw a water jogger. "Very difficult; like running in suction cups," Mark always said. He did it in training. She'd never tried it.

She took a long, satisfying swallow of her drink and propped her elbows up on the table and looked out, unseeing, at the crashing, melodramatic Pacific. Suddenly she felt a surge of self-pity, felt her eyes fill with tears and, in an attempt to conceal them in the event someone was watching her, she turned at an extreme angle and looked directly out across the ocean and through the couples strolling along the sand. From this angle she discovered

221

that the large plate-glass window gave off a perfect reflection of the café behind her—a mirrorlike image, all the colors reflecting perfectly on black night and crashing waves. How curious, to be looking in one direction and seeing more clearly in the opposite direction!

Gerald would have liked this place—intimate and small, simple. He'd have liked the reflection as well, would have seen philosophy in it and symbol. He was a good man, in spite of—

As the self-pity increased instead of subsiding, she started to reach back for her drink, thinking to numb all feeling—at least temporarily. But, just as she was in the process of turning away from the reflected image of the café, she saw a woman. Apparently she'd just come in the front door and was now standing on the elevation near the cash register as though waiting to be seated. In the reflection, Brett looked more closely, suffering a degree of recognition. She'd seen her before someplace—or at least she thought she had.

For several moments the woman stood and waited, looking out over the sparsely populated restaurant as though she were looking for someone.

Who was she?

Compelled by this urgent question, Brett turned too quickly away from the reflection and in her haste the edge of her arm knocked over her drink. As the old-fashioned spilled out over the small table, she pushed instantly back in an attempt to avoid the sticky cascade which was moving perilously close to the edge of the table.

Within the instant the young waiter was there, cloth in hand. "Here, that's okay," he soothed, and quickly lifted the edge of the tablecloth nearest to her and folded it back on itself, while at the same time lifting the salt and pepper and sugar bowl off the table entirely.

"I'm . . . so sorry," Brett murmured, embarrassed, and felt a new heat cut a searing path up the sides of her cheeks.

"It really is okay," the boy repeated graciously. "You should have been here last week when I dropped a full plate of spaghetti with shrimp sauce right over there." He pointed to a place close to the cash register.

Still suffering waves of mortification, Brett laughed nervously and followed the direction of his hand toward the spot and, in the process, saw the area near the cash register where the woman had recently stood.

Empty.

"You just sit tight," the waiter continued to soothe. "I'll get a fresh tablecloth and"—pointedly he held up the empty glass—"and a fresh one of these."

"No, it . . . isn't . . ." She'd started to say "necessary" but the boy had already departed, either without heeding or hearing.

Still embarrassed, she saw a couple at a nearby table staring at her. Both looked quickly away as she made eye contact.

But her main interest now, despite the stares and embarrassment, was the whereabouts of the woman. Accordingly she looked out across the small room, searching carefully each occupied table—no more than half a dozen in all—but saw no one who resembled the woman she'd seen in the reflection of the glass. Again she did a quick survey of the room, found nothing—no red dress, no dated hairdo, no features which had reminded her of—

Rita Manning.

Impossible! Rita disappeared—presumed dead.

At the third quick, but thorough, survey of the room, she turned slowly back around in her chair in time to see the young waiter hurrying toward her, a fresh tablecloth over his arm.

"Here, this will fix you up."

"I . . . am sorry."

"Hey, don't think anything about it, you hear? I told you."

She assisted him as much as possible with the cloth, smoothing down edges, wanting very much to look out over the restaurant again but lacking the courage to meet all those staring eyes.

"Good as new," the boy smiled pleasantly. "Be right back with your drink."

"No, it isn't . . ." Again she tried to stop him but again too late. In an attempt to ease her sense of mortification, she looked out toward the ocean and shortened her vision to the reflected image of the restaurant itself.

And saw her again. The red dress, high pompadour. Unmistakable.

This time Brett stood and pushed back her chair with such force that it collided with a heavy brass planter situated on the window ledge, which in turn struck the glass itself. Like a bolt of lightning a jagged crack climbed instantaneously to the top of the window.

Reflexively, Brett moved back. At the same time a woman screamed somewhere in the restaurant.

Suddenly Brett felt strong hands pushing her away from the glass with such force that she almost lost her balance. The hands that were pushing also held her upright and continued to move her out of harm's way—all the way back to the cash register, where several other patrons had already retreated.

For several taut seconds no one spoke, all focused with fearful apprehension on the cracked window, the crack still slowly climbing like the reverberating echo of thunder.

"It'll hold." This voice was male, deep and filled with authority. "Only a dumb ass would put anything but shatterproof glass on the Coast."

At first Brett didn't turn—couldn't turn. The embarrassment, the shock at seeing the woman, the residual effects of the mysterious and difficult day had all taken a toll. The hands that had pushed her away from the window now guided her down into a chair. She sat without resistance, head down, and wondered when in her life she'd ever felt more bereft, alone and abandoned.

"It's okay," the young voice whispered, hovering over her.

Then she heard the same voice that a few moments earlier had reassured the entire restaurant with the news of shatterproof glass. "Okay, everybody. It's going to be okay. You can go on back to your tables now. You two up there, the waiter will move your stuff to one of these tables."

Still she lacked the courage to look up, though she knew she'd have to speak soon, for everyone seemed to be drifting away from her.

"Come on," the young waiter urged kindly. "Let me move you as well. We don't want to test our luck."

Then at last, motivated by a single desire not to make a bigger fool of herself, Brett stood up with dispatch and moved away from the suggestion. "No, thank you. I think I'd better go now."

"Agreed." This voice belonged to the manager, owner, whatever.

Stunned by his cold expression, Brett faltered.

As though spying her weakness, the heavyset man moved in for the kill. "Before you go, honey, I need your name and address and insurance company. That sort of damage doesn't come with the price of a bowl of shrimp."

Beginning to feel like a criminal, Brett nodded, not trusting herself to speak, and looked helplessly about for her purse. The fact of tears did not aid her vision, quite the contrary. She saw everything blurred as though under water, even the young waiter who now extended toward her a small, brown, leather clutch purse which she recognized as the one she'd come in with. Grateful, she looked up and saw the boy back away from the encounter and saw as well the look of silent encouragement on his face and a quick smile.

"Just your name and address and insurance, lady, that's all. Then you can go."

Again she nodded and dug blindly in her purse for pad and pencil and couldn't find either. "I . . . need . . ."

She'd just looked up when he thrust a pad and pen at her. She took both, and with trembling hands scribbled the information, feeling new waves of embarrassment from the humiliation. As she handed the paper back she murmured, "I . . . owe for four drinks . . ."

"On the house, lady. Move on now, please. This ain't no singles bar."

She nodded, without looking up and stood on uncertain legs. She reached quickly for the back of the chair and would perhaps have fallen had it not been for the arm that suddenly went around her shoulders, grasped her firmly and started her toward the door with a breezy explanation.

"I'll see her to her car and be right back."

"Well, hurry. Chivalry comes out of *your* paycheck, not mine. Let's get back to normal as soon as possible."

Brett wanted to protest the assistance but knew better. She needed it. Once outside, she felt the first cool blast of salt-scented ocean breeze and lifted her face toward it, feeling almost instantly its reviving power.

"Where's your car?"

"Over there," she murmured, looking out over the small parking lot and finding her trusted, though aging, VW.

"Hey, what happened in there, lady?" the young waiter asked now, still giving her assistance though she needed it less now and was beginning, with fresh air, to feel stronger.

"I . . . thought I saw someone," she said, not absolutely certain she owed him an explanation. Perhaps she did. He had been kind.

"Must have been someone special the way you reacted," the boy marveled. "But, hey, don't worry about Morelli. He'll survive a cracked window. This way it'll match the crack in his head."

As she reached out for the door handle, Brett pulled free of his support and instantly slipped into the driver's seat and closed the door, as though she wanted to shut him out or shut herself in. Slowly she rolled down the window, appalled at how her hands were still shaking. "Thank you for . . . everything," she said simply

225

and fished the keys out of the pocket of her jacket and started the ignition.

Over the rumble and growl of the motor she saw him smile and touch his hand to his forehead. Then a quick look of concern crossed his face. "Are you sure you're okay? To drive, I mean."

She nodded and shifted into gear, wanting to speed them both on their respective ways. Belatedly she thought she ought to have tipped him. He had been kind. But she didn't take the time, wanted nothing so much as the dark privacy of her car, away from all embarrassment and loneliness and humiliation and tension. To this end she waved a final time and backed her car out of its slot, angling toward the drive, the access road and the coastal highway beyond. In the rearview mirror she saw him, still standing in the parking lot, his white jacket and face bathed in red from the taillights of her car.

What had happened? Who had she seen? Why had everything been so terribly wrong and threatening today?

She must get home and call Mark. She didn't want to smother him but she was worried about him, worried for him. Surely a brief ten minutes—

Her thoughts broke off as she eased the car off the access road that led to the busy highway. There was another way back. She didn't have to take this highway. In fact, she wished now she'd taken the winding route through the coastal communities. But she hadn't and the commitment was made now. There was no way she could get off this access road, not with someone behind her and—

Suddenly the mammoth truck blew its sirenlike horn, clearly warning her to take her chances with the constant flow of fast-moving traffic.

Who could the woman have been?

The sirenlike blast came again. She tilted the rearview mirror for a better look at the bastard and saw nothing but the chrome teeth and the blinding white lights of a monstrous truck.

Keep your mind on what you're doing. The highway was the quickest way home and she wanted to go home as badly as she'd ever wanted anything in her life.

Now she heard other horns joining the truck's impatient one. Suddenly it seemed to her as if she were standing in the way of the entire world, blocking everyone. Without looking, she pressed her foot down on the accelerator and started off at too rapid a speed—and did not see the camper trailer bearing down on her from the left until too late, the truck coming right behind her as though it too were part of the conspiracy.

In the moment before the collision, she knew it was going to happen and, strangely enough, did not fear it. Her only regret was for Mark, that she'd not had time to warn him about certain hazards.

The collision was monstrous, violent and fiery, the small VW no match for the camper trailer and even less of a match for the huge gasoline semi which followed her too closely into the conflagration, one fireball contributing to another. Immediately several other cars careened into them at top speed, unable to brake. In a matter of seconds the entire highway resembled a small atomic blast, none surviving in the circle of the fireball itself.

Fed by spilled gasoline, the fire burned out of control for over an hour. When it was over there would be nothing recognizable.

Identification impossible.

Campus Corner

The fire was over, though the charred remains appeared to stand in the center of a lake which had been caused by the residual spill from the firemen's hoses. It was a red-black scene with the watery reflection catching and holding flashing red lights.

Yet as Mark turned the corner on the street which led to the campus shops, the charred remains of Uncle Polly's café were not uppermost in his mind. Location and pursuit of that oversized white shirt were.

When precisely the idea of surreptitious pursuit had come to him he did not remember. All he knew for certain was the decision had been formed and reached on the walk back from the base. He loved her. He had to see more of her, and yet for some reason she insisted upon keeping some sort of mysterious barrier between them. Thus, he rationalized, the secret pursuit was for her good as much as his. Whatever it was she was trying to hide, he wanted to reassure her there was no need. Perhaps the only way to do that would be to see for himself the location and conditions under which she lived.

There still were many people milling about. Straight ahead he saw police setting up wooden horses, forming a barricade to all save officials. Obviously the barricades had done nothing to discourage foot traffic, as the street which ran in front of the campus shops now resembled a block party. There must have been two hundred, milling and laughing and generally getting in the way of the firemen who were trying to restore hoses and other pieces of equipment.

Mark still had only one goal. Cass. As far as he could tell, she'd disappeared through that mass over there and he'd better go find her if he didn't want to lose her.

228

Suddenly, whatever it was—the suggestion of the word "lose" or perhaps just the devastating damage of the fire itself or the fact that the white shirt had been preceding him like a beacon for several blocks and then had suddenly deserted him, whatever—at this moment and quite unexpectedly he felt a mysterious sense of loss so sharp and so penetrating that it amounted almost to physical pain.

He drew slowly to one side out of the ragged, uneven flow of traffic and took brief refuge beneath a tree. Nearby was a wooden bench donated by local merchants for the convenience of people awaiting a bus. The bench was empty and he walked toward it as rapidly as the mysterious ailment would permit. His knees felt weak, his forehead hot and his palms damp.

He sat slowly and bent over, resting his head in his hands. Still the black feeling persisted, growing worse, like all the premonitions in the world rolled into one.

Something had happened. Something had changed his life, altered it in some way. How, he didn't know.

The awful weight continued to grow and expand until, to his complete bewilderment, he felt tears, hot and stinging, behind his eyes, and he let them come because he had no choice. For a few moments he was rational enough to know how stupid he must look, seated alone on a bus-stop bench, bawling. But as the mysterious grief built, he ceased to think on occurrences and gave in to the strong emotion and wept for someone, the loss of someone, and felt such profound feelings of lostness that his breath seemed to catch in his throat, incapacitating him even further.

After several moments he felt a brief cessation of pain and searched through his pockets for a handkerchief or a tissue and found neither and had to make do with trying to wipe his eyes clear with the back of his hand. When he managed to look up, the chaos was still constant, as was the black mood of mysterious grief. He would have to find out soon what it was that had prompted such a mood.

For now the only thing that was capable of righting the mood—or at least of neutralizing it—was his dire need to find Cass. To that end he pushed up from the bench and looked beyond the barricades to the confusion of the street itself. From this distance he saw nothing that even resembled the long, oversized white shirt.

For the first time he wondered if Uncle Polly was all right—or had he—

229

"Was anyone hurt?" he called out to a nearby policeman, surprised and pleased at the force in his voice.

The man didn't answer but did manage to shake his head once vigorously, which Mark assumed was a negative reply. If it was accurate, that was good news. Now, as he drew nearer to what was left of the café itself, he had serious doubts. The place was literally leveled—roof gone, the adjoining roofs of the shops next door on either side collapsed as well, charred and still smoking. Fallen, blackened timbers protruded up from the wreckage at distorted angles, resembling burned limbs.

As he made his way slowly through the milling crowds recording the macabre scene, he felt again that peculiar and devastating sense of grief and mourning.

Dead.

Someone was dead, Mark's life forever altered. Uncle Polly? He hadn't known Uncle Polly that well. Cass? He'd just left Cass, but suddenly it was absolutely imperative that he find her.

Once again he searched the immediate faces, trying to single out the close-cropped blond hair, the wide-set eyes that looked alternately naive and wise. It made sense to him that she would stop here. She did know Uncle Polly, on several occasions had appeared to be very fond of him. Surely she would stop here and check on him.

Now, convinced that he was in the right place and it was simply a matter of sorting through the faces, he began a slow, methodical inspection, his heart quickening on several occasions when he'd seen from the rear a blond head or the expanse of a white shirt, but on all occasions he was mistaken.

She'd come this way. He was certain of it. He'd followed her, hadn't he? Unless that too had been an illusion.

Please!

He found himself saying the single word over and over again as he was jostled and pushed by the crowd. The kids seemed in a celebrating mood for some reason, as though any excuse—tragedy or not—that dragged them away from their books was cause for celebration. Nearby he saw several beer cans hoisted aloft.

Dead. Someone was dead.

As the weight of grief moved with him through the jostling crowds, twice he considered giving up. At some point one must learn to be philosophical. If he was meant to find her, he would. Let fate do the work for a while. He was weary from futile effort.

With that brief surrender he backed away through the crowds, still looking, even in retreat, but headed ultimately toward the quiet sidewalk on the opposite side of the street, the one that still appeared to be relatively dry—unlike the shallow lake underfoot which the kids were now stomping in and splashing through.

Tired, still suffering from that mysterious, heavy sense of grief, he searched the perimeter of the crowd and looked ahead to the quiet darkness across the street. There were clusters of people there, all quietly looking, mostly older, their faces reflecting the loss, the awesome strength and courage needed to begin again. Those faces he could relate to, not these callow, raucous, mindless ones with beer dripping from their unused and untested faces.

My God, he sounded like an old man, bitter and cynical.

As he approached the curb on the far side, he stepped up and turned for one last look from this slightly elevated position which enabled him to see over most of the heads to the burned café itself—a spectacle which did not improve with distance nor elevation, something out of a nightmare, a blackened oven in which nothing could have survived.

Gazing toward the ruins that once had been a café, he shifted his eye just a short distance to the front of the shop next door—a small dress shop, he thought, though now it too had suffered extensive damage, its roof partially collapsed. Several agitated people stood on the sidewalk, pointing in first one direction and then the other.

But it wasn't this group that had attracted Mark's attention. It wasn't the group at all but two figures that stood just on the edge of the light still coming from the fire trucks and police cars, a very different and mismatched two, he noticed. One was tall, portly, the other short, slim. They were talking earnestly, these two, nose to nose as it were. What initially had attracted Mark was the vivid field of an oversized white shirt on the smaller figure.

Cass!

His heart sped up, then stopped for a moment. From this distance it was impossible to tell for sure. He'd have to move closer without being detected. For some reason he didn't want to be seen by anybody.

Dead. Someone was dead.

Beginning to feel a little mindless with unclear grief and fatigue, he stepped slowly off the curb, always keeping his eye on the shadowed two across the street. The man—and he noticed now that it was a man—appeared to have something draped over his shoulder. A blanket, Indian fashion. He seemed to be holding his right arm rigid, encased in white. It appeared to be bandaged.

Uncle Polly?

231

The thought occurred and along with it a feeling of joy that the old man had somehow survived the conflagration.

He started off the curb heading directly into the center of the laughing, noisy crowd—then changed his mind. He'd circumvent the crowd and, by taking the sidewalk on the opposite side of the street, he would use that police car for cover and be able to move to within a few yards of where the two were talking. To this end he stepped back onto the curb and moved quickly down the street forty yards—well past the bulk of the crowd—to where the single police car was parked sideways in the street to prevent other vehicles from entering. Flashing red and blue lights cast multicolored and distorted shadows over everything.

Still Mark moved forward, alternately checking his footing on the narrow curb and the two across the street, whose conversation—whatever its nature—appeared to be growing even more agitated. He was fairly certain it was Cass now, standing in a position of defiance, hands on hips, feet spread as though challenging the old man in some way.

Quickly he moved forward across the street, coming up on the police car and then crouching down, making certain he was well concealed, though suddenly he felt idiotic and looked nervously behind him, hoping, praying no one was watching.

"But I did nothing!"

This plaintive protest came from the opposite direction, from Cass—though he was less certain of the tone he heard in her voice, one he'd never heard before and one which alarmed him. She sounded afraid, as though she'd been accused of something, a serious something for which there were serious consequences.

He raised himself to the level edge of the window and peered out and over, fully expecting to see the two deep in animated conversation.

Instead he saw nothing but the shadowy sidewalk itself, the many, colored, flashing lights casting the area in sad and muted tones, like an abandoned carnival.

Frustrated, he raised partially up and was on the verge of standing upright when, glancing to the left, he saw a familiar sight—that large, oversized white shirt, tail out, moving at a rapid pace away from the flashing lights and the core of excitement. In the opposite direction he saw the man—Uncle Polly, he assumed—walking with equal determination and what appeared to be anger away from the confrontation.

While Cass was moving away from the campus shops in the area of the fire, Uncle Polly was moving directly into the area. He

232

stopped in front of his café and surveyed the destruction. For a moment it seemed to Mark that he could literally feel the man's defeat, his beefy arms going limp, his entire body seeming to slump, as though someone had delivered a stunning blow to his midsection. The last to collapse was his head, as though, having looked his fill on the charred remains of what once had been a restaurant, he'd now seen enough.

At that same moment Mark saw two police officers approach the bowed, defeated man, a third man trailing behind. He looked closely, some faint recognition dawning despite the distance and distorting lights. The third man trailing behind the cops was Terry Crawford.

What was Crawford doing here and in the company of cops?

Mark watched the three a moment longer as they approached Uncle Polly. All stopped short, as though they had run into an invisible barrier. Terry took the lead in the approach to the old man and Mark wondered why he was watching this trio when his main interest was moving steadily off into the night on her way to disappearing—again.

This thought, amounting almost to fear, spurred him into movement and, without hesitating, he started off down the street in the direction in which he'd seen her go. Only at the last minute did he catch sight of her at the far end, briefly illuminated by the streetlight, which appeared to cast a blue glow across the white shirt. Then she was gone, having turned the far corner, heading east.

Still moving forward, Mark broke into a run. He gained the end of the block, breathing heavily, looked eagerly ahead and saw her just turning that corner, heading north now.

He moved forward, crossing the street with his first burst of speed and foolishly keeping his eye on the exact spot he'd last seen her, as if he had only to stare hard enough and she might reappear. He knew she wouldn't and knew further that, even if he made the next corner in time, he might have lost her, for that street was residential, dark, no colored neon or shop fronts, nothing but the sparsely placed streetlights and the fainter light that managed to slip through drawn front drapes.

As he approached the end of the block, he broke speed to the extent that he could manipulate the turn. As he did he saw the street as he had imagined it—dark, shadowy, the houses on either side large, Victorian in design. The town's first money, he decided, oldest money, possibly the last in the way of sizable fortunes. He paused for a moment, looked ahead and for a second

233

saw only the thickly tree-shaded street, itself diminishing at midblock to total darkness, and reemerging into the faint light of the streetlamp at the opposite end.

Then he spied her in the split second she passed in and out of the shadowed trees, moving with less urgency now—or so it seemed—scuffling, head down like a child fatigued at the end of a day.

Good, then he could break his speed as well, and did, proceeding at a pace that matched hers. Suddenly he ached to catch up with her, take her hand, hold her, soothe her and tell her not to be afraid.

From where he stood with three quarters of the block separating them, he saw her come to an abrupt halt and stand perfectly still as though listening.

As he waited with her, a safe distance behind, he looked about and observed that all the houses on this street were oversized in the fashion of the turn of the century. Also the street fairly reeked with respectability.

From where he stood all he could see was her bowed head, her shoulders limp, as though suddenly all the life and vitality had gone out of her. For a lost number of moments she seemed more than content merely to stand there, unmoving, not looking up or in any direction.

For the second time Mark considered going to her, calling to her, reminding her in whatever way was necessary that she wasn't alone—for that's what her posture and attitude seemed to be saying. Yet again he resisted.

Since she'd refused to tell him, he had to know where she lived, what her life was when she wasn't prowling the base with him. With that bit of information, perhaps he wouldn't feel so desolate every time they separated, as if he'd never see her again.

Wait, she was moving again. Ever so slowly, but walking past the gingerbread-trimmed Victorian showplaces, hands rather rigidly held at her sides, as though she'd reached a hard-fought decision and was now proceeding reluctantly to see it through.

Mark stepped out of his safe shadows behind a huge native elm and started down the street after her. Her pace was extremely slow as she approached the corner and stood, clearly illuminated, beneath the streetlamp. But there was something different about her now. No longer was her head in a bowed position. Now she appeared to be gazing at the house on the corner across the street, an architectural specimen as large and murky as all the others on the block. From where he stood at midblock, he saw a single light

234

coming from a second-story window. The rest of the house was dark, as though uninhabited. A huge house, it seemed to rise forever in the night sky with extravagances of gingerbread trimming every window.

Mark held his distance and watched as at last Cass stepped off the curb, looking neither to the right nor to the left for oncoming traffic. Fortunately there was none at this late hour and in this neighborhood. In fact most of the houses were completely dark as though everyone had gone to bed.

Crossing the street, he watched Cass, still hesitant, her head seeming to lift, as though she felt it necessary to keep the huge and looming house forever in her sights. For some reason he knew it was hers. This was where she belonged, this great piled mausoleum with the single glow of low-wattage light slipping out of the second-story window. He tried to conceive of growing up in such a place and couldn't. The house seemed to boast of its built-in loneliness.

Now he saw Cass turn abruptly and look over her shoulder, as though she'd heard something—or perhaps she had sensed his presence. Quickly he fell back into near shadows—a large bush near a mailbox—and dropped down and held his position, despite his absence of breath and pounding heart. He held himself absolutely motionless in his position of concealment for several moments and finally dared to raise up to peer through the foliage toward the spot where he'd last seen her.

He saw her now across the street, standing on the opposite curb, her attention riveted on the house, the white picket fence, the gate which she was slowly approaching.

He knew it. This *was* hers, where she lived. Pleased with his hard-gained knowledge, though still stunned by the size and the feeling of ugliness of the place, he dared to venture out of his concealment and start once again down the sidewalk, always staying well outside the periphery of light which spilled out from the lamppost. He proceeded on to the end of the natural shadow, then held his position, confident now that he'd found her that he could take his time in his pursuit.

Clearly she was turning into the walk, reaching over to unlatch the gate, her head still lifted to the imposing facade of the house, her attention—like his—attracted by that dim yellow light coming from the second floor—the only light in the entire huge house as far as he could see. She was moving down the walk, her pace slowed even more, as though her reluctance to enter the house had yet increased.

235

He'd never seen her like this, so hesitant and uncertain. Again he felt a strong compulsion to call out to her, to inform her that she was not alone. But of course he couldn't. For one thing, the quiet night was not right for calling out. Even the distant traffic sounds seemed to have abated. No dogs barking, no crickets, no night noise—friendly or otherwise.

He looked up from his brooding on the silence of the night to see her just starting up the stairs which led to the broad wooden portico. For a moment the shadows seemed to devour her. Alarmed at losing sight of her, he stepped nearer to the spill of streetlight, forgetting the need for his own concealment. As he hurried across the street he continuously searched the darkened porch.

Fully prepared for her to call out to him, he took the opposite curb at renewed speed and approached the end of the picket fence, trying again to peer through the shadows and see her.

There she was now, standing before the broad closed front doors, head down, body limp, as though she'd suffered a small collapse of nerve. Unless she turned inadvertently in her distress, she'd never see him. Something about that small, partial collapse suggested that she was totally unaware of anyone or anything else in the world but her own distress.

Then he saw her slowly twist the knob, her own slight weight causing the door to creak but not to open. Then, as she obviously exerted more strength, the heavy door opened—at least far enough for her to slip inside and disappear from his sight into the darkness of the house itself.

For several moments he stared transfixed at the vacuum as though he expected her to return. When she didn't, he concentrated on the low, large, heavily draped windows flanking the front door. Light would shine at any moment. He was certain of it. It was the customary thing to do, wasn't it, to enter one's house and turn on lights?

After several moments when no new illumination had been added to that faint yellow glow coming from the second floor, he started carefully down the walk, his hands running lightly along the pickets, feeling a need to retain connection with something for fear that he too might simply drift off into the dark silence along with the rest of the world. It was as though this place, this house, was trying to clear the world of all superfluous interference.

He stopped at the gate and debated for a moment whether he should go farther. A single word occurred to him. *Trespassing.* He considered for a moment all its ramifications, then pushed with

236

his knee against the low gate and discovered that she'd left it unlatched.

Someone or something—fate perhaps—was making it easy for him. Even as he climbed the stairs—freezing on the third as the old wood cracked noisily, as loud as a pistol shot in the quiet night—he knew but was unable to say how he knew that the front door would be open and available to him.

Suddenly, as he climbed the last step to the old wooden portico, he stopped. Not because he'd run into any new obstacles but because it suddenly struck him that everything, everything was being made too easy. Quickly he glanced over his shoulder to the sidewalk behind, for a moment considering it as an escape route. But the consideration lasted only a moment. Despite the risks involved, he had to take them. He had to know what she was going to confront inside that house.

As no light had come on, he moved slowly, stealthily toward the front door, which, like the gate, swung open. With only a moment's hesitation he placed both hands on the weathered, rough surface and exerted only the slightest of pressures and felt the door give. As Cass before him, he opened it only wide enough to slip through, then quietly closed it and turned to confront the vacuum of darkness.

For a moment he saw nothing but a million swirling dots, as though his vision had suddenly become impaired. His ears listened closely and heard something—a voice, very distant, speaking very low. Two voices? He couldn't tell.

He opened his eyes to see the microcosm of swirling dots gone, merely a black abyss again confronting him. Now and then it altered even as he stared at it, revealing very slowly the specifics of a large, high-ceilinged entrance hall, two double doors on each side flanking the front door. His interest was straight ahead toward the broad staircase that led up to the only source of light in the entire house, for from that direction, as his eyes began to adjust, he saw a sepia-colored spill which seemed to creep across the floor and ease down the uppermost steps of the staircase as though it was coming from beneath a closed door.

He stood a moment longer, testing the silence and the darkness.

I live with my mother. My grandfather's dead.

Rita Manning was missing and ultimately presumed dead.

Then no one else should be in the house but Cass—and her.

He held his position at the closed front door, waiting for the commonsense impulse, the engines of reason, the old lessons of morality and decency to turn him about and send him back into the anonymous safety of the darkened porch, sidewalk and street beyond where everyone had a right to pass. But what he feared more was leaving Cass alone in this great silent tomb with only that distant spill of sepia-colored illumination for comfort. So the choice was his, as were the risks, and he willingly took them if they would give him access to her, her life, her needs, her fears.

He heard the voices again. Female—or at least he thought they were. Speaking very softly. Coming from up there.

He moved on down the hall to the bottom of the staircase, glancing ahead as well to the right where he saw a long, dark corridor which seemed to narrow as it led deeper into the house, saw additional doors, endless doors which led off it. Again he thought how somber and gloomy all this would be for a child growing up with no one for company or comfort save a mother and the oppressing and oppressive memories of a larger-than-life father.

The perception of resentment coming so unexpectedly stopped him just as he approached the bottom of the staircase. The oppressing and oppressive memories? Did he feel that way about his father? He'd never known it before. The living room had been his shrine, that oil portrait his god. He looked up toward the faint light as though for understanding. Cass would know what he meant. He wondered where in this great wooden tomb was her god, her altar, her oil portrait of Alec Manning.

Mother.

My God, what was it, that awful crushing weight which momentarily rendered him breathless and caused him to reach out for the wooden banister for support and grasp it with all of the available strength at his command?

Mother.

He must call her, must talk to her, must tell her—no, ask her to tell him—about Rita Manning and Alec Manning and what they were to her or she to them. And his father.

He heard a new sound coming from the stairs. Music. The same, tinny, poor quality of Cass's portable radio with its rolled top, the tune familiar as well, one that had driven him batty several weeks ago when they'd explored the old barracks together. . .

"Is that where Uncle Polly went?"

"Yes."

"He said it was my fault."

"Turn it off, Cassie, for heaven's sake. I never liked that song since—"

238

This voice he heard clearly, and he halted again in his faltering progress up the stairs, impressed by the beauty of the voice, its melodious quality. Surely a cultivated and trained voice—yet not a theatrical voice, for there was no attempt at projection nor was there any of the built-in artifice of a theatrical voice. This was natural and soothing, even in its plea for Cass to turn off the maddeningly repetitious music.

He held his position at the third step and heard the song end abruptly in midphrase. For a moment he heard nothing but static. Clearly the radio was Cass's favorite toy. Then he heard a man's voice, a radio news commentator, coming as though over great distance.

"At 3:09 P.M. there was a mighty explosion. The whole piece of heaven seemed to catch fire. Jap torpedoes had hit near the carrier *Wasp*'s gasoline system, which was particularly vulnerable because the carrier's planes were then being refueled. Gasoline fires spread to the magazines. Bombs and gasoline caused the . . ."

"Oh, Cassie, that's no better. I've heard all that before and so have you. Just turn it off, please. Let's listen to the silence."

Mark bowed his head during this curious news announcement, the better to hear over and around the heavy curtain of static. Now as he heard the radio being turned off he looked up, baffled. The *Wasp*? A World War II carrier, if he remembered correctly. What kind of news bulletin was that, announcing an event over twenty years in the past?

But he overlooked the absence of an answer in the beauty of that woman's voice. A more appealing voice he'd never heard before in his life—part maternal, part seductress, all female.

Cass's mother is Rita Manning. The voice is Rita Manning's! It had to be. No other possibility. Not dead, not missing, as his mother had frequently told him.

Then voices again—or rather a voice, that same musical and very compelling one. "Cass, come sit by me. You don't have to get sleepy yet, do you?"

"No, Mother."

"Then forget all about Uncle Polly and where he's gone. Come and sit here. Put your head in my lap, that's a good girl."

"Mother, I'm . . ."

"And don't talk. You mustn't talk. It's my turn, not yours. You know it's my turn."

"I said I was . . ."

"Sit down, Cass, right here. Now."

Mark listened, head down, one hand on the banister, intrigued

239

by the changing tone and mood of the woman. The beautiful voice had commenced as soft as a summer breeze and the final "Now" had resembled winter. He considered moving up another step or two, then changed his mind. Wait until they were talking again. Let their voices obscure the creaking wood.

"Now, are you ready for me to talk? Are you quite comfortable? I want you to be comfortable."

Another step executed just in time before her voice fell silent.

"What we must talk about, as you so well know, is our declaration of loyalty to each other. Isn't that right, Cass? You must tell me that you know you need me. Because you do, don't you? Isn't that right, Cass?"

"Yes, Mother."

"Is that loyalty still intact?"

"You know it is, Mother."

"No, I don't know that, Cass. That's why this need to talk before we move on. I must know for certain."

In this rapid exchange Mark accomplished three more steps and got caught midway up the fourth. Although he was mystified by the curious conversation, he was even more mystified by the sound of Cass's voice—so flat and unresponding and uncharacteristic.

"You are dependent on me, Cass. For everything. You understand that, don't you? I ask nothing in return except loyalty, the bond that stretches between us, has forever. If it should ever break you'd be the loser. Do you realize that?"

"Yes, Mother."

"Nothing would happen to me. I can go on forever, but you're the one who needs me."

"I said, 'Yes,' Mother."

Four more steps. And only four to go, he noticed, rising high enough on the staircase for a full-length view of the double doors spilling forth a crack of light along with the strange conversation. Silence. In this new silence he observed to his right what appeared to be a rolled-up carpet runner, as though someone had taken it up in preparation of putting a new one down. In the shadowy upper corridor it resembled a lumpy body.

"Cass, listen!" This strong and imperative command came from behind the double doors and caused Mark to freeze anew.

"What, Mother?"

"I heard something."

"What?"

"Listen!"

Slowly Mark bowed his head and closed his eyes, as though

240

those movements were capable of making noise. What she'd undoubtedly heard was the pounding of his heart.

"Mother, please. Don't . . ."

With his eyes closed it sounded as though Cass were crying or on the verge of it.

"Did someone follow you, Cass?"

"No, Mother. I swear it!"

"We're not alone."

"No, it's Grandfather."

"Not your grandfather. Someone else."

Even as she spoke, Mark heard her voice changing from that low and melodious, compelling one to one that was harsh and threatening. For several moments, which seemed like several lifetimes, the taut, suspicious silence held. There was not a sound coming from within the large house or without.

Precisely what she'd heard, Mark had no idea. For one fleeting moment he was tempted to reverse his steps and flee this place as quickly as possible. He had no business being here and—though his initial motivation was concern for Cass—he had gained what he'd come for. He'd wanted to see where she lived and if she was all right.

"Mother, let me go now. I'm tired."

"When I say, dear. Are you sure you heard nothing?"

"Yes, Mother."

"Very well. I'll take your word. I thought I felt something strange . . ."

"Nothing, Mother."

"Very well. Then look at me. I need a reaffirmation. For your own sake, you must know who you are. Do you?"

"Yes, Mother."

"You know the very source of life, don't you?"

"Yes, Mother. Please don't . . ."

"Sit still. I'm not hurting you and you know it. Such a crybaby!"

Throughout this exchange Mark made it to the top of the landing, his attention torn between the rolled-up carpet on his right and the now clearly threatening dialogue coming from behind the closed doors. What was she talking about and what was she doing to Cass, who sounded very tired? Drugged, almost. And hurt.

He needed to see, though the very moment that this impossible thought occurred to him he rejected it. What he really needed to do was to get out of here. He had no business being here and if he were discovered—

"Put your head down, Cass, right here in my lap. That's a good girl. You know how much I love you, don't you, how much I've always loved you?"

"Yes, Mother."

"And you love me as much."

"Yes, Mother."

"Will you promise always to do exactly as I say and never to leave me?"

"Yes, Mother."

"What if some young man comes along? Will you leave me for him?"

"No, Mother."

"Promise? Cass, promise."

"Yes, Mother."

Mark felt a moment of disappointment, keen and sharp. Why had she made that promise?

From where he now stood the central keyhole of the double doors was less than three feet away. Two steps, a quick look. How would it hurt? Then he would leave immediately and say nothing to anyone. He had no idea what was going on here. Maybe nothing but a loving mother and daughter. One look.

As the woman's voice started up again on basically the same theme of Cass's extreme need for and dependence on her, Mark took one hesitant step, refraining at first from placing his full weight on the old floorboards. Then at last he dared to do so and heard nothing in the way of a betraying crack, heard instead the woman's voice—stronger, nearer—speaking the same nonsense as ever—her favorite subject apparently Cass's complete dependence on her for everything.

Another step. Another testing of weight. One more and he'd be close enough.

"So you see, Cass, we are locked in a bond, aren't we? And you mustn't get our friends in trouble anymore, like Uncle Polly. Poor Uncle Polly."

"I'm sorry."

"But of course you are. Of course, he's really quite ruined here and must go away. But there are others who must be taught and you must help me."

As Mark approached the double doors, he started down on one knee, his mind frantically recording the bizarre comments.

You mustn't get our friends in trouble. Poor Uncle Polly. He must go away.

In his tension he forgot to test the weight of his knee and, as he made contact with the floor, the old board gave a faint crack. His first instinct was to stand rapidly, but he realized that that could cause a greater disturbance. So he held his position—and held his breath as well—bending forward and pressing his left eye to the large, old-fashioned keyhole.

At first glance the room resembled a storeroom in which nothing had been stored—or everything had been recently removed. He couldn't see the light source at first, then he did. A single bare bulb, hanging suspended on a long cord in the center of the ceiling. Low wattage cast half shadows on everything as well as distortions.

Her mother's voice was droning on about caution and consequences. Mark angled slightly to the left, sensing that was the direction of her voice. At last he found Cass, seated upon the bare floor beside a rocker, her head resting to one side on the seat of the chair, the rest of her body curled, relaxed, legs drawn up, arms limp in her lap. She appeared to be drowsing. Perhaps asleep. Eyes closed, no sign of movement.

But where was the other voice coming from? On the chair—or more accurately draped over the chair—he saw a bright red dress. The long sleeves extended over the arms of the rocker, the skirt neatly arranged as though someone had just stepped out of it—or was on the verge of just stepping into it.

Mark pressed closer to the keyhole, not paying too much attention to the draped dress or—and he'd only now just noticed—the pair of white, high-heeled shoes which, like the dress, had been neatly arranged on the floor in front of the rocker, again as though someone had just stepped out of them or was preparing to step into them.

He leaned farther to the left, and at the exact moment of his movement he thought he saw the red sleeve lift into the air and hang there suspended for a moment before falling back down onto the chair arm. He blinked at the tableau and tried to keep the sleeve in close focus—which was difficult to do as his eyes were burning now.

Optical illusion. Peripheral vision. Nothing more.

Where was the woman? Once again he tried to coax his vision around the corner. Then he saw—or thought he saw—one of the high-heeled shoes move, tap once before settling back into safe and reasonable inaction.

His bent leg ached and he longed to straighten it but dared not move. Not now. Not until he could clear his vision and at least make some kind of sense out of what he thought he'd seen. He'd still not located the woman talking. Only Cass—who appeared to be asleep, for she hadn't moved.

At the thought of her, he looked back toward the rocking chair

243

and saw it commence slowly to rock, Cass's head and shoulders limply moving it, though clearly not the source or cause of the momentum.

He gaped forward and felt his heart accelerate, tempted at first to break away from what he could not believe, let alone understand.

Those two white, high-heeled platform shoes, ankle straps straining against the movement, pushed rhythmically against the floor. That was the cause of the faint momentum of the chair. That and—

His bewilderment grew to shock and both to a kind of quiet terror, for the reasonable part of him knew there was no reasonable explanation for what he saw. Still on his knees, he moved backward, his mind not ready to concede anything, his emotions struggling to hold themselves in check. Curiously, his first coherent thought was to advance, not to retreat, advance at least long enough to rouse Cass from her strange stupor.

But there was still that unexplained phenomenon confronting him, and against the reality of that he faltered, thinking to call to Cass, to rouse her through the closed doors, try to—

Suddenly he heard a new sound comingling with the faint creaking of the old rocker, a rush—like air displaced by something large with wings—coming up from behind. As the noise increased in volume he stood and felt the objecting muscles of the knee too long bent and searched the shadowy upper hallway for the sound that was only now familiar to him. He'd heard it before.

Then he saw it, the large wingspan, swooping up the staircase, emitting from its beak a curious whispering, whimpering, breathless sound, as though it did not fly effortlessly but had to expend great energy and concentration.

Frozen by that fear, he flattened himself against the near wall and watched as it made several passes over the stairwell itself, swooping higher and lower with each demonstration, as though performing for him, showing him its skill.

Over the swoop of the wings he heard the rocker, still creaking, something still propelling it, though no longer did he hear the voice. The voice was silent. All was silent, save for the swooping of the airborne thing that with each pass now was coming closer.

Slowly he eased down the hall away from the double doors, not certain it had seen him yet, but somehow knowing better. At least now he was in perfect alignment with the staircase. It was his briefly formed plan to flee down that staircase and out of the front door into the relative safety of night. Later he'd try to make

244

sense out of what he thought he'd heard and seen here tonight—though he knew down deep it would never make sense except as—

His thoughts were interrupted by a sudden swooping which came from very close, directly in front of him. In the absence of light, he looked to see what appeared to be a hawk perched on top of the banister, its wings withdrawn now, though still enormous, that curious whimpering, breathless sound filling the hall and Mark's ears. But most bizarre of all, he could see the hawk's eyes clearly. Bright red, as was its beak. A nightmare creature's face staring directly at him. Nothing moving. No sound. Not even the faint creaking of the rocker.

Then the bird lifted off with a great, noisy flapping of wings and appeared to hang suspended in the air directly over the staircase, as though defying Mark to make his escape. When he didn't, the bird altered its suspended state and flew directly toward him with such ready and sudden speed that though Mark raised his left arm in quick defense, it wasn't quick enough, and he felt a sharp, knifelike pain directly beneath his left eye—only inches below his eye, as though the bird had aimed for that specific spot.

As the wings lifted high above Mark in a clear attempt to reconnoiter, he didn't hesitate but pushed violently away from the wall, moving from motionless to top speed in less than a second, his goal the top of the stairs, then down, and out.

Less than a foot before he reached the stairs, he felt something rolled and thick collide with his forward motion, felt himself, almost airborne, colliding with the obstruction. Now he remembered the rolled carpet.

There was no defense against the fall, only the natural and powerful instinct to break it some way by flailing out on both sides. Feeling his left hand come into painful collision with the banister, he grabbed hold, despite the pain, despite his descent, which blessedly had been partially blunted by that one hand, which continued to grab even though the weight of his body continued to dislodge it.

Down. Down. His spine took the brunt of his weight, then his shoulders, then his head, though always spared by that one hand which did its best to relieve the burden and brunt of the fall itself. Where was the bottom? He'd have to stop soon.

Then he did. Though his first and most powerful instinct was to lie absolutely still and give the entire bruised and aching body a chance to reorganize and check its wounds, he nonetheless heard

245

over his fear that rushing displacement of air and knew the adversary was still close at hand, knew there was no time for examination, and he scrambled immediately to his feet. His knee buckled in rebellion but he managed to move forward, crablike, for a few feet.

At last his fear impressed the desperate need to move upon his entire system and this time the knees held. He stumbled as though drunk, but still upright, down the corridor which led to the front door, hearing the thing behind him, that awful half-human, half-animal noise, as though it were in as much stress as he was.

There, the door. He hurled himself at it with unexpected strength and panicked as he felt it refuse to give, tried again, and felt another knife-sharp attack in the center of his back. It had caught up with him, its beak being its main weapon. As the rushed swooping lifted over his head, Mark knew he had less than a few seconds to try again for escape. Somehow he knew if he didn't make it this time it would be difficult—if not impossible—to attempt it again.

Pull! Damn it, pull it open!

This he did, and at the exact moment heard the sound behind him, the whimpering breathlessness coming for him. He gave the door one enormous pull and felt the first blast of cool autumn air upon his face. He saw the darkened portico and steps, the cracked sidewalk, the lower white gate and beyond—freedom.

It approached him now like a dive bomber. He could hear it coming, dared not look up, and as he ran he tried to cover his head and the back of his neck with his arms. He received a knifelike wound on the back of his left hand. Blindly, still struggling against the pain and fear, he tried to wave his arms at the creature and experienced a brief, short-lived relief as he heard the telltale rush of wings ascend through the night sky and knew it would only be a matter of seconds before it returned to finish its kill.

At the gate now, he jerked it back with such force he heard the hinges crack and was tempted to look up into the night sky to locate and identify the thing that was attacking him. Better judgment won out and he took the darkened sidewalk running, searching up and down for cars, pedestrians, anyone who might lend him assistance. But, as earlier, the quiet, secluded residential street was deserted. No one in sight. No car moving. No friendly light.

Then he heard it again, louder this time, as though it were

coming from a great height. He dared not consider the damage that knifelike beak could do with such force and power behind it. For a moment he stood on the curb at the intersection and the battle raged within.

Run and hide!

Stay and fight!

Then there was no time to wait for the outcome of the battle. The whimpering was coming closer, accompanied by a sound which resembled an increasing wind. There wasn't even time to run. He was in the process of dropping to his knees, both arms laced tightly over his neck and head, eyes closed. Despite the enclosed position he heard the sirenlike sound, as though the velocity of the fall produced a whine in itself.

His fear vaulted. This would be more than a knife prick.

"Simpson, in here. Hurry!"

At first he thought he'd imagined the voice, but he glanced quickly out from his crouched, bowed position and saw a car before him, the door pushed open, motor ancient and rattling though still going.

"Simpson, did you hear me? Get your ass . . ."

He did, without a second invitation. Even as he scrambled off the curb and into the safety of the car, he heard the siren whine reach decibel level, heard a sharp noise on top of the car. Without raising all the way up, he reached out to close the door and felt something like teeth close instantaneously on his arm and tear out a small piece of flesh.

The car was moving forward for half a block with the door still open before finally he was aware of someone reaching across him and giving it a mighty slam. Then he heard the old engine growl and whine as the driver insisted on instant speed.

But that was the extent of Mark's awareness, all his energies focused on his bleeding right arm and the sensation of teeth closing upon his flesh. The blood, despite his grasp on the wound, continued to pour rivers, which seeped out and around his fingers, coating his arm a glistening, shiny red in minutes.

"Christ, you're going to fuck up my car good! Here, wrap that around it."

Within the range of his downward and tortured vision, Mark suddenly saw a large white towel thrust toward him. He took it and wrapped it tightly about his forearm, applied pressure to the open wound and at last dared to look up.

Was it still in pursuit? It couldn't be. The driver was taking him for a high-speed ride through the streets, running several stop

247

signs on the way. Mark glanced out of his right window and saw nothing but the ragged end of town.

In the distortion of a flashing red light, Mark looked to his left into the weathered, middle-aged face of—

Amos Foster.

Apparently the man saw his close scrutiny and grinned cockily and lifted his hand to his forehead in a mock salute.

"Good evening. If you ask me, I got your ass out of there just in time. From where I sat, it looked like Cassie's feathered friend wanted to make mincemeat out of you. How are you feeling?"

Stunned to the point of paralysis, fear still robbing him of much of his energy, Mark gaped at the question. In the silence he found himself working on the question:

Amos Foster. Why Amos Foster?

"You may want to get a doctor to look at that arm, you know. Sometimes those things can be rabid."

"Wh-what things?" Mark stammered, and considered those two words a major accomplishment.

Amos Foster gave him a look of massive incredulity. "The hawk, you silly bastard. That great big thing with big wings, you know, that was ready to chew your balls off." This was followed by a laugh as the man seemed to relax behind the wheel and break his speed. One arm rested across the back of the seat, the other manipulated the steering wheel with the help of a steering knob. Mark hadn't seen one since his California hot-rod days.

Apparently Amos Foster was aware of his lack of response and asked with greater concern now, "Are you okay, kid? You should never ever tangle with that thing. Only Cassie knows . . ."

"I didn't tangle with it. It tangled with me. What . . . was it?"

Again Amos gave him a look of weary patience. "I told you. That's Cassie's hawk. From the base. She feeds the bitch, don't you see? I've told her she oughtn't to. Wild things ought to be left wild. But, no. She takes meat out to it. Sometimes the thing follows her home and . . ."

Suddenly he broke off and concentrated on a left-hand turn into traffic heading out toward the busy interstate. Once the turn had been completed, he settled back again and drove with one hand. A new mood seemed to come over him, a new seriousness. "What the hell were you doing at Cassie's?"

Mark put new tension on the white towel and noticed a large red coin beginning to appear on the white terry-cloth surface. "I . . . went to see her," he said distractedly. "I wanted to see where she lived."

"Why? What business is it of yours?"

Suddenly, despite the rescue, Mark resented the man's tone and attitude. "I might ask the same thing."

"Now you listen, you son of a bitch!" The anger in the man's voice was hot and immediate.

Mark looked up to see him glowering at him, another flashing red light coating his lined face with nightmare shadows.

"I could have just left you there to be picked to death, you know. But I saved your hide and now you owe me one, do you hear?"

Mark didn't particularly agree, but he was grateful and now he nodded.

"Then I'm asking you to get the hell out of here. Cassie ain't for you. Pay no attention to Cassie. Cassie ain't nobody. Go home. Clear on back to California. If I'm not mistaken, your old lady needs you now."

Mother.

"Thank you," Mark said politely, "for coming along when you did." He stared out the window and failed to recognize his location. "If you'll drop me off somewhere near the center of the campus, I'll . . ."

"Did you understand what I said to you, Simpson? I can't be there again. I shouldn't have been there this time, but Cassie . . ." Suddenly he broke off and gripped the steering wheel with both hands.

In the faint light coming from the dash, Mark could see a new expression on his face, one he couldn't really identify, one which he'd never seen before. As Amos Foster made a sharp turn to the right heading back toward the university, Mark felt a strange compulsion to ask a few questions of his own. But first an expression of gratitude did seem in order.

"I am grateful," he began falteringly, looking down on his arm. The bleeding apparently was subsiding, though beneath the towel he still could feel teeth closing on his flesh, and the sensation momentarily distracted him.

"No thanks are needed, Simpson. Just listen to me and get the hell out of here."

"I . . . can't just leave here. I'm on scholarship."

"Fuck the scholarship!"

"You wouldn't say that if you were a student or an athlete." He paused. "Are you?"

Amos Foster laughed. "Hell, no. Bartender by trade and a damned good one."

249

"How did you meet Cass?"

"Oh, hell, everyone in town knows Cassie Manning. Her mother, too."

Abruptly he broke off, and in the faint light of the dash Mark saw a new grim determination on his face, a new set to his mouth and jaw.

"Here you go, Simpson."

Startled, Mark looked out of the window to see the athletic dorm. They must have taken a different route. He'd recognized none of his familiar landmarks of the campus corner.

"Now go on in and get someone to take a look at your hand, arm—and your face, too. You got nicked there as well. And call your old lady in California and tell her to put the light in the window because you're coming home. You don't belong here."

Mark started to object and decided he'd just ignore the guy's rambling and thank him again for another timely rescue. "Thanks again," he said politely, and crawled slowly out of the car. He started to say more—wanted to say more—but Amos gunned the motor and took off with such speed that the front door flew shut of its own volition.

At that moment Mark was concerned with the slow-dawning recognition: The car.

He'd seen that car, that Chevy of ancient vintage with the smoked window glass. He'd seen it idling at an intersection on the base. He was certain of it. He stood on the curb and watched the old car disappear into the night and tried to find a logical explanation for the car, for the wounds on his hand, arms, face and back, for what he'd witnessed in the large house on Sorrento.

"Hey, Simpson, who the hell did you tangle with?"

The voice evolved out of the night and passed close behind him. He didn't respond, for there was no possible response.

"Simpson, you okay? You haven't seen Terry Crawford, have you? We were supposed to go . . ."

Mark abruptly shook his head and, holding his towel-wrapped arm close to his body, started down the walk which led to the dorm and the blessed and safe privacy of his room.

The voice called after him, "Hey, what's the matter? You too good to talk to us? Well, I've got a message for you. You're supposed to call home, Your Royal Highness, you hear? Your mother."

Less than three feet from the dorm door he stopped and looked back, adding remorse to his already burgeoning emotional baggage. How would it hurt for him to be civil? They thought he'd been in a fight. Good, let them. He really had no idea where

250

Crawford was and he would have liked to have asked a question or two about the message from home, but they were gone now, whoever they were.

Call home.

It was his intention to do so just as soon as he examined and assessed the damage done by "Cassie's friend." Maybe Amos Foster was right. Maybe he should just go home. There was something here he didn't understand. His father—

Later. He'd think about it later. For now he'd clean off the blood and try to cleanse his head as well of that god-awful sound, the rushing hiss of wings, the whimpering breathlessness, as though someone were as trapped as he was.

"Crap, Simpson, you'd better not let Coach see you. He don't go for his boys fightin'."

"Neither do I," Mark called back in answer to the voice, and hurried on up the steps, desperate for the privacy of his own room.

Terry Crawford knew that Uncle Polly had lied and that stuck sideways with him about the same way that Coach Herbert's order for him to spy had stuck sideways. And not just once. He'd heard Uncle Polly lie repeatedly to the cops, off and on all evening long. To the fire inspector as well.

Was there anyone with you in the restaurant, Mr. Zelius?

No, sir, Officer, sir. I was alone, waiting for customers.

A lie. Terry knew it was a lie, and once he'd started to tell the cops what he'd seen when he'd heard Uncle Polly shout back to someone. But he'd kept still and tried to figure out why Uncle Polly had wanted to lie—and why he wouldn't let anyone look at his arm. It obviously had been cut by glass or something. The old man had insisted on two things to the point of getting mad, one, that he was all alone in his café when the fire broke out, and, two, that his arm was okay and he needed nothing.

Now Terry continued to perch on the curb opposite Uncle Polly's fire-blackened café and watch the mop-up crew, the weary, blackened firemen keeping an eye on every piece of the still-smoldering timbers, while Uncle Polly stood to one side, his arm still bandaged, looking at his ruined café as though permanently defeated.

In a way Terry felt responsible. That's why he was still here. After all, he'd been here at the beginning, had heard Uncle Polly's angry accusations aimed at someone out of sight in the kitchen, had seen the soundless explosion.

251

A patrol car pulled up from the end of the street and parked in front of the destroyed restaurant. The officer driving said something to one of the firemen, who in turn pointed back toward Uncle Polly.

"Hey!" the officer shouted. "One or two questions, okay? Then we'll find you a place to go."

Terry had just remembered the old man slept in the room behind the café. Gone now. Everything gone. All his personal belongings.

Slowly, wearily, Uncle Polly approached the police car and Terry heard his response.

"No, no more questions. A man has a limit. I passed mine long ago. And I not stay here. I leave this state, go someplace else. Texas, maybe."

"You won't leave right away, will you? Maybe we can talk tomorrow."

"Maybe tomorrow. I might talk tomorrow."

The police officer nodded and expressed his sympathy. A time was set to talk in the morning and then the patrol car started slowly down the street, running over the thick fire hoses, which were now being used simply to wet down still-smoldering areas.

Clustered around the one remaining fire truck, Terry saw a few firemen sipping hot coffee, talking among themselves. Still alone—an island—was Uncle Polly. Go talk to him, Terry advised himself. Maybe you can find out why he lied. Maybe there's a good reason.

"Uncle Polly?" As Terry pushed himself up from his awkward position on the curb, he called out to the man and saw him look nervously in his direction, as though under attack. "It's just me. Terry Crawford." He smiled and hurried into the light spill from the streetlamps so the man could see who it was and not be alarmed.

"I . . . don't . . ."

"Maybe not," Terry grinned, "but I was on the scene first and just wanted to see if you're okay, Your arm . . ."

"Who are you?" Uncle Polly demanded, all his defenses in place, backing away as Terry approached.

"Don't worry, Uncle Polly," he tried to soothe. "I just want to talk to you for a minute, that's all."

"Talk, talk. That's all everybody wants to do. Ruined. Uncle Polly ruined."

"Who was with you in the kitchen, Uncle Polly? Before the fire started, I mean."

252

The bluntness of the question seemed to catch the man off guard. For a moment he blinked up at Terry, his face a map of defiance, fear and disbelief.

With an innate openness and honesty, Terry blustered on, hiding nothing, simply wanting the story set straight. "I was hungry, you see," he grinned. "Always hungry, according to Coach. I passed by your café and it was empty, but all the lights were on. I have a friend who comes in all the time and I was kind of looking for him, but I saw you instead. You were really mad as hell at someone in the kitchen because you were yelling back something about how they talked all the time and now it was your turn."

As Terry talked, Uncle Polly started to shake his head and backed away from the words, as though they were, in themselves, an assault and a threat.

"No, please, Uncle Polly. I don't mean to . . . I just wanted to know why you said you were alone. There was someone."

"Leave . . . me . . . be!" The fear on the man's face was clear, and now he had increased the speed of his movement away from Terry, an awkward backward movement, stumbling on almost every step but still shaking his head, as though he felt a need to constantly challenge and refute Terry's accusation.

When it occurred to Terry he was doing more harm than good, he stopped in his pursuit of the old man and held up both hands, palms out, as though to say, Enough. Stop. "Okay, okay, Uncle Polly, you were alone. Though I . . . I just wanted to help. If there had been someone, then . . ."

"You want to *help*?" the old man cried.

Terry heard a deep wheezing sound coming from Uncle Polly's throat and knew that a lot of smoke had gone down and done damage.

"Of course I do," Terry nodded, feeling sorry for the old man. Normally he appeared so cheerful and self-possessed. Now something had undermined him, something more than just the destruction of his café.

"Then you help," Uncle Polly said in a strong announcement, holding his position at last, though supporting his wounded arm with his opposite hand and coughing, a violent paroxysm that left him bent over and breathless, his eyes tearing.

Terry started toward him with the idea of guiding him away from this place where smoke still hung thick and heavy in the air.

Again Uncle Polly scrambled backward as best he could under the circumstances, still waving away all efforts of assistance, despite his weakened condition. "I see you," Uncle Polly began after the coughing spasm was over. "I see you every night outside my window looking in on the California boy. You know him?"

Baffled by this line of questioning and a little embarrassed that he'd been observed in his clandestine activity, Terry ducked his head and heard the last of the firemen shouting behind while rewinding their long hoses. "Yes," he muttered, still embarrassed. "I know him. Of course I know him. We're both runners."

"Why you spy on him, then, if you friends?"

"I really wasn't syping, you see, Uncle Polly. Oh, hell, yes, I was. It wasn't my idea. It was the coach."

"Why?"

"I don't know. He's worried."

"Why?"

"Because he's afraid that Mark . . ."

"As well he should be," Uncle Polly agreed massively. His agreement drew him several steps back toward Terry where, in a conspiratorial tone, he now whispered, "If you want to help, go find your California friend Mark Simpson. If you're truly his friend, knock him in the head, take him to the airport and put him on a plane to—anywhere."

Terry listened carefully and tried to make sense out of what he was hearing, though his efforts were undermined by the rather comical image of himself hitting Mark Simpson in the head, kidnapping him and taking him to the airport. "Uncle Polly, I can't do that!"

"You must! The boy's in danger." In his zeal to convince Terry of this totally insane course of action, he started coughing again, the rattles in his lungs increasing.

Terry felt himself torn between assisting the old man and resisting his crazy ideas concerning Mark Simpson. If he could find out how and why and from whom Mark was in danger—if it was real—it might be better just to go back and talk with Coach Herbert. He'd know what to do.

"Uncle Polly, can you tell me . . .?"

"I will say no more. All the time I say too much." Abruptly he broke off and looked distractedly about at the ground. "Go get your friend," he repeated now. "While there's still time, go get him and *make* him leave."

"I can't just . . . Can't you tell me?"

"No!"

This single word seemed to drag the old man backward, a never-ending protest in the night, an awesome sound, as though a lifetime of protest and rebellion had been contained too long and was now at last being released. "No more bargaining," he cried out, moving steadily away from Terry. "Never any room to bargain. Cannot be changed. Remember that. Tell him that. Tell him!"

Then suddenly he disappeared into the darkness at the end of the street.

His voice ceased and Terry heard nothing but a few of the remaining firemen calling out for slack here, tension there, as they worked at rewinding their long hoses. Terry looked back over his shoulder, baffled that the firemen had not heard the recent hysterical outburst.

Quickly he looked back, waiting for Uncle Polly to reappear in the spill of the streetlight at the opposite end of the block. Seconds, minutes passed. Still the man did not reappear. He could have—

No, he couldn't. There was no alley, no midblock escape route, the street lined solid on both sides. Then where was he?

And what did he mean about Mark, and what in the name of God was Terry supposed to do now? As the fragmented confusion increased inside his head, he found only vague relief in one direction.

Coach Herbert. Go tell the coach exactly what had happened, what the old man had said, the works. Maybe that was what Coach had wanted all along. Maybe he knew what the old man was saying. Anyway, get rid of it. Dump it in the coach's lap.

He took one look back over his shoulder and saw the last of the firemen climbing aboard the fire truck. The pavement resembled a large reflecting pond that seemed still to contain the glow of the fire. He focused only a moment on the phenomenon then turned his back on it, got his bearings, selecting the quickest route to Coach's house and knowing he was probably in bed. But he'd just have to get up, for now—whether he liked it or not—there was news of his fair-haired boy from California.

At the first intersection Terry paused in the spill of light into which he'd expected Uncle Polly to appear. The street corner was deserted, no one in sight. No cars, nothing. This peculiar vacuum caused Terry to wonder exactly what time it was. In the dim light he lifted his left wrist, angled his watch—a gift from his dad— toward the yellow glow.

What the—

The glass face was shattered, the clock's hands gone. All that remained were the Roman numerals marching in precise but useless formation around the outer rim. He looked down on the ruined watch with real regret. His dad would be furious.

Well, he'd have to deal with that later. For now, on to Coach Herbert's. Anything to clear his head of this screwed-up night.

He stepped off the curb, heading north toward the residential section that bordered the campus, and then stopped. He'd heard something. A sound that didn't belong to the night.

He looked around, thinking someone had come up behind him. That's what it had sounded like. Uncle Polly maybe? Nothing. The sidewalk, the corner, was as deserted as it had been moments before.

Freaked out, that's what he was, and no small wonder. Again he took a long remorseful glance down at his broken watch, then proceeded on down the shadowy street. Even the porch lights had been turned off. A line of cars were parked patiently at the curb, waiting for daybreak to give them permission to move.

Terry moved quickly into the dark vacuum and considered whistling. He used to do that as a kid. At least it would be a sound he could account for—and that would be reassuring. He tried now, but his mouth was dry, his lips worse.

Hurry! Two blocks straight ahead, then turn to the—

Listen.

He stopped midblock, head lifted, some instinct telling him to stop and listen. Then he heard it again. An undecipherable sound, really. Neither footsteps nor voice nor anything that he could identify. Like a sudden rush of air. Like something moving. Not in front of or behind him, but—

Above him?

Despite this curious and irrational thought, he looked up through the lace network of night trees, a spidery effect, as most of the leaves had already fallen in preparation for winter. Nothing. Only the traceries of dead branches, stiff and brittle-appearing, like arthritic old women.

While he was looking up he heard it yet increase, the very sound whose source he was searching for. Still increasing, the sound was made more complex now by an equally curious whimpering, a low moan which immediately was drowned out by a breathlessness, as though someone were breathing heavily close to his ears.

As the mystery vaulted—along with his fear—he turned rapidly in an erratic circle, his head lifted, as though he knew a threat was approaching and he could protect himself if only—

Then came the first stab, a knife-sharp probe to the center of

256

his back that sent both his hands moving at an awkward angle to the injured area. A reverberating pain seemed to spread out in concentric circles, causing him to stagger from the sidewalk to the middle of the street where, without benefit of light, he collided with several of the parked cars, as though he were drunk.

His fingers now found the torn fabric of his shirt and, beneath that, his flesh torn, a gaping hole spilling something sticky and wet, which trickled down his back and seemed to collect at the obstruction of his belt.

He had no idea what had attacked him, but neither did he have any intention of staying around to find out. Yet, just as he was recovering from the first attack, he heard the sound again. He looked fearfully up and only at the last moment realized the fatal error of that.

Before he could alter the line of his vision, he saw what appeared to be a great winged shadow swoop directly down upon him. At the center of that shadow was the sharp, probing thing that he saw too late, and from then on he was forced to rely upon the incoherence of pain, for in twin stabbing motions he felt both his eyes set aflame, small but powerful fires behind each retina, pain so excruciating that he let forth an animal howl of anguish, his hands now rushing away from his back to his eyes, where he felt the same hot, sticky moisture pouring from the blank holes, the sensation of heat so strong that all his hands could do were to hover helplessly in the general vicinity of his face.

Ultimately the agony toppled him. He fell face forward and felt the knifelike drill now attacking his shoulders, a cool rush of air across his bare back, accompanied by the unidentifiable whimpering and breathlessness and the flapping of great wings and a strong odor.

An incision now ran the length of his back, the fire from his eyes spreading, an interior fire which seemed to burn through his brain and emerge on the back of his neck. Tear after tear, cut after cut, his head lifting as each strip of his flesh was torn from his back.

The living, coherent Terry Crawford was gone, blessedly removed from this world. All that remained on the darkened residential street was a piece of bloody carrion—

"Hello? Hello?" Mark shouted into the receiver of the public telephone on the third floor of his dorm, wondering who it was on the opposite end of the line. He had called his mother's number but a woman's voice—not his mother's, one he'd never heard before—had answered. Then he'd lost her for a moment. Static. Then a curious silence.

"Hello? Is anybody there? Can you hear me?"

"Of course I can hear you, Mark. No need to shout. No need at all."

There was that voice again, well modulated, quite attractive, but who in the hell was it?

"I'm . . . sorry," Mark apologized. "The connection was bad there for a moment. I . . ." He broke off, listening. There was some peculiar sound in the background like— He couldn't identify it. "I was told to call home. There was a message," he began again. "Is my mother there? I do have the right number, don't I? Brett Simpson, Area Code . . ."

"Of course. I'm a good friend of your mother's, Mark. She asked me to call you. So it's my call you're returning."

Alarmed for some reason, Mark gripped the receiver and stared at the graffiti-covered walls surrounding the telephone box. "Is anything wrong? Is she . . . is she all right? My mother, I mean."

"She's fine, Mark. She's really fine. She wanted me to call you and tell you that she had a chance to go down to Baja. You know how she loves it, and a mutual friend of ours who runs a travel agency was taking a group down and invited your mother to go along. So . . ."

Mark covered his free ear in an attempt to screen out the dorm noise. In the process the blood-spotted towel fell off his arm and he saw a small gaping hole on his forearm as though something had literally taken a bite out of him. "Baja?" he repeated, his sense of bewilderment growing. To the best of his knowledge, his mother had never been to Baja in her life—nor had she ever expressed a desire to go. As for "loving it"—

"I beg your pardon," he said politely, pleased to hear the static clear, the reception good, the mysterious sound gone, "what did you say your name was?"

The woman laughed, a beautiful sound, an uncultivated voice but a naturally beautiful one. "Oh, you wouldn't know me, Mark. At least you wouldn't remember me. I met you when you were just a baby. I moved in down the street after you left for school. But, like I said, I've known your mother for a long time. All the way back to our Navy days."

Navy days? Then he would know her.

"Could you tell me," he began, still courteous, "is there any way I can get in touch with her? A phone number, surely."

"In Baja?" There was that laugh again, irresistible. "You have to be kidding, Mark. That's where people go to get away from telephones."

"When did she leave?"

"Well, let's see. A few days ago."

"I can't understand why she didn't call me."

"Oh, she tried, Mark. She really did. You're a hard man to pin down."

The woman laughed again and he thought of wind chimes. Still, what she said was true. He'd been in and out a lot.

"Well, listen, Mark, I have to go now. I really do. I've done my duty." Again she laughed. "I promised your mom I'd call you. Don't worry. She's a big girl and can take care of herself. So you just settle down and run your races, get good grades and break all the little girls' hearts, you hear?"

For some reason he shivered and felt a cold blast of air, as though someone had opened the door on a deep freeze. "Wait!" he called into the receiver, wanting more information, wanting at least this woman's name and number.

But then he heard the connection broken, the line go dead, heard a steady hum interrupted occasionally by static. And then heard—nothing.

"You through, Simpson?" someone called out from the end of the hall. "It ain't a private line, you know."

He looked toward the owner of the voice and didn't recognize him. He nodded vaguely and hung up the receiver, his eye falling again on the graffiti-covered wall, the innocence of hearts and flowers mixed with crude drawings and cruder gestures. Just as he was turning away, at the very edge of the scrambled messages and artworks, he read two words.

See Cass.

He stood for a moment as though transfixed at the visual images that bombarded his mind, confused and confusing. He saw her as they had made love, and that image blended with the one he'd recently left of the young girl seated on the floor beside the rocker, head resting on the seat—

See Cass.

Suddenly the wall, the phone, every solid object in the hall began to waver as though underwater. He closed his eyes and held onto the phone box and waited out the dizziness. No big deal.

259

"Hey, Simpson, have you seen Terry Crawford? He was supposed to . . ."

Slowly Mark shook his head, as though fearful of adding to these feelings of weakness.

"Well, where the hell could he have gone?" The voice drew near, then broke off sharply. "What the hell happened to you, Simpson?" There was awe in this voice, a kind of marvel, as the boy drew closer.

But Mark moved quickly away and tried to dismiss him. "You should see the other guy," he quipped, and tried to cover the dried blood spots on the white towel, courtesy of Amos Foster.

"You'd better see Doc Robbins," the boy called after him. "Doc likes to know every time you nick yourself shaving."

"I will, I will," Mark called cheerily back. He turned the corner of the upstairs corridor, breaking into a light run which deposited him in front of his own door—a sight which he viewed now with all the simple reverence of a pilgrim.

"Thank God!" he muttered and pushed open the door, closed it immediately behind him and then slid the bolt. Better than nothing. He was more than content for several minutes to inhabit the darkness, leaning against the door, as he realized he literally lacked the energy for any further movement.

In the darkness he closed his eyes, as though he needed a double blindness for protection against that which he did not understand. In the dark vacuum he heard a woman's voice again, an echo.

She's gone to Baja with a mutual friend and she told you not to worry.

There had been nothing wrong with the message. Of course it was without precedent. His mother never even went to the store without telling him. Still, he could live with that. After all, they were eighteen hundred miles apart and it was past time for them to organize and follow their own lives without each other.

No, the trouble with the message had been the messenger. Who was she and why hadn't she identified herself? Mark knew all of his mother's friends—and rather well at that. He'd not even recognized the voice, though she'd claimed to be an old friend of his mother's from Navy days.

Suddenly a new weariness compounded the old and at the same time multiple throbbings erupted on his body—one in the exact center of his back, one on his hand, one on his left cheek and one—the worst—on his arm.

Feeling a new momentum—a kind of unexpected energy brought on, no doubt, by at last being alone—he peeled off his shirt, grabbed the gooseneck lamp from the desk and hurried, bare-chested, to the dresser mirror. The cord reached and he flipped on the brighter illumination of his desk lamp, angling it toward the glass and looked.

The wound beneath his left eye resembled a puncture. That it had bled was evident in the multiple network of dried bloodstains which now coated Mark's face. In addition, the tender flesh around the eye had already commenced to swell and turn blue. It was going to be one hell of an eye. Upon closer examination he saw that, beyond the damage of the puncture itself, the eye was unharmed. Certainly no stitches were required. A shot, perhaps, but he could wait on that until morning.

Now he angled himself around and tried to see his back. Basically there was the same damage—a blue-black puncture hole, slightly swollen, and a dried network of blood culminating at the obstruction of his belt.

Then there was the third—his arm—the one that had hurt the most, as though something with teeth had tried to tear flesh from the bone. As he moved the light down he saw that this one was more than a puncture. Here a sizable piece of skin had been torn off and his forearm bore the same dried and rusted appearance as the other two wounds, extensive bleeding in all three places, as well as a slight cut on his hand.

As though the careful assessment of his wounds had contributed to his weakness, suddenly he felt his stomach turn, felt his knees give. Using the end of the dresser, then the chair for support, he cut a wobbly path to the bed and sat heavily, kicking the stained towel as he moved. Once down, he closed his eyes and rested his head in his hands. Maybe Doc Robbins had better take a suture or two on the arm. But no sooner had he reached the decision than he canceled it. Had he lost his mind? He renewed his grasp on his head as though literally to hold it together.

Outside in the hall he continued to hear voices. Someone shouted, "Anybody seen Crawford?"

"Try the sack. You know Terry."

Briefly Mark saw an image of the tall, red-haired boy. Open, honest, uncomplicated. Lucky.

With the toe of his shoe he kicked halfheartedly at the soiled towel. Amos Foster. Why had he just happened along? Don't ask questions. Just be grateful.

On the curled hem of the towel he saw stitching. A tag of some sort, one end curling free from the towel itself. Indulging in idle curiosity, he bent over and felt a new throbbing on his face and ignored it. Lifting the hem of the towel, he straightened the name tag and held it toward the light of the lamp.

Slowly he stood, taking the towel with him to the source of the light itself and read it again.

RITA MANNING.

For several moments he stared at it, as though if he stared long enough, he might be given the gift of at least partial understanding. He longed to talk with his mother, to tell her that the presumption made years ago after Rita Manning's disappearance had been very wrong.

Now he was convinced that it was Rita Manning who had been talking to Cass about loyalty and dependence. Had it been Rita Manning in the chapel as well? And why had the dress appeared to move of its own volition? And why did Cass appear so fearful whenever her mother was mentioned.

His mind cut off, as though overloaded. At last it had reached the limits of its natural endurance. He slumped against the dresser and somehow found enough energy to make his way back to the bed, where gingerly he let himself down, angling away from the cut on his back, his head at last coming into reassuring and comforting contact with the pillow.

It wasn't exactly sleep, for he continued to see splintered images from the day. When he saw the golden glow of cotton-woods and the gemlike chapel he felt a degree of ease—though paradoxically he was forced to admit the peace was a bogus one, for at the same time he knew he'd never felt so lonely, so alone, so abandoned in his life.

With a kind of mindless concentration Coach Herbert smoothed the fringed border of his woven place mat, waiting for the sound of Peg's car to leave his hearing as she backed down the drive on her way to Doc Robbins's house. He heard the car go from reverse to low, listened as she pulled away from the curb and realized he should be going with her.

But he couldn't. Not just yet. He needed some time alone. Women, by nature, were better equipped to handle these things anyway. The car was gone now and Peg with it, her eyes red-rimmed from silent weeping. But, Lord, what she'd accomplished since the call had come a mere two hours ago at six A.M.!

Although he'd been expecting it, he still couldn't believe it. Ellie Robbins—dead. The wasting cancer had at last claimed her. Old

Doc had had one of the nurses call directly from the hospital. They wouldn't let him go home until someone came to pick him up, take him home and stay with him. As the son and only child was in Seattle, Peg—bless her heart—had volunteered, and Coach Herbert had said he'd walk over in a little while.

He carried his oversized coffee mug to the stove and filled it again with steaming coffee, snagged a sticky cinnamon roll from the pan, warm from the oven, and carried both back to the kitchen table where Peg had thoughtfully left the morning paper, still folded.

He sat down and drew his bathrobe about him and stared at the steam from the coffee and the tender flesh of the roll and felt himself growing hard and philosophical. Peg was halfway right. He wasn't absolutely certain that Ellie Robbins was with God, as Peg believed, for he'd never in his busy life had time to work out such problems, but at least he knew one thing for certain. She didn't hurt anymore. And that was a blessing. And she didn't have to suffer any more indignities. That too was a blessing. And she didn't have to feel herself growing weaker, more incapacitated.

A sip of coffee. Feeling better, really better. Thus fortified, he opened the paper. He angled the headlines toward the bright spill of sunlight coming through the starched yellow curtains: SKELETON FOUND ON LOCAL STREET.

The macabre words seemed to leap out at him. Of course it had to be a prank. Med students, no doubt. At least once a year they pulled something obscene and indecent and outraged the entire town.

Still shocked, he lifted the paper and read the lead story. The grisly sight had been found by a couple out for a late-night stroll on Sorrento Avenue. The young girl was still in a state of shock. Small wonder. They said they were walking down the middle of the street and stumbled over it.

In mounting horror, Coach Herbert slammed the paper down on the table and soothed his disgust in the rest of the cinnamon roll and a large swallow of hot coffee. Well, if you asked him, the future docs had gone too far this time and he, for one, hoped the police nabbed the pranksters and literally threw the book at them.

Enjoying his anger—at least it kept him from feeling grief—he lifted the paper and read:

> Authorities are puzzled by what appeared to
> be large amounts of fresh, though dried, blood

263

in the general area of the skeleton. A pathology
report is due later this evening which authorities
hope might give some clue concerning the age
of the skeleton. For now the area has been
cordoned off as the investigation continues.

For several minutes he read the rest of the paper, then read it
again and groaned as he reread that authorities were in the dark
as to the identity of the remains and how such a grisly sight had
come to be found on a city street.

Coach Herbert stood and stretched, continuing to feel better,
despite the depressing headline. The heavy pall lifted at least for
a few minutes. As he headed back toward the stove and another
cup of coffee, he eyed the phone at the end of the kitchen
counter. He would phone the dorm and check in with Crawford.
Not a bad idea. Next best to going over there himself, which of
course he couldn't do now under the circumstances. He veered to
the right, grabbed the phone and carried it back to the kitchen
table, pushing aside the newspaper in the process, seeing again
the macabre headline.

Quickly he dialed the dorm number and glanced up at the
yellow-daisy face of the kitchen clock. Eight-fifteen. Everyone up
or they'd damned well better be!

"Hello? Who's there?" He bent over the receiver and cupped
his hand around it, trying to identify the male voice at the other
end. "Who? Dick? Dick, this is Coach Herbert. Would you go find
Terry Crawford for me? It's important."

He heard eager respect in the boy's voice and was pleased by it.
Holding the receiver clamped between his jaw and his shoulder,
he reached for his mug and the paper. Searching for other items
of interest, he turned the paper over.

CAMPUS CAFÉ BURNS TO THE GROUND.

Again he lifted the newspaper, astonished by the dramatic
events of the night. Apollo Zelius. It had been his restaurant, the
House of Greek, which had been leveled. Cause of fire as yet
unknown.

In the background on the phone Coach Herbert heard the
shouts of young men. They'd be finished with breakfast now and
on their way to classes or training sessions.

"Coach?"

"Yeah. Here."

"The guys say Terry didn't come in last night."

264

This announcement—so blunt and incredible—seemed to echo for a moment before it fully penetrated. "Didn't . . . what?" Coach Herbert tried to repeat.

"The guys say Terry Crawford didn't come back to the dorm last night. He didn't sleep in his bed."

The repetition was faithful and without variation, as though the speaker knew the seriousness of what he was saying. For a moment Coach Herbert stared at the receiver in his hand, as though that inanimate object held a clue to the mystery.

"Sir, are you there?"

He heard the distant voice coming through the receiver and belatedly realized he was keeping the boy waiting. Coach Herbert said at last, "Would you do me a favor?"

"Sure, anything. What?"

Now Coach Herbert focused on the folded newspaper where he'd dropped it on the kitchen table. Upside down the news made even less sense.

"What, sir? What do you want me to do?"

"Uh . . . nothing. Nothing, I'm sorry. I'll be in later. Oh, wait! You might pass the word that Doc Robbins's wife died last night." He waited, expecting some sort of reaction from the voice on the other end of the line. "Did you hear me?" he asked sharply.

"Yes, sir, I heard you. And I will, sir. Pass the word, I mean."

"Thanks," Coach Herbert muttered now. Without a further word he hung up and held his hand on the receiver for several moments as though to isolate the unfeeling voice on the other end of the line.

Terry Crawford didn't come in last night. The kid had a girl—he'd told Coach Herbert that himself—and he was a red-blooded all-American boy in all respects. Probably shacked up in one of the motels out on old Highway 45. Well, he'd call them both on the carpet later in the day, both Simpson and Crawford. It would be a good excuse to leave Doc's house anyway. Peg had told him she planned to stay all day and be of whatever service she could.

Slowly he returned to the kitchen table and sat heavily, feeling midnight tired at eight in the morning. He lifted up his coffee mug and made a face at the now cold and bitter coffee. Even the cinnamon rolls were too gooey with icing—and cold. Everything cold—including himself.

As he pushed up from the kitchen table he held his position for a moment, poised halfway up, leaning, palms down, on the table. The newspaper, right side up, stared back at him, a blurred gray newspaper photo of tree-shaded, quiet, placid Sorrento Avenue, one of the town's most respected streets. Several faceless figures in the photo—the police, he assumed—cordoning off the area where the skeleton had been found.

Put it out of your mind. You have enough problems of your own this morning.

On that note he quickly left the kitchen, heading for a long, hot shower and—hopefully—a cessation of thoughts of death—

Cass slept deeply—as she knew she would—and upon awakening remembered instantly what she had to do this day, had always known, but now dreaded it more than she had anticipated.

Don't think about it. Don't think about anything.

She slipped out of bed. For a moment, once standing, she felt a pleasurable ache in her legs and remembered the reason. The memory left her weak and she sat on the edge of her mussed bed, closed her eyes and saw him so clearly. Briefly the child within her wept with longing and loneliness.

"Cass?"

She looked up at the voice, knew where it was coming from and knew she had no choice but to obey it. "Coming."

"Don't dress. Remember, Cass, you're not to dress today. I'll help you. Just your robe, that's enough."

"When did you get back, Mother?"

"Late. I'm fine. Are you as excited as I am?"

Again Cass bowed her head, then reached for her robe at the foot of her bed and slowly drew it on, knotting it about her waist. Briefly she wondered where her mother had gone last night. It had been late when she'd heard her go out.

"Are you coming, Cass?"

"Coming." As she started toward her bedroom door she felt again a wave of dread like an ordeal long awaited, finally arrived, the specifics of which she didn't know or couldn't remember or wouldn't remember. At the door she stopped and leaned against it as a thought occurred. Why did it have to be today? Her mother had waited this long, what harm another week, another month? But she knew the answer, knew the uselessness of even posing the question. It would only make it more difficult.

"Good girl, Cass. Come along now."

Thus resolved, Cass pushed open the door and stepped out into the cold, shadowy corridor and for a moment missed her

266

grandfather with an ache that amounted to physical pain. Since his death she'd had no one to bridge the gap. Uncle Polly had tried, but Uncle Polly was her mother's friend and spy, not hers, as was Amos Foster.

"Cass, are you coming?"

For a moment she turned in an aimless and disoriented circle, feeling lost in the upstairs corridor. Then she looked down the hall toward the stairs, on one side her mother's room, her's on the other. From where she stood the double doors appeared to be closed.

"Come closer, Cass. Sit outside. I'm not quite ready for you yet. I can talk to you through the door."

A bad sign. Either her mother was angry with her or—

"Did you know about last night, Cass? Did you know that he was here?"

As she approached the closed doors she felt new apprehension. "Who, Mother?"

"Don't play games with me. You know perfectly well whom I mean."

The tone, the words, the closed doors—all three frightened her. Surely there wouldn't be punishment. Not today.

"Sit down, Cass. You need to be reminded of a few things."

"Yes, Mother." Docilely she sat on the floor outside the doors, drew her robe about her and crossed her arms in weak defense against the chill. She leaned her head back against the wall, closed her eyes and found herself hoping only that it would be over soon.

"He followed you here, didn't he?" she heard her mother accuse.

"If he did, I was unaware of it."

"You're a liar!"

This voice screeched at her so close her ears hurt. She bent over and covered them with her hands and for a moment was thankful for the new silence.

"Did you sleep with him? Cass, answer me! Did you sleep with him?"

"Yes."

"Bitch!"

"You told me to make him helpless."

"But don't make yourself helpless in the process."

"I'm not, Mother."

"Then you're resolved?"

Cass closed her eyes again and felt strangely dead. "Yes."

There was a pause, then, "Good girl. Smart girl. Grandfather used to say that you weren't smart, but I insisted that you were and you are, aren't you?"

The betrayal by her grandfather hurt. In an attempt to cancel the tears, she closed her eyes tighter. She knew how her mother hated tears.

"Nothing to cry about, Cass. I'll never abandon you like he did. You'll be with me always because you need me, don't you?"

"Yes, Mother."

"Where does your strength come from?"

"From you, Mother."

"And I have only your best interest at heart, correct?"

"Yes, Mother."

"When this is all over I think we'll go away. Would you like that?"

"Yes, Mother."

"Italy. I think you'd love Italy."

"Yes, Mother."

"You are a good girl, Cass. I would hate it if something terrible happened to you."

"Thank you, Mother."

"He was here last night."

"I'm . . . sorry, Mother. He must have . . . followed me."

"Amos is gone now."

Cass looked up, startled by this news. "Why?"

"He betrayed me. Just like Uncle Polly did. Surely you knew that. You were probably in on it as well."

"No!"

"Amos helped him, the bastard."

"What . . .?"

"Oh, never mind your pretty head about it. I may let him come back later on."

The news was upsetting. She liked Amos. He'd been a good friend. "Can I take my radio this evening?"

"Of course. I always let you take your radio, even when you're careless and leave it lying about."

"I found it."

"You didn't find it at all. He did. The bastard did."

"Why do you call him that?"

"I could call him worse if you prefer that."

"No."

"You really think he's harmless? You do, don't you?"

A dangerous question. Be wary of the answer. Then there was no need.

"Well, that's one of the purposes of this day. To reeducate you as it were. To let you see for yourself the duplicity of all men. Once you learn that, then we're finished here and can leave. You'd like that, wouldn't you?"

Again Cass nodded.

"Then why are you sitting out there? Come on in. We have so much work to do."

Cass opened her eyes at the sudden transition.

"Are you coming, Cass? If you're hungry, don't bother. We'll find enough food to make gluttons of ourselves. You mark my words."

All the time her mother talked, Cass pulled herself slowly to her feet, not always understanding what was being said but knowing that the momentous day had finally arrived, one that her mother had been planning for and waiting for and anticipating for years. As for Mark, it was just as well. Nothing could have ever come of it.

"Cass, don't dawdle. We have so much to do today and I really don't have time to punish you. Don't make me. I want today to be perfect in every way—for both of us."

"Coming." She glanced down the stairs before she went into her mother's room and thought she could detect traces of him—his scent, the curious manner in which his presence registered on the air like an imprint. If she only knew precisely what this day would hold for him and for her! It was like a coming of age for both of them, performers in a drama in which they lacked a script.

No matter. She would do her best for her mother's sake.

Cass pushed open the door to the shadowy interior of her mother's room and smelled something strong and acrid. She saw several fresh red stains on the hardwood floor, most dried, though a few were still wet and glistening.

He'd never felt so alone, cut off, isolated. All morning long his only companion had been his father's ghost. For the rest of it, his room was quiet. The dorm was quiet, everyone taken off, freed from training in memory of Doc Robbins's wife. Even the world outside his window seemed to have gone unnaturally quiet.

Every attempt he'd made today to alter his aloneness had been blunted. He'd even ventured down to the dining room at noon, thinking he'd try mending some of the broken fences with his teammates. But the dining hall had been closed, and all training sessions had been canceled. He'd even gone by Terry Crawford's room but found that empty too.

Now, sitting alone in his room on the end of his bed, it almost seemed as though the world had purposefully cut him off and isolated him.

As he bowed his head he thought he'd give anything to alter the silence—which really wasn't a true silence at all, for he kept hearing things, voices.

Along with the fragmented voices constantly hovering over him was the remembered image of his father as he'd grown up with him—that fixed, boyish face, so confident, the backward collar, the enormous and overstated silver crucifix, like God—

With his eyes closed he could still see his father vividly. The longer he stared, the more poses presented themselves to him, as though all the hundreds of snapshots in his mother's old photo albums had suddenly come to life. His father—still looking starched in old clothes—moving stiffly down a walkway. His father standing behind a baby carriage. His father and three others, all looking tense and uncomfortable.

Suddenly Mark stood, fearing that if he didn't get out of his room he would surely lose his mind. Someone was in pursuit of him and he knew who it was and suspected that he would know no peace until he met him head-on.

His father.

In a way he'd known it all along. His father was the one who'd wanted him back here.

Why?

Slowly he walked to the window and looked down on the empty street. Usually bustling at mid-afternoon—kids passing to and from classes, in and out of the gym—now, no one. All off in a beer joint somewhere breaking training. When the cat's away . . .

Enough. Get out.

This interior voice was so urgent that he started immediately toward his door, pulled it open and stepped out into the shadowy hall and saw someone standing at the far end. A man, his back to Mark. Not a student. He was wearing a dark, slightly out of fashion suit.

Mark froze. "Who's there?" he called out, and heard his voice echo endlessly about the empty corridor.

270

As the door to his room slammed shut behind him, the noise startled Mark. He looked quickly over his shoulder at the sudden sound, then looked back toward the end of the hall, ready to call again.

The man was gone.

Father.

Try to think. Where had he last seen him? At the Officers' Club, sitting at that table. For several minutes Mark stood in the hall, nervously inspecting every shadow as though it contained a threat.

Leave.

Again, as the voice in his head gave him a direct command, he backed a few steps down the hall away from the place where he'd seen the man. Correction, thought he'd seen the man.

Keep it all in perspective.

Suddenly he heard a phone ringing and looked toward the public phone box at the end of the corridor.

Go answer the phone. He needed a human voice. He'd be all right then.

As he ran past the closed doors on the third floor, he wondered why everyone had closed their doors. Usually they were wide open.

Even as he lifted the receiver he shouted a greeting, "Hello?" Quickly he held it to his ear, half afraid that he'd arrived too late. "Hello? Who is it? Anybody there?" he shouted again. "Please . . ."

Although he did not hear the irritating buzz of a disconnection, he did hear a hollow silence that begged to be filled—which unfortunately matched the silence he'd inhabited all morning long.

"Hello? Who's calling please?" No answer. Only that vacuum, that empty silence. The longer he listened to it the more alarmed he became.

Father.

What does he want? Why had he become suddenly aggressive? The images and the memories and that awful silence could only be described as aggressive. Someone was trying to manipulate him, to tell him something.

Suddenly he hung up the receiver and removed his hand as though it were hot and he was in danger of burning himself.

Cass.

Suddenly he heard a telephone again. Not this one, for he was still standing directly in front of it.

271

He heard the ring in echoing shrillness and realized it must be coming from the second floor, directly beneath him. No concern of his. Whereas before he'd run to lift the receiver in time, now he moved at quite a deliberate pace down the hall, uncaring whether he reached the phone in time or not.

Yet as he moved leisurely down the third-floor corridor, the phone on the floor below seemed to be ringing with rhythmical insistence. Even as he started down the stairs he knew the phone would persist, that he could take his time and still arrive before the ringing stopped.

Someone was trying to reach him.

If only he could talk with his mother! What the hell, Baja wasn't the end of the world. Surely there was a phone there someplace. Maybe that was Sally with news of his mother. Maybe it had been Sally upstairs, a bad connection.

Then suddenly it became imperative that he reach the phone in time. He took the second-floor landing in a run and stumbled, righted himself with the help of the banister and dashed down the second-floor corridor. As he ran he counted the telephone rings and prayed that someone's stubbornness held out.

Still several feet away, he reached out and jerked the receiver free, held it to his ear and closed his eyes as again he shouted, "Hello? Who is it? What do you want?"

There was silence, then, "I beg your pardon, sir. You're wanted at the chapel."

Mark gaped at the voice as well as at the message. "Who do you want to speak with?" he asked.

"You, sir. Sorry to bother you but you're needed at the chapel right away. Could you come?"

Suddenly Mark slammed down the receiver, held his hand on it and saw that hand trembling.

He needed Cass.

He listened intently, longing to hear just one human voice, one sound of this world. A screech of tires, a shouted obscenity, the roar of a jet passing overhead. But nothing. He heard nothing. At last surrendering to the vacuum, he slowly took his hand off the phone.

You're wanted at the chapel, sir.

Then he really didn't have a choice, did he? Whatever it was that had drawn him back here had specific need of him now. How foolish it would be to pay heed for this long, to follow every capricious whim and then suddenly go deaf. Carefully he started down the steps that led to the first floor and the street.

He wanted Cass desperately. As he stepped out into the direct rays of a late-afternoon sun, he considered again returning to the large house on Sorrento. Maybe they could go to the chapel together.

But an equally strong instinct commanded him to go alone. Whatever was awaiting him at the chapel had to be faced and dealt with alone.

A remarkably short time later—after a walk of which he could remember nothing—he found himself on the long boulevard that led directly toward the chapel. The same late-afternoon glow of autumn sun on golden cottonwoods transformed the area into an unreal color. So exaggerated were the tones that it resembled a child's fairy tale or a Disney cartoon. No colors of this world were that vibrant, that compelling.

As he turned into the rounded driveway, he thought it seemed in better condition than the last time —a smooth, curved, unbroken ribbon of concrete, as though it had only recently been laid and smoothed. If the chapel had appeared in mint condition before, now it literally glistened with a fresh coat of white-satin paint. Mark saw it first like a jigsaw through the scattered golden leaves, combined with the beauty of the late autumn sky.

He proceeded slowly down the drive, suffering the distinct sensation of passing through a golden curtain, leaving the tenuous present behind for the certain and predetermined past. He wouldn't have been too surprised to have looked about and seen clusters of white uniforms on the boulevard.

Father.

Close by. He was close by and Mark knew it. He could feel that presence, the same presence he'd grown up with.

He noticed the chapel doors were open. As he approached the front steps, for some reason he felt a compulsion to do so in stealth, trying not to announce his presence in any way. Halfway up the steps, coming ever so faintly into the golden silence, he heard voices. Only a low hum at first. Male and female, as nearly as he could tell.

Still moving as quietly as possible, Mark stepped into the shaded darkness of the vestibule and heard the voices growing louder. Definitely a man and a woman, coming from—

There.

At the back of the chapel he stopped and looked down to the front pew, where earlier he'd seen the woman dressed in black as though in mourning. No mourning female this time, but rather a familiar sight and sound. The red dress, the thick auburn hair,

273

the irresistibly beautiful voice. She sat straight in the pew, facing the pulpit, as though someone had commanded her to sit up straight and keep silent and pay attention. Again he couldn't see her face, but he experienced a surge of mysterious joy at having found her again.

Seated next to her on the front pew was a man dressed in a dark suit, the angle of his body obscuring his face. He gestured occasionally, wild and erratic movements, as though he were going slightly mad. Mark heard him whisper fiercely, "You must listen to me!" as though the woman had been paying no attention to him. "Listen to me, I beg you! We can go ahead. I can request a . . ."

"No."

"Why not?"

"Mainly because I don't want to."

This declaration, so breezy and uninvolved, seemed to fall in cold counterpoint on the man's fervent passion. "What do you mean you don't want to?" he now demanded, and leaned closer.

Mark suspected that he'd grasped the woman's arm, applying subtle pressure.

"As I said"—the woman was speaking—"there are others to consider. Besides ourselves. Anyway, we did nothing wrong."

"Nothing wrong!" the man repeated, his shocked incredulity seeming to render him speechless for a few moments.

"Oh, come on, now," she chided, something very young and adolescent in her voice. "We had a good time together, that's all. You know that."

"No!"

"Yes."

This short, intense debate involving only two small words seemed to put an end to the conversation for several minutes. Embarrassed, Mark considered leaving. Obviously he'd stumbled on a very personal argument and he had no desire to stay and eavesdrop.

"Rita, it's more than that and you know it!"

Mark had just turned about when he heard the man's plaintive cry, his voice breaking.

"You . . . told me . . . at the time . . ."

"Oh, for heaven's sake! You should know by now not to take anything I say too seriously. You can't. I play games. Surely you see that?"

Suddenly the man stood up. Mark could feel his fury—like a

poison—increasing. For a moment he thought the man would strike her, this capricious woman who now disclaimed any feeling between them.

"Then I've ruined my life! For you! For nothing!" The man stared straight up toward the pulpit as he spoke.

Mark continued to stare at the man's back, some fearful element of recognition dawning.

"Oh, don't be so melodramatic," the woman chided, her impelling voice as beautiful as ever, despite the ugliness of what she was saying. "Surely you don't think you're the first!"

"You . . . spoke . . . of love, Rita," he now said falteringly.

"Of course I did. I speak of love always. It's the only thing worth speaking about."

"You led me to believe . . ."

"You've believed what you wanted to believe."

"Damn you!"

"My, that doesn't sound very much like a man of God."

"You're evil!"

"Of course I'm evil. And so are you, or else you wouldn't have given in."

Suddenly the man buckled. He sat back down on the pew, as though someone had struck him, and covered his face with his hands. Again Mark could feel his torment and longed to share it—or relieve it. Out of the man's dreadful agony Mark heard one word, scarcely audible but clear nonetheless.

"Brett."

"Oh, your sweet little wife. She'll survive, flourish even, as the widow of a naval hero."

Then the recognition was complete, for, though stunned and wounded, the man slowly rose, gazing down on the woman as though staring into an open coffin. Before he could speak, the woman laughed, a resounding music like wind chimes, and moved carefully to the far end of the pew.

"What greater gift could I give you, Gerald, in return for your . . . love, than permanent release from all that guilt? My heavens, in only a few years it would turn you inside out. You'd destroy yourself and take several others with you. Instead, I'm going to let you be a war hero, loved and revered and remembered by all. Even sweet little Brett. She'll never know of your fall, I promise you. It'll be my secret as well."

Mark tightened his grip on the back of the pew, as though fearful of losing his balance. He'd wandered into another world—

275

or been summoned. Now all he wanted was a way out. What business was it of his that his father and Rita Manning had—

He saw his father pull himself to his feet and turn toward the red dress just exiting through a side door of the chapel. In his cry was the torment of all men—weak regardless, doomed regardless.

"Damn you!" he shouted. "Damn you! God damn you!"

The cry echoed over and over again, dragging the man the length of the pew, where he stumbled finally in his rage, grief and guilt, and went down on his knees before the pew, disappearing from sight.

Mark stared ahead, expecting the man to reappear. Then go to him. Try to understand later. Pass no judgments, just go to him. As he started down the center aisle he heard his own belabored breathing and approached the front pew with hesitancy, looked down on the place where he'd seen his father fall and saw—

Nothing. Gone. Both of them.

He looked up to the side door, which had been left open, and saw an unexpected sight—Amos Foster's old Chevy parked and idling right outside the door.

"Hurry!" he shouted at Mark. "We don't have much time. Neither you nor I. I'll take you there."

As Mark didn't move immediately, he heard Amos shout again, his head halfway out of the car. "Are you going to move or not, you silly bastard? Your old man needs you. Now!"

Again Mark put aside the need to understand. He was being manipulated. At least now there was something honest about it, the past coming forward and identifying itself as past, pushing aside the present in the process.

Nothing really is ever lost. Nothing really is ever lost from the past.

He heard Amos curse. "You've come this far and I'll help you go the rest of the way. But we've got to hurry! That's it!"

His shouts and obscenities ceased as Mark moved toward the side door, giving the end of the pew a wide passage and close inspection. He'd seen the man—his father—go down. Where was he now?

"Crawl in. Hurry! I'll take you where you have to be."

As Mark obliged he recognized the old car, having been a passenger in it several times before. But it seemed older now, less well cared for. The seat cover was torn, as was the fabric overhead, which now hung down in ragged strips.

"Where are . . .?"

"Not far."

"Who are you?"

276

The question, though blunt and simple, seemed appropriate and did not warrant the great belly laugh which Amos Foster was now giving it. "Just get ready for what you have to do."

As the old Chevy careened down the streets of the base, Mark tried to get his bearings. Something had changed. Everything had changed. All of the buildings now were in mint condition, all freshly painted, the lawns mowed, the plantings and shrubs and bushes young and small. Here and there Mark saw groups of men moving off in various directions, all talking quietly, no one paying the slightest attention to the rattle and growl of the old Chevy motor, which sounded as if each turn would be its last.

A block from the extreme south edge of the base, Amos Foster guided the old Chevy to the right side of the street and tried to pump life into it a moment longer, but the car sputtered and died.

"End of line," the man announced.

Mark wished Cass were here.

"Go on, now," Amos insisted, leaning back against the torn seat covers. "Run on down to Coffin Pond. Your old man needs you there. He really was a good man and he tried to come back and help us, but . . ."

The man seemed suddenly to become massively tired. His breathing became labored. His head thrashed once or twice, then he turned away from Mark. "H-hurry!" he gasped. "Go on. Get out of here. It's all up to you now."

Not wanting to anger the man, Mark opened the car door and felt the handle fall off in his hand. He stepped out and at the same time saw the tires go flat, an immediate and consummate disintegration, as though some foreign chemical substance was causing the collapse to speed up.

"Amos!"

He bent over and tried to look back through the window, concerned for the man and wanting more information. But he was gone, the driver's seat empty, the car itself continuing to disintegrate before his eyes like time-lapse photography—the paint peeling, patches of rust appearing. All the tires flat now, then turning liquid, leaving the old car resting unevenly on rims.

Shocked, Mark backed away from the disintegration, not understanding it, concerned for Amos, yet knowing his concern was a matter of monumental insignificance in the face of this new and powerful sphere he'd entered.

Turning his back on the mysterious death of the car, Mark started off at a trot toward no-man's-land and heard something like an enormous machine working somewhere—

Then he saw it, just as he turned the last corner, atop the high embankment which overlooked Coffin Pond. From this distance it seemed to be an enormous yellow earthmover.

It hadn't been there before. But now he realized that "before" had no definition in this new sphere. Here there were no such designations as "before." Perhaps not even "after" either. "Now," that was the only viable reference point. "Now" and what did he see "now"?

The earthmover vibrated, as though someone were testing the motor. At the same time the huge jaws lined with steel teeth opened and closed again in a testing manner.

Who? he wondered, and quickly crossed the street, scrambling up the high embankment and feeling the coolness of an autumn breeze. He tried to see around the dazzling, fiery evening sun as it struck with blinding accuracy on the broad, front windshield of the earthmover, rendering sight useless. He started to call out, but knew that it was useless trying to project his voice over the din of the machine.

As he reached up for the door, the sun suddenly withdrew its blinding rays and slipped behind a cloud. Through the mud-streaked window he saw an apparition from a nightmare—a figure, head bleeding, blood streaming from his eyes, his nose, his mouth, his clothes burnt, still smoking, as was the flesh on both his arms. Around his neck, with bits of flesh clinging to it, Mark saw the crucifix—the large silver one that he'd looked at every day of his life.

"Help . . . me," came the words that somehow escaped through bleeding lips. "Help . . . me . . . Mark." This voice was growing stronger, despite the agony that was apparent in all respects.

Mark clung to the door of the high cab, looking up, part of his mind trying to reject what he saw and the other part responding with the need of a lifetime.

He could feel the powerful motor still vibrating beneath his feet as he stepped up closer to the plea for help.

"I . . . tried . . . twenty years ago. She must be destroyed. But my . . . spirit wasn't strong enough. I need you. You must help."

Through the blood and burnt skin, Mark now saw a superimposed image from the oil portrait and felt a sharp confirmation as it fit. Recognition complete. This was his father from his watery grave on the *Lexington* in the Coral Sea.

"Help me, Mark. She's evil. She'll destroy you. Evil must be destroyed."

The apparition did not look at Mark at any time while he spoke. Rather the dead eyes looked straight ahead with such intensity, such a weight of hate, that Mark was compelled to see the object of such ready poison.

Then he saw her.

The woman, dressed in red, the glimmering auburn hair falling liquidly down her back, standing on the precise edge of the high embankment, something relaxed, at ease, about her, as though she wasn't even aware of the large machine behind her angled directly toward her—or as though she didn't care.

"This is why I called you back, Mark. I need your help. I'm not strong enough by myself. Help me, please."

Still the woman had not looked back, had not in any way acknowledged the powerful machine which was aimed directly at her. If only she would turn, she would see the danger for herself.

"Mark, she'll destroy you, as she destroyed me, as she has destroyed your mother, and Alec, and everyone whose life she touches. Please come close and help me. I need . . ." The voice seemed to be growing fainter, though the hideous image was still clear.

The grim apparition had not moved from its original position behind the controls of the earthmover, yet Mark saw the enormous gearshift move, plunge forward, a single action which set the machine into a slow, lumbering course of forward motion. Not moving rapidly, for there was no need for speed. The killing aspect of this machine was its enormous weight. It would simply crush to death anything in its path.

"Come, Mark. Help me. You must help me. Good must always destroy evil. Please help me."

Turn around and look, for God's sake!

To Mark's surprise he heard an interior voice aimed at the woman. Why didn't she turn? Why did she continue to stand, unmoving, gazing out at the ghost base, as though—

Less than thirty feet now. He glanced at the apparition behind the controls and saw the wounded and blood-coated features fixed on its prey with the same intensity as the woman's gaze was fixed on the blank horizon.

As the machine rumbled closer and closer, Mark felt a splintering of emotion and instinct.

No!

Whoever she was, whatever she was, this was not the way.

"No!" he shouted again, aloud now, and reached into the high cab in an attempt to grab the gearshift, but a swollen, blue, blood-encrusted hand lifted at the same time, as though to hold him at bay.

"No, you musn't!" Mark cried, seeing the woman yet closer.

Why didn't she hear the machine? Why didn't she move? Why didn't she turn?

Less than twenty feet now and drawing nearer. The specter seemed to be trying to coax greater speed out of the earthmover. Repeatedly Mark heard the growl of an acceleration, the high-pitched squeal of gears abused.

Look! Turn around! Please!

But she didn't and somehow Mark knew she wouldn't, knew that both the apparition and the woman were playing roles preconceived in time. This had already happened.

"Take the controls, Mark. You do it with me. Together . . ." This voice reached him over the roar of the machine and he looked up to see the bloodied image smiling at him. "Hurry! We're almost . . ."

"No!" Mark protested a final time. Seeing the woman through the streaked windshield less than ten feet away now, he reached again for the gearshift and at the same time pushed hard against the specter's shoulder and felt the flesh of his hand come into contact with something winter-cold and looked back to find the apparition—

Gone. The driver's seat was empty, only a smeared residue of blood and water on the seat—that and a strong scent of seawater.

But while the apparition of his father was gone, the gigantic machine was still moving, still on course at a lumbering, but steady, pace, the large teeth-lined jaws aimed straight for the woman. For several terrifying moments Mark struggled with the controls, trying to find the one that would shut it off, turn it about. But he couldn't. The collision was inevitable.

Help me destroy her.

Then, assessing his time to be only a matter of seconds, he at last stumbled free of the earthmover and ran ahead at top speed and took a falling lunge in the direction of the woman.

The force of the impact carried them out of the path of the machine and, as it rumbled past, driverless, heading now for the edge of the abyss below the embankment, Mark covered the woman with his own body in a protective manner and felt her breathing beneath him and tried to look toward the embankment where the earthmover was just going over.

Quickly he bowed his head over her and warned, "Keep your eyes closed, head down!" Then he waited for the explosion which would surely come, the weight of the machine crushing everything, spilled fuel contributing to the fire and confusion and final explosion.

But nothing came. He dared once again to look carefully up and saw the earthmover gone over the side of the embankment.

He'd seen it, had tracked it, had watched it.

But still no explosion.

While his attention was riveted on the place where by now there should have been a fireball, he felt movement beneath him, the woman trying to accommodate the crush of his weight. As he moved to one side, he saw her, still facedown, saw her right hand lift to the crown of her long auburn hair, saw the fingers close tightly around the top and pull, the entire headpiece falling free.

A wig!

Mark raised up in stunned recognition. "Cass?"

She turned and he saw tears on her face. He had started to move completely free of her when he saw her attention fixed on something high overhead, the fear on her face beginning to mingle with new fear.

He followed the direction of her gaze and saw as well the enormous wingspan circling high above them, something about the darting and feinting movement that suggested rage.

"Don't move," Cass gasped. "She's . . ."

But she never finished, for suddenly he heard that nightmare sound, the same one that had pursued him out of Cass's house, that same displacement of air, followed by a curious breathless whimpering. The face was visible now—a hawk's face, beak open. The feinting and darting in midair over, the bird approached them now in dive-bomber fashion. It would be a killing collision and he knew it. Whoever those claws and that knifelike beak were intended for could not survive.

Then let it be him. Now he had more cause than ever to protect the woman beneath him.

"Hang on," he whispered. Again he covered her completely and found the softness of that short-cut blond hair. In the last moment before the attack, he murmured, "I love you."

Then he closed his eyes and waited for the first strike.

But it never came. The hissing displacement of air increased until it became a shrill whine and now it seemed to be hovering directly over them.

For a moment he dared to look back over his shoulder, still maintaining a protective position above Cass. As he did he saw the hawk hovering less than three feet above them, larger than any hawk he'd ever seen, suspended, still airborne but unmoving. As he watched, the hawk's face became liquid and blended with that of a woman's face—one he'd seen before on that first day in the Officers' Club.

Then suddenly the bird/woman shrieked—a sirenlike sound that seemed to explode endlessly against his ears—and at the same time the wings moved. The air around them became increasingly cold and all light left the sky. In total blackness, he heard the wings lift, heard the screams yet increase and saw a faint light returning along the rim of the world. The hawk was high above them now and the shrill, sirenlike scream grew fainter with height and distance.

Cass was watching now as well, her face still fearful, a powerful invasion which caused her entire body to tremble inside the red dress. Her first word was scarcely audible.

"Gone," was what she whispered.

Slowly she began to sit up, though not once did she release her grasp on Mark's hand. "Gone," she repeated, still fearfully searching the sky. All at once she bent over and covered her face with both hands and cried.

Mark watched, helpless, on his knees before her, trying to understand. "Why were you the one standing on . . .?"

"She made me. Said that you would commit the same act of violence against me that your father committed against her."

Mark was stunned. "She wouldn't have let you die!"

"No. She would have destroyed you first, as she tried to destroy your father but couldn't. It was his spirit that attempted to kill her years ago. She had no power against the dead. So, in her fury that night, she killed Amos Foster instead."

"Then why didn't she attack me a minute ago? Attack both of us."

Slowly Cass looked up at him, her remarkable face still a mass of fear, but she was beginning to relax. Now she sat hesitantly back on her heels and looked at him for several moments before she spoke.

"You," she said simply. "Because of you, what you did. My grandfather, too. He did the same thing. He tried to return all of her evil with love. He told me that was the only defense against her, told me that evil couldn't exist where there was love."

Her face seemed like that of a child as she spoke and, watching

282

closely, Mark could see the fear beginning to ease, her eyes clear as she realized she no longer had any need to be afraid.

"Your father thought that he had to destroy her. You can't destroy evil. In order to destroy it, you have to hate it—and it feeds on hate. Where there is no hate, evil will die—or go away."

"Will she . . . die?"

"No. But she won't come back here." Cass smiled softly. "And now I'm free. My grandfather told me something would happen one day that would free me."

"What will she do?"

Cass sat on the earth, legs crossed, fingers caressing the long grasses. "She'll have to find Uncle Polly first, but that won't be hard."

Bewildered, Mark sat opposite her. "Why Uncle Polly?"

"He's her true father. Like her, not of this world. Uncle Polly chose my grandfather and grandmother to give her a human birth, nourish her and try to blunt her powers. My grandfather loved Greek mythology, so Uncle Polly knew he would understand. My grandfather was not her father; Uncle Polly is. He's looked after her for a long time. Since the beginning."

Mark was tempted to ask since the beginning of what, but didn't. From childhood books on mythology, he remembered vividly the image of a bird's body and a woman's head, and knew that the words "since the beginning" probably were beyond his comprehension.

Slowly he bowed his head, trying to digest Cass's words as well as the events of the last few minutes, days, weeks. All he knew for certain was that time had been a matter of total insignificance, that the unresolved passions of twenty years ago had surfaced as raw and as painful and as real as though they had just happened.

Was it possible?

Was it true that on certain rare occasions there literally were no protective barriers to keep one safely anchored in his own place, his own time?

The implication of the question and worse, his fear of the answer dragged his head upward where he saw Cass looking at him with an expression of sweet compassion and understanding.

"Mark—" She spoke his name softly and reached for his hand and simply held it for a moment before speaking.

"Do you want me to tell you everything, at least what I know? My grandfather told me before he died. Sometimes I'm glad he did and other times I find myself wishing he hadn't."

As she spoke of the safety of ignorance, he found himself as always captivated by her quiet beauty, a peace that seemed to radiate from within. What a joy it would be to gaze upon that face every day.

"Tell me," he invited quietly, realizing he had to know, if not for himself, at least in order to share her burden of knowledge.

With her first words, his worst fears were confirmed. His logical, practical twentieth-century mind would have to struggle even to comprehend.

"She was not of this world, not like us. She was a diviner, a siren, capable of rising above the limitations of flesh and blood and becoming whatever she wanted, for whatever purpose."

He shifted on the ground, though never broke contact with her hand. For some reason, now more than ever, that one bond, that one link had become very important to him.

"Go on," he invited, and saw new stress on her face and realized that it was even more difficult for her than for him.

"My grandfather loved her and understood her and tried to put her at ease in this world. But he told me it had not been of her choosing, this place, that it was a kind of exile for her, that she had never been happy, that—"

With her eyes down, she appeared to be smoothing the grass, running the palm of her hand lightly over it, first in one direction, then the other, as though she had to find something that she could smoothe, soothe, control.

"She lured my father into marriage," she went on with new bluntness, as though interested only in getting it over with. "Though she seduced him, my grandfather told me that they were happy together for a while. But—"

It was an ominous break and one tinged slightly with cynicism, as though in her world, it was the nature of happiness never to last—for anyone.

"She grew restless and selected her next amusement, *your* father."

Mark looked up, recalling the ugly scene he'd witnessed in the chapel, the distraught and despairing man pleading for love and receiving only the woman's contempt.

Incongruously Cass smiled, though it was short-lived and replaced by a new somberness. "My father begged her to leave your father alone. They were devoted to each other, Alec Manning and Gerald Simpson, and my father knew that such an alliance, though it would be less than meaningless to my mother, would destroy your father; he knew at that point what she was and knew that your father would not be able to resist her and would be unable to reconcile his actions with his faith and dedication."

284

Mark reached for the small hand that was compulsively smoothing the grass, as though to inform her that his comfort was close by, that she was not alone. "Did your father know, from the beginning, what she was?"

She shook her head. "Not from the beginning. But later, when she used her powers to get your father sent to the Coral Sea and ultimately to his death—"

Mark looked up at the sky in search of more air. He thought again of that massive oil painting that had literally dominated his life from boyhood. How much more he would have preferred the flesh and blood man.

"Do you want me to go on?" The gentle voice was Cass, apparently seeing something on his face.

"Yes," he nodded and looked away and tried to digest the sense of a new loss mingled with old grief.

"After your father's death, my father moved out of the house, an act which enraged her. She tried to lure him back."

"And that's when she arranged—"

—"his death, yes. By then she had reverted almost wholly back to the spirit world. My grandfather had lost all control because she was growing stronger on my father's hate—"

For several moments she was silent, as though she, too, were hearing her words clearly for the first time, was seeing clearly the nightmare past out of which she had evolved and hopefully had survived.

When she started speaking again, her voice was almost a monotone, everything within her trying to resist her own words. "When your father's spirit returned in an attempt to destroy her, she then had all the sustenance she needed in that single act, though it was a mixed victory, for a while it restored all her powers, those powers were useless against his spirit. There was little she could do to a dead man except—"

Again her voice broke. In this new suspense, he looked up. "Except what?"

She looked directly at him. "Lure his son back and destroy *him*."

The words so gently delivered seemed to echo endlessly in his head. He recalled his peculiar inability to understand his presence here, as though someone were manipulating and controlling him, the mysterious way in which he'd turned his back on the California school, his home, everything he'd known and loved and felt familiar with. "I thought it was my father who—"

"It was both of them," Cass confirmed, "both drawing you back for their own purposes. Your father needed your help and Rita wanted—"

"My death."

Whereas before there had been an endless echo, now there was nothing except a deafening silence. He had the curious sensation that they both had become fixed at this point in time.

Suddenly a thought occurred. "My mother."

He felt Cass's hand tighten about his. He waited for her to speak and when she didn't, he felt his fear increase.

"Cass, what—"

"I'm not certain," she said quickly, as though she knew she had to say something. "Rita hated your mother because she always thought that Alec Manning had left her and had gone to Brett Simpson. Rita left your mother alone after your father's death because she felt that her loneliness would be far worse than any death—"

In his mind, Mark saw his mother, her perpetually mourning eyes, her dark moods, her sense of being lost even when in a group of people. Rita Manning had made a correct and brutal assumption. His mother's loneliness had been torture.

"But—" As Cass started speaking again, Mark dragged himself back.

"But what?"

"Mark, I'm afraid that she's done something to your mother now."

"Why?" Suddenly he was on his knees before her, angry and fearful all at the same time.

"Because she was afraid your mother would warn you about her, afraid she would call you home before she'd had a chance to—"

He remembered his deep and mysterious sense of grief the night of the fire. He must go home. "Where do I start?" Ultimately his incoherence diminished though his sense of fresh grief, and mourning remained.

Cass knelt before him. "I hope I'm wrong, Mark," she whispered. "But I'm afraid we're both alone now."

For several moments neither spoke, a curious sense of self-consciousness seeming to weigh on both.

"Mark, I'm sorry."

"No need."

"Your father called you back here."

"I know. It's all over." He reached for her hand and enclosed it between his own and looked up into the early evening sky and saw nothing more than a very distant, very friendly-appearing jet, trailing a silver vapor ribbon behind.

Evil cannot exist where there is love. It feeds on hate.

"After she finds Uncle Polly, what will she do?" he asked, feeling suddenly sorry for Rita Manning, lost in time as she was, forever condemned.

For several moments Cass didn't answer. "Uncle Polly will stay with her, help her. He'll find her sailors. She's happiest with sailors, but she always destroys them."

Slowly Mark stood and walked to the edge of the embankment and looked over and knew what he would find—nothing but the placid charm of the little pond. No fiery, destroyed earthmoving machine, no smoldering ruins, nothing. Time was back on track now—at least for a while.

He did see something else in the long grasses below, silver, glistening in the dying light of day. He scrambled down and retrieved Cass's old portable radio where she'd obviously left it before the grim charade had started. As he drew near Cass, he saw her still brooding, head down, looking bereft and alone. In an attempt to comfort her, he turned the radio on in search of the old music that she seemed to love so much.

Evil cannot exist where there is love. It feeds on hate.

But the music was gone. All he could find was heavy static, alternating with the low, droning voice of a news commentator announcing that Congress was cordial, though not swayed by civil rights leaders meeting at the Capitol, that the Vietnam crisis looked extremely grave, and that President Kennedy would definitely visit Dallas next week, despite advisers warning against it.

Quickly he flipped it off.

"Let's go," he whispered, and helped her to her feet, enclosing her in his arms.

"Where?" she asked, pressing close to him, as though for sanctuary.

He shut his eyes and rested the side of his face on the softness of her hair. For the first time in his life he felt peace.

"Where shall we go?" she asked again, looking up as though afraid he hadn't heard or lacked an answer.

He'd heard—and he had an answer.

"Wherever we can be together. Always."

00752494 6

Harris   C. 4
  The diviner.